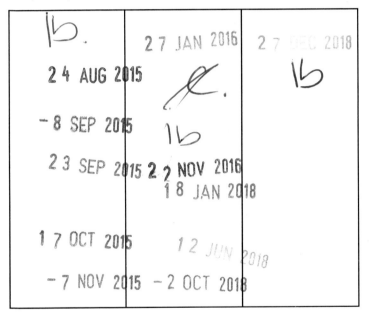

ENDANGERED

C. J. BOX is the winner of the Anthony Award, Prix Calibre .38 (France), the Macavity Award, the Gumshoe Award, the Barry Award, the Edgar Award and is an L.A. Times Book Prize finalist. He lives in Wyoming.

ENDANGERED

JOE PICKETT, BOOK 15

ENDANGERED

JOE PICKETT, BOOK 15

C. J. BOX

HEAD of ZEUS

First published in the United States of America in 2015
by G.P. Putnam's Sons, New York

This edition first published in 2015 by Head of Zeus Ltd

9 7 5 3 1 2 4 6 8

A catalogue record for this book is available
from the British Library

ISBN (HB) 9781781852767
ISBN (TPB) 9781781852774
ISBN (E) 9781781852798

Printed and bound in Germany
by GGP Media GmbH, Pössneck

Head of Zeus Ltd
Clerkenwell House
45-47 Clerkenwell Green
London EC1R 0HT

WWW.HEADOFZEUS.COM

To Ivy

And Laurie, always

Men are what their mothers made them.

—RALPH WALDO EMERSON, *The Conduct of Life*

Therefore I did not know that I would grow to be
My mother's evil seed and do these evil deeds.

—EMINEM, "Evil Deeds"

LEK 64

1

When Wyoming game warden Joe Pickett received the call every parent dreads, he was standing knee-high in thick sagebrush, counting the carcasses of sage grouse. He was up to twenty-one.

Feathers carpeted the dry soil and clung to the waxy blue-green leaves of the sagebrush within a fifty-foot radius. The air smelled of dust, sage, and blood.

It was late morning in mid-March on a vast brush-covered flat managed by the federal Bureau of Land Management. There wasn't a single tree for eighteen miles to the west on the BLM land until the rolling hills rocked back on their heels and began their sharp ascent into the snow-covered Bighorn Mountains, which were managed by the U.S. Forest Service. The summits of the mountains were obscured by a sudden late-season snowstorm, and the sky was leaden and close. Joe's green Game and Fish Ford pickup straddled the ancient two-track road that had brought him up there, the engine idling and the front driver's door still open from when he'd leapt out. His yellow Labrador, Daisy, was trembling in the bed of the truck, her front paws poised on the top of the bed wall as she stared out at the expanse of land. Twin strings of drool hung from her mouth. She smelled the carnage out on the flat, and she wanted to be a part of it.

"Stay," Joe commanded.

Daisy moaned, reset her paws, and trembled some more.

Joe wore his red uniform shirt with the pronghorn patch on the sleeve, Wrangler jeans, cowboy boots, and a Filson vest against the chill. His worn gray Stetson was clamped on tight. A rarely drawn .40 Glock semiauto was on his hip.

Twenty-one dead sage grouse.

In his youth, everyone called them "prairie chickens," and he knew the young ones were good to eat when roasted because they'd been a staple in his poverty-filled college days. They were odd birds: chicken-sized, pear-shaped, ungainly when flying. They were the largest of the grouse species, and their habitat once included most of the western United States and Canada. Wyoming contained one hundred thousand of them, forty percent of the North American population.

Of this flock, he'd noted only three survivors: all three with injuries. He'd seen their teardrop-shaped forms ghosting from brush to brush on the periphery of the location. They didn't fly away, he knew, because they couldn't yet.

It was obvious what had happened.

Fat tire tracks churned through the sagebrush, crushing some plants and snapping others at their woody stalks. Spent 12-gauge shotgun shells littered the ground: Federal four-shot. He speared one through its open end with his pen and sniffed. It still smelled of gunpowder. He retrieved eighteen spent shells and bagged them. Later, after he'd sealed the evidence bag, he found two more shells. Since eighteen shells were more than a representative sample, he tossed the two errant casings into the back of his pickup.

There was a single empty Coors Light can on the northeast corner of the site. He bagged it and tagged it, and hoped the forensics lab in Laramie could pull prints from the outside or DNA from the lip. Problem was, the can looked much older than the spent shotgun shells and he couldn't determine if it hadn't simply been discarded along the road a few weeks prior to the slaughter.

Joe guessed that the incident had occurred either the night or day before, because the exploded carcasses hadn't yet been picked over by predators. Small spoors of blood in the dirt had not yet dried black. Whoever had done it had shot them "on the lek," a lek being an annual gathering of the birds where the males strutted and clucked to attract females for breeding. The lek was a concentric circle of birds with the strutting male grouse in the center of it. Some leks were so large and predictable that locals would drive out to the location to watch the avian meat market in action.

The birds bred in mid-March, nested, and produced chicks in June. If someone was to choose the most opportune time to slaughter an entire flock, this was it, Joe knew.

So "Lek 64," as it had been designated by a multiagency team of biologists charged with counting the number of healthy groupings within the state, was no more.

JOE TOOK A DEEP BREATH and put his hands on his hips. He was angry, and he worked his jaw. It would take hours to photograph the carcasses and measure and photograph the tire tracks. He knew he'd have to do it himself because the county forensics tech was an hour away—provided the tech was on call and would even respond to a game violation. Joe knew he was responsible for the gathering of all evidence to send to the state lab in Laramie, and it would have to get done before the snow that was falling on top of the mountains worked its way east and obscured the evidence. Since it was Friday and the lab technicians didn't work over the weekend, at best he'd hear something by the end of next week.

He'd find whoever did this, he thought. It might take time, but he'd find the shooter or shooters. Fingerprints on the brass of the shells, tire analysis, the beer can, gossipy neighbors, or a drunken boast would lead him to the bad guys. Sometimes it was ridiculously easy to solve these kinds of crimes because the kind of person who would leave such a naked scene often wasn't very smart. Joe had apprehended poachers in the past by finding photos of them posing with dead game on Facebook posts or by looking at the taxidermy mounts in their homes. Or by simply going to their front door, knocking, and saying, "I guess you know why I'm here."

It had been amazing what kinds of answers that inquiry sometimes brought.

But he wasn't angry because of the work ahead of him. There was also that special directive recently put out by Governor Rulon and his agency director about sage grouse. Preserving them, that is. Game and Fish biologists and wardens had been ordered to pay special attention to where the grouse were located and how many there were. The status of the sage grouse population, according to Rulon, was "pivotal" to the future economic well-being of the state.

Sage grouse in Wyoming had shifted from the status of a game bird regulated by the state into politics and economics on a national level. The U.S. Fish and Wildlife Service was threatening to list the bird as an endangered species because the overall population had declined, and if they did, it would remove hundreds of thousands of acres from any kind of use, including energy development—whether gas and oil, wind, hydrothermal, or solar. The federal government proposed mandating an off-limits zone consisting of one to four miles for every lek found. That would impact ranchers, developers, and everyone else.

That was the reason Joe had been on the old two-track in the first place and stumbled onto the killing ground. During the winter, he'd seen the flock more than once from the window of his pickup, and sage grouse didn't range far. Sage grouse did not exhibit the brightest of bird behavior. He recalled an incident from the year before, when a big male—called a "bomber" by hunters—flew into the passenger door of his pickup and bounced off, killing itself in the process. Joe's truck hadn't been moving at the time.

Years before, prior to the national decline in the sage grouse population, Joe had accompanied outlaw falconer Nate Romanowski to this very sagebrush bench. At the time, Nate flew a prairie falcon and a red-tailed hawk. Joe and Nate served as bird dogs, walking through the brush to dislodge the grouse while the raptors hunted from the air. Grouse defended themselves against the falcons by flopping over onto their backs and windmilling their sharp claws, but the raptors got them anyway, in an explosion of feathers.

Joe wondered if he'd ever hunt with Nate again, and not just because of the sage grouse problem. With a half-dozen serious allegations hanging over his head by the feds, Nate had agreed to turn state's witness against his former employer, a high-society killer for hire. Nate had not touched base with Joe, or Marybeth, or their daughter Sheridan in months. Joe had no idea if Nate's long-ago pledge to protect the Pickett family still held. And Joe was still angry with him for getting mixed up in a murder-for-hire operation, even if the targets richly deserved killing.

JOE SHOOK HIS HEAD to clear it, and looked at the carnage. Half a year after being named "Special Liaison to the Executive Branch" by Rulon himself, in the middle of Joe's own five-thousand-square-mile district, he'd discovered the site of the wanton destruction of twenty-one rare game birds whose deaths could bring down the state of Wyoming.

That's when the call came. And suddenly he was no longer thinking about birds.

THE DISPLAY SAID **MIKE REED.**

Reed was sheriff of Twelve Sleep County, and had been for two years. He was a personal friend of Joe's and had cleaned up the department, ridding it of the old cronies and flunkies who had been collected by the previous chief, Kyle McLanahan. Reed was a paraplegic due to gunshot wounds he'd received in the line of duty and he traveled in a specially outfitted van. His injuries had never prevented him from getting around or performing his job.

Reed's voice was tense. Joe could hear the sound of a motor in the background. He was speeding somewhere in his van.

Reed said, "Joe, we've got a situation. Are you in a place where you can sit down?"

"No, but go ahead."

"I'm running out to meet my deputy on Dunbar Road. He responded to a call from a couple of hunters this morning. They claimed they found a victim in a ditch."

Joe knew Dunbar Road. It was south of Saddlestring, an obscure county road that ended up at a couple of old reservoirs in the breaklands. It was a road to nowhere, really, used only by hunters, anglers, and people who were lost.

"The victim is a young woman, Joe," Reed said. "She was found by Deputy Boner."

Joe felt himself squeezing his cell phone as if to kill it.

"My deputy thinks she looks a lot like April. He says he knew April from when she worked at Welton's Western Wear, and it might be her."

Joe's knees weakened, and he took a step back. April was their eighteen-year-old adopted daughter. She'd disappeared the previous November with a professional rodeo cowboy and they'd only heard from her two or three times. Each time she called, she said not to worry about her. She was, she said, "having the time of her life."

Because she'd turned eighteen, there was little Joe or Marybeth could do, except encourage her to come home.

"She's alive?" Joe asked, his mouth dry.

"Maybe. Barely. We're not sure. It might not be her, Joe. There's no ID on her."

"Where is she now?"

"In the backseat of my deputy's cruiser," Reed said. "He didn't want to wait for the EMTs to get out there. He said it looks touch and go whether she'll even make it as far as the hospital."

Joe took a quivering breath. The storm cloud was moving down the face of the mountains, the snow blotting out the blue-black forest of pine trees.

"Whether it's April or not," Reed said, "it's a terrible thing."

"Mike, was she in an accident?"

"Doesn't sound like it," Reed said. "There was no vehicle around. It looks like she was dumped there."

"Dumped?" Joe asked. "Why didn't she walk toward town?"

"She's been beaten," Reed said. "Man, I hate to be the one telling you this. But my guy says it looks like she was beaten to a pulp and dumped. Whoever did it might have thought she was already dead. Obviously, I don't know the extent of her injuries, how long she's been there, or if there was, you know, a sexual assault."

Joe leaned against the front fender of his pickup. He couldn't recall walking back to his truck, but there he was. The phone was pressed so tightly against his face, it hurt.

March and April were usually the snowiest months in high-country Wyoming, when huge dumps of spring snow arrived between short bursts of false spring. The last week had been unseasonably warm, so he was grateful she hadn't died of exposure.

Joe said, "So you're going to meet your deputy and escort him to the hospital?"

"Roger that," Reed said. "How quick can you get there? I'm about to scramble Life Flight and get them down here so they can transport her to the trauma center in Billings. These injuries are beyond what our clinic can handle. Can you get there and . . . identify her?"

"I'm twenty miles out on bad roads, but yes, I'll be there," Joe said, motioning for Daisy to leap down from the bed of the truck and take her usual spot on the passenger seat. He followed her in and slammed the door. "Does Marybeth know?"

Marybeth was now the director of the Twelve Sleep County

Library. She'd be at the building until five-thirty p.m., but she was known to monitor the police band.

"I haven't told her," Reed said, "and I asked my guys to keep a lid on this until I reached you. I thought maybe you'd want to tell her."

Joe engaged the transmission and roared down the old two-track.

"I'll call her," Joe said, raising his voice because the road was rough and the cab was rattling with vibration. Citation books, maps, and assorted paperwork fluttered down through the cab from where they had been parked beneath the sun visors. "We'll meet you there."

"I'm sorry, Joe," Reed said with pain in his voice. "But keep in mind we don't know for sure it's her."

Joe said, "It's her," and punched off.

He called Marybeth's cell phone. When she answered, he slowed down enough so that he could hear her.

"Mike Reed just told me they're transporting a female victim to the hospital," he said. "She was found dumped south of town. Mike says there's a possibility the girl could be—"

"April," Marybeth said, finishing the sentence for him. "How bad is she?"

"Bad," Joe said, and he told her about the Life Flight helicopter en route to the hospital from Billings.

"I'll meet you there," she said.

Before he could agree, she said, "I've had nightmares about this for months. Ever since she left with that cowboy." Joe thought, *She can't even say his name.*

Joe disconnected the call, dropped his phone into his breast pocket, and jammed down on the accelerator. Twin plumes of dust from his back tires filled the rearview mirror.

"Hang on," he said to Daisy.

Then: "I'm going to kill Dallas Cates."

Daisy looked back as if to say *We'll kill him together.*

2

fter what seemed like the longest forty-five minutes of his life, Joe arrived at the Twelve Sleep County Hospital and found Marybeth in the emergency entrance lobby. Sheriff Mike Reed was with her, as was Deputy Edgar Jess Boner, who had found the victim and transported her into town.

Marybeth was calm and in control, but her face was drained of color. She had the ability to shift into a cool and pragmatic demeanor when a situation was at its worst. She was blond with green eyes, and was wearing a skirt, blazer, and pumps: her library director's outfit.

She turned to him as he walked in and said, "Sorry that took so long."

He was unsettled from being nearly shaken to death on the ride down from the sagebrush foothills. His hands shook from gripping the steering wheel. He saw the subtle but scared look in her eyes and went to her and pulled her close.

"I saw her when they brought her in," Marybeth said into his ear. "It's April. She looks terrible, Joe. The emergency doctor called it blunt force trauma. Someone hit her in the head, and her face was bloody."

"I was hoping it wasn't her," Joe said, realizing how callous that sounded. It shouldn't be *anyone*.

"She's alive," Marybeth said. "That's all they can say. She isn't conscious, and as far as I know she hasn't opened her eyes or tried to speak. I keep seeing doctors and nurses rushing back there, but I don't know what they're doing other than trying to stabilize her for the Life Flight."

"This is so terrible," he said.

"I kept telling her . . ." Marybeth started to say, but let her voice trail off. After a beat, she gently pushed away from Joe and said, "I'm going with her in the helicopter to Billings. We just have to hope that, with all she's been through, she can hold on another hour.

"I called the high school and left a message with the principal that you would pick Lucy up," Marybeth continued. "Maybe you can take her out to dinner tonight, but you'll need to feed the horses when you get home."

Joe started to argue, started to tell her not to worry about his dinner or anything else, but he knew this was how she processed a crisis—by making sure her family was taken care of. Only after it passed would she allow herself to break down. So he nodded instead.

"I'll call Sheridan as soon as I know something," she said. "I've already made arrangements to be gone a few days from work. They were very good about it."

Sheridan was a junior at the University of Wyoming and had chosen not to be a resident assistant in the dormitory another semester. She was living with three other girls in a rental house and making noises about staying in Laramie for the summer to work. Joe and Marybeth didn't like the idea, but Sheridan was stubborn. She was also not close to April, and the two of them had often clashed when they'd lived in the same house together.

Lucy was Joe and Marybeth's sixteen-year-old daughter, a tenth grader at Saddlestring High School. She was blond like her mother and maturing into self-sufficiency. Lucy had been a careful observer of her two older sisters and had avoided their mistakes and errors in judgment. April had stayed in contact with Lucy more than anyone else, although Lucy had relayed what she'd been told to Marybeth.

Joe said to Marybeth, "You know who did this."

"We can't jump to that conclusion."

"Already did," Joe said.

In his peripheral vision, he saw Sheriff Mike Reed roll his chair toward them. If Reed hadn't overheard Joe, he'd at least gotten the gist of what had been said, Joe thought.

"When you have a minute . . ." Reed said.

Joe turned to Reed and Boner, then shook Boner's hand. "Thanks for bringing her here. We appreciate it. You made the right call not waiting for the ambulance to show up."

Boner was new to the department and Joe didn't know the man well.

"Just doing my job," Boner said softly. "I've got a three-year-old girl at home. I can't imagine . . ." He didn't finish the thought, but looked away, his face flushed red.

Joe said to Reed, "It was Dallas Cates. That's who she left with. We need to find him."

"Whoa," Reed said, showing Joe the palm of his hand. "I know you've got your suspicions, and I do, too, but right now we've got nothing to go on."

"It was him."

"Marybeth is right," Reed said. "You're emotional right now and you're jumping to conclusions. I know it's against your nature, but you need to let this thing work. I've got my guys working on the investigation and my evidence tech out there on Dunbar Road to see what we can find. It's only been a couple of hours, Joe."

Joe said, "If you don't find him, I will."

"Joe, damn you," Reed said, shaking his head. "Slow down. Just slow down. You know as well as I do that we could screw the whole thing up if we put blinders on and make accusations that turn out to be false."

Joe smoldered.

After a moment, he felt Marybeth's hand on his shoulder and he looked back at her.

She was grave. She said, "Promise me you won't do anything crazy while I'm gone. I need you here with Lucy, and this is too close to home. Promise me, Joe."

"It's obvious," Joe said to both Marybeth and Reed. "A twenty-four-year-old local-hero cowboy takes a liking to my middle daughter and convinces her to take off with him on the rodeo circuit. She doesn't know about his past, or what he's capable of, so she goes. A few months later, she gets left in a ditch outside of town. Who *else* would we suspect?"

Marybeth didn't respond, but Reed said, "Joe, we're already on it. I sent two guys out to the Cates house fifteen minutes ago. Supposedly Dallas is at home recuperating from a rodeo injury right now."

"He's home?" Joe said. "When did he come home?"

"Don't know," Reed said. "We'll find out."

"April was probably dumped yesterday," Joe said. "Do you feel the dots connecting, Mike?"

"We're asking him to come in for questioning," Reed said.

"I want to sit in."

"Not a chance in hell, Joe. I was thinking about letting you watch the monitor down the hall, but if you keep up your attitude, I'll ban you from the building."

Joe looked to Marybeth for support, but she shook her head with sympathy instead.

Reed said, "All we need is for you to draw down on our suspect during the initial inquiry and for him to press charges against us and you. No, Joe, if we want to do this right, we do it by the book."

"Promise me," Marybeth said.

Joe looked down at his boots.

He said, "I promise."

She squeezed his hand.

Then he looked hard at Mike Reed from under the brim of his hat. He said, "Mike, I know you'll do your best and I'll behave. But if something goes pear-shaped, things are going to get western around here."

"I expected you to say that," Reed said with a sigh.

BLUNT FORCE TRAUMA.

The very words were brutal in and of themselves, Joe thought as he and Marybeth trailed April's gurney down the hallway. He could hear the helicopter approaching outside, hovering over the helipad on the roof of the hospital.

April was bundled up and he couldn't see her face. He wasn't sure he wanted to. Joe was grateful Marybeth had positively identified her earlier.

He was unnerved by the number of suspended plastic packets that dripped fluids into tubes that snaked beneath the sheets. An orderly rolled a monitor on wheels alongside the gurney. Her body looked small and frail beneath the covers, and she didn't respond when the orderlies secured her to the gurney with straps.

Joe reached down and squeezed her hand through the blankets. It was supple, but there was no pressure back.

"Let me know how it goes," Joe said to Marybeth, raising his voice so as to be heard over the wash of the rotors.

"Of course," she said, pulling him close one last time before she left. Her eyes glistened with tears.

Joe watched as the gurney was hoisted into the helicopter. A crew member reached down from the hatch and helped Marybeth step up inside. Seconds later, the door was secured and the helicopter lifted.

Joe clamped his hat tight on his head with his right hand and silently asked God to save April, because she'd suffered enough in her short life, and to give Marybeth the strength to carry on.

"How well do you know the Cates family?" Reed asked Joe as he drove them to the Twelve Sleep County Building. Joe was in the passenger seat of the specially equipped van. Deputy Boner had volunteered to follow them in Joe's pickup and to keep an eye on Daisy until Joe could retrieve his vehicle and his dog.

"I've tangled with them before," Joe said. "Mainly with Bull, the oldest son. I've met the old man, Eldon, and I've been to his elk camp a few times."

He knew the Cateses lived on twelve acres in the breaklands. The property contained a smattering of old structures in the scrub pine, including the shambled main house, a barn, and several falling-down outbuildings. Their place was about twenty minutes from town.

"What do you know about them?" Reed asked.

Joe told Reed that the Cates family ran a hunting-guide business called Dull Knife Outfitters. Dull Knife was one of the oldest big-game outfitters in the Bighorns, and one of the most notorious. There were rumors that Eldon was involved in taking elk out of season as well as in the wrong hunt areas, on behalf of clients, and that he made deals with hunters to obtain prime licenses on their behalf without going through the lottery, if they paid his special fee. Joe had even heard that Eldon had a secret elk camp deep in the mountains that he operated completely above the law, where he guaranteed certain wealthy hunters a kill that would make the record books.

But they were rumors only. Joe had never caught Eldon committing a crime, and no accuser had ever come forward. He'd interviewed several Dull Knife clients over the years and none of them would implicate Eldon. Despite spending years on horseback in the most remote areas of the mountains, he'd not yet found Eldon's secret camp—if it existed at all.

Eldon had a unique reputation among the other, more respectable outfitters in the district. Although sniping among competing hunting guides was normal, the one thing Eldon's competitors could agree on was that *they didn't like Eldon.* They thought he used his reputation as the oldest outfitter in the mountains as a slam against them, and they didn't like how he challenged the ethics of the profession—which reflected poorly on *them.* Guides said that Eldon sometimes claimed kills made by their clients by tagging them on behalf of *his* clients, and that he refused to respect the boundaries of the Wyoming Outfitters Board's designated hunting areas. He would also bad-mouth other outfitters to his clients, calling them "amateurs," "greenhorns," and worse. For a number of years, Eldon drove his four-wheel-drive pickup around town with a magnetic sign on the door that read DULL KNIFE OUTFITTERS: SATISFYING OUR CUSTOMERS WHEN THE OTHER GUIDES WERE STILL IN DIAPERS.

Joe had been asked by several outfitters to talk to Eldon about it, but Joe told them there was nothing he could legally do. When the magnetic sign was stolen from the truck while Eldon was in a bar, Eldon had vowed to press charges for theft against the other outfitters in the county, but he never did.

Joe had always considered Eldon Cates to be an aggravating throwback who would someday foul up. When he did, Joe wanted to be there.

Bull was another story. Bull was bigger and dumber than his dad, and two years earlier, Joe had caught the son and his unpleasant wife, Cora Lee, red-handed with a trophy bull elk in the back of their pickup three days before the season opener.

Bull's hunting rig could be identified instantly because it had been retrofitted as a kind of rolling meat wagon. He'd welded a steel pole and crossbeam into the bed and strung a steel cable and hook from a turnbuckle. With the device, Bull could back up to a big-game carcass, hook the cable through its back legs, and hoist it up in order to field dress and skin it on the spot.

Bull's scheme had been to kill the bull prior to the arrival of two hunters from Pennsylvania. If either of the two hunters didn't get their own trophy bull elk, Bull was going to tag the carcass with their license and let them take it home, thus guaranteeing a one hundred percent successful hunt. The Pennsylvania clients hadn't been in on the scheme, from what Joe could determine.

Judge Hewitt was a hunter himself, and he came down hard on Bull Cates.

The violations had cost the outfitter several thousand dollars in fines, the forfeiture of his rifles and pickup, and the loss of his outfitter's license from the state association. Bull was bitter and claimed Joe had "deprived him of his livelihood" and that he would someday even the score. Cora Lee acted out during the sentencing and hurled epithets at Joe and Judge Hewitt and was forcibly removed from the courtroom by deputies.

It wasn't uncommon for a game violator to talk big in bars about getting even with the local game warden, and Bull wasn't the first to ever make threats. For Joe, it was part of the job. He knew that in the past the threats had always dissipated with the onslaught of the next morning's hangover.

Nevertheless, for months after, Joe had taken measures to avoid running into Bull and Cora Lee. There was no reason to pour fuel on the embers. Joe wasn't as young as he used to be, and Bull had six inches and fifty pounds on him.

So when Joe would see Bull's pickup—a 2007 Ford F-250 with a DULL KNIFE OUTFITTERS decal crudely scraped off the driver's-side door—in the parking lot of the grocery store, he would drive around the block until it was gone. When the vehicle was parked in front of the Stockman's Bar, Joe would keep driving.

When there were no hunting seasons open, the Cateses operated C&C Sewer and Septic Tank Service. C&C stood for "Cates & Cates." It was a dirty job, pumping out rural septic tanks. The

Cateses owned several circa-1980 pump trucks, and Joe often saw them on remote roads in the spring and fall. When he spotted one in front of him on the highway, he gave it a wide berth.

"So you know Bull, all right," Reed said with a chuckle. "Did you ever run across Timber, the second son?"

"Timber?" Joe said. "What's with these names?"

"If you think Bull is a problem, he's a piece of cake compared to son number two. Timber was a hell of a high school athlete. He was quarterback in the late eighties, the last time the Saddlestring Wranglers won state, back before you came into this country. Timber walked on at UW, and he might have played eventually, but he got into some kind of bar fight at the Buckhorn in Laramie and they threw him off the team. Unfortunately, he moved back home. And he was *crazy*. He'd get so violent when he drank, it would take four of us deputies to get him down. When he discovered meth, he got even worse. Finally, he was arrested up in Park County for carjacking some old lady on her way to Yellowstone Park because he'd run out of gas and he wanted her Mustang. Lucky for all of us, Timber is doing three years in Rawlins. I hear he isn't exactly a model prisoner, or he would have been out and back here by now."

Reed took a deep breath. "However . . . I got word from a buddy of mine, a prison guard, that Timber could be released any day now. I've sent a memo to my guys to keep an eye out for him. My guess is he'll go straight home to Mama. Then it'll be a matter of time before he gets in trouble again."

"Then there's Dallas," Joe said.

"Then there's Dallas," Reed echoed.

Joe had met him four months ago at his house. Dallas had been invited there by April, who at the time had worked at Welton's Western Wear. Dallas was a local hero, winner of the National High School Finals Rodeo, then the College National Finals Rodeo, and at that time he was in second place in the standings in bull riding and bound for the National Finals Rodeo in Las Vegas. His lean, hard face was so well-known among rodeo fans that his likeness was used to sell jeans in western stores, and he'd visit local retailers to promote the brand when he wasn't riding bulls. That's how Dallas and April met.

Dallas Cates was shorter than Joe, but had wider shoulders, and biceps that strained at the fabric of his snap-button western shirt. He had a compact frame that suggested he was spring-loaded and ready to explode at a moment's notice. His neck was as wide as his jaw, and he projected raw physical power.

There was a two-inch scar on his left cheek that tugged at the edge of his mouth in an inadvertent sneer. Supposedly, Dallas got the scar when he jumped from a moving snowmobile onto the back of a bull elk, in an attempt to wrestle the animal to the ground like a rodeo cowboy did with a running steer. The sharp tip of one of the antlers had ripped Dallas's cheek. Joe didn't know if the story was true, but he'd heard it several times.

Dallas was also somewhere on the periphery of a terrible crime that had occurred when he was an all-state wrestler for Saddlestring High School, when a girl was abducted, raped, and dumped outside of town by at least four high school–aged suspects. Unfortunately, the victim, named Serda Tibbs, couldn't identify her assailants because she'd been slipped a date-rape drug that rendered her unconscious. Were there four of them, or five? Four seniors were arrested, tried, and convicted. None of the four would finger Dallas Cates, even though several other students anonymously claimed

Cates was the ringleader. That was the power Dallas held over the other student criminals.

"So have you met the matriarch, Brenda Cates?" Reed asked Joe, cocking his head as he pulled into his designated parking spot on the side of the county building.

The way he'd asked, Joe surmised, held significance.

"No. Marybeth's met her at the library. Brenda wanted her support on creating signs to post at the entrances to town bragging about Dallas."

Reed nodded. "She wants signage put up declaring Saddlestring the 'hometown of PRCA bull-riding champion Dallas Cates.'"

Joe snorted.

"Let's just say she's very proud and protective of her family," Reed said as he swung his seat around and lifted himself into his wheelchair in a single fluid motion.

Before Joe could ask what that meant, Reed's cell phone burred and the sheriff held it up to his ear. He listened for a minute, then asked, "What about Dallas?" before listening more and punching off.

"What *about* Dallas?" Joe asked.

"That was my deputy. Dallas's parents say he's laid up and can't make the trip into town right now. But Eldon and Brenda Cates themselves should be here any minute. They're being very cooperative, I'm told."

Joe said, "I'll bet."

Sheriff Reed said, "If Dallas Cates is that banged-up and has actually been home for a while, he might not have been the one, Joe."

"I want to see him. I want a doctor to evaluate his condition."

"We can do that," Reed said, "and we will. But first I think we should hear out Eldon and Brenda, don't you?"

Joe agreed.

"Brenda is the one you should be interested in," Reed said, arching his eyebrows and sliding the van door open.

Eldon and Brenda Cates sat in hard-backed chairs across from Sheriff Reed's desk in his office. Joe stood off to the side with his arms folded over his chest, leaning against the radiator. He'd agreed to observe only and to not ask questions. Dulcie Schalk, the county prosecutor, had taken a side chair next to Reed's desk. She'd positioned herself in such a way as to keep a close eye on both Joe and the Cateses.

Eldon asked, "Has April said what happened to her?"

Sheriff Reed shook his head. "Not yet. She wasn't conscious when we found her."

"That's what we figured," Eldon said, and he and Brenda exchanged knowing glances. "Because if she could talk she'd a told you our boy Dallas didn't have nothing to do with it."

"That's what we're here to find out," Reed said.

"We can guess what you all might be thinking," Eldon said. "But it ain't like that. When your guys came out and told us what'd happened, we figured we ought to come in here right away and nip this in the bud." When he said it, he cast a quick look toward Joe.

Eldon was tall and rawboned, with broad shoulders and a weather-beaten face. He had thin straw-colored hair and a heavy lantern jaw. His hands were large and red and crablike, and it appeared to Joe that Eldon didn't know what to do with them when he was seated.

First they were on his lap, then rested on his thighs, then hanging down on either side like twin slabs of meat in a cooler. He wore a heavy wool hunting shirt, worn jeans, and lace-up high-heeled outfitter boots for riding that were covered with years of bloodstains from dead deer, antelope, and elk.

"What is it you think we're thinking?" Reed asked without a hint of aggressiveness.

Eldon glanced at Joe again, then at Dulcie. He said, "That Dallas might have had something to do with this."

"Why would we think that?" Dulcie asked.

She was tightly coiled, as always. Dulcie Schalk was in her mid-thirties, with soft, dark hair, dark brown eyes, and a trim, athletic figure. She was dressed in a dark suit with a ruffled white blouse. She was single and considered one of the prime catches in Twelve Sleep County, although there were rumors about her sexual preference. Joe had once wondered as well, until she'd asked him some provocative questions about his friend Nate Romanowski. Dulcie was tough and thorough, and never went to court unless she was absolutely convinced she had the evidence to obtain a conviction. Her success rate was more than ninety-five percent, and she'd recently won her first reelection.

"Because that's how you people think," Eldon said in answer to Dulcie's question. He leaned back and said, "You people sit up here and look down on the little people out in the county just trying to make a living."

Reed reacted with scorn and shook his head. He said, "I'm the sheriff of the whole county, Eldon. I'm not just sheriff of Saddlestring."

Dulcie said to Eldon, "I don't believe at this point a single accusation has been made, so I hope we can put your prejudices and assumptions aside and start over. We're just in an information-gathering phase. Now, from what I understand, you two volunteered to come in here. We want to hear what you have to say."

"So we can rule things out," Reed added.

Eldon nodded slightly. He had heavy-lidded eyes and virtually no expression. Brenda looked over at him approvingly but had yet to say a word.

Brenda Cates was heavy, with a round face and permed auburn hair. She wore a faded blue dress and heavy sensible shoes, and she clutched her overlarge purse on her lap with both hands. Her face was hangdog, jowly, matronly pleasant at first glance. She looked like the type of woman who baked lots of cookies and took in stray cats, Joe thought. She wore no makeup.

Joe couldn't figure out why Reed had suggested she was the one to watch instead of Eldon.

Eldon looked over to Joe again and said directly to him, "I should'a said earlier we're just both real damned sorry about what happened to your girl."

"Thank you," Joe said.

Eldon said, "Dallas feels damned bad, too. He'd have been here if he wasn't so buggered up. He's got busted ribs and a shitload of other injuries from the Houston Rodeo last week. He drew a bull that pounded the crap outta him. That bull got him down on the arena floor and threw him around like a cat playing with a mouse. Them bullfighters tried to get him out, but you know how a bull is when its mind is made up. We seen it on TV and it was a damned bad wreck."

Brenda visibly shuddered and clutched her purse even tighter when she seemed to recall viewing the ride.

"So Dallas has been home awhile?" Reed asked.

"Yes, sir," Eldon said.

"Was April here with him?"

"Nope."

"Where was she?" Reed asked.

"Your guess is as good as mine," Eldon said. "Dallas said she took off a while back, after they broke up. She left with some other buckle bunnies and he ain't seen her since."

Dulcie asked, "Buckle bunnies?"

"That's what some folks call girls who hang around rodeo cowboys," Reed told her. "Kind of like rodeo groupies, I guess. You can see 'em strutting around in tight clothes by the ready area during the rodeo. That's where the cowboys get ready to ride."

When he realized what he'd said, Reed turned to Joe and mouthed, *"Sorry."*

"Buckle bunnies," Dulcie repeated, shaking her head.

"When was the last time Dallas was with her?" Reed asked.

"Oh, it's been a while."

This was all news to Joe, but he kept his promise to Reed and Marybeth and didn't speak. As far as he and his wife knew, April had been with Dallas since she'd left months ago. The idea of April traveling with a pack of girls from rodeo to rodeo—being known as a *buckle bunny*—made his stomach lurch.

"What is 'a while'?" Reed asked Eldon.

The man looked back at him dully, then turned his head toward Brenda. Joe saw her nod quickly to him, as if prodding him on.

"A few weeks, I guess. A while. I don't know," Eldon said.

"He'll be able to tell us?" Reed asked.

"I'm sure he will," Eldon said.

"So how long has he been home with you after his injury?"

"'Bout a week," Eldon said. Then something went even deader in his face. Brenda glared at him, but he wouldn't meet her eyes.

"A *week*?" Joe asked. "I thought I heard you say it was a couple of *days*."

Eldon didn't even move his head when Joe spoke.

"Joe," Reed said, "we had a deal. I ask the questions."

Joe looked to the sheriff with an exasperated *Then ask them* look. Dulcie carefully observed Eldon and Brenda Cates.

"Which is it, then?" Reed said. "A couple of days or a week? It's important that we know."

He didn't go on, but Joe thought everyone in the room knew what he was saying. If Dallas had been home a week, that meant he'd been injured during the first few days of the Houston Rodeo and was at home recovering while April was . . . out there somewhere. But if he'd just returned home the day before, he could have had April with him. Until he didn't.

Brenda put her hand on Eldon's thigh. It shut him up. She took over. She said, "Do you know why some people call my husband 'Snake' when his real first name is Eldon?"

"No," Reed said, "but I don't know what that has to do with this."

"They call him Snake because he has a strange gift for being bitten by rattlers," she said. Brenda had a husky voice, but it was smooth and convincing, Joe thought. "How many times have you been bitten by rattlesnakes, Eldon?" she asked her husband.

After a long pause, Eldon said, "I don't remember. Seven, maybe eight times."

"Nine times," Brenda corrected him, then looked from Joe to Reed to Dulcie with wide-open eyes to hammer home her point. "Six times since we've been married. We don't know what it is, or why it is. Whether Eldon has some kind of smell that attracts poisonous snakes or what. But if three men are walking across a pasture and one of them gets bit—it's Eldon. I don't know how many times he's been out hunting with clients or on a septic tank job when he calls me on the radio and says, 'Brenda, I got bit again.' So I drop whatever I'm doing and take him to the hospital for treatment. But the thing is, all that venom has affected his memory. He can't remember days or dates anymore. So when he says Dallas has been home for a day or a week, well, you can't really believe him."

She turned to Eldon and said, "Sorry. I had to tell them."

He didn't react.

Brenda looked directly at Joe and said, "Dallas used to love that girl of yours. Eldon and I met her at the National Finals in Las Vegas last year and the two of them couldn't have been happier. That's the kind of boy he is: Dallas bought our plane tickets and put us up in the Mandalay Bay Hotel. Eldon hadn't been on a plane in years.

"You should have seen them together, Mr. Pickett. He doted on her. Just doted on her. They were like the Barbie and Ken of the rodeo set. Now, I don't know what happened between them. Dallas doesn't talk about things like that. I know she watched him like a hawk when other girls were around. He told me once she got real jealous for no reason, and he thought she was smothering him.

Dallas has always been the social type, and I'm sure she didn't appreciate that very much. I think that's why he broke it off with her, that jealousy. I'm guessing she didn't take it well at all. I'm just speculating, but I'm a pretty good observer of human nature. April is as fierce as she is good-looking, and I can't see her just shrugging her shoulders and moving on."

Joe shook his head, not understanding. Dulcie picked up his cue.

"Did April try to get back at him somehow?" she asked.

"Oh, he never told me anything like that," Brenda said. "But I think the breakup affected him. It happened just before Houston, which is probably why his head wasn't in the game and he got bucked off and hurt so bad."

"So it was April's fault?" Joe asked. He'd once again broken his agreement by speaking up, and Reed gave him a disapproving look.

"I didn't mean it that way," Brenda said, looking aghast. "I just meant that he didn't ride with the kind of total confidence and concentration he's known for. You can watch the tape of it and see for yourself. I'm not blaming that poor girl for anything at all."

"So he came home alone," Reed broke in. "Did you two pick him up at the airport?"

"He drove," Eldon said.

"He drove back from Houston with broken ribs?" Joe asked, incredulous.

He noted that Brenda again gripped Eldon's thigh with her hand. This time, she appeared to be applying real pressure, but the man looked ahead stoically.

"Like a lot of boys around here, Dallas has a thing about his pickup," Brenda said. "He'd never leave it, no matter what. He never likes to be without it. Even if he was dying, he'd drive. Imagine how tough that kid must be. He drove from Houston to Saddlestring all alone with broken ribs and a dislocated shoulder. I don't know how he did it."

Joe raised his eyebrows and caught Dulcie's eye. The dislocated shoulder was new information. She'd caught it also.

"Which arm is dislocated?" she asked Brenda.

"His left, thank goodness," Brenda said. "That's because he has to grip that bull with his right hand. So he'll still be able to do that."

Joe visualized the act he'd seen many times. Bull riders lowered themselves carefully into a steel chute filled with a two-thousand-pound animal. Often, the bull was so big there was barely enough clearance on either side of it for the cowboy to mount it. A flanking strap lined with lamb's wool was cinched to the rear quarters of the bull with an easy-release snap. After the cowboy had jammed his gloved hand into the opening of his bull rope, which was cinched around the middle of the bull, the gate was opened. It was a common misconception that the flanking strap was attached to the bull's genitals, when it wasn't at all. As much as trying to get the rider off its back, the bull was just as concerned about ridding himself of the flanking strap, which was alternately pulled tight and released and served as an irritant. It took a tremendous amount of upper-body strength and balance for a rider to stay on the bull while it spun, twisted, and bucked.

That kind of upper-body strength, Joe knew, could produce a hell of a beating.

"So how long has he been home?" Reed asked them.

"Three days, two nights," Brenda said with finality. "And from what I understand from your deputies, poor April was just found this morning. And since she definitely wasn't with us, that means she got here with someone else."

She pushed the bulk of her weight forward on the chair and leaned across the desk toward Reed.

She said to the sheriff, "I hope you find whoever did it and put that man in a cage. And if he resists arrest and gets himself shot in the process, I don't think anyone would have a problem with that. Dallas feels the same way."

"Then where is he?" Joe asked. "Why isn't he here now?"

Brenda's eyes flashed when she turned to Joe. There was real anger there, and it surprised him.

"Eldon is right," she said. "You people look down on folks like us. I see it all the time. When Eldon and Bull take their pump truck out, the property owners act like it's their fault they're swimming in their own feces. I saw it when I talked to your wife in the library about supporting our effort to recognize the fact that this town produced a national champion bull rider named Dallas Cates. She just looked at me and nodded her head like she couldn't wait for me to leave and go back to whatever rock I crawled out from under. And I could see you all setting a trap for that poor kid and putting him in your jail. That's why Eldon and I came down here. We wanted to set the record straight before you jumped to the wrong conclusion."

She narrowed her eyes and said, "Dallas was at home when April was beat up and dumped outside of town. She fell in with the wrong crowd. That wasn't his fault. He'd be here right now if he was healthy enough to drive into town with us. I know you're thinking that if he drove here all the way from Houston then he should be able to drive the twenty miles from our place, but it isn't like that.

Dallas is the toughest kid you'll ever meet. He gritted his teeth and drove all the way from Houston in terrible pain, but he didn't let it get to him until he was home and safe. It's like he stored up all that pain and waited to let it hit him, and it has now. With all of his injuries and maybe months of recuperating ahead of him, Dallas fought the pain and drove all the way back here to a town that refuses to appreciate anything he's accomplished."

To Joe, it was a tour de force of smoke and misdirection. Reed was right. Brenda had coached Eldon on what to say, but Eldon had fouled it up so she had to step in and take over. Brenda was running the show and she no doubt ran the family. Now he knew what he was dealing with.

"Even in his condition, he wanted to come into town with us and see April," Brenda said, tears forming in her eyes. "He wanted to make sure she was okay, but I told him to stay."

"Why?" Dulcie asked her.

"Because I know how you people could stack the deck against him," Brenda said, narrowing her eyes again. "He's on pain meds and you could get him to say something and twist it back around on him later."

"We'd never do that," Reed said defensively.

"*He* would," Brenda said, pointing at Joe. "I saw how he railroaded Bull right out of our outfitting business."

Joe said, "I caught him and Cora Lee with a dead six-by-six elk in the back of his pickup three days before the season opener. How is that railroading?"

Brenda Cates ignored the question, and this time Reed didn't glare at Joe for talking.

She said, "Do you want to know what I think happened to April?

I know you probably don't want to hear it because you all have your sights set on my Dallas, but I thought you might be interested anyway."

"What's that, Brenda?" Reed asked. Joe could tell by the set of the sheriff's jaw that he was trying hard to remain civil.

Brenda looked around, as if inviting everyone else in the room into her conspiracy theory. She lowered her voice and said, "I think April took up with another man—maybe another cowboy. She has the looks, she could pick anyone she wants and they'd go with her. I think she did it to rub Dallas's nose in it, hoping he'd want to get back together with her. But she picked the wrong man to make Dallas jealous. Maybe that cowboy figured out what she was up to and lost his temper.

"Either that," Brenda continued, raising her hand and showing two fingers, "or she was hitchhiking her way back home and she got picked up by the wrong people. It could have been just as simple as that. Didn't I hear that she didn't have her purse or ID on her?"

Reed nodded.

"Maybe that's because the people who beat her, robbed her as well. And they probably left her for dead out there."

Reed and Dulcie looked skeptical.

Brenda pressed on. "I hope you don't go at this thing with blinders on. You've got to consider other possibilities."

"We'll consider them all," Reed said. "But it just seems more likely she was with someone she knew."

"It wasn't Dallas."

"We get that," Reed said.

"It could have been anyone," Brenda said fervently. "It could be someone you'd never suspect. It could'a been those other buckle bunnies she was with. Or it could'a been someone local who picked her up on the highway and offered her a ride to town. I've seen some strange people driving around on the highways. Who knows what they're looking for. Maybe a young, pretty girl wearing cowboy boots?"

Convinced she'd made her point, Brenda said, "There's another reason why I didn't want Dallas to come here with us."

Reed arched his eyebrows and said, "Yes?"

"There's nothing more vengeful than a woman scorned," Brenda said. "If she regained consciousness, I wouldn't put it past her to say Dallas was responsible. That way she could get back at him once and for all."

At that moment, the room seemed to turn red to Joe. He bit his lower lip with his teeth and looked away so that he wouldn't go after both Brenda and Eldon.

"You have interesting theories," Reed said. "And don't think we don't appreciate you coming in on your own to talk with us." His words sounded hollow.

Dulcie said, "I hope you don't mind if I come out and talk with you again and ask some follow-up questions. Plus, I'd like to meet Dallas. I've heard a lot about him."

Joe said, "Like this isn't the first girl he's been around who ended up beaten and dumped."

Eldon's face went white while Brenda rotated her bulk in the chair and stabbed a finger toward Joe.

"My Dallas had nothing to do with that Tibbs girl. Nothing!"

She turned back to Reed. "He has no right to say that to us."

"You're right," Reed said, looking witheringly at Joe.

"This is what I mean," Brenda said, gathering herself onto her feet. "We try to do the right thing and this is what happens."

Eldon stood in a single motion, but never took his cold, dead eyes off Joe. Joe stared right back.

Dulcie moved quickly and stood between them.

"We're sorry," she said to Brenda. "I hope you can understand that Joe is upset right now. If something like that had happened to your daughter . . ."

Brenda nodded. She said, "If you need to talk to us, just make sure to call first. Out at our place, we're always on the watch for poachers and trespassers. Eldon and Bull are known to shoot first and ask questions later."

Eldon gestured toward Joe and said, "If you bring him with you, there'll be trouble."

"I won't. And I'll call first," Dulcie said, looking down at her notebook. Joe could tell she was angry.

AFTER THE CATESES HAD LEFT, Sheriff Reed said to Joe, "That was real smooth."

Joe shrugged and waited for more. Instead, Reed wheeled over to his window and parted the blinds. His office overlooked the parking lot.

Eldon and Brenda were in the cab of their huge SUV, Eldon behind the wheel. The vehicle was old enough that it still had the name SUBURBAN on it, and not the revamped YUKON XL that Chevrolet had taken when they rechristened the exact same vehicle with a less controversial brand. The man stared blankly ahead while Brenda reamed him out, jabbing him in the arm with the same finger she'd pointed at Joe.

"I'd give my right arm to hear what they're saying," Dulcie said.

After five minutes, the truck backed out of the lot and pulled away.

"They're gone," Reed said.

"There are so many holes in their story, I don't know where to start," Dulcie said. "Is it possible for a man with cracked ribs and a dislocated shoulder to drive fifteen hundred miles across the country?"

"It was obvious Brenda wanted Eldon to tell the story," Reed said. "She coached him and set him loose. But he's too damned dumb to keep his days or his story straight. I don't know whether to believe that rattlesnake story or not."

"They're lying," Joe said.

Reed said to Joe, "I know how it looks. But we've got to build a box around Dallas. It shouldn't take too long to establish if and when he was injured and when he got back. There's obviously a video of his ride, and we should be able to find credit card receipts for fifteen hundred miles' worth of gas. We'll see if he'll consent to a doctor going out there. Plus, we don't have any of April's lab results yet or the tech report on the samples taken from where we found her. We might even find Dallas's DNA on her, which destroys their story."

Dulcie snapped her notebook closed. She said, "What is it with their attitude toward us? The county is filled with rural people. We don't look down on anyone."

"That's the way they are," Reed said. "Brenda, especially. She's got a chip on her shoulder and always has. Something about a land deal her father got screwed out of. I don't know the details."

"I don't care about the details," Joe said. "Dallas Cates is guilty as hell."

"But you are *not* to get any further involved in the investigation," Dulcie said, pointing her finger at him. "You already made them mad. If this looks like an angry father going after an innocent kid, it blows up the prosecution."

Joe looked over at Reed. He didn't need to say it again.

"We'll nail the bastard," Reed said. "And maybe we'll charge Eldon and Brenda with obstruction and being accessories to the crime. And if April dies . . ."

Joe cringed.

Reed said, "Sorry. You know where I was going with that. This is why you need to step aside."

As JOE AND DULCIE left Reed's office, she put her hand on his shoulder.

"How is Marybeth holding up?"

"Better than can be expected," Joe said. "I'm waiting for her to call from Billings."

"Give her my best."

"I will."

"We'll get him, Joe."

He looked at her and said, "You better."

"I wasn't kidding about you staying out of this," she said. "If I need to go all the way to the governor, I will."

He nodded, but he didn't commit.

"And you shouldn't get Nate Romanowski involved, either. In

fact, I'd suggest you not tell him until we've got Dallas behind bars. The last thing we need around here is Nate's brand of justice."

"Haven't you heard?" Joe said. "He's gone straight."

"Riiiight," she said, drawing out the word.

WHILE JOE WAS CLAMPING on his hat to go outside to his pickup and Daisy, Dulcie put her hands on her hips.

"Do you think there's anything to Brenda's denials?" she asked.

"No."

"She's right about one thing, though. We need to look beyond Dallas. We need to consider this other mystery cowboy or even the hitchhiking theory. And we need to be open to any other kind of idea, whether we heard it from Brenda Cates or not."

Joe didn't respond.

"We've got a lot of work to do," she said. "We need to verify Brenda's story and track down where April has been for the past month—who she was with, what rodeos she attended, all of that. We need to verify when Dallas was injured—if he was—in Houston. And I need to talk with Dallas himself, without his mother in the room."

Joe nodded.

"Of course, if April recovers, she can tell us who did it, even though Brenda tried pretty hard to discount that even before it happens," she said.

"Which is why her son is guilty as hell," Joe said.

4

J oe sat sullenly in his pickup with his phone in his hand on the outer circle of Saddlestring High School, waiting for Lucy to come out. He was midway in a long line of parents in pickups and SUVs who were waiting for their teenagers to emerge. Even though, officially, he was prohibited from using his state pickup to transport family members, it seemed like the least of his worries at the moment.

He re-litigated the scene from Sheriff Reed's office the hour before, trying to open himself up to the possibility that Dallas had nothing to do with April's injuries. He mulled over Brenda's theories. A mystery cowboy? A stranger picking up hitchhikers? He couldn't square the circle.

He recalled how relentlessly Brenda and Eldon had defended their son. It bothered him on a couple of levels. Although it could be expected that parents would protect their own, it seemed not to have even occurred to them that Dallas could be responsible for the crime. They simply refused to believe it, which made them less than credible. To have such an unshakable belief that Dallas was innocent reminded Joe of other parents he'd encountered over the years: couples who attacked teachers because of their child's failing grades, or coaches because their child was a poor athlete, or *him* because he'd given a citation to their boy for fishing without a valid license.

For some parents, their offspring were perfect beings. It was a cancer on society, he thought, and it was getting out of control. The Cateses were the worst example of it he'd encountered.

He grinned cruelly to himself when he imagined their reaction when Dallas was convicted and sent to the Wyoming State Penitentiary in Rawlins. *Oh,* he thought, *the rending of garments, the gnashing of teeth . . .*

MARYBETH HAD SENT a series of cryptic texts while Joe waited.

> Landing at the trauma center now.

> Doctors evaluating her in the ICU.

> Still hasn't regained consciousness.

> Good doctors, thank God.

> Did you remember to pick up L?

He'd responded: *Yup.*

STUDENTS BEGAN TO POUR out of the front doors of the school moments after the bell rang. Groups of upperclassmen came out and turned for the parking lot and their cars. Tenth graders and those who didn't have vehicles searched the line of cars for their rides.

Joe waited, and waited some more. No Lucy.

Only after he had raised his phone to call her did she come out. She wasn't alone.

Joe had been cursed with three attractive daughters. They stood out in a crowd. Especially Lucy. She was blond, lithe, lively, and stylish. He cringed when he was in a public place with her and saw the looks males gave her, but he understood. She was not as studious as Sheridan or as brooding as April, and she'd come into her own as a genuinely warm personality who looked at the bright side of every situation. Marybeth had once said that Lucy seemed to move across the earth in her own personal sunbeam.

And she did so slowly, Joe thought as he drummed his fingers on the steering wheel. Lucy was a girl without urgency, and she seemed to float through life at her own smiling but unhurried pace.

With her was Noah After Buffalo, her debate club partner. Lucy wore black leggings and knee-high boots with her golden hair cascading over the shoulders of her tight down coat.

Noah was a Northern Arapaho whose parents had recently moved off the reservation and into town. He was smart and polite and seemed to have grown a foot taller in the last few months. He was a year older than Lucy and had his own battered pickup. Sometimes he brought her home after school. Marybeth liked him, and Joe tolerated him as much as he tolerated any male in the vicinity of his daughters.

Lucy and Noah walked closer together than Joe would have liked, and he saw Lucy look over and scan the remaining cars for Marybeth's van. When she saw Joe's green pickup, she mouthed, *"My dad is here"* to Noah, who waved.

Joe waved back, and Lucy separated from Noah and made her way toward his pickup. But before she did, she reached back and squeezed Noah's hand behind her back in an intimate gesture.

"I saw that," Joe said as Lucy slid into the passenger side and Daisy greeted her by pressing her head under Lucy's chin.

"Oh, Dad," Lucy said, vigorously scratching Daisy until the dog moaned.

He thought: *One daughter took up with a cowboy. Another is taking up with an Indian.*

Joe wasn't sure what to make of that.

AS THEY PULLED OUT, Lucy said, "Why isn't Mom here? Not that I mind that you pick me up, but . . ."

She studied him and apparently sensed that bad news was coming. He could see it in her eyes. She was intuitive like that, and had the ability to read people in a way Joe never could. He attributed it to all the years that Lucy had hung back and observed family interactions from the standpoint of the youngest.

He said, "The sheriff's office responded to a call today that a girl had been badly beaten and left by the side of a road. Lucy, it was—"

"April," Lucy said, tears filling her eyes. "Is she okay?"

Joe took a deep breath and told Lucy all he knew, in workmanlike fashion. Lucy listened without comment, but the tears kept coming. She dried her cheeks with the back of her hand. He finished by telling her that Marybeth said the doctors were good.

"Maybe she'll be okay," Lucy said. "One thing about April—she's tough. Sometimes that's scary, like when she's mad at me or thinks I stole her boots or something, but in this case it might get her through."

Joe almost smiled. He recalled the incident a year before when April had launched across the dinner table at Lucy for borrowing her best cowboy boots. Later, they had been found under April's bed. Lucy, to her credit, hadn't backed down.

"So it's you and me," Joe said. "We can stop and get something to eat in town or I can fix you something at home for dinner."

"What?" Lucy asked. "Red meat and bread?"

"What's wrong with that?" He knew he had plenty of elk steaks in the freezer.

"Let's get pizza."

Joe nodded.

JOE ASKED LUCY, "When was the last time you heard from April? You're the only one in the family she really communicated with." They were making the eight-mile drive from Saddlestring to his rural state-owned home on Bighorn Road. The warm pizza was in a box on the seat between them. Strings of drool hung from Daisy's mouth.

"A week ago, I guess," Lucy said. "She posted a photo of herself in a bikini by a swimming pool. It was at some hotel in a big city."

April had blocked both Marybeth and Sheridan from her Facebook and Twitter pages. Only Lucy was allowed to follow her.

"Can you be more specific?" Joe asked.

"It was in Texas somewhere."

"Houston, maybe?"

"That sounds right. But she didn't post much of anything beyond the photo. She never does—there are just lots of photos of her and Dallas doing cool things. I think she wanted to impress me. You know, goofing around in airports, partying with cowboys. Selfies, you know."

Joe grunted. Then: "Did April tell you she and Dallas Cates had broken up?"

"*What?*"

He told her what Brenda Cates had said.

"A month ago?" Lucy said. "No way. If that had happened I'd know about it even if she didn't tell me directly. She wouldn't keep posting photos on her page of the two of them if it was over. April is strange, but she isn't crazy. If they'd broken up—and especially if he'd broken up with *her*—the world would know it by now. She would have started up an 'I Hate Dallas Cates' site."

"If they did break up, do you think April would come back here?" Joe asked.

Lucy shrugged and said, "I never know what April will do next." After a beat, she said again, "No way April and Dallas broke up."

Joe said, "I believe you."

THERE WAS a white late-model pickup parked at Joe's house with two people sitting inside. They were obviously waiting for him to arrive. The vehicle had U.S. government plates.

Joe moaned.

"Who is that?" Lucy asked.

"I call them the sage grouse twins," Joe said. "Go ahead and take Daisy and the pizza inside. I'll be in shortly, after I talk to them."

ANNIE HATCH of the Bureau of Land Management and Revis Wentworth of the U.S. Fish and Wildlife Service waited for Lucy and Daisy to enter the house before they got out of their pickup. Joe remembered that Wentworth had a thing about dogs—one had bitten him once on a local ranch he was visiting and now he insisted that he wouldn't get out of his vehicle until all canines were secured.

Hatch and Wentworth were members of the Interagency Sage Grouse Task Force (ISGTF), which had been created by the federal government two years earlier to oversee state efforts to manage the species. Governor Rulon had loudly objected to the creation of the task force and had threatened to lock up any federal government employees who entered his state, but he'd eventually acquiesced when Washington threatened to withhold highway repair and Medicare funds. An agreement had been reached that the task force would keep the governor's office informed as to their activities and findings and that they'd restrict their jurisdiction to the public lands of the state. That meant literally half of Wyoming, though, and the governor's feelings about *that* situation were well known.

Joe liked Annie Hatch just fine. She was in her mid-thirties, pleasant, and friendly in just a mildly bureaucratic way. She had long, curly brown hair and an athletic build, and she dressed in an "outdoor girl" style: jeans, hiking boots, fishing shirts, fleece jackets. Her personal car was a Prius and she taught yoga classes in the evenings. Unlike Wentworth, who resided in Denver and was renting a room at the Holiday Inn in Saddlestring, Annie lived in a small house in town and was a member of the community.

"Hey, Joe," she said as she got out of the pickup.

"Annie," Joe said. "What brings you here?"

"Sage grouse."

"Imagine that," Joe said wearily.

Revis Wentworth got out and cast a cautionary look toward the front door of the Pickett home.

"Daisy is inside and she's harmless," Joe said to him.

"Supposedly, so was the dog that bit me. I needed eleven stitches," Wentworth said back.

Joe shrugged.

Wentworth said, "We got a report that there's been a massacre on BLM land."

Wentworth was slight, serious, and more than a little in love with his position, Joe thought. He was pale and wore black-framed hipster glasses. Joe had never seen him smile or make a joke. Wentworth always wore a sport jacket, but kept it unbuttoned so the people he met could see the semiauto hanging from a shoulder holster underneath. As one of 250 special agents for the USFW, he was authorized to carry a weapon.

"Yup," Joe said, gesturing toward the foothills to the west. "Lek Sixty-four. I counted twenty-one dead birds."

"My God, an entire lek," Hatch said, covering her open mouth with her hand as she gasped. "That's horrible."

"Were you going to inform ISGTF about it at any point?" Wentworth asked. He pronounced the acronym "Izg-Tiff."

"Probably."

"Is there some reason you didn't call right away?"

"By the time I had thought about it, I checked my watch and it was already after five," Joe said. It was a dig, but it was also true.

"You have my cell phone number," Wentworth said.

"Actually, I don't."

"Please," Hatch said, stepping between them. "Let's settle this later. We're talking about an entire lek of sage grouse."

"This is nothing more than a provocation," Wentworth said, shaking his head. Joe eyed him carefully to determine that he was talking about the slaughter and not about him.

"I wouldn't read too much into it yet," Joe said, sidling past the special agents so that he was positioned to open his gate and go inside. He hoped they would let him. He said, "I gathered evidence and took a bunch of photos. I've got spent shotgun shells, tire tracks, and maybe even a DNA sample. It looked to me like a couple of yahoos stumbled onto those birds and went postal. We'll get 'em."

"Locals, no doubt," Wentworth said with disdain.

"Probably."

"You'll need to turn over all the items you found so we can send them to our forensics lab," Wentworth said.

"I'm sending them to our own lab in Laramie on Monday," Joe said, annoyed with Wentworth's attitude. "They're the best when it comes to wildlife crimes."

"Do you want me to go over your head?" Wentworth asked, arching his eyebrows.

"Go ahead," Joe said with a flash of anger. Then he took a breath and said, "Revis, why can't we talk to each other like a couple of adults? Why do you need to act like the federal alpha dog? I know how to do my job, and we're just talking about sage grouse here."

It was another shot.

"Just sage grouse," Wentworth repeated, as if he couldn't believe Joe's insolence. "I suppose if you spend every day with hunters and dead animals, a few dead birds don't seem like much. Did you forget the entire population is on the brink?"

Hatch put her hand on Wentworth's shoulder and said to Joe, "There's no reason we can't work together on this, is there?"

"No, of course not. By the way, how did you find out about the incident?"

"Someone called our tip line," Wentworth said.

"Who?"

"It was anonymous."

"Male? Female? Age? That area up there where I found the birds isn't a place where someone would just happen by."

"I can't give you any of that without authorization," Wentworth said, looking over the top of his hipster glasses. "But we need you to take us up there to Lek Sixty-four."

"Really?"

"We don't want to get lost. You can guide us there."

"There you go again," Joe said. "Giving me another order I'm going to ignore."

"Please, Joe?" Hatch pleaded.

Joe paused by his gate and looked over his shoulder at her. He said, "Not tonight. I've got a personal situation going on and I need to be home with my daughter.

"I'll give you precise directions if you want, but I'm surprised you don't know where it is. Believe me when I tell you there isn't much more to find up there, and by the time you locate the site, it'll be dark and snowing."

"Let us decide that," Wentworth said.

Joe turned and went to his truck and found his topo map of the benchland foothills. He spread it out on the hood of his truck and circled the location, then handed the map to Hatch.

"I'll need that back when you're through," he said.

"I'll return it," she said with a smile.

Joe looked toward the Bighorns. They were obscured by storm clouds.

"You might want to wait until tomorrow," he said.

"We heard you the first time," Wentworth said. Then: "C'mon, Annie. Let's go do the game warden's job for him."

"You do that," Joe said, and turned to the house.

"Joe, is everything okay?" Hatch asked.

"Nope, it isn't," he said, and went inside.

LUCY SAID, "They're in love," when Joe entered the mudroom and kicked off his cowboy boots. She was sitting on the couch with their Lab/corgi mix, Tube, in her lap. Since Sheridan and April had left the house, Tube had become Lucy's dog.

"What?"

"They're in love, those two. Or at least he's in love with her. I was watching them through the window. What are their names?"

Joe told her, then said, "Lucy, they just work together."

"Are they single?"

Joe said, "I don't know. Annie Hatch is. I'm not sure about Wentworth. I saw a wedding ring on his finger when I first met him, but I don't think he has it on now."

Lucy nodded smugly. She had a gleam in her eye. She said, "He's definitely not wearing it now."

"How do you know he's in love with her?" Joe asked, a bit flummoxed by his youngest daughter.

"Didn't you notice their body language? She's nice and friendly, but he's very protective of her. He acts like he wants everyone to know he's in charge. And when she put her hand on his shoulder, it calmed him down immediately. That wouldn't happen if they just worked together."

"I never would have noticed," Joe said.

"No kidding," Lucy said.

If Lucy was correct, Joe thought, it helped explain the almost religious fervor the sage grouse twins brought to their jobs. They'd been brought together by a single mission: to save a species. They spent hours and days together and they came from a certain bureaucratic mind-set. It made sense, and he wondered why he'd never noticed it before.

"Why didn't you tell them about April?" Lucy asked. "I'm sure they'd understand."

"It just didn't seem right," Joe muttered.

"They'll know soon enough," she said. "The word will get out."

He nodded. Of course she was right. And the information would have wiped the smirk off Wentworth's face.

Still, though . . .

"HEY," Lucy said to Joe as she ate a slice of pizza at the dining room table, "I want to show you something."

She'd been browsing on her iPad while Joe skimmed the weekly Saddlestring *Roundup*. She turned the iPad in his direction.

"What are we watching?" Joe asked. He could see she'd already queued up a YouTube video.

"It took me about ten seconds to find Dallas Cates's ride."

Joe was suddenly interested. Lucy started the video. It was titled "Dallas Cates Riding Bushwhacker at the Houston Livestock Show and Rodeo." The date the video had been posted was three days before, but he knew that didn't necessarily mean it was when it was taken.

It was an amateur video, shot by someone standing behind the chutes with a shaky handheld camera phone. There was no narration.

It began with a shot of Dallas buckling on the mandatory flak vest, then pulling his cowboy hat on tight. His face was grim and determined and practically set in stone. Then he turned and mounted the chute where Bushwhacker stood waiting.

The crowd sounds were loud in the background and there were snippets of conversation nearby. It was shoulder-to-shoulder behind the chutes: contestants, stock contractors, cowboys who were there to help their friends and offer advice. The visual swooped around at times as the videographer was jostled, and there were brief shots of the astrodome roof, the crowd, and dirt on the floor. Then the videographer managed to secure a good location right next to the chute itself.

The announcer said, *"Now, folks, you can turn your attention to chute number two, where the world champion bull rider from two years ago, Dallas Cates of Saddlestring, Wyoming, and Stephenville, Texas, prepares to go mano a mano with Bushwhacker, the 2014 Bull of the Year."*

Joe and Lucy exchanged glances.

"Watch this close," she said.

Dallas Cates lowered himself down on the back of the bull. He jammed his gloved right hand through the rope and used his left hand to pull his fingers through farther. The camera jostled again, and for a moment the screen was filled with overhead lights. Then it settled back on Dallas. He was hunched forward on the back of the bull, his left hand already poised in the air.

Someone shouted, "Ride 'im, Cates!"

The announcer said, *"Dallas Cates enters this go-round at number two in the world and number three in the standings. A good ride on this bull will vault him to first place! Folks, Dallas Cates is eight seconds away from shocking the world."*

Behind the chute where Cates was mounted, a rodeo official pulled back hard on the flanking strap. The official would release it the moment the gate was thrown open.

Cates broke his concentration for a moment and glanced over at the stands. The camera followed, and there, for no more than a second, was April. She flashed a smile at Dallas and offered him two thumbs up.

Then Dallas turned back to the task at hand and nodded to the men outside the gate waiting for the signal to open it. Dallas had a certain something, Joe noted as he watched. He had a presence about him, real charisma. As much as Joe hated him, he couldn't take his eyes off the man. No wonder the jeans company chose him as a spokesman, he thought.

Almost imperceptibly, Cates nodded to the men in the arena that he was ready.

Bushwhacker and Dallas exploded into the arena in a whirling combination of twists and bucks. The crowd went wild. Although the videographer missed part of it, Dallas Cates was thrown forward on the front shoulders of the bull, then rocked back. The cowboy flew through the air and landed flat on his back in the dirt behind the bull.

While the announcer said, *"Dallas Cates gets Bushwhacked in two-point-eight-seven seconds!"* the bull wheeled and lowered its head and charged Dallas, who scrambled backward like a crab.

Bullfighters dressed as clowns swooped in a second too late to distract the animal, and the bull either hooked or head-butted Cates with enough power to send him airborne again. There was an audible gasp from the fans, but despite the unreliable camerawork, Joe could see Cates roll to his feet and scramble up the chute boards to safety.

Then it was over.

"Let's see it again," Joe said.

They watched it three more times. It was April, all right, and it didn't look like the two of them were at odds. After all, Dallas had looked over to her for last-second encouragement. She'd been beaming. Joe had rarely seen her look so happy or so excited.

"I told you," Lucy said. She was focused on the relationship.

Joe was focused on the wreck of the ride.

The last glimpse of Dallas was of him climbing the chute boards and vaulting over the top into the ready area.

"That bull got Dallas," Joe said, "but he looks pretty darned healthy when he runs away. I know adrenaline can make a man do all kinds of things, but I also know how much it hurts to get your ribs broken. There's nothing worse. Dallas doesn't look like he's got broken ribs the way he's flying over that chute gate. Plus, he was wearing one of those flak vests they all have to wear these days."

Lucy looked over and said, "Does that mean those Cates people are lying?"

"I think it does," Joe said.

HE WAS FEEDING THE HORSES in the barn after dinner when Marybeth called. She sounded shaken.

"The doctors say April has severe brain damage. She was hit multiple times in the head. There's swelling around her brain."

"Oh no," he said, once again feeling his knees wobble.

"They say they want to put her into a medically induced coma."

"A what?"

"A medically induced coma."

"How bad is it, Marybeth?"

She said, "They really don't know. They say she's on the low end of the Glasgow Coma Scale, whatever that means. There's no eye, verbal, or motor response. They need our permission to put her under, so I wanted to talk with you first."

Joe shook his head. As if Marybeth could see him do it, she said, "The idea is to keep her unconscious and healing until the swelling in her brain goes down. They want to give her a drug called propofol to put her into the coma. The doctors say shutting down her functions will lower her blood pressure and reduce the swelling in her brain in case they have to do surgery later. It'll give the brain time to heal. It's what they did for Gabrielle Giffords, the U.S. representative who got shot in the head in Arizona, and what they do with other victims of blunt force trauma."

Joe recalled the Giffords incident. He asked, "What do you think?"

"If they leave her the way she is, her body may shut off blood flow to the damaged parts of her brain. She'd be brain-dead."

"Oh, man."

When Marybeth didn't speak for a moment, he realized she had lowered the phone to cry. He waited.

"It's not a sure thing, so we have to brace ourselves," she said after a moment, once she'd gathered herself together. He could imagine her wiping away tears on her cheeks as she talked. "It's possible she'll never come out of it. It's also possible that they could bring her out of it, but there's been so much damage, she'd never really be the same. But they're good doctors and I trust them. They have a neurosurgeon on call in case they need to do surgery. All we can do is trust them and pray for her."

Joe tried to swallow, but his mouth was dry.

"How long?" he asked.

"Days, weeks, maybe months. They use propofol because it's easily controlled and it has a short length. That's so they can reduce the dosage when the swelling goes down and bring her out of the coma periodically. When they do, they can measure her Glasgow scale to see if she's responding. They also measure brain activity through catheters in her brain."

"Then we have to say yes," Joe said.

"I agree. I'll go sign whatever it is I have to sign and I'll call you later tonight."

JOE WENT INSIDE and told Lucy what Marybeth had said. Lucy nodded, wide-eyed, then got up and started toward her room to call her big sister, Sheridan.

In the threshold of the doorway, she asked, "Did April say for sure who did this to her?"

Joe shook his head.

"Will she ever be able to tell us?"

"We don't know, Lucy."

Lucy closed her eyes briefly, then shut the door behind her.

WHEN JOE'S CELL PHONE lit up an hour later, he lunged for it. He was halfway through his first bourbon and water. The television was on, but he had no idea what network it was tuned to.

He looked at the phone screen and scowled, then punched it live.

Annie Hatch said, "It's a blizzard up here, Joe. We can't see well enough to find the road to get back to town. Revis and I were hoping you could drive up here and kind of lead us back."

"Did you find the site?"

"We think so, but we're not sure. There's so much snow in the sagebrush—"

"I told you not to go up there tonight," he said.

"I know, I know," she said wearily. "Do you think we wanted to call you?"

"Sit tight," Joe said with irritation. "Don't keep driving around. Just sit tight with your headlights on. How far did you go off the county road?"

"Not far, I don't think."

"Tell him to hurry," Wentworth said in the background.

She didn't, but Joe said, "Wentworth better keep his mouth shut or you'll both be there all night."

He heard her shush her partner.

As Joe laced on his boots in the mudroom, his phone lit up again. Reed.

"Mike," Joe said.

"Are you sitting down?"

Joe braced for it, whatever it was.

"After you left this afternoon, the dispatcher got a 911 call. The reporting party said she heard about April through someone she knows at the hospital, and she recalled seeing a man she identified as Tilden Cudmore force a girl matching April's description into his vehicle on the highway yesterday morning. She said she didn't call it in at the time because she thought maybe Cudmore was her father and the girl was a runaway or something."

Joe tried to process what Reed had just told him.

"Who made that call?" Joe asked.

"I don't know," the sheriff said. "She wouldn't identify herself to the dispatcher."

"But you think it was legitimate?"

"Yeah," Reed said. "We've had run-ins with Cudmore a few times. He's a survivalist type who lives by himself in a trailer out in the county. He's a real piece of work. There have been rumors about him cruising the highways, driving well below the speed limit, like he's looking for somebody, but we couldn't hardly pick him up for that.

"Anyway, I sent a deputy out to his place, but he wasn't home and his Humvee was gone. The deputy happened to look in the man's dumpster and he found a purse inside with April's ID. There's also a backpack and some clothing we hope you can identify."

Joe said, "Tilden Cudmore. You've thrown me for a loop."

"Join the club," Reed said. Then: "Here's the address. I'm on my way out there now."

———

Joe knocked and opened Lucy's bedroom door. She was still on the phone with Sheridan.

He said, "Get dressed and bundled up. I need your help. They may have found some of April's things and you'll be better at recognizing them than I am."

"Did Dallas Cates have them?" Lucy asked.

"Some guy named Tilden Cudmore."

"Who's he?"

"I have no idea," Joe said. "But we're going to find out."

5

Tilden Cudmore, fifty-two, lived alone on a sagebrush-covered swale by the wastewater treatment plant six miles west of Saddlestring. From the county road, Joe saw the pulsing lights of the law enforcement vehicles, so he knew where to turn.

He and Lucy passed under a wrought iron archway that was strung with bleached-white animal skulls, a naked and shackled storefront mannequin made to look as if it were being frog-marched to meet its fate, and a tattered DON'T TREAD ON ME Gadsden flag that rippled in the cold, light breeze.

"This place is creepy," Lucy said, her eyes wide.

Joe grunted a response. He tried not to think of April being brought here the night before. That shackled mannequin alone, if she had seen it, seemed to foretell a horrible fate.

Lucy hugged herself. No doubt she was spooked, Joe thought. While Sheridan often used to ride along on his patrols and had experienced crime scenes, raucous elk camps, and sometimes tense confrontations, Lucy had never been eager to accompany him into the field. He understood. Lucy preferred happy situations and happy people, while Sheridan was intrigued by the procedures involved with law enforcement. Joe appreciated the differences in the way each girl was wired since birth.

The two-track entry road to the dark trailer was muddy and

rutted. Old ranch equipment—broken-down tractors, a hay-baling machine, a slumped-over wooden wagon—lined both sides of the path. Unlike many remote ranches that had a graveyard of broken machinery and trucks, it was obvious someone had deliberately placed the equipment there, just as someone had erected the arch-way and wired on the skulls. Sheriff Reed's van, as well as two county SUVs, were parked in front of a ramshackle double-wide trailer that looked like a flatbed had backed up and dumped it off years before. There were dead trees on the windward side of the structure and a litter-strewn front yard. A hand-painted sign was mounted on the front of the trailer near the door that read:

STAY OUT
SURVIVORS WILL BE PROSECUTED

Joe noted a ten-foot chain-link enclosure on the side of the trailer. The gravel floor of the cage was covered with feces, and lengths of chain snaked through the gravel. Obviously, Cudmore housed dogs there.

Dulcie Schalk's Subaru Outback sat off to the side.

Joe wheeled in and killed the motor. He said to Lucy, "How about you stay in the truck until I figure out what's going on?"

"Okay."

She seemed to be in no hurry to get out. He reached over and pat-ted her shoulder before opening his door.

Dulcie was in the middle of a heated conversation with Deputy Boner. Sheriff Reed was in his wheelchair between the two of them as if he were a referee.

"What we've got here is an illegal search," Dulcie said to Boner.

"You entered private property without a warrant and went through his garbage. I could see Judge Hewitt rule that whatever you found here is inadmissible as evidence."

"It wasn't like that," Boner said, crossing his arms over his chest. "I drove out here in response to a call to ask Mr. Cudmore some questions about his whereabouts yesterday. The subject wasn't home, and as I was heading back to my vehicle, I heard what I thought was a baby crying."

That silenced Dulcie, and she looked to Reed. Reed was non-committal.

"The crying sound was coming from the dumpster," Boner said, pointing toward a dented metal box on the edge of the lot. "I thought it sounded human, so I had probable cause to look inside to make sure there wasn't anyone in imminent danger."

"He had probable cause," Reed said, nodding his head.

"A crying sound?" Dulcie asked, skeptical.

"Turned out to be a cat," Boner said. "There was a cat in there. But it sure sounded like a baby crying."

"And where is it now?" Dulcie asked.

"As soon as I lifted the lid, it ran away."

"And this evidence you found was just sitting on top in plain view?"

Boner looked over at Reed, then said, "Sort of."

Dulcie moaned. "What does that mean?"

"I shined my light in there and saw some fabric poking out of the garbage. So I kind of pushed some trash aside."

"Think of his state of mind," Reed said. "At this point, he was still thinking *baby*, not *cat*."

Dulcie asked Boner, "What color was it? The cat, I mean."

Boner hesitated a second before saying, "Black."

"A black cat," Reed echoed.

"With white feet," Boner said, as if just then recalling the detail.

"Did you and the sheriff cook this up together?" Dulcie asked, but her tone had softened.

"Would we ever do anything like that?" Reed asked. Then, looking up, he said, "Hey, Joe."

"Mike."

"I'm glad you're here. We've got a couple of things to show you."

"That's why I brought my daughter Lucy," Joe said. "She knows April's clothing and such."

He winked at Dulcie. "We would have gotten here sooner," he said, "but I had to slow down to let a black cat cross the road."

"Hmph," Dulcie said, shaking her head. But she didn't continue with her objections.

AFTER JOE WAS ASSURED by Boner and Reed that nothing Lucy would see should upset her, she joined them near the dumpster. The items Boner had found inside were displayed on a blue plastic tarp and covered with a clear sheet of plastic. Evidence numbers and tags were already attached and the display was ready to be photographed. Beads of moisture dotted the outside plastic from snowflakes that had melted on it.

Boner swept the beam of his flashlight from item to item.

"That's her sweater," Lucy said, pointing at a thick beige garment. "I know because I used to borrow it from her closet. She yelled at me when she found out, so I stopped."

"What about the coat?" Reed asked gently.

He was referring to a multicolored leather jacket embroidered with NFR logos and insignias.

"I've never seen that in person," Lucy said, "because I think it's new. It *looks* new. I'm pretty sure there are a couple of photos on Facebook of her wearing it, though. That's easy to check."

Reed and Dulcie exchanged looks, and Dulcie nodded that she'd follow up.

"And there's this," Reed said, gesturing toward what looked like a leather shoulder bag with a western buckle strap on it. Joe recognized it himself from the last time he'd seen April. She had slung the bag into the cab of his truck when he'd picked her up after work at Welton's Western Wear. All she could talk about that day as they drove home was having met Dallas Cates, who had been at the store that day to promote his line of denim jeans.

"That's her purse," Lucy said. Joe noticed her eyes were moist.

"We found a wallet inside with her Wyoming driver's license," Reed said to Joe. "There were no credit cards or cash, though. I assume she has a cell phone, but we haven't found it yet."

"She has a phone," Lucy said.

Deputy Boner said, "We're waiting for a generator and lights before we crawl back in the dumpster. There's a lot of stuff in there, and heavier things like a phone or keys might have settled to the bottom. There may be other items in there, too. These things were obvious because they were on top."

"Under the black cat," Dulcie said, rolling her eyes.

"Yes, ma'am," Boner said with what sounded like sincerity.

"Where's this Tilden Cudmore?" Joe asked.

"He looks like our perp," Boner said.

"Whoa there," Reed said. "Who's to say he didn't find these things on the highway and bring them home to throw away after pocketing the credit cards and cash?"

Boner said, "He still looks like our perp. Especially since somebody saw him forcing April into his car."

"There's that," Reed said.

"Again," Dulcie said, raising her voice, "I want everyone here to proceed with caution. I'll grant that it looks bad for Mr. Cudmore, but we only know what we know . . . *about this son of a bitch.*"

Joe almost smiled. Dulcie had revealed more about her thoughts than she had wanted to, he thought.

"HAVE YOU BEEN INSIDE?" Joe asked Reed, nodding toward the dark trailer.

"We're waiting on a warrant from Judge Hewitt," Reed said. "Dulcie put that in motion earlier, and we tracked him down having dinner at the Burg-O-Pardner. He signed it. We should have it within the half hour. The evidence tech is also on the way."

Joe nodded. They were near Reed's van. Boner and the other deputies were establishing a crime scene perimeter by threading yellow tape along the barbed-wire fence and entry arch. Lucy was in Joe's truck on her cell, filling in her mother and Sheridan. Dulcie was leaning against her car, talking on her cell phone as well.

"I've got to admit this really surprised me," Reed said. "He wasn't on our radar at all. Maybe Brenda kind of had a point about going at this with blinders on."

"I'm still not sold," Joe said. "What can you tell me about Tilden Cudmore?"

"He's a nut," Reed said without hesitation. "I've had quite a few encounters with him over the years—enough that when we get that warrant I want everyone to take their time going through that trailer of his. I wouldn't be surprised to find out it's booby-trapped. He's probably got fragmentation grenades rigged up to trip wires and shotguns cocked and aimed toward the doors. I might even leave it alone for now and ask the state bomb squad to open it up as soon as they can get here."

He looked up at Joe, and the ambient light from errant flashlights highlighted the spray of stress wrinkles that fanned out from the corners of his eyes.

Reed said, "Cudmore thinks of himself as a patriot and survivalist type, but he's just a walking bundle of paranoid conspiracy theories. He moved here two or three years ago from southern Illinois, I think, hoping to find a bunch of like-minded individuals. For the most part, I think he was disappointed.

"I've heard him go on at city council meetings about the Trilateral Commission, the Bilderbergers, Agenda 21, all that crap. He's a 9/11 truther who thinks Bush and Cheney brought down the towers so they could invade Iraq for oil. Cudmore's politics are all over the map. We threw him out of the local Tea Party because he's such a lunatic."

"*We?*" Joe asked.

"I'm on board with my largest constituency," Reed said, a little on the defensive. "You know that."

Wyoming had a larger per capita membership in the Tea Party than any other state.

"What does he do for a living?" Joe asked.

"He can run a backhoe, I guess. But basically he does a whole lot of nothing," Reed said, shaking his head. "He's supposedly got some kind of disability and he lives off welfare payments."

Joe said, "He hates the government but lives off welfare?"

"Yeah, I know," Reed said.

Joe gestured to Reed to continue.

"You've never run into him?" the sheriff asked. "He drives an army-surplus Humvee. Bumper stickers and signs all over it?"

Joe now recalled the Humvee and some of the messages on it: KILL A COMMIE FOR MOMMY, 9/11 WAS AN INSIDE JOB, THE TREE OF LIBERTY MUST BE REFRESHED FROM TIME TO TIME WITH THE BLOOD OF TYRANTS, RON PAUL FOR PRESIDENT, ONE NATION UNDER CCTV, OBAMA LOVES AMERICA LIKE O.J. LOVED NICOLE. A miniature Gadsden flag flew from the radio antenna.

"That's his?" Joe said. "Yeah—I've seen it around town. But I guess he's not a hunter or a fisherman, because I've never run across him out in the field in my district. I'll run a license check, but if he was a sportsman I think I would know it. I thought survivalists hunted at least. How else would they survive?"

"Some, like Tilden Cudmore, buy their five years' supply of food and have it delivered by UPS," Reed said. "We should assume Cudmore is armed and dangerous. He's an open-carry type— wears a .357 revolver in a holster over his coat. He's been thrown out of county commissioners' meetings because he refuses to take it off."

"Any sex crimes on his record?" Joe asked softly, looking over to make sure Lucy was still in his pickup. She was.

"No," Reed said with a sigh. "No felonies at all. A few DUIs, resisting arrest, refusing to comply—that sort of thing. I think he's in the middle of a tax dispute with the IRS, but they haven't involved our department. So his misdemeanor convictions have been for civil disobedience stuff—except for the DUIs. But, as I told you earlier, we've had a few calls about him cruising way below the speed limit out on the interstate. He alarms people when they see him driving around in that Humvee of his. But we've never had a reason to arrest him for it.

"I sent an officer out here once to ask him why he drives around like that. Cudmore claimed he was looking for beer cans and bottles to claim the deposit on them. That doesn't exactly square with his personality, but that's what he said."

"Is he prowling for hitchhikers?" Joe asked.

"That would be my guess," Reed said. "But again, the first time we've ever received a report of him forcing someone into his car came a few hours ago. Thank goodness the RP put two and two together and let us know."

Joe asked, "Who is the reporting party?"

"A female. I'm not sure she identified herself to the dispatcher."

"Can we find out?" Joe asked.

"We'll have a recording," Reed said, looking skeptically at Joe. "Why—what are you thinking?"

Joe shrugged.

"Anyway," Reed said, "we've put out a statewide BOLO on him and his Humvee. He won't get far if he stays in that vehicle. It's a rolling billboard."

Deputy Boner appeared from the dark and held a cell phone out to Reed. "Chief Williamson for you."

Reed frowned and shook his head before taking it.

"Yes, Rocky," Reed said.

Joe could only hear Reed's side of the conversation, but he got the gist of what was going on.

"No, we've got it handled. There's no need for that now . . .

"I'd say sit tight and put your resources into finding Cudmore . . .

"I know he's always armed, but sending that thing out here might play into his worldview and set him off, you know? I'd rather not do that . . .

"I understand. You're just offering help and I appreciate that. But we've got the situation under control."

Reed punched off and handed the phone back to Boner. To Joe, he said, "Our overeager police chief offered to send out his new toy. I politely declined."

Joe rolled his eyes.

The Saddlestring Police Department, like so many police departments across the country, had received a twenty-ton military MRAP—a mine-resistant ambush protected vehicle—from the Pentagon and the Department of Homeland Security the month before. The vehicle had been designed for and used in the Iraq War. Although it had cost the government more than a half-million dollars, it was given to Chief Williamson and his six-person police department free of charge. Helmets, body armor, combat boots, and camouflage uniforms were also provided. Williamson, who was as eager to make a show of force as Sheriff Reed was to refrain from it, had also procured a .50-caliber machine gun for the turret on top.

To Joe's knowledge, the MRAP had been used twice: once to arrest a meth cook operating out of a garage, and also to serve papers on a derelict ex-husband for failure to pay child support. There had been a column in the Saddlestring *Roundup* by Chief Williamson apologizing for the damage to curbs, gutters, and lawns the MRAP had crushed en route, as well as a vow to only use it in the future for more appropriate situations.

Joe left Reed to check on Lucy. It had gotten cooler. Hard pellets of snow came in waves, bouncing off the windshields and the packed ground.

It was then that he remembered the plight of the sage grouse twins.

He pulled his cell phone out of his pocket and called Annie Hatch.

"I'm really sorry," he said. "Something came up. I can be up there in a couple of hours—"

"Fuck you!" Wentworth screamed back. He'd obviously snatched the phone from Hatch. "Don't even bother. We found Lek Sixty-four just after the snow paused for a few minutes, and we managed to find the road, no thanks to you."

Joe punched off before he said something he'd later regret.

Ten minutes later, a set of bright headlights appeared on the access road. Because of his job and the long nights he had spent perching and patrolling his district, Joe had become a student of headlights in the dark. He could discern the make and model of an off-road vehicle by the spacing, height, and intensity of the headlamps. They were like faces to him. These headlights were far apart and higher and brighter than normal, and Joe shouted, "It looks like a Hummer!"

"Oh shit," Reed said. "Here he comes."

As he wheeled toward his van, Reed said to his officers, "Get ready for anything. Think of your safety first—and no hero antics. We just want to take him in and question him at this point."

Deputies jogged toward their vehicles with their hands on their weapons.

Joe grasped Dulcie by the arm and guided her toward his pickup. Lucy opened her door when she saw what he was doing.

"Please get in there with Lucy, and both of you stay on the floor," Joe said. "Don't raise your heads until I tell you to, okay?"

Lucy nodded, and scooted across the seat to make room for Dulcie. Joe retrieved his Remington Wingmaster 12-gauge shotgun from behind the seat. If there was a firefight coming, he thought, the last thing he wanted was to be dependent on his sidearm. He racked a double-ought shell into the receiver.

When the pickup door was closed, Joe looked across the hood toward the oncoming vehicle. Rather than slow down at the band of crime scene tape, the Hummer accelerated through it.

H e knows we're here!" Reed shouted.

Joe crouched down behind the front fender of his pickup and rotated on his heels so he could survey the situation behind him. Reed had wheeled his chair back to his van and was positioned near the grille. Joe saw a glimmer of red from the wigwag lights wink from the barrel of Reed's drawn semiauto. The deputies were well positioned behind their vehicles and were locked and loaded. Boner was crouched behind the back hatch of his SUV.

The Humvee roared into the yard and steered around two sheriff's department SUVs, headed toward the trailer. Joe popped his head up over the hood of his pickup and was instantly blinded by the Humvee's headlights. He dropped back down, squeezing his eyes shut. All he could see on the inside of his eyelids were the pulsing green orbs of an afterimage.

As the Humvee shot past Joe's truck, he heard several deputies shout for Cudmore to stop, but he didn't. Joe kept his head down, but no one fired at the passing vehicle.

The driver powered through a small front fence and across the lawn, turning around the side of the trailer and out of view. But rather than keep on going, the vehicle braked to a stop in the backyard.

"He's going inside!" Reed shouted. He ordered two deputies to flank the trailer, and they moved out on foot.

"Should we storm it?" Boner asked Reed.

"Negative," Reed said back. "I don't want to get anybody hurt."

"He's inside," someone said.

Joe looked up. A dim light had been turned on inside the trailer in what looked like the living room. A moment later, the window was thrown open.

"You sons of bitches have no right to be on my property, so get the hell off!"

He sounded enraged.

"Get in your goddamned cars and get the hell off my property, you fascist, jackbooted thugs!" he hollered. "Unless I see warrants and an order signed by the sheriff of this county—*the only authority I recognize*—you're trespassing on my place and I'll have all your asses. You have no right to be here!"

He had a thundering voice, Joe thought, but slightly slurred. Joe blinked his eyes, trying to force away the effects of the exposure to the headlights so he could see again.

"I'm right here, Tilden," Reed responded from behind his van. "It's Sheriff Reed. The warrant is on the way. So calm yourself down and stop yelling. Nobody wants any trouble if we can avoid it."

Reed had a patient, reasonable timbre to his voice.

That seemed to startle Cudmore into silence.

Reed said, "If you're packing that pistol you carry around, you need to take it out of your holster and put it down and come out of the house. I need to see your hands."

"Sheriff, why are you here?" Cudmore asked.

"I think you know why, Tilden," Reed said.

"Whatever it is, it's bullshit."

"So calm down and let's talk about it."

Joe took a deep breath. The situation seemed to be cooling. He chanced a glimpse around the front of his truck, keeping low this time so the headlights wouldn't hit him again.

In the background, he could hear one of the deputies on his radio calling for additional personnel. He hoped that Chief Williamson wasn't monitoring the channel.

Joe caught a glimpse of Cudmore as he lumbered past the dining room window. He was a huge man, blocky and solid. He had a massive Neanderthal brow and deep-set eyes. His unshaven face sparkled with silver whiskers. He wore a kind of slouch hat and there was a spray of wild thin hair that flowed from beneath the sweatband to his shoulders. The wispy hair glowed in the beams of flashlights and spotlights, and then he was gone.

A few seconds later, his face appeared in the bottom corner of the window. Cudmore squinted into the light, his mouth curled with anger. "How many of you jackbooted thugs are out there, anyway?"

"Quit saying we're jackbooted thugs, Tilden," Reed said with annoyance. "It's my sheriff's department. I don't even know what a jackboot is."

"How many?"

"Half my department, Tilden," Reed said.

"Well, shit, it'll take more than that if you want to arrest me."

"Lower your weapon and come out," Reed said. Not so reasonable-sounding this time.

"Ain't you heard?" Cudmore said. "There's this thing called the Second Amendment. I got a right to keep and bear arms."

"Of course you do," Reed responded. "But we've got a situation here and I'm getting impatient. We'll give you your weapons back after we ask you a few questions at my office. If there's been a mistake, you'll be back here within an hour or so."

"To hell with that. I know how your so-called justice system works. Get your men off my place. All of 'em. I'll talk to you, but only to you."

"That's not going to happen, Tilden," Reed said.

Joe didn't know all the reasoning or philosophy behind it, but he'd heard that some survivalists made it part of their governing philosophy to recognize the local sheriff as the only authority in the country because, for whatever reason, the rest of the government—especially the federal government—was considered illegitimate. At the moment, Joe couldn't care less about Cudmore's reasons. He wanted him in a cage—or worse.

"You're not arresting anyone," Cudmore boomed. "This is my private property and you have no business being on it."

"Back to that," Reed said.

"Yes, goddamnit, back to that," Cudmore said. "Why are you here, anyway?"

"We need to ask you some questions about a girl you might have picked up on the highway yesterday. We found her, Tilden."

There was a long pause. Then Cudmore said, "What girl?"

It was an unconvincing reply, Joe thought. There was a hint of panic in it.

"If I come out, you promise you won't shoot me?" Cudmore asked.

"I promise. My guys are professionals, and they won't shoot, either, as long as you don't make any threatening moves. So come out slow and relaxed, Tilden. We'll go to my office and we can talk this out."

Cudmore's face disappeared from the window.

Joe looked at the front door: it wasn't opening. He wondered if Cudmore would be dumb enough to try to escape through the back, where two deputies were waiting. Judging by his performance thus far, Joe thought, Cudmore was dumb enough to do just about anything.

For the first time, Joe heard something beneath the sound of the Humvee's engine: the snarling of dogs. He changed his angle and could see the tops of black shapes inside the trailer: blocky heads, and glimpses of eyes and white teeth. The insides of the windows were smeared with spittle.

"Mike," Joe said, "he's got his dogs in there with him."

Cudmore's face reappeared and he looked toward where he'd heard Joe's voice. He seemed to be thinking, trying to decide what he was going to do next.

"I've got my dogs in here," Cudmore said. "I suppose you're going to arrest me for that, too?"

"Of course not," Reed said. "Just keep them inside when you come out. We don't want to hurt your animals, either."

After another long pause, Cudmore said, "Okay, I'm coming out." He sounded resigned.

Joe tensed for what might happen next.

The front door opened slightly and Cudmore squeezed out. The dogs tried to exit as well, but he blocked them with his body until he could close the door behind him. A flashlight beam raked Cudmore over, pausing at his empty holster.

"Deputy Boner," Reed said, "please approach Mr. Cudmore and place him under arrest."

"Yes, sir," Boner said, rising from behind his vehicle. His weapon was out and extended in front of him.

"I thought we was just going to talk," Cudmore said. "Did you lie to me?"

"No. We *are* going to talk."

Just then, Joe heard a heavy rumbling sound from behind him. It was actually causing the ground to tremble.

"Oh no," Reed said.

The Saddlestring Police Department's MRAP turned in off the highway and flattened the wrought iron archway. Plumes of dust billowed out from its undercarriage and dual sets of back tires.

"You fuckin' lied to me!" Cudmore cried.

Then he leaned over and opened his front door and stepped aside.

"Get 'em, boys!" Cudmore commanded.

Four massive pit bulls boiled out: teeth flashing in the ambient light, ropes of saliva flapping in the air. Two of them were on Boner before he got a chance to retreat or fire.

Boner went down, the dogs on top of him. It was a savage attack.

Cudmore pumped his fist with joy.

Joe pushed himself to his feet. The third dog was streaking across the yard toward Reed, who was in the process of raising his weapon. Reed fired, but missed.

Joe raised his shotgun and fired instinctively, an orange gout of flame exploding from the muzzle. He hit the pit bull behind its front shoulder with a full load that rolled it across the grass less than a foot from Reed's feet in the chair. The concussion was loud, but Joe barely heard it over the roaring in his ears. He *hated* killing a dog.

The fourth dog retreated from the others and took refuge behind Cudmore's legs. Cudmore cursed and kicked it hard in the ribs, but instead of attacking like the others, the dog hunkered down in the mud.

The other deputies had surrounded the two snarling dogs on top of Boner. One of them yelled to be careful not to hit Boner, who writhed on the ground in a tornado of solid muscle and red-stained teeth.

Cudmore rocked back on his heels with his hands on his hips and hooted. Then he bent toward the whimpering dog and yelled, "Go help your brothers, you coward."

There were several flashes and thumps and loud yelps as rounds hit the two dogs on top of Boner, then the whimper of a dying creature who'd been thrown to the side by the impact of the bullets. Boner thrashed, rolling, grasping at his face and throat. Blood, bits of flesh, and fur were everywhere.

A harsh spotlight from the top of the MRAP illuminated it all.

Joe was a beat too late when Cudmore drew a weapon he'd had tucked in his waistband under his jacket. The man did it tentatively, as if he were having second thoughts even as the semiauto cleared.

A volley of shots from the deputies cut him down and he fell straight back like a felled tree. A deafening burst from the .50-caliber machine gun on the MRAP ripped through the night and tore a twisted chunk of aluminum off the roof of the trailer. The fourth dog managed to scramble out of the way of Cudmore's crashing body.

Joe ran to where Tilden Cudmore lay, and he kicked the .357

from the man's hand. Cudmore grunted from the blow—he was still alive—and Joe wheeled and pressed his shotgun barrel into the man's doughy cheek.

"Stay right where you are," Joe said.

"I'm not goin' anywhere, but I ain't dyin', neither," Cudmore said, revealing a mouthful of long yellow teeth in what was either a grimace or a grin. "I was prepared for your gestapo tactics."

It was then Joe saw the collar of the body armor vest that Cudmore wore beneath his coat. Although the body armor had prevented rounds from entering his body, their impact had done damage. Cudmore hugged himself and whimpered.

"You're going to pay for what you did to April," Joe said, leaning in hard with the shotgun.

In Cudmore's rheumy eyes was confusion at what Joe had said, then a slow realization.

"So that's why you're here," the man said. "You think I done something to some girl. You people—"

The fourth pit bull charged Cudmore as if to attack him, but feinted at the last second and ran away. It got close enough to scare Cudmore, though. Joe admired the dog and watched it run off into the night.

"GET THAT THING OUT OF HERE!" Sheriff Reed yelled, wheeling his chair across the yard until it thumped into the front bumper of the MRAP.

The local cop garbed in camo and an army helmet who had fired the burst with the machine gun that missed Cudmore and nearly the entire trailer, said, "Sheriff—"

"Get that thing the hell out of here or I'll arrest the lot of you!" Reed shouted. Joe had never seen him so mad.

The MRAP backed away, crushing a snow fence.

FIVE MINUTES LATER, with his ears still ringing from the explosion of gunshots, Joe heard Reed fume to Dulcie, "I just about had him in custody without anyone getting hurt. Then Williamson showed up with his goddamned *tank.*"

REED SAID, "If it weren't for Deputy Boner's injuries, I might ask the EMTs to slow down on their way out of here, and maybe we grab us some coffee while Cudmore rolls around in pain. But that wouldn't be right, would it?"

"Um, *no,*" Dulcie said, her face white with shock at what had just happened.

Reed wheeled over to Joe. "Thank you for your restraint in not shooting him."

"It didn't seem right," Joe said. "I really hated to shoot those dogs, though."

"That last dog must have really hated him," Reed said, shaking his head. "He finally got the chance to show him how much, is what I think."

Joe barely heard him. His nerves jangled from the release of adrenaline and his throat ached from having witnessed—and participated in—such a scene of savagery.

He had his arm around Lucy, who had stayed silent since the shooting was over. He hoped she hadn't seen much, but he was afraid she had. He wondered what she thought of her father if she'd seen him prodding a shotgun into the face of an injured man lying flat on his back on the ground.

"But we got our man," Reed said.

Joe took a deep breath and recalled the confusion in Cudmore's eyes just before he'd been attacked. He said, "Are you sure about that?"

"Maybe this will help," a deputy named Woods said as he backed out of Cudmore's Humvee, where he'd been searching the front cab.

He held up a Visa card and an iPhone.

"The credit card belongs to April Pickett," Woods said. "I found it under the seat."

Lucy shrugged out of Joe's arm and approached Woods with her hand out. Woods turned over the phone.

Lucy swiped it on and punched a four-digit code and the phone lit up. She held it up so Joe could see the backlit image of April and Dallas Cates taking a selfie. They were grinning like fools with their cheeks pressed together, looking up at the camera.

PART TWO

YARAK, INC.

7

On Monday morning, Nate Romanowski blinked against the harsh interior lighting of the interrogation room in the Federal Building in downtown Cheyenne. He wore a loose orange jumpsuit stenciled with DOJ over the breast pocket and large red Crocs on his feet. His long blond hair cascaded past his shoulders. His complexion was waxen and pale and his sharp blue eyes looked out as if from behind a mask. His hands and wrists were bound by a Smith & Wesson Cuff-Maxx high-security belly chain and restraints, even though his trip had consisted only of an elevator ride from the basement cell to the seventh floor.

The guard guided him through the door and shut it behind him.

"Was this really necessary?" he asked as he rattled his wrist chains at the bulky man on the other side of the interrogation table. A slim manila folder was on the surface of the table.

"Probably not," the man answered with a slight grin. He wore a suit jacket, tie, and a white shirt that strained over his belly. His name was Stan Dudley, and he was the FBI special agent in charge of Nate's case. Dudley was in his mid-forties, with a fleshy bland face and pasted-down light brown hair that would rise away from his scalp as the day went on. He had close-set eyes, a rounded nose, and ancient acne scars beneath his cheekbones. His thick neck bulged over the collar of his shirt, and sometimes when he talked, the swell of fat under his jaw trembled.

"Then why did you bring me up this way?"

"People talk," Dudley said. "We don't want the guards and other staff to think we're letting you walk, do we?"

Nate grunted.

"Have a seat."

"Do you have a key for these?" Nate asked, thrusting his arms out.

"Someone does. Sit down."

Dudley liked this, Nate knew. He liked telling Nate what to do and how to do it and when he wanted it done. And he liked stringing him along, reminding Nate who was in charge and who was in custody.

As he repositioned the hard-backed chair with his foot so he could sit down in it, Nate thought how easy it would be to quickly reach across the table and twist Dudley's ears off. The chain between his wrists was long enough that he could grab both of them.

But because he wanted out and he knew that Dudley would love the excuse to keep him inside, Nate sat.

Dudley reached out and tapped the file. "You know I fought against this, don't you?"

Nate didn't respond.

"I think it's a despicable deal. If it was up to me, I'd unleash the federal prosecutors on you and put you away for a hundred years. I know—and you know—that you've been responsible for murder and mayhem across most of the continental U.S. People just can't go around serving as judge, jury, and executioner based on some kind of personal code. We have laws for that. To that, we can agree."

Nate agreed to nothing.

"But we've gotten the word to back off. All they care about at the Department of Justice right now is this deal," Dudley said, again tapping the file. "I don't know if you realize how flipping lucky you are."

"I'm Mr. Luck," Nate said sourly. He'd been held in the basement of the Federal Building in detention for four months. He'd not flown his falcons, or breathed mountain air, or eaten his normal diet of lean game meat he killed himself. Although he'd done thousands of push-ups, pull-ups, squats, and other exercises in his cell, and he was in many respects in the best physical shape since he'd been in Special Operations, mentally he felt bloated, flabby, dull, and completely off his game. His brain was foggy, and he had trouble concentrating. Nate had come to understand the vacant-eyed tigers he'd seen pacing rhythmically back and forth in the zoo because he felt like one of them.

"Rulon didn't help, either," Dudley scoffed, referring to the governor of Wyoming, who had two and a half years left in his second and final term of office. "I don't know what you ever did for him, or if you have illicit photos of him or what, but he went to bat for you. He somehow convinced my superiors you'd be of better service to us out there than in here. I think he's full of shit, but he must have been pretty convincing."

Nate raised his eyebrows in surprise. He wasn't aware that Rulon had been involved in the negotiations, but he was grateful for it.

"We've got your gun," Dudley said. "And you're not getting it back."

"I've got a right to defend myself," Nate said.

"When you sign these papers, you sign away your rights. You have no rights beyond that, unless I say so."

"I want my weapon back."

Nate had surrendered his .50-caliber five-shot Freedom Arms .500 Wyoming Express revolver when he gave himself up. It was a hand-gun that could take out a moose a mile away or kill a car. The gun was a part of him and he knew how to use it.

Dudley placed his hand on the file and said, "If you're stupid enough to arm yourself again, you'll be right back here, and I'll be happy to expedite the paperwork."

Nate looked away.

"I'm sure you'll be happy to know that even though I lost the argument against releasing you, the DOJ agreed to retain me as your case manager, since we have such a special relationship and all."

He said, "You know, before I took this job out here, I was warned about people like you. I was told there were still a number of lone-wolf survivalist types who lived out here in places like Wyoming, Montana, and Idaho. I thought we'd stomped them out years ago, but here we are. There still may be a few of you left, but as of today the number is one less, which makes me feel very . . . *patriotic*."

Dudley grinned at that.

"THE NEGOTIATIONS WERE LIKE five monkeys fucking a foot-ball," Dudley complained. "You've got career federal prosecutors, a military JAG because of your Special Forces background, DOJ po-litical lackeys, and the governor's office all fighting about what to do with you. My solution was real simple: put you on trial and send you to the supermax in Florence, Colorado."

Dudley looked up to see if he could get a reaction out of Nate. He couldn't.

"But our biggest problem, *as you know*, was placing you at the scene of your most heinous crimes, because you were literally off the grid. No credit card receipts, no hotel registries, no cell phone records, no loans, no CC videotape, no arrests, no *nothing*. No direct or circumstantial evidence. Don't get me wrong—I'm convinced that with enough time and manpower we'd be able to nail you. We can nail *anyone* if we set our mind to it. *Anyone*."

Nate tried not to sigh. He'd heard the threat from Dudley a half-dozen times. He knew better than to rise to the bait.

What he wanted to say was simple: *I've never killed anyone who didn't need killing.*

THE FACT WAS, Nate knew, the feds couldn't convict him on the murder, conspiracy, kidnapping, or other charges they'd originally filed against him. As Dudley had admitted, the evidence wasn't there.

But what they could do was put him away for not filing tax returns for the last twelve years. While the crime didn't even re-motely rise to the level of the original charges, a conviction on tax evasion could put him into federal prison for years. It was the "Al Capone method" of going after a target indirectly, and it could be devastatingly effective if the prosecutors were motivated to pursue it.

The original charges had been quietly dropped and replaced with new charges while the negotiations were under way. However it went, he knew, they had him.

———

"So LET ME BE the first to welcome you back to the modern world," Dudley said, showing his teeth. "Consider your wings clipped. You can't make a move without me knowing about it. If you decide to try and go underground again, I'll be on you with a team within minutes and we'll drag your ass back here, unless, you know, something bad happens during the arrest that results in your demise.

"I'll know where you drive, what you eat, where you sleep, and how long you sit on the toilet. You'll be just another American citizen. We'll know everything about you and we can take you down anytime we want. And believe me, I'll be paying attention to those things because I'm . . . motivated. Motivated to putting you away. Do you understand that?"

Nate grunted again.

"Did you read the agreement?" Dudley asked.

"Yes."

"Are you ready to sign it? Because if you aren't, I'll happily call the guard and send you back to your home away from home in the basement. Even the governor would have to understand that we couldn't release you if you refused to play ball."

"I need a pen," Nate said.

"That's my boy."

Then, turning toward the two-way mirror, Dudley said, "Bring in the devices."

A HIGH-TECH TRACKING BRACELET was secured to Nate's left wrist and another was fastened to his ankle by two young DOJ technical support staffers. Nate barely listened to what they were telling him about the devices, but he got the gist. Neither of the techs would meet his eye as they worked.

The monitors were waterproof, shockproof, and permanent, and could only be removed by a DOJ specialist. The devices looped around his limbs and were locked in place by a coded infrared beam. They were thin and unobtrusive and reminded him of plastic-coated steel cables.

If he tried to cut them off or remove them, a homing signal would alert the feds—meaning Dudley as well as full-time surveillance staff stationed in Virginia—and "the wrath of God will descend upon you," Dudley said. The devices would provide Nate's precise GPS coordinates to the meter at all times and could be tracked by satellites and, if necessary, drones.

Even local private closed-circuit cameras could be hacked and overridden to provide video evidence of his whereabouts if they wanted to watch him. It was experimental technology, Dudley said with pride, but it had worked in beta experiments thus far.

One of the techs placed a cell phone and charger on the table in front of Nate.

Dudley said, "That's your new BlackBerry. Don't lose it, don't use it for anything other than to check in every day, and don't ever turn it off. There's a single number stored inside that goes direct to an operations center in Langley, Virginia. When we say check in every day, we mean check in every day. Let us know what you're doing, where you're going, and who you're with. You won't be talking to me directly, but I'll get a daily update from your contact. If you don't call in, we'll come looking for you. Got that?"

Nate frowned at the phone. Not only did he hate cell phones, but Dudley had given him a *BlackBerry*.

NATE BREATHED IN and looked up at the camera mounted over the two-way mirror in the wall. The red light was on. Someone, somewhere, was watching him.

He was back on the grid.

"I'M OBLIGATED BY PROCEDURE to go over the agreement with you so you fully understand what you're about to sign," Dudley said. "You claim that you've read it, so this is for the record." The record meant the overhead camera, Nate knew.

Dudley opened the folder.

"'Agreement between the U.S. Department of Justice and one Nathaniel Romanowski,' blah-blah-blah, legalese boilerplate . . ." Dudley said in a singsong voice until he got to the third page. "Okay, page three: the terms. If you want me to read the actual language, please indicate by saying that you do. Otherwise, I'll paraphrase."

Nate sneered.

"Okay then, I'll take that as permission to paraphrase.

"Subject agrees to cooperate with all ongoing federal investigations concerning one Wolfgang Templeton and his criminal network. Subject agrees to provide testimony in court if requested by the DOJ. Subject agrees to participate in any local operations if asked by the DOJ involving Wolfgang Templeton and to serve as an agent of the prosecution during said investigation. Got that?"

Nate nodded.

"You know what it means, right?"

"I'm offering myself up as bait."

"Correcto," Dudley said. "We're assuming Templeton isn't too pleased with you for blowing up his operation. If he knows you're out on the street, we think he'll come after you. That's when we'll nail him. So, yes, 'bait' is a good word for it."

Nate had crossed the line the year before. He had willingly become a part of a high-class murder-for-hire operation with the understanding that only elite society's untouchable scum would be targeted. Nate had wholly approved of the concept. Templeton ran the operation from his remote Black Hills ranch in Medicine Wheel County, Wyoming. But Templeton had overreached and the operation had gone sour. Nate had realized too late what had happened and he'd been the catalyst in Templeton's final undoing. Templeton got away in one of his private planes, along with his new fiancée: Joe Pickett's mother-in-law, Missy Vankueren. Their whereabouts were unknown.

Nate had discerned that the FBI wanted Templeton bad due to political pressure placed on them by members of the administration who'd had friends and crony capitalist colleagues "disappeared" by Templeton's operation. He'd heard there were cabinet secretaries as well as the attorney general himself who wanted revenge, and they were willing to influence the prosecution of Nate to expedite it. He was to become a tool of the same elites Templeton had targeted. At the same time, Nate had no doubt that Templeton was under pressure from former clients—many of whom were prominent in government and industry—to eliminate the threat of Nate ever talking about the operations he knew about and had been personally involved in.

"There are other terms," Dudley said. "You already know about not carrying a weapon so we won't go there again. Oh—and this: 'Subject waives his rights to access the federal witness relocation project.' That means if Templeton turns up the heat and comes after you, you can't come crying to us to hide you away."

Nate gritted his teeth. He said, "I've never gone crying to anyone about anything."

Dudley smiled and went on to the next item.

"'Subject agrees to commit no more crimes in the state of Wyoming.'"

Nate snorted at that.

"That was Governor Rulon's provision," Dudley said. "He said he did some research and a former governor of Wyoming made the same deal with Butch Cassidy before he released him from the territorial prison over in Laramie. Apparently, Butch was an honorable outlaw and he never committed another crime in Wyoming, even though he used to use the state as his hideout. It seems like a stupid provision to me, but the governor insisted. Are you as honorable an outlaw as Butch Cassidy?"

Nate's face didn't twitch.

"Oh, and this is mine," Dudley said, looking up. "'Subject agrees to have no more contact with one Joe Pickett of Twelve Sleep County—or his family.'"

"*What?* That wasn't there earlier," Nate said angrily.

Years before, Nate had made a pact with Joe to watch out for the Picketts after Joe managed to get Nate released from jail for a crime he didn't commit. Since then, they'd been through a lot together and it was Joe who'd convinced Nate to turn himself in after the Templeton scheme blew up. It wasn't a vow he was willing to break.

"I just added that this morning," Dudley said. "It's for your own protection and for ours. I talked to the DOJ and I pointed out that every time you get involved with that friend of yours, people end up dead. I know it, you know it, everybody in the state knows it. This will prevent that from happening until we've nailed Templeton. Maybe after that, we can revisit the language."

"I won't agree to it," Nate said. "You can't put in terms that weren't negotiated earlier."

"We can do whatever we want," Dudley said, thrusting out his jaw. "We're the government."

Nate smoldered. He had relented on every point over months and he was minutes away from being released. Now this.

"What about my right to freedom of association?" Nate said.

"I think we went over that rights thing already," Dudley said impatiently.

"Joe is a good man. I'm obligated to him."

"Not anymore."

"You can't do this."

"Do I have to say it again?"

"AND THE LAST THING," Dudley said. "'Subject agrees to go seek legitimate employment.' That's right—you need to go straight. Meaning you'll actually get a job, go to work, pay your taxes, and exist like a normal human being until Templeton decides to find you. This, for you, might be the toughest thing of all."

"It's not," Nate countered.

Dudley leaned back and arched his eyebrows. "Are you gonna tell me this falconry business you dreamed up is actually going to work?"

"Yes."

"What is it you plan to do again?"

Nate said, "There are people out there who have a need for falconry services, mainly for the purpose of chasing off problem species. Over the years, invasive bird species have been introduced throughout North America and they've multiplied by the millions. We're talking about starlings, English sparrows, house finches, Eurasian collared doves. Their populations have exploded. Crows and pigeons are always a problem, too.

"Refineries don't want pigeons roosting in their equipment. Ranchers don't want starlings taking over their barns and pooping on their livestock. Growers don't want starlings and crows eating their produce. All these birds are terrified of certain predators like peregrines or gyrfalcons. They know and fear a falcon's silhouette in the sky even if they've never actually seen a real raptor—it's imprinted in their DNA. They know that if a falcon is around, they better leave the premises or they'll get smacked. Starlings will travel a hundred miles to avoid a falcon in the sky. Hiring an experienced falconer costs a lot less than trying to poison or shoot the pest birds, or to rig up netting or spikes or whatever. That's what I'm going to do."

Dudley rolled his eyes. He said, "And this girlfriend of yours has it all organized and ready to go?"

Nate nodded. He'd met Liv Brannan in Medicine Wheel County and they'd connected instantly. Liv had a sharp business mind and the capital from years of working for Templeton to launch Yarak, Inc., a falconry services enterprise. He couldn't wait to see her. She had milk-chocolate skin, big brown eyes, and a trim figure, and she was smart as a whip. She had spent hours convincing him through the Plexiglas window of the visiting room that he should negotiate his way out of jail—and that she'd be waiting for him. They'd go straight together, she'd said.

Liv had talked to proprietors of other falconry outfits around the country and learned that experienced master falconers could make $400 to $750 per day from winegrowers, refinery owners, farmers, ranchers, and other commercial operators. She'd obtained the equipment, registered the new company with the Wyoming secretary of state, filed the tax forms, set up a website, and had already begun marketing Yarak, Inc.

The classic falconry definition of *yarak* was a Turkish phrase describing the peak condition of a falcon to fly and hunt. It was described as "full of stamina, well muscled, alert, neither too fat nor too thin, perfect condition for hunting and killing prey. This state is rarely achieved but a wonder to behold when observed."

"It sounds like a stupid idea to me," Dudley said.

"That's why I hate explaining a business plan to a bureaucrat who's never worked in the private sector in his life."

Dudley narrowed his eyes and set his jaw.

He said, "I know what's going to happen to you. You'll either be back here or you'll be dead. I'm okay with either one."

Nate reached out and pulled the sets of documents closer and spun them around. He said, "One of the greatest and most mystical things about falconry is that when you release a bird to the sky— even a bird you've worked with for years and years—you never know if it's going to come back. Eventually, that falcon may take off and it's the last you ever see of it. Years of work and dedication are re- leased to the wind. There's satisfaction in the partnership, but no certainty. If you're a person who needs certainty, falconry isn't an art you should try to master."

Nate signed the papers and shoved them back to Dudley, who sat back, screwed up his face, and said, "I'm not sure I understand a word of what you're saying."

"I'm not surprised," Nate said, holding out his hands. "Get the key."

As Nate passed by the armed security guards manning the metal detector in the entry lobby, they nodded at him in a way that suggested they knew much more about him than he knew about them. He nodded back. He was aware from several disparaging remarks from Dudley that a kind of unwelcome (by Dudley) legend had grown about Nate among certain types. Nate had never fostered any admiration or following, and he didn't plan to start now. But those security guards seemed to admire him in a way he found uncomfortable.

He was wearing the same clothes he'd worn when he was taken into custody months before: jeans, heavy lace-up boots, a T-shirt under a gray hoodie, a canvas tactical vest. A leather falcon jess bound his hair into a ponytail.

When he pushed through the double doors of the vestibule's entrance and stepped outside, his senses were overwhelmed. The sky was cloudless and the spring's high-altitude sun was intense. The air smelled of leaves budding out, pollen, and car exhaust. He could hear birds chirping, motors racing, and a light din of traffic from downtown.

Idling on the street in front of the Federal Building was a white panel van. A graphic of a peregrine falcon in full-attack stoop had been painted on the side over the words YARAK, INC., lettered in a rough stencil format. In script beneath the graphic it read: *Falconry Services* and contained a website address.

Liv was at the wheel, and when she saw him come out of the building, her grin exploded. It seemed bright enough, he thought, to cast shadows.

He waved hello, then walked around the back of the van and jumped into the passenger seat and shut the door.

"You are a sight for sore eyes," she said, still beaming. "I've been dreaming of this day."

Liv wore jeans, knee-high boots, a T-shirt, and a blazer with a sheer violet scarf. She looked good.

Nate overlooked that and said, "We need to talk."

She shook her head defiantly and pulled away from the curb.

The golden dome of the state capitol building reflected the harsh afternoon sun. Nate thought: *Thank you, Governor Rulon. You did me a solid.* But he knew to expect a call someday from the governor's people. Rulon was wily and he'd expect something in return.

"There's nothing to talk about," she said.

"Liv . . ."

"Forget about it. I know you. You're going to try to convince me that I'm in danger being close to you. That we should go our separate ways for my own safety."

Nate nodded. He said, "It's a matter of time before Templeton finds me. When he finds me, he'll find you. I can't risk losing you. You deserve a better life."

"That's nice," she said, guiding the van north through the blocks of old Victorian homes that once belonged to absentee cattle ranchers who had ranches in the north. The buildings were now law offices or the headquarters of associations.

She said, "I'm not going anywhere. This is a partnership, remember? We're going straight and we're doing it together. We're putting Mr. Templeton behind us and we're getting right with God and country. It's a new chapter in our lives. This is where the outlaw falconer and the formerly wayward sister from Louisiana join forces. We're going to be normal together like we talked about. So save your breath."

He moaned.

"Forget all that and think about this moment," she said. "You're out of jail and back among the living. This is what we've been waiting for."

"I wish it felt better," Nate said.

She reacted as if he'd slapped her, and he quickly tried to explain. "It's not you," he said. "I'd rather be here with you right now than with anyone on earth. But I thought I'd feel free on this day— emancipated. Instead, I feel like a eunuch."

He lifted his arm to show her the monitor. "There's one on my ankle, too. They're tracking every move I make, so they can swoop down on me if I stray or if Templeton finds me. And they didn't return my weapon."

"That was part of the agreement," she said, patting the center console. "But nowhere on that paper did it say *I* couldn't carry."

Nate opened the console to find a deadly looking snub-nosed revolver.

"It's a Smith and Wesson Governor," she said. "The man at the gun store said it's very versatile and a real stopper. You can load it with .410 shotgun shells, .45 ACP rounds, or .45 Colts. Or you can mix and match—three shotgun shells, three bullets. I thought you might like it, and I think even *I* could hit something with a shotgun shell at close range."

"Interesting choice," Nate said. He was proud of her.

"Look over your shoulder," she said.

He turned. There were no seats in the back of the van. His two peregrines and the red-tailed hawk stood erect and hooded in wire cages on the floor. They looked healthy and still. The ability raptors had for remaining still for hours and then exploding into furious action was a trait Nate had always admired.

A large plastic cooler—no doubt containing dead rabbits and pigeons for feed—was behind the cages. Falconry gloves, lures, and whistles were packed in translucent boxes that had been fixed to the interior side wall of the van. On the other wall was heavy winter clothing and a small desk that would pop down for communications and bookkeeping.

"Just like you described it," Nate said. "You did a great job."

"We're open for business," she said with a grin. "In fact, there's some news on that front."

He waited.

"Our first job," she said. "It came this morning. A rancher in northern Wyoming named Wells needs to chase starlings out of his horse barn."

"So that's where we're headed?" Nate asked as they cleared the city limits and merged onto I-25 North.

"Only as far as Casper tonight," she said, looking over and crinkling her nose. "We have a reservation at a hotel—the honeymoon suite. You and I have some catching up to do."

Nate sat back and smiled.

She said, "Those bracelet monitors can't hear us, can they?"

"No."

"Good. I don't want to scorch some bureaucrat's ears tonight."

8

The next day, as they drove north on I-25, near the gnomish dryland formation known as the Teapot Dome, Nate pressed the send button on the BlackBerry that Dudley had given him. His call went straight through.

A woman answered.

"This is Nate Romanowski," he said.

"I know who you are."

"Okay, well who is this?"

"That's not important."

"How about I call you Olga, then? That's a good Soviet name."

"Hmph."

Her voice was calm and businesslike, and she clipped off her words. There were no background conversations going on or ambient noises. She sounded to be in her mid-fifties, he thought, but it was only a guess. He imagined a hatchet-faced woman with short hair wearing a headset with a computer monitor in front of her. She was divorced but had two adult children who never called her. She'd worked for the federal government all of her life and she knew how many days she had left until retirement. She vacationed in Florida for three weeks every year, but never got tan.

Of course the conversation was being recorded, he thought. Probably by multiple agencies.

"I'm going north for a job," Nate said.

"I see that. What kind of vehicle are you in?"

"We've got the Yarak, Inc. van. I'm not driving."

"Who is with you?"

Nate hesitated. He was sure Olga knew the answer to her question, and he didn't want to bring Liv into the conversation.

"My partner," he said.

"Olivia Brannan?" the woman said.

Nate sighed. He noticed that Liv was looking over at him, curious about the conversation.

"What is the location of the job?" Olga asked.

Nate covered the mouthpiece on the BlackBerry and asked Liv. She told him what she knew.

"It's a ranch outside of Saddlestring," Nate said. "The HF Bar Ranch. It's been there for generations and I know where it is, but I've never been on it before. It's a working ranch, but also a dude ranch. From what we know, the wranglers want starlings chased out of the barn before the guests start to arrive this summer so the backs of the horses and the saddles aren't covered with bird poop. I'm telling you this so you don't think we're being lured up there by the bad guys."

He could hear her tapping keys on a keyboard.

She said, "Saddlestring. Isn't that where Mr. Pickett lives?"

"It is."

"Do we have a problem?"

"No, Olga. We don't have a problem. The county itself is nine thousand, three hundred and fifty square miles. That's as big as New Hampshire. It's not likely I'll just run into Joe." Nate felt his face flush hot.

"I see," Olga said. "Special Agent Dudley will be interested in this information."

"Tell Mr. Dudley to piss up a rope, Olga," Nate said. "I signed the agreement. I'll abide by it."

"Noted."

"Until tomorrow, Olga," he said, and punched off.

Nate dropped the phone on the seat between them and rubbed his eyes with the heels of his hands.

"I'm not going to be able to do this," he said.

"It'll be a process," Liv said, but she looked worried.

DESPITE BEING WITH LIV AGAIN, despite the champagne she'd arranged for and the honeymoon suite she'd reserved, Nate had not been able to perform the night before. She'd been patient, alluring, and enthusiastic, but he couldn't get aroused. He loved her, but something was wrong. He drank too much Wyoming Whiskey and fell asleep, and when he woke up in the middle of the night, he didn't know where he was. He thought he was back in his cell.

Liv had held him tight the rest of the night, skin to skin.

She'd awakened him gently that morning.

He'd said, "What's wrong with me?"

"You're not yourself," she assured him. "You've been through a lot and your feet aren't on the ground yet."

He told her how he'd thought of her constantly, how he'd fantasized about being with her again. In none of his dreams had it gone like it had in real life the night before.

He'd said, "I feel like I've been emasculated."

"Is it because they took away your gun?" she asked.

"No. It's because they took away my honor," he responded. "That's all I've ever had."

THE SPRING SKY ROILED with thunderheads, and Nate could see downspouts miles away that looked like Greek columns connecting the high plains to the sky. Small herds of pronghorn antelope grazed on the fresh carpet of green grass, their burnished-copper and white color scheme making them stand out like highway cones. The smell of moist sage was thick in the air, as was ozone.

"I almost forgot what it smelled like when it's about to rain," he said to Liv.

"Maybe it'll help bring you back," she said. "And once you get your birds in the air and you have a job to do, I think it'll get better. Work is good for the soul. Every man needs work."

He nodded, and said, "I knew you were beautiful and smart, but I didn't realize until recently that you are also very wise."

She laughed. She had a great laugh, he thought, an all-out Louisiana low country belly laugh.

"No one's ever called me wise before," she said.

AS THEY PASSED the town of Kaycee, Nate lifted an imaginary glass and said, "Here's to Chris LeDoux."

"Who?" Liv asked.

"He used to live here," Nate said. "Chris LeDoux was a championship professional rodeo cowboy and a country singer. He's a Wyoming icon. Garth Brooks sang a song that mentions him called

'Much Too Young to Feel This Damn Old.' Joe and I always salute his memory whenever we pass by."

Liv took a deep breath. She said, "Speaking of Joe, there's some bad news."

Nate looked over, concerned.

"His daughter April was found beaten and left for dead outside of Saddlestring," Liv said.

Nate sat up immediately. His first thought was to remove the Governor out of the console and strap it on, agreement or no agreement.

"They caught the guy who did it," Liv said.

"Who was he?"

"Some local weirdo," she said. "From what I read about it, the case is pretty much open-and-shut."

Nate said, "I can only imagine what Joe and Marybeth are going through. They dote on their daughters. I never knew April that well, but Sheridan is my falconry apprentice."

Liv told him the few facts of the case she'd read in that morning's *Casper Star-Tribune*.

Nate said, "I'd like five minutes in a room with that guy. I'd guess Joe would say the same thing."

"Except Joe's on the right side of the law," Liv said.

"He is. Man, I'd like to be able to see him and Marybeth," Nate said. "I'd like to tell them I'm thinking about them."

"We'll be in the general area," Liv said, nodding toward the Bighorn Mountains that had risen on the horizon to the west. "I know you're not supposed to make contact with him. But what if he makes it with you? Like if some little bird let him know you're working on the HF Bar Ranch for a few days?"

Nate smiled. "And who would that little bird be?"

"Gee, I have no idea," she said with a wink.

IT WAS AN HOUR before dusk when Nate and Liv drove the van under the ancient pole archway decorated with whitened antlers and a hanging wrought iron sign that indicated they'd arrived at the historic HF Bar Ranch in the Bighorn Mountains. Gates made of weathered pine poles had been swung open, and the chain that had locked them together hung from the top rail of the left-side gate.

The van left the pavement and climbed through dark pine forests and open alpine meadows bursting with wildflowers on a gravel corduroy road. Rain had swept through the foothills in the previous hour, freshening the air and darkening the roadbed. Moisture glistened on the tips of pine needles like tears.

From the looks of the sky to the north, another thunderhead was on its way.

For the first time since he'd walked out of the Federal Building the day before, Nate began to feel good. Whether it was the smell of the pine-rich mountain air or simply being in Liv's company, he felt his equilibrium start to level out.

The ranch road wound through groves of pine and aspen. Deep in the shadows of the trees, there were still crusty log-shaped snowdrifts from the winter. Mule deer grazed on spring grass that had grown from the benefit of sunlight shafts through the canopy. At least one set of tire tracks glistened in the muddy road on the way to the ranch. No doubt the tracks had been made by whoever had unlocked the gate for them, Nate thought.

The trees opened onto a sprawling ranch headquarters: a main lodge, wings of guest cabins, a network of roads and trails that spun off from the center like spokes on a wagon wheel. Liv parked in front of the lodge near a sign that said LOBBY.

There were no cars, trucks, or ranch vehicles to be seen, and the lower-floor windows of the lodge building were covered by weathered plywood.

"It doesn't look like there's anyone here," Liv said, leaning forward so she could see the top-floor windows of the lodge. "Why would they board it up like that?"

"Snow," Nate said. "It gets deep up here. It doesn't look like anyone has been here to open it up yet. So who are we meeting?"

"I guess he's the caretaker," Liv said. "John Wells. I didn't get a lot of detail from him."

"Where's this horse barn?" Nate asked, looking around. It made sense that the barn wouldn't be too far away from the lodge and cabins, since guests needed easy access to it for daily trail rides.

"Is that it?" Liv asked, pointing out her driver's-side window.

A weathered roof peeked over the tops of the trees to the west. Nate noted that the tire tracks they'd followed went in that direction.

"I think so," he said.

Liv backed up and took the road.

The massive old log horse barn was actually closer than it had seemed—less than a hundred yards from the lodge, but the timber was too thick in between for them to have seen the structure in full from the ranch yard. The barn was dark and weathered and the rain had temporarily stained the logs a deep brown. Hitching posts that looked a hundred years old stretched across the front of the building. A huge sliding barn door was partially open.

On the left side of the structure was a rusting GMC Suburban with Twelve Sleep County plates.

"There's his car," Nate said.

"There's someone in it," Liv said as they got closer to the Suburban. "It looks like a woman. Probably his wife."

Liv parked on the right side of the barn and waved toward the woman in the SUV. The woman, who looked stout and immobile, waved back.

"So do we get the birds out?" Liv asked Nate.

"Not yet," he said. "First I need to scout out the place. I need to see how many problem birds there are inside and where they're nesting. I probably won't put the falcons up tonight as it is. I don't want them flying around in the dark in unfamiliar terrain. I'd rather release them in the morning when we know what we've got here."

"You're the falconer," she said cheerfully. "I'm the businessperson. While you're looking things over inside, I'll go talk to our client over there and ask her to sign a contract. We agreed to seven hundred and fifty dollars per day with a maximum of three days, unless there are still starlings around. If that's the case, they'll only pay us two hundred and fifty dollars for two more days until all the problem birds are gone. If it goes beyond five days, it's gratis."

"Oh, they'll be gone," Nate said with a cruel smile.

He turned in his seat and found a long Maglite flashlight to take into the barn with him.

"Meet you back here in a minute," he said to Liv.

Liv shouldered on a light rain jacket, looped her violet scarf around her neck, and, grabbing her clipboard, approached the old

Suburban. The bulky woman in the passenger seat watched her with hooded eyes. She looked like a tough old ranch wife, Liv thought.

The woman rolled down her rain-beaded window and arched her eyebrows as if to say, *What?*

"Hello. I'm Liv from Yarak, Inc. Are you Mrs. Wells? The one who sent me the email that you needed some falconry services done?"

The woman nodded. She seemed placid and stoic. There was no smile. Her eyes seemed intelligent, though.

"I didn't realize there would be two of you," the woman said.

"We cover our own expenses and accommodations and such," Liv told her. "You don't have to worry about that."

The woman tipped her head back slightly in a way that indicated Liv's answer hadn't addressed her statement. She said, "My husband is in the barn. That's where the birds are."

Liv looked over her shoulder to see Nate pause at the open barn door, test the flashlight, and walk inside.

"Well," Liv said. "Do you want to look over the agreement before you sign it?"

"We always do that," the woman said. "But this is my husband's deal. He's the one with the key to the gate. He watches over the place in the winter when the owners are away. I'm just along for the ride."

Liv said, "So should I go inside and find him?"

"In a minute," the woman said. "Let's let your guy talk with him first. Let them get their business out of the way."

Liv was slightly puzzled. The woman wore a plastic rain bonnet to cover her hair and an old dark green coat. Liv knew style, and guessed the coat may have been fashionable in the mid-sixties.

Liv said uncomfortably, "Well, we'll have to get these contracts signed before any work can be done."

"You'll have to take that up with John," the woman said. "Like I told you, I'm just along for the ride."

The woman had penetrating eyes, Liv thought. They were the same eyes she saw when she took the hoods off Nate's falcons to feed them.

"We don't see a lot of Negroes around here," the woman said.

"Excuse me?"

"You're very pretty. I can see why he took up with you."

"Do you know Nate?" Liv asked, confused.

"I just know of him," the woman said.

"I'm sorry, I didn't get your name," Liv said, trying not to sound as offended as she felt.

"Kitty," the woman said. "Kitty Wells."

Liv cocked her head, thinking. The name was familiar, but she couldn't place it.

INSIDE, Nate swept the beam of his flashlight across the high rafters. He saw old splashes of white excrement from birds who'd inhabited the building years before, but no starlings.

The barn smelled pleasantly of decades of horses. Hay and manure lingered in the air. The dirt floor was packed down to the consistency of cement. A series of empty stalls lined both walls of the barn. Obviously, the owners hadn't brought the guest horses to the ranch yet for the season. In the rear of the barn was a closed-up tack room.

"Are you Nate Romanowski, the falcon guy?" a harsh male voice asked from inside one of the closest stalls.

"I am," Nate said. "Where are your problem birds?"

"Oh, they're here," the voice said.

"Where?"

"Keep lookin'."

Nate lowered the flashlight until the beam illuminated the lantern-jawed face of an old man wearing bib overalls and a crumpled straw hat. Nate could see only his face and the top of his shoulders above the uppermost rail of the stall.

"Who are you?" Nate asked.

"John Wells. I'm the caretaker." He paused. "I'm the man who gets you out of our way."

Then, raising his voice, the man said, "Now, son."

The muzzle of a shotgun suddenly poked out from between two planks of the stall. Nate heard the unique *snick* sound of two safeties being thumbed off simultaneously.

He thought: *Ambush*.

Nate instinctively crouched and reached under his left arm for the handgrip of the weapon that wasn't there.

With a heavy boom, an orange fireball erupted from the hayloft over the old man's head, followed closely by the discharge of Wells's shotgun.

Nate staggered back. The flashlight dropped from his hand. He'd been hit. It was as if he'd been whacked in the chest several times with a baseball bat by someone swinging for the fences. There was a hot stinging sensation in his cheek and on the right side of his neck.

Wells fired again.

Nate went down. His mind was sharp and he knew what had happened. Two men had fired on him with shotguns likely loaded with double-ought buckshot. Each shell contained at least eight pellets that were the equivalent of .33-caliber bullets. Most of the pellets had ripped into his flesh.

He thought that, in the past, he would have drawn his weapon and taken out Wells before the first shot, and then put down the other man above him in the hayloft.

But now, he was flat on his back. His arms and legs were dancing to their own rhythm. He could smell gunpowder in the still barn and his own hot blood coursing through hay on the floor.

Outside, Liv screamed.

He thought: *I tried to tell you.*

Through what seemed like a tunnel, he heard the old man say, "Get down out of there, boy. We got to get the hell out of Dodge."

"That wasn't so hard," the son said with a surprised laugh. "I thought the guy was supposed to be tough."

"He don't have that gun of his," the old man said.

A moment later, heavy footfalls thundered by Nate toward the open door.

LIV HAD FROZEN momentarily at the sound of the first shot. It seemed so loud and harsh in the quiet mountain air. She was too stunned to react when the woman reached out of the Suburban and grabbed a handful of her scarf and pulled her close. Kitty was remarkably strong, given her appearance.

There were two more heavy booms from inside the barn, but Kitty had cinched the scarf tight and pulled most of it inside the vehicle. She rolled up the window to secure the scarf—and Liv—in place.

Liv screamed, but she couldn't twist away. Kitty had hardly moved, but she'd taken action. Now her hawklike eyes raked Liv's face with smug triumph through the dirty passenger-side window.

In Liv's peripheral vision, she saw two big and rough men run toward the Suburban from the barn door. They each carried a long gun.

Nate wasn't with them.

9

That night in Billings, Marybeth Pickett tossed aside a magazine she'd been scanning in the waiting lounge of the ICU and rubbed her eyes. She'd realized she'd read the magazine before—twice—and she wished she'd thought to bring the charger for her iPad. Before it ran out of power, she'd answered a dozen library-related emails and had updated Joe, Sheridan, and Lucy on April's condition, like she had every few hours since they'd arrived on Friday.

April had looked peaceful as the propofol was administered via IV, Marybeth told them. Her shallow breathing and severely reduced vital signs were normal responses to a drug-induced coma. One of the doctors compared the procedure they were doing to April to a bear hibernating in the winter. Her metabolism and heartbeat slowed drastically as the beeps on the monitor came farther apart. Marybeth had held April's limp hand and massaged her knuckles while she slept. Her daughter's total lack of response was troubling and upsetting, but that was normal, too.

The worst thing, she'd told her family, was how impotent she felt. There was nothing she could do now. She couldn't really comfort April, but she wrote that she'd feel horribly guilty leaving the hospital. What if she was gone when April suddenly showed improvement? Or if April's condition rapidly deteriorated? Marybeth couldn't stomach the thought of her daughter somehow realizing she was alone in a strange room and in a strange city, even though she knew rationally it was unlikely April would be able to think those thoughts.

Marybeth stood and paced. The hospital at night was a lonely and spooky place. The waiting lounge was empty except for her, and the low hum of medical equipment throughout the floor was like emotional white noise. She looked up every time a nurse or doctor walked down the hall and she'd come to recognize most of them. She knew their shifts, their speech patterns, and the way they walked. She'd gotten to know a couple of the staffers, particularly the night nurse. But Marybeth felt she could never get comfortable, that she was in the facility with nothing to do or offer while the outside world spun on.

This was her new self-contained world. It was horrible.

SHE'D BEEN SHOCKED to learn from Lucy and Joe about the apprehension of Tilden Cudmore. Unlike Joe, she knew the man personally—she'd met him several times at the library.

Cudmore was an unpleasant man who spent a good deal of time in the library to get on the Internet, read newspapers, and harass patrons. His body odor was the subject of pained jokes among the staff, and his sour smell lingered even after he'd left the building. He loved getting into political arguments with people, and Marybeth had been pulled out of her office several times to intervene. It was also suspected that he used the men's room to shave.

She'd heard there were library users who steered away from the building if they saw his Humvee in the parking lot.

There was something clearly off about him, she thought, but

she'd *never* gotten a vibe from him that he was a predator. A nutcase, yes. A paranoid schizophrenic, possibly.

She'd told Joe she would not have even thought of Cudmore in relation to April's attack.

That she'd misjudged the man so completely gnawed at her. Marybeth was perceptive when it came to judging others and to assessing potential threats, especially when it concerned her children. She couldn't believe she hadn't picked up on anything with Cudmore.

ALL THE DOCTORS could tell her was that it could be days, it could be weeks, it could be months. Marybeth had a long meeting with the hospital bookkeeper that morning and it had been both frustrating and fairly traumatic. Long-term care for April would cost hundreds of thousands of dollars. No one knew how much. Marybeth made several calls to their insurance company and received few answers.

"Things are so crazy right now," one of the insurance staffers told her. "They change the rules on us every week. We don't know which end is up. So at the moment, I can't tell you for sure what we can cover and what we can't."

"Then what am I supposed to do?" Marybeth asked.

"I wish I could tell you," the woman said with genuine empathy. "Health care right now is a nightmare. I hope you can be patient while we try and sort it out."

"I CAN BE PATIENT while we go bankrupt," Marybeth answered.

She tried not to think about the enormous costs of keeping April alive, but she couldn't help it. She was in charge of family finances, and she knew this could wipe them out. And no one seemed to be able to answer her questions.

She tried not to think about a possible answer to their financial woes, if it came down to that, but she couldn't help it. Her mother, Missy, was a multimillionaire. She was also on the run with Wolfgang Templeton. Missy had not been in contact in any way since they had flown away from Templeton's Wyoming ranch in his plane. But even if Marybeth reached out to her, would Missy help out? She'd never really liked April, and she *hated* Joe.

Missy would be her last possible option, Marybeth concluded. And it might be preferable to declare bankruptcy over that.

The combination of Tilden Cudmore, April's condition, and the insurance problems—plus being away from her home and family— were weighing her down mightily. After visiting hours the previous two evenings, she'd drunk a bottle of wine by herself in her hotel room so she could sleep through the night.

As she paced, she felt a tremor in the floor. It felt at first like heavy equipment being moved down the hallway. Then she realized the vibration didn't come from inside the building, but from the roof. The Life Flight helicopter, likely the same one that had transported April and her a few days before, was landing on the helipad.

Her observation was confirmed when the hallway came alive with emergency room doctors and technicians. An empty gurney sizzled down the hallway with nurses on either side.

Curious, Marybeth stepped out into the hallway after they'd gone by.

"Hi," she said to the night nurse at the station. "What's going on?"

They'd gotten to know each other since Marybeth arrived. The nurse was named Shri Reckling. She had three daughters, and a husband who worked for the state of Montana. Because of their similar families and situations, Marybeth and Shri had bonded instantly.

"Emergency landing," Reckling said. "A gunshot victim in critical condition. He's from Wyoming, just like you."

"Really," Marybeth said. "My husband says that because the state has such a low population, there is only one degree of separation. If you don't actually know a particular person, you know someone who knows him or her."

"Montana is the same way," Reckling said with a sly smile. "Is that your way of asking who is in the helicopter?"

"Yes," Marybeth said.

"I don't have a name yet," Reckling said. "When they do the admittance paperwork, we'll know more. All I know at this point is the FBI is involved somehow."

"So he's with the FBI? Or a fugitive?"

She knew Joe had worked closely over the years with the FBI, particularly a special agent named Chuck Coon. So the one degree of separation would likely come to fruition.

Nurse Reckling leaned back and shrugged. "I'm not supposed to release the names of patients, you know."

"I know," Marybeth said. "I don't want to get you in trouble."

Reckling looked up and down the hall, then whispered, "Stay in the lounge. I'll drop by when I know something."

Marybeth winked at her. Waiting would give her something to look forward to besides deciding what kind of wine to buy on her way to the hotel.

Less than five minutes later, the team of emergency doctors rushed the gurney back down the hallway from the elevator. Marybeth looked up from her magazine—which she was reading again—to see a scrum of alarmed men and women clatter by. All she saw of the shooting victim was a glimpse of a man's large and lifeless hand hanging down from under the sheets.

The hallway went quiet again when the double doors to surgery wheezed closed.

She waited another half hour, checking her watch every few minutes.

Finally, Nurse Reckling leaned in the doorway.

"He's in emergency surgery," she said. "He's likely to be in there for hours."

Marybeth arched her eyebrows, as if anticipating more.

Reckling raised an electronic tablet and said, "It says here 'N. Romanowski.'"

Marybeth went cold and the magazine slid from her hands and dropped to the floor.

"Nate Romanowski?"

"No first name given," Reckling said. Then: "Oh no. Do you know him?"

"God, yes," Marybeth said, standing up unsteadily. She reached out for the back of the chair to steady herself. "Is it bad?"

Reckling took a deep breath. She said, "I'm not in the ER."

"Please."

"I heard one of the doctors talking to somebody with the FBI," Reckling said with a sigh. "Special Agent Dudley was his name. He insisted I put him through to surgery. The surgeon there told him it doesn't look good. The injuries are massive and he doesn't think Mr. Romanowski can make it. I heard the FBI guy on the other end screaming at him until the doctor just hung up on him."

Marybeth was stunned.

The phone rang at the nurses' station, and Shri Reckling said, "That's probably him again. I don't really want to answer it. Are all those FBI types so pushy?"

PART THREE

ALL RISE

10

The arraignment for Tilden Cudmore began at nine-thirty on Wednesday morning in the Twelve Sleep County courthouse, Judge Hewitt presiding.

Joe sat in the third row from the back, his hat crown-down next to him on the bench. His mind was still reeling from what Marybeth had told him about Nate the night before. He would miss his friend. Joe had a lot of questions Marybeth couldn't answer—like when did Nate get out of federal lockup? And why was he in Twelve Sleep County?

He hoped she'd have more information when he picked her up in Billings later that day, after the preliminary hearing had concluded. She was as ready to come home as he was ready for her to. Marybeth said the doctors recommended she leave. April's condition was stable and they'd keep her that way. The question wasn't bringing her out of the coma—that could be done at any time. The question was April's recovery or lack of it when they brought her out from under the propofol. She could be healed or she could be brain-dead. Marybeth's voice had broken when she said it.

Lucy had been a good sport while her mother was gone, but there was no doubt she was sick of frozen pizzas and elk steak. Plus, Joe had learned that morning that he didn't know how the washing machine worked. He hoped no one would comment on his rumpled uniform shirt.

The judge was still in his chambers. The gallery consisted of Joe, a bandaged-up Deputy Boner, and an older woman with steel-gray hair, who was sitting in the front row and knitting, by the looks of it, a garish afghan. She didn't seem to be connected to the case in any way, he thought. She was likely one of those people who just liked attending court.

Cudmore sat with his back to Joe in an orange county jumpsuit. His hair was tousled and there was a four-day growth of beard on his face. Next to him was the public defender, Duane Patterson, who was intently scribbling something on a legal pad. Cudmore turned his head and sized up his attorney and seemed to regard him with sneering contempt.

At the prosecutor's table was County Attorney Dulcie Schalk. She sat completely still with her hands clasped in front of her on the table, staring at the closed door of Hewitt's chambers like a cat poised over a gopher hole. Joe recognized her dark gray pin-striped power suit, as she called it. She once told Joe she had never lost a case while wearing that suit. If she was wearing her blood-red ruffled blouse—which he couldn't see because she hadn't turned around— it meant she was going for the kill. Or in this case, the maximum sentence possible.

He'd heard Cudmore would be charged with aggravated assault, attempted murder, and kidnapping. That was just for starters. Joe knew Dulcie well enough to surmise that an indictment for first-degree murder—if April didn't pull through—was already written and in her top desk drawer.

Joe felt a breeze on his neck as the courtroom door opened and he looked over to see Sheriff Reed wheel himself in. He stopped at Joe's row and beckoned him over. Joe slid to the end of the bench so they could talk softly to each other.

"I had a dream about that damned tank last night," Reed said. "In my dream, it drove across my front yard and a bunch of idiots playing army were behind the wheel. It made me so mad, I called Williamson at home and yelled at him again. Woke him up."

Joe nodded.

"I heard about your friend Romanowski," Reed said. "What a hell of a run you're having."

"Not as bad as the run April and Nate are having."

"Both at the same hospital at the same time? Who would have put odds on that?"

Joe shook his head. He'd wondered that himself during his sleepless night.

"Why was he at that ranch?" Joe asked. "Any ideas?"

Reed said, "I talked to the owners of the HF Bar and they're clueless. They're still at their winter home in Arizona and they weren't even planning to come back until next week. Apparently, that's when they traditionally start opening up the guest ranch. They've never heard of Nate Romanowski and they don't know why he was there."

Reed leaned in closer to Joe. "It's impossible to say how he even got up there, unless he was dumped. There were no vehicles on the ranch. Hell, the last I knew he was in federal lockup in Cheyenne. The first I heard he was out was last night, when the FBI called me at my house to tell me they were sending a helicopter up here to my county. They said Romanowski was wearing a tracking device of some kind, and when it went haywire that meant it had been damaged in some way. At the time, they suspected he'd tried to cut it off.

They didn't know he'd been shot up until they found him. Apparently, he was found in the road between the barn and the main lodge. I get the impression he'd crawled there."

"I've got a call in to Chuck Coon with the FBI," Joe said. "The feds sprung him for some reason. Coon can tell me why and how long he's been out."

"Strange Nate didn't contact you," Reed said.

Joe shrugged. He'd wondered the same thing. So had Marybeth.

"How did he get to the ranch?" Joe asked.

"The FBI guy in charge of the case is named Dudley. When I talked to him, he said Nate was last seen the day before getting into a white van in front of the Federal Building. A fetching, dark-skinned woman was driving. They've got it on closed-circuit video."

"Liv Brannan," Joe said. "That fits."

"But she's not at the HF Bar—and neither is the van. We've got an APB out on it. The markings on the side of it say 'Yarak, Inc. Falconry Services.' Does that make any sense to you?"

Joe nodded. It had been a while since he'd heard the word *yarak*.

Reed shook his head. "The front gate was locked, so he must have jumped the fence. But he couldn't have walked all the way from Cheyenne to the HF Bar. We've got to assume this Brannan woman drove him."

"Any tracks?" Joe asked.

"If there were any tracks on the road, the rain washed them away. Our evidence tech may find something, though. He's up there today poking around."

Joe said, "I've met Liv Brannan. She was mixed up with Wolfgang Templeton, but she's a good person. Pretty, smart, and in love. Nate feels the same about her. I know you can never guess what goes on between two people, but it doesn't make sense to me that she'd cut him loose the day after she picked him up."

"I hope we find her," Reed said. "She could shine some light on this thing."

"How many people besides the owners have a key to the front gate?" Joe asked.

"I asked the owners that same question," Reed said. "They could think of at least a dozen. Maintenance people, plumbers, the local utility companies, contractors, employees, state licensing inspectors, et cetera. I asked them for a complete list of names."

"*I* have a key," Joe said.

"You do?"

"Yup. They gave me one a few years ago, after I'd had to call them in Arizona. A hunter wounded a bull elk that went on the property. We wanted to go get it so it wouldn't go to waste. The owners had one of their seasonal employees meet me at the gate and he handed me a spare key. It's possible there are more keys than we know about floating around."

"That makes things tougher," Reed said. "But we're on it."

"Let me know, okay?" Joe asked.

"I will."

Reed hesitated a moment, then said, "I hear he's not going to make it."

Joe nodded. "That's what Marybeth said, but Nate is the toughest guy I've ever met. I know Nate, and he'd have taken some guys with him if he was bushwhacked."

Reed said, "Maybe our tech will find some blood or spent shells up there. That's providing he was shot on the HF Bar and not shot somewhere else and dumped."

"I'll stop by there on my way to Billings," Joe said, raising his eyebrows as if to ask for permission.

"I guess it can't hurt," Reed said. "Another set of eyes and all. And because this isn't connected to"—he paused and gestured toward Cudmore—"*this.*"

Joe said nothing.

"ALL RISE," the bailiff sang.

Joe got to his feet as Judge Hewitt blew into the courtroom from his chambers behind the bench. The judge was short, dark, and twitchy, and his eyes narrowed for a second when he discerned that two occupants of his court had remained seated. One was Sheriff Reed, and Hewitt acknowledged his error with a quick nod of regret. The other was Tilden Cudmore. Cudmore was slouched in his chair, his legs splayed toward the bench, his head slumped to the side.

Joe observed Patterson surreptitiously prompt Cudmore to stand by jabbing him in the arm with his finger. The public defender faced the bench while he did it. In reaction, Cudmore rolled his shoulder away from his counsel.

Joe thought: *Uh-oh.*

Hewitt took his seat and glared at Cudmore. He was still glaring when he said, "Mr. Patterson, does your client have a problem?"

"Your Honor?" Patterson said. Even at a distance, Joe could tell Patterson was flushing red.

Hewitt jabbed his finger impatiently at Cudmore. "There he sits," he said. "Are we going to have to start talking about contempt charges before this hearing even begins?"

Patterson knelt down next to Cudmore and emphatically whispered into his ear. Finally, with a heavy sigh, Cudmore lumbered to his feet. He stood hip out, his body language saying to Joe, *This is ridiculous.*

"You may all be seated," Judge Hewitt said through clenched teeth. "Except for you," he said, boring in on Cudmore. "You keep standing for a few minutes until I tell you to sit down."

Joe hadn't seen that maneuver before, and he'd testified in Judge Hewitt's court many times over the years. Hewitt was a no-nonsense tyrant of a judge who ripped through every procedure like his hair was on fire. He hated it when a lawyer meandered or stalled, and he was quick with a threat or a sarcastic put-down if either the prosecution or the defense didn't respond to his questions quickly enough or if they appeared to be wasting his time. He'd been brusque to Joe a few times, but Joe learned later it wasn't personal. The judge wanted the trial to end so he could go hunting or fishing. Joe had encountered Judge Hewitt wading waist-deep and fly-fishing in the Twelve Sleep River many times. Hewitt was only relaxed, it seemed, when he was on the water. They'd had several conversations about dry flies, nymphs, and streamers. They never talked about particular cases before the court or about law enforcement in general.

Personally, Joe and Marybeth owed a debt of gratitude to Judge Hewitt and it had to do with April's status as their adopted daughter. Finally, after years of April's existence in a legal netherworld, the judge had informally recommended to Joe and Marybeth a clear path for settling April's legal status once and for all.

April had been abandoned by her mother at age five, when the Picketts took her in. Due to circumstances, the birth mother's brief interference, and Joe and Marybeth receiving bad advice, the family hadn't formally adopted April when she was returned to them, and for a while it seemed April didn't *want* to be adopted. When April reached her late teens and demanded that she wanted to "know who she was," Joe went to the judge for advice.

Hewitt recommended an experienced family lawyer in Jackson Hole he'd once partnered with, and he made a call to her to smooth the way. The lawyer took up the case and provided her opinion that, despite the unusual circumstances of the case, the facts spoke for themselves—April had lived with Joe and Marybeth for a sufficient length of time with no support or contact from April's extended family—and that what was pertinent was the "intent of both par- ties." In a sense, they were already common-law parents. The lawyer drew up an adoption petition signed by Joe, Marybeth, and April, which was filed with the court.

Judge Hewitt approved the petition in a proceeding that lasted five minutes. He signed off on it with a wink to Joe and Marybeth.

And she took on her new name: April Pickett.

"Counsel, approach," Hewitt snapped.

Patterson and Dulcie Schalk responded by practically sprinting to the bench. They'd both been in Judge Hewitt's courtroom many times. Despite that, Joe knew the judge was reading each the riot act: telling them to move things along, keep things clean and profes- sional, and most of all to not waste his time. Joe could see Patterson and Dulcie nodding along.

When they returned to their tables, the bailiff read off the formal title of the case as well as the docket number.

Cudmore was still standing.

Dulcie rose to present an affidavit prepared by Sheriff Reed that supported the charges. After Dulcie finished her presentation, Patterson would then do his best to argue that the affidavit contained insufficient evidence to warrant going forward with a trial.

He had a hard job, Joe thought. Patterson was tall, thin, and ungainly, and wore a suit that was too large for him and hung on his slim frame like a tarp covering an outdoor barbecue grill. Judge Hewitt was rarely magnanimous to the defense, and Tilden Cudmore hadn't helped his cause by refusing to stand up.

"Let's get this show on the road," Hewitt said, scanning the papers in front of him. "Let's hear the charges."

Dulcie approached the podium. Before she spoke, she looked around to see who was in the gallery. When she saw Joe, she smiled. When he noticed she was wearing her blood-red attack blouse, he smiled back.

"Okay, you'll probably want to be sitting down for this," Hewitt said to Cudmore.

Cudmore remained standing.

"Didn't you hear me?" Hewitt asked, raising his voice. Patterson tugged on Cudmore's sleeve.

"I got something to say, Your Excellency," Cudmore grumbled. "I've been sittin' in your jail since Friday night. I've done enough sittin'."

"That's not how it works," Hewitt said impatiently. "There's a procedure here, and in my courtroom we follow it. Miss Schalk reads the charges. When she's done, I'll ask you if you plead guilty or not guilty. Then I determine if there's enough evidence to proceed. Got that?"

It didn't stop Cudmore. "I want to fire this guy," he said, pointing at Patterson a foot away. "I don't want him to represent me one more minute. He's a part of our corrupt legal system, just like everybody in this damned room. I ain't gonna let myself get railroaded by treacherous elites with an incompetent boob by my side."

"Tilden . . ." Patterson said. "Come on now. You don't know what you're doing."

"I sure as hell do know what I'm doing, Your Excellency," Cudmore said too loudly to Judge Hewitt. "He might as well be over there with Schalk, rubbing her feet, that's how close they are. This is a damned joke, this trial. I ain't done nothing wrong and you are all just actors performing a part in a play called *Let's Screw Tilden Cudmore Because He Knows the Truth About Obama and 9/11.*"

Dulcie scowled at Cudmore, then turned to the judge.

"Your Honor, I move that the defendant be gagged and restrained if he says another word out of order."

"Fine idea," Hewitt said, nodding toward the bailiff. "I was thinking about having him tased first. Do you have your Taser on you?"

"Um, yes, Your Honor," the bailiff said, instinctively checking his equipment belt to make sure the Taser was there.

"Though I'm kind of starting to like the term 'Your Excellency,'" Judge Hewitt said with a grin.

Then he turned to Cudmore and the grin vanished.

Joe looked over at the woman in the front row. She'd lowered her knitting to her lap. She was transfixed and had a slight grin on her face.

Judge Hewitt said to Cudmore, "Sit down and shut up. That is your first and only warning. The only reason I haven't had you dragged back to jail with a whole slew of new charges is because a local girl was horribly beaten and she deserves swift justice."

"Like this is justice," Cudmore said, his voice rising again. "First they send an armored personnel carrier onto my property to arrest me, like this was Cuba or Russia or some damned Third World dictatorship. Then they blow off the roof of my house with a .50-caliber machine gun. *Then* they drag me in here in front of you.

"This is a kangaroo court, a show trial just like the Commies used to run. I done nothing wrong, but here I am. They set me up and brought me in because of my political beliefs. I'm a political prisoner. If that girl got hurt, it's because she brought it on herself. Hell, everybody in this town knows April Pickett is nothing more than a two-bit buckle bunny out there spreading her legs wide and just asking for something like this to happen. This is bullshit, Your Excellency."

Judge Hewitt turned white. He banged his gavel down so hard— *bam-bam-bam-bam*—the shaft snapped.

Joe was five steps down the aisle before he even realized he had launched out of his seat. He was headed toward the bar, into the well of the court itself. Cudmore stood with his back to him not twelve feet away through the short batwing doors. Joe fixed his eyes on the back of Cudmore's head and neck, where the first blows would land.

Sheriff Reed said, "Joe, no," and wheeled his chair to block the entrance.

Joe reached down to shove the wheelchair aside, but Reed's pleading eyes penetrated his rage, and he hesitated.

"I'm not moving," Reed said firmly. His grip on the outside push rim of his back wheels was like iron.

Joe took a breath and looked up. Dulcie had turned and was shaking her head apologetically. Patterson covered his face with his hands. And Tilden Cudmore puffed up his chest.

"Sorry, but some things just need to be said."

The bailiff moved toward Cudmore while fumbling for his hand-cuffs. Cudmore had six inches and fifty pounds on the man and stiff-armed him when he got close, rocking the bailiff back on his heels.

"Mr. Cudmore!" Judge Hewitt roared from the bench. "Sit your ass down and shut up, or I'll light you up right here and now."

Hewitt was on his feet, holding a black semiauto Sig Sauer aimed at Cudmore. It wasn't a secret that he always carried a concealed weapon out on the street. But until that moment, Joe didn't realize he packed heat under his robe as well.

"You don't need to shoot me," Cudmore whined. He turned to Patterson. "He can't do that, can he?"

Patterson moaned into his hands.

The courtroom door burst open and two of Reed's deputies came in, guns drawn.

"Here they come!" Cudmore sang out. "The jackbooted thugs again!"

Reed gestured to Cudmore and rolled his chair back. Joe stepped aside to let them pass, but he thought about joining them. He wanted a piece of Cudmore.

"Throw him in a cage," Hewitt said when the deputies secured Cudmore on each side. "Get him out of here."

Cudmore didn't fight them, but he made himself go limp so they had to practically drag him to the side door.

To Patterson, Hewitt said, "Is he prepared to make a plea? Or do I have to send him for a psych evaluation first?"

"We talked about a plea of not guilty," Patterson said sullenly. "Either that, or nolo contendere."

"There's a difference, Mr. Patterson."

"I know that, Your Honor. He can't make up his mind."

"He better make up his mind."

"If he'll even talk to me," Patterson said, shaking his head from side to side.

To Dulcie, Judge Hewitt said, "We'll bring him back in tomorrow morning with leg and hand restraints and a gag over his mouth and try this again."

Hewitt lifted his robe, holstered his handgun, and let the robe drop. He said to Joe, "I'm sorry you had to hear that. And I'm sorry I lost control of my courtroom. This is the first time that's ever happened."

Joe nodded.

"If it happens again," Hewitt said, "I'll let you have a go at him, if you promise me I get a shot at him when you're through."

"That's a deal," Joe said. But his face was still flushed with anger.

WHEN HE TURNED to get his hat, Joe saw that Brenda and Bull Cates had come into the courtroom during the fracas. Bull wore bib overalls with a C&C SEWER AND SEPTIC TANK SERVICE patch over the breast pocket, and he had a length of straw in his mouth. He wouldn't meet Joe's eyes.

Brenda used the backrest of the bench in front of her to stand up. She looked at Joe with profound sadness.

"So that's the animal who did it," she said. "Just like I tried to tell you people. He drives around on the highway just looking for victims. I tried to tell you people, but you were all so sure it was Dallas. Maybe next time you'll listen to an old lady when she tells you something, even if you think she's no better than poor white trash."

Joe grunted.

"I heard what he said about April. I'm just grateful Dallas wasn't here to hear that. I'm sure he still has feelings for her and he probably would have killed Cudmore with his fists. He's faster than you."

Joe's blood was still running hot, so he clamped his mouth shut and retrieved his hat from the bench.

"He would have been here if he was healthy enough," Brenda said. "He really wanted to come to support you and your family."

Joe fit his hat on his head.

"Has she had a chance to say anything yet?" Brenda asked.

11

H *as she had a chance to say anything yet?"*
Of all the things that had been said that morning in that courtroom, it was Brenda's parting question that lingered in Joe's mind as the most bitter and profound. It hung in the air in the cab of his pickup like a foul smell, and it lingered as he exited the town limits and merged onto Bighorn Road. He needed to feed the horses and Daisy before embarking on his two-and-a-half-hour trip north to Billings.

It wasn't: "How is she doing?"

Or: "When is she expected to recover?"

Or: "When can we see her?"

But: *"Has she had a chance to say anything yet?"*

Joe answered aloud: "What are you afraid she might say, Brenda?"

DESPITE TILDEN CUDMORE'S crazy guilt dance of a performance in the courtroom that morning, which seemed designed to show Judge Hewitt he was mentally incompetent to stand trial, and what he had said about April—who he'd not admitted to even knowing when he was arrested—Joe wondered why Brenda had asked that particular question.

And he wondered why the Cateses had shown up for the arraignment.

HE MADE THE LAST straight ascent to his home. In the distance, Wolf Mountain was budding green through his passenger-side window. And when he approached his house, he saw the white pickup with U.S. government plates parked in front.

For a moment, he wondered if the horses and Daisy could wait to eat until late that night. Then he groaned and continued into the driveway.

Annie Hatch opened the passenger-side door and walked over to greet him with her hands stuffed in the back pockets of her jeans. Her body language said: *I am remorseful.* Revis Wentworth stayed behind the wheel of the pickup. Apparently, he wasn't as remorseful, Joe thought.

Joe parked and got out. "Now isn't a good time, Annie," he said.

"That's why we're here," she said, looking up from her boot tops to Joe. "Why didn't you tell us about what had happened to your daughter? I—we—feel terrible about pressuring you during this time in your life."

"You're doing your job," Joe said. "I didn't want to bring my own personal stuff into it."

"But if you would have told us . . ."

Joe chinned toward Wentworth, who seemed to be studying something fascinating on the dashboard. "It wouldn't have mattered," Joe said.

"It would have to me," she said.

"Thank you, Annie."

"How is your daughter?"

"She's stable. It's complicated."

"Good, good," Hatch said. "I'm so glad to hear that."

Joe nodded. It was apparent there was more on her mind, but he didn't want to hear what it was. He said, "Well, it was nice of you to come by, but I'm on my way to the hospital right now."

Because she didn't turn around and walk back to her truck, Joe knew that she definitely had more to say.

"What?" he asked.

"Well, I almost hate to ask," she said, "but we were wondering if you'd sent that box of evidence from Lek Sixty-four to your people at the lab."

Joe took a deep breath and closed his eyes for a moment. The anger he'd felt in the courtroom had dissipated, but it was still within reach.

"No, I haven't," he said. The evidence box had been taped up and labeled, but was still on his desk in his cluttered office. He hadn't even thought about it the past few days.

"In that case, Revis was wondering if you wouldn't mind handing it over to us. We'd like to FedEx it to our experts in Denver. The word is getting out that an entire lek was massacred, and, well, you know how it is. We've got people breathing down our necks, wondering what we're doing about it. Revis even got a call from D.C."

Joe put his hands on his hips.

From the open window of the pickup, Wentworth spoke up. "Like you said, *we* still have a job to do."

Joe knew he'd screwed up, and he wanted the sage grouse twins to go away.

He said to Hatch, "I'll go get it. Just let me know what you hear back, okay?"

"Thank you, Joe."

"One more thing," he said.

"Yes?"

He pointed at Wentworth. "Keep him away from me."

USING A BROKEN GREEN PINE BOUGH he'd found on the side of the road, Joe propped up the yellow crime scene tape that was stretched across the open gate of the HF Bar Ranch and then drove his pickup underneath it.

Gary Norwood was leaning against his SUV and eating an apple when Joe pulled into the ranch yard. Norwood had been on the job less than two years and had taken it straight out of college. He looked it. He wore a loose oversized cowboy shirt over a black concert T-shirt, baggy jeans, and a backwards baseball cap. He had a shaved head and a soul patch beneath his lower lip. He'd not taken off his latex gloves to eat the apple.

"The sheriff said you might stop by," Norwood said. "I don't mind the company, since it's just me: the entire Twelve Sleep County Evidence Tech Department."

"I can't stay long," Joe said, getting out of his pickup. "What have you found?"

"Follow me," Norwood said, opening the back door of his SUV and tossing the apple core onto the floorboard, into a month's worth of fast-food wrappers and other trash. "Just make sure to walk clear of the evidence markers. I've got everything prepped for when the feds show up later."

He led Joe through the ranch yard on foot toward an ancient log horse barn.

"This is quite a place," Norwood said over his shoulder. "It would be cool to see it in full operation. I might come up this summer when it's in full swing. I bet there are some good-looking rich women who come out here to play cowgirl."

"That's usually the case," Joe said. He knew how the local single cowboys and wranglers made sure they got the night off during the summer—usually Wednesdays—when the guest ranches brought their clients into town. Many liaisons between rawboned local boys and well-heeled women executives from the east had occurred over the years at the Stockman's Bar.

"Did I hear it right that you know the guy they found here last night?" Norwood asked.

"Yup."

"He going to make it?"

"It doesn't sound good."

"I can see why," Norwood said, matter-of-fact. "Because some-body lost a hell of a lot of blood."

Norwood walked Joe through his best reconstruction of what had happened.

"He was found here," Norwood said, pointing toward a clearing on the near end of the ranch yard marked with a yellow plastic evidence marker. "I don't know whether he was trying to crawl far-ther and just played out, or what."

"Can you tell where it happened?" Joe asked.

"I think I've got a pretty good idea," Norwood said. "I just wish it hadn't rained yesterday. Any footprints or tire tracks I might have been able to find in the dirt were washed away. But I can show you where he was shot."

Joe followed, and Norwood shined his flashlight on a massive spoor of blood on the floor of the barn. Evidence markers were spaced around the pool.

"He bled quite a bit here, so I think this is where he first went down. There's an intermittent blood trail going out the open door and through those trees toward the ranch yard. That's where the FBI guys found him."

Joe said, "So as far as you know, the FBI guys never came into the barn?"

"As far as I know. I think they landed the helicopter and scooped him up and took him to Saddlestring Airport. They were met there by the Billings Life Flight chopper that took him to the hospital."

"Why didn't the FBI take him there?" Joe asked.

"Their chopper was too big to land on the roof, from what I understand, so they had to move him onto a smaller aircraft. You know how the feds are—only the biggest and best equipment for them."

"Anyway," Joe said, prompting Norwood. "Could you determine where the shots were fired from? Or how many shooters there were?"

Norwood dug out an ultraviolet flashlight from his gear bag and shined it on the back of the sliding barn door. A pattern of tiny flecks appeared under the light and glowed like a frozen starburst.

"It appears from the blood spatter that he was shot from shoulder height from one of those empty stalls over there. There's also some blood spatter near the baseboard—see it?"

"Yup."

"That indicates a second shooter from up there in the loft, because the spatter is nearly on the ground. So two shooters at least—one at ground level and one from above—but it's just a guess."

Joe rubbed his chin. "Did you find any spent casings?"

"No," Norwood said. "The shooters must have had the presence of mind to pick them up before they left. But I think I know what kind of weapons they used."

Joe arched his eyebrows.

"Shotguns. Both of 'em."

Norwood walked to the doorframe of the sliding barn door while opening a pocketknife. He jabbed the point into the old wood and started digging. In a moment, Joe heard the knife click on something metallic. Norwood dug it out and handed it to Joe.

"A shotgun pellet. Pretty big, too. I'm guessing double-ought, but I'll have to gather up a few more and measure them in my lab. It could be a zero buck, but I think it's too big to be an 'F' or a 'T.'"

"Yup," Joe said, rolling it around in his palm.

Hunters in Wyoming didn't use buckshot for deer. That was a southern thing, using shotguns in heavy brush at close range. Wyoming deer hunters used rifles because there was rarely much cover and most shots were at a distance. The only real use for buckshot was to kill men or bears at close range.

Norwood said, "And as you know, this makes identifying the weapons much tougher. Spent bullets have unique marks on them from the rifling of the barrel. We can identify the caliber and match up a test round fired from the same gun. But shotgun pellets? No markings. Even if we find someone with a half-empty box of double-ought shells it's difficult to make a match that'll stand up in court."

"So this was a trap from the get-go," Joe said. "Somehow, they lured him up here with the express purpose of shooting him down."

"That's what I'm thinking," Norwood said.

JOE CONNECTED on the phone with FBI Special Agent Chuck Coon when he was in sight of the WELCOME TO MONTANA sign on I-90. The snowcapped Bighorns were in his rearview mirror and the vast rolling terrain was a carpet of brilliant green grass.

Coon was in charge of the Wyoming office of the FBI in Cheyenne. He was intense and honest, a by-the-book G-man as distressed by some of the goings-on in Washington as the locals. Which meant, Coon had told Joe, that he'd be stationed in far-off Wyoming for the rest of his career.

Joe said, "Nate Romanowski walked into an ambush and, from what I can tell, he wasn't armed. How did you people let that happen?"

Coon sighed and said, "Hold on." That was code for closing his office door so he couldn't be overheard.

"Look," Coon said, "the deal with your pal Romanowski was negotiated directly with the DOJ, with your governor playing a supporting role. They didn't include us local guys in the deal and they didn't let us see the final agreement. I didn't even know he was gone until after the whole thing came down."

"But they took away his weapon," Joe said. "They sent him to his death."

"I wouldn't have done that," Coon said, "but then, I wouldn't have agreed to let Romanowski out of the basement for the rest of my natural life. Everywhere he goes, somebody winds up dead or with their ears twisted off. But this isn't any secret to you."

"No, it isn't," Joe said. "So who is the agent in charge?"

"His name is Stan Dudley."

"Can you patch me through to him?"

"No can do," Coon said. "The only way I can talk to him is if I go through the DOJ channels in D.C. That's the way they have it set up. Besides, I don't think he's in the building. I think he's hovering around Romanowski on his deathbed, hoping he'll find out who shot him with your pal's last words."

"Dudley's in Billings?"

"I think so," Coon said. "That's the last I heard. But don't hold me to it. Like I said, Dudley's operating on a separate track. Frankly, I don't really like the man, but that's neither here nor there. He probably doesn't like me, either."

Joe paused, then asked, "But do you know what's going on? Why would they want Nate out? Not that I'm against it, but it doesn't make sense to me."

"Me, either," Coon said. "I've heard some things, though. Governor Rulon wanted him out because, well, he likes him. He made Romanowski promise not to commit another felony in Wyoming. But for the feds—my understanding is they wanted to put him out there to serve as bait to Wolfgang Templeton. They wanted to snare Templeton when he came after Romanowski."

"And Nate agreed to that?"

"Apparently," Coon said. "He agreed to stay out of trouble, but it sounds like that didn't last very long."

"Nope," Joe said. "Why is the DOJ even involved? Don't they have enough on their plate these days?"

Coon snorted. "What I'm going to tell you is complete speculation on my part. And if you repeat where you heard it, you and I are going to have a problem."

"Shoot," Joe said.

"Some of Templeton's victims were crony capitalists or friends of big fund-raisers for the current administration. It's personal. Officials who shall remain nameless want revenge on Templeton and they want to shut him up. Simple as that. Romanowski is just a means to an end."

Joe felt his ire rising once again. "So Templeton, or Templeton's men, found Romanowski and they took him out? Is that what you're saying?"

"I'm purely speculating. Who else would want him dead? I'm surprised they even knew that quickly he was out. Unless, of course, someone on the inside let them know."

That possibility gave Joe an instant headache. "You mean like someone in your building?"

"Like I said, I'm speculating," Coon said.

"Who else could it be?"

"Gee, I don't know," Coon said. "Maybe someone at DOJ tipped Templeton off. Maybe Templeton acted a lot more quickly than the bureaucracy thought possible and they weren't prepared yet. Have you thought of that? We're a big agency and we move slow. Someone may have started something that quickly went over their head."

"They wouldn't want anyone to know that," Joe said. "There would be some big-time CYA action going on right now."

Joe drove on. He could hear Coon breathing on the other end.

"Are you done?" Coon asked.

"I guess so. I've got a lot to think about."

"You do." Then, with his voice softening, Coon asked, "How's your girl, Joe? I hear she's in the same hospital."

Joe brought Coon up to speed, and told him briefly about the calamity in the courtroom that morning.

Coon said, "It's a good thing you've got Marybeth. If I had all that going on . . . I don't know what the hell I'd do."

Joe agreed.

"Chuck," Joe said before punching off, "please let me know if you hear anything about Nate or Templeton."

"Not officially," Coon said. "But I may give you a call from time to time on your cell phone."

"Thank you."

"Hang in there, man," Coon said.

12

April's hospital room was dimly lit and quiet except for the muffled hum of the HVAC and an occasional soft click from one of the many electronic monitors hovering over her bed. Thin wires from embedded catheters coiled up from her head. She was being fed intravenously through a tube, and other tubes delivered hydration and medication. Additional tubes carried waste away into receptacles underneath the bed. Because she was so still, it seemed to Joe she was simply serving as a disinterested processing center for the transfer of incoming fluids.

Marybeth was with him when he entered the room and she stood behind him as he approached the bed.

"I haven't seen her since she left," he said, reaching out and brushing April's cheek with the back of his hand. She was battered but sleeping, her expression untroubled. He could not tell from looking at her that she had brain trauma. Her hair was brushed neatly, although the part was wrong. How would the nurses know?

Joe listened as Marybeth explained the procedure the doctors had undertaken, and she pointed out what the readings on the monitors meant. She showed Joe the all-important readout that would indicate an increase—or decrease—in brain activity when she was brought out of the coma.

He found April's limp hand under the blanket. It was warm but unresponsive.

"I've seen her eyelids flutter a couple of times," Marybeth said softly. "That's not supposed to happen unless there's brain activity. But when I asked, I was told the monitors didn't pick it up. But I swear I saw it happen."

Joe looked over. He believed her, of course. But he didn't want to read too much into it.

"She's got great doctors and nurses," Marybeth said. "They'll look out for her. They know to call or text me the minute they determine they want to bring her back, or if her situation changes in any way. I want to make sure I'm here if either happens."

Joe nodded. He had trouble speaking. His job was to take care of his family, to protect them. He hated it that there was nothing he could do to help April now. Her fate was up to doctors he didn't know, to April herself, and to God. He could only hope that some- where in her sleeping body she had the ability and the will to get better.

He leaned down close enough to April that he could smell her hair. It smelled medicinal, not like it used to smell. She belonged to the hospital now. He started to say something, but his throat was constricted.

He rose and took a deep breath. Then two.

After a few moments, he leaned back down to her and said, "I just wish you could wake up and tell me who did this to you. I'll get the man who did it."

He hoped against hope for a fluttering of her eyelids or a sign— any sign—of a reaction.

Nothing.

Marybeth reached under the covers and gently placed her hand on Joe's. She whispered to him, "Don't you dare lose hope."

In the hallway, Joe said to Marybeth, "Do you know where Nate is?"

"They haven't let me see him."

"Who told you that?"

She said, "There's a special agent in charge. Kind of an unpleasant man, if you ask me. I know there are rules about only family members in ICU, but . . ."

"Is his name Stan Dudley?"

"He didn't introduce himself."

Joe said, "Let's go find him."

Shri Reckling had just come on the night shift and she agreed to help them. She used her key card to open the secure ICU door. When the nurse on duty looked up to see three people come into the hallway, Reckling said, "It's okay. They're with me."

"We're here to see Nate Romanowski," Joe said.

Before the ICU nurse could respond, a portly man in an ill-fitting suit leaned out from the waiting lounge and said, "Forget it. He's back in surgery again. Patching this guy up just so he can die in a couple of days is going to bust my budget."

Joe said, "You must be Stan Dudley."

Dudley looked Joe over carefully, from his lace-up outfitter boots to his Wranglers to his red uniform shirt and weathered Stetson. He said, "And you must be Joe Pickett."

"I'm Marybeth," she interjected, stepping forward.

"The two of you, then," Dudley said. He seemed to be contemplating what he'd say next. Then: "Well, it doesn't really matter that you're here, because there's no chance to see Romanowski. They took him back into surgery about half an hour ago. More internal bleeding, I guess. He hasn't regained consciousness and he hasn't said a damned word since we found him. It wouldn't do anybody any good to try and see him now anyway. The doctors won't let you into the room."

Joe said, "I hope their bedside manner is better than yours."

Dudley puffed out his chest. "I don't sugarcoat things. I'm a straight shooter."

"I think you're an ass," Joe said.

Marybeth shouldered past Joe and stood in front of him so he couldn't advance on Dudley.

Her voice was calm. "How long will he be in surgery?"

Dudley shrugged. "Your guess is as good as mine. He's been in there twice already. The doctors removed something like seventeen hunks of buckshot. There are a couple near his heart they may just leave there because it's too dangerous to try and get them. Plus, he lost a lot of blood. One more hour of him lying in the dirt on that ranch and we wouldn't even be talking here right now.

"So," Dudley said, gesturing with his hand at Joe and Marybeth as if shooing them away, "you two should just scoot on out of here. You can't see him, and he's not likely to ever sit naked in a tree again, or whatever it is he supposedly does for fun."

"Not so fast," Joe said, lowering his voice.

"Come again?" Dudley said, glancing back inside the lounge, where, Joe guessed, there were a couple of backup agents.

"Who bushwhacked him?" Joe asked.

"Your guess is as good as mine," Dudley said. "But my guess includes the name Templeton."

"How would he know Nate would be there?"

"The guy probably has his tentacles in everything," Dudley said. "Somebody must have tipped him off. But I do know who could probably answer that question. Do you know Olivia Brannan?"

Joe heard Marybeth gasp in front of him and saw her raise her hand to her mouth.

"I know that's your theory," Joe said. "But it doesn't wash."

"So where is she?" Dudley asked with a forced grin. "She picks him up, takes him to that ranch, and vanishes off the face of the earth. It isn't a stretch to guess she colluded with the shooters."

Joe shook his head.

"Do *you* know where she is?" Dudley asked. "Does anybody? She wasn't at the scene, and her and her van are AWOL."

Marybeth said, "She's head over heels for Nate, and he feels the same way about her."

"She devoted years of her life to working for Wolfgang Templeton," Dudley countered. "She's known Romanowski for what—six months?"

"I'm not buying it," Joe said. But his mind was spinning because it made sense.

"Maybe we can ask her," Dudley said. "If she can *ever be found*."

LATER, AS JOE'S PICKUP rose above the rimrocks that defined Billings and the dark prairie was stretched out in front of them, Marybeth said, "If both April and Nate are taken away from us . . ."

Joe said, "Don't you dare lose hope."

As they crossed the border back into Wyoming, Joe's cell phone lit up. Dulcie Schalk.

"Hello, Dulcie," he said.

He could tell by her long pause that bad news was coming.

She said, "Tilden Cudmore hanged himself in his cell. They found his body an hour ago."

Joe tapped his brakes so he could pull over to the shoulder of the highway. Marybeth studied his face. Joe repeated what he had just heard, and Marybeth closed her eyes.

"How did it happen?" Joe asked, holding the phone away from his face and punching the speaker button so Marybeth could hear the conversation as well.

"He used a bedsheet for a rope and he tied it to the light fixture," Dulcie said.

"Where were the deputies?"

"We just interviewed them. They checked on him at eight-fifty p.m. and he appeared to be sleeping in his bunk. When they went back in at five past nine, he was dead. They did CPR on him when they cut him down, and the clinic tried to revive him, but he was DOA."

Joe said, "He didn't seem like the kind of man who would do himself in."

"I agree," Dulcie said. "Otherwise, we would have put him on a suicide watch. You just never know what's going on in a man's head. Especially that man's head."

"Is it possible someone got to him?" Joe asked.

She sighed. "No. It's all on videotape. He waited until the deputy left the cell and he jumped up and went to work. No one was watching the monitor at the time he did it. So, no. He killed himself."

"His guilt got to him," Marybeth said. "Or he was a coward who couldn't face jail."

"I'm guessing the latter," Dulcie said. Then: "Marybeth, I'm sorry I had to call you with this news."

Marybeth said, "Don't be. I would have gladly handed a rope to the man who assaulted April."

"That's one way to look at it," Dulcie said. "I'd rather have sent him to Rawlins, but in a sense, we've got justice—just not the kind I prefer."

After a pause, she asked, "So how *is* April?"

Joe turned off the speaker and handed the phone to Marybeth.

While Dulcie and Marybeth talked, he eased the pickup back out onto the highway.

He could not have predicted this turn of events. It was not at all satisfying to him. He couldn't get over the fact that he wasn't sure justice had been served at all.

Cudmore was a creep and a paranoid conspiracy theorist. The evidence was stacked against him. The things he had said and done at the arraignment hearing had almost convinced Joe he was capable of beating and dumping April. Dulcie obviously believed Cudmore had done it. Marybeth seemed to think the same thing.

Joe wasn't so sure. And he couldn't reach out to Nate for help because Nate was dying.

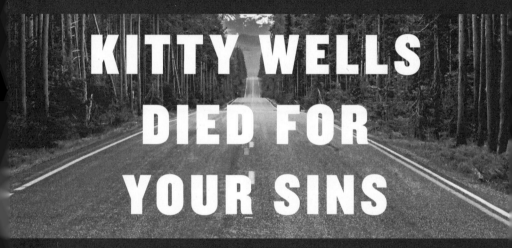

PART FOUR

KITTY WELLS DIED FOR YOUR SINS

13

Two days later, Liv Brannan looked up when she heard the heavy oncoming footfalls approach the root cellar from outside. She'd come to recognize the day-to-day routine.

It was dinnertime on Friday night, March 21. It was her thirty-third birthday, but she didn't plan on telling anyone about it because she knew they wouldn't care. When a single tear leaked out of her left eye, she violently wiped it away.

She sat on a rickety hard-backed chair near the air mattress and a mass of rumpled sleeping bags. It was the only chair available.

By the looks of it, the cellar had been dug into the earth many years ago, probably before the motley collection of houses, double-wide trailers, and metal buildings had been assembled above ground. She'd seen glimpses of the compound through a tiny gap at the bottom of her blindfold when they brought her here after the shooting. There were old trucks and cars rusting in a field, a pack of dogs that had rushed out to greet the Suburban, and stray chickens in the yard. Elk, moose, and deer antlers whitened by age and sun covered the entire side of an old clapboard barn. She thought: *White trash.*

By the glow of a utility light that hung from a slit in the double doors, she'd studied every inch of the root cellar. She didn't have anything else to do except reread the dozen magazines—*American Hunter, National Enquirer, Taste of Home*—they'd left for her. Someone had torn off the address labels on the front of each one so she wouldn't know who the subscriptions were for—or the address they'd been sent to. All she knew was that the compound was about an hour from the HF Bar Ranch. She had no idea which direction they'd come from, and she hadn't seen which roads they had taken, because she hadn't been allowed to get off the floor of the second row of seats in the SUV until they arrived. She knew they'd been on gravel roads, asphalt, and finally a rutted dirt road that was a bruiser.

The walls of the cellar were hard dry clay. It had been dug by hand tools and she could make out the pick marks. Webs of dried roots reached out of the walls like gnarled hands. Several rows of empty shelving covered each wall, no doubt where someone used to store canned vegetables or jam. She'd heard that people out here used to can trout and wild game in Mason jars as well. The shelves were held up by rusted metal L-shaped braces. She'd tried to pull one out, but it was stuck fast. She'd continue to try to get one free because it was the only thing she had that could possibly serve as a weapon.

Plotting her escape was better than crying to herself. Liv was cried out.

The other items in the cellar—the blankets, the ancient thick sleeping bags lined with deer and elk montages that were no doubt used in a hunting camp, the humming electric space heater, the five-gallon white bucket that served as her toilet, the case of bottled water—were harmless.

THE HASP WAS THROWN on the double doors twelve feet above her. The left door was opened, then the right. The particular smell

of the place—the mixture of spilled diesel fuel, manure, and sage—
wafted down from outside. She could see a square of pure blue sky.

"Stand back," the man said. "I'm puttin' the ladder down."

Liv stood and moved the chair, then retreated to the wall in back
of her as the aluminum extension ladder was lowered until the feet
were solidly on the floor. She looked up as the opening filled with
the shoulders and head of a man. He wore a cowboy hat with sharp
upturned side brims like he always did, and he appeared to be
grinning.

"*There* you are," he said finally. "It took me a minute to see where
you were."

"I'm here," she said.

"I got your supper."

He backed off for a second and then reappeared. His cowboy
boots descended rung by rung. His back was to her as he came
down, but he had his head turned so he could watch her and make
sure she didn't try anything. He steadied himself with his left hand
on the rail. A black feed bucket with a small quilt over the mouth of
it hung from his right.

"You've got a hell of a treat coming your way. Fried chicken, corn
on a cob, rolls, butter, and salad with Thousand Island dressing,"
he said.

When he got to the bottom, he turned. He was big, with wide
shoulders and a barrel chest. His head was blocky and he had a lantern jaw and small, close-set eyes. As always, he had her Smith &
Wesson Governor tucked into the front of his jeans and an electric
hot-shot, designed for livestock, sticking out of his back pocket. She
knew he wouldn't hesitate to use it on her if he felt the need. Or
maybe just for fun.

She could smell the aroma of fried chicken from the bucket.

"How long are you going to keep me down here?" she asked. "It gets really cold at night."

He snorted and pointed at the space heater that glowed red.

"It doesn't exactly keep it toasty in here."

He said, "I woke up once in the woods with five inches of snow on me. This ain't so bad."

"It is for *me*."

He shrugged. "That ain't my call."

"Whose call is it?"

"Why do we have to get into all this again?" he said. "Can't we ever just have a nice conversation? Why do you always have to be so feisty?"

"*I'm in a hole in the ground.* What if it rains or snows?"

"That's why we put them blankets down here, I think."

"What if it rains hard and this cellar fills with water?"

"Yeah, well," he said after a long pause. As if he really had to think that over, she thought.

"Why did you kill him?"

"I just do what I'm told to do for the good of the family. It wasn't nothing personal. Mom always says we gotta cover all the bases."

Those were the same words he'd used when she'd asked him the last time. The same words he used every time she asked.

"*'Cover all the bases'?* What does that even mean?"

He shrugged again and said, "She's always thinking a few steps ahead of everybody else. I don't even try to outguess her on this kind of thing."

"Are you sure he's dead?" she asked.

That made him think. It was as if he'd never even considered the question.

He said, "We hit him with three full loads of buckshot. That'd kill any man."

"Nate's not any man. He's a good man. And he was unarmed."

"Yeah, I know," he said. Then: "Why was that? Why didn't he have that famous gun of his on him?"

"The feds took it away."

"Damned feds anyway," he said. "That's what they're tryin' to do with all of us—take away our guns. That's what your president wants to do."

Liv said, "Why is he *my* president?"

He reddened. "You know. Jeez, it seems like everything I say makes you mad."

"I'm in a hole."

"Could be worse," he said.

"What did you do with the van?"

"We took care of it."

"What's that mean?"

"It's okay if you don't eat it all," he said, lowering the bucket to the floor. "I noticed you don't eat everything I bring you. That's probably why you're so skinny."

She sighed.

"Man, that chicken smells good, don't it?" he said, nudging the black bucket with his boot tip. "I bet you can't wait to dig into that."

"Why?" she asked. "Because that's what my people eat?"

"Shit, that ain't what I meant," he said, looking down for a second. "Me, I love fried chicken, and as you can see, I'm a white man.

Mom makes it once a week, on Friday night, and I always make sure I'm around. It's my favorite thing. I usually eat six or seven thighs." He paused. Then: "I'm a thigh man. I love that dark meat."

"There you go again," she said.

When he looked up, this time he wasn't embarrassed at all, and she realized he'd meant to say it. He'd probably been practicing it to himself on his walk over from the main house. He probably thought he was clever.

"Oh," she said, sickened by the realization, but trying not to show it. She refused to show him weakness.

Above, Liv heard a door slam shut in the distance, then a woman shout.

"Bull? What are you doing down there?"

The man rolled his eyes and boomed, "No names, Cora Lee!"

He looked at Liv and shook his head as if he expected her to agree with him what a dolt Cora Lee was.

"Bull and Cora Lee," Liv said. "So was that your mother I met at the ranch?"

"Quit asking me all these damned questions," Bull said, irritated. She couldn't tell if he was angry at her or at Cora Lee. Or both.

"Bull!" Cora Lee shouted. "We're all fuckin' waiting on you to eat! You're supposed to lower that bucket down to her. You ain't supposed to deliver it like you was fuckin' room service."

"She's got a mouth on her," Bull said as an aside to Liv. "And she could probably afford to miss a few meals, if you know what I mean."

Liv forced herself to grin. She could tell he liked that.

"Bull, goddamnit!" Cora Lee yelled.

"I'm coming!" he yelled back. "I'm coming."

Before he climbed back up the ladder, he asked, "You need anything?" His tone was much gentler than the one he'd used to answer Cora Lee.

"Yes. Let me out of here."

"Very funny," he said with a chuckle.

He climbed to the top. She heard Cora Lee say, "Jesus, man. There you are. Hurry the fuck up."

"Shut up, Cora Lee," Bull said as he pulled the ladder up and swung the doors closed and locked them.

TWO HOURS LATER, the footfalls came back. Lighter this time, but not much.

Instead of Bull, it was Cora Lee. Liv recognized her by her voice.

"I'm doin' the shit run," Cora Lee said, dropping the coil of thin rope to the floor. It nearly hit Liv. "Tie it on your feed bucket first. Then I'll drop it back down for the chamber pot."

While Liv bent down to fix the rope to the black bucket handle, Cora Lee said, "What is it you and Bull was talking about for so long?"

"I wasn't the one talking," Liv said.

"Goddamn that man," Cora Lee said under her breath. "You just stay the hell away from him."

Liv looked up, exasperated. "I'm not the one coming down the ladder."

Cora Lee narrowed her eyes. She was a sturdy, rough-looking blonde. She looked like she'd lived hard. Liv could see where she had once been pretty, twenty years and fifty pounds ago. Now, though, she had a weathered face set in a scowl.

"Tell them to let me go and I'll never breathe a word of this to anyone," Liv said.

"Like I'm gonna believe that," Cora Lee said, untying the feed bucket and setting it aside. She dropped the rope back down. "Now your shitter."

As Cora Lee hoisted the white bucket, it thumped on each rung of the ladder. Liv retreated to the far corner of the cellar before any of the contents could splash out and hit her. A few foul drops stained the floor near the feet of the ladder.

"Oh, sorry," Cora Lee said, not sorry at all.

Liv heard Cora Lee empty the bucket on the ground a few steps away from the cellar door, then she returned to lower it back down.

"Would you mind rinsing it out first?" Liv asked.

"Yeah, I mind," Cora Lee said. "I gotta get myself ready. Me and Bull are goin' to town later."

Liv thought, *His name again*. Either Cora Lee was especially stupid or she knew Liv would never have the chance to identify them to anyone.

So there were four of them at least, Liv thought to herself. Bull and his wife, Cora Lee. A man—the father?—called Eldon. She knew that name because she'd heard Cora Lee call to him a day ago. Eldon had responded with "No names!" and Liv could picture him pointing toward the root cellar in the distance. At other times, though, she could hear conversations between family members where they seemed to either have forgotten about her or didn't think she could overhear. Or they just didn't care, like Cora Lee.

She'd heard a couple of references to someone named Dallas, but she'd not heard Dallas speak for himself. Either Dallas was away or he'd not left the house.

Then there was the mother. The woman who "covered all the bases." The woman who originally claimed she was Kitty Wells. Liv cursed herself for falling for that. Kitty Wells had been a country singer back in the fifties and sixties. Liv's mother used to sing "It Wasn't God Who Made Honky Tonk Angels" around the house, and she sang it better than Kitty Wells.

Liv hummed,

Too many times married men think they're still single
And that's caused many a good girl to go wrong.

Her head snapped up when she recalled the lyrics. Maybe, she thought, she had a weapon after all.

She was still thinking it through later that night when she realized it had become remarkably colder in the cellar, and the outside seemed oddly hushed. Only when a few rivulets of precipitation trickled down the clay walls did she know it was snowing.

14

On Saturday afternoon, Joe Pickett rumbled his pickup slowly down the muddy two-track that cut through the sagebrush toward the site of what had once been Lek 64. Daisy sat in the passenger seat with her front paws on the dashboard. The four inches of heavy spring snow that had fallen the night before had mostly thawed, but the moisture released a panorama of scents that kept his dog's attention.

Clouds shrouded the summits of the Bighorns, parked there as if gathering strength before they loosened their grip and snow descended again. There was no spring in the Rockies, Joe knew. There was winter, summer, fall, and March-through-June, which was made up of various highlights of the other three.

While he often worked weekends in the summer to check fishermen and -women and in the fall to check hunters, he tried to take weekends off during the winter and March-through-June. But the night before, he'd received an email from his director, Lisa Greene-Dempsey, with the subject line "CRISIS." Most subject lines on LGD's emails were versions of "CRISIS" or "EMERGENCY." The body of the email was written in her particular style: all capital letters and no punctuation except ". . ." between thoughts. To Joe, her messages all came across like shouted rants. She wanted him to "GET OUT TO THE LOCATION OF LEK 64 . . .

RECOVER ANY SURVIVORS OF THE SAGE GROUSE MASSACRE . . ."

Apparently, the news of the slaughter had gone viral within the agency due to notices sent out from the Sage Grouse Task Force. LGD wanted to mitigate her report to the governor about the incident by saying that her man in the district, game warden Joe Pickett, had rescued the survivors.

Joe had groaned. He knew there would be no survivors because it had been more than a week since he'd discovered the killing field. The few cripples he'd seen darting through the brush would have long ago been eaten by predators, because they lacked the protection of the concentric circle of birds. On their own, they were history. It was the brutal but natural circle of life and death in the wild.

He knew LGD wouldn't be satisfied until he assured her he'd returned to the scene and looked it over. Even then, he knew she wouldn't be pleased with his report. She was a political animal and not a favorite of Governor Rulon, who had appointed her as a favor to his wife. There were rumors that LGD was positioning herself to run for governor once Rulon completed his second and final term. She was sensitive to anything that might cause her a public relations hit—especially from the feds and her environmental support groups. Being in charge of an agency that let dozens of potentially endangered sage grouse be decimated on her watch wouldn't help her ambitions. Her email to Joe was carefully crafted outrage that she could later use as evidence of the immediate action she had taken. She even referred to the loss of Lek 64 as "SPECIES GENOCIDE."

LGD had not asked about April's condition but, to be fair, Joe wasn't sure she knew about what had happened.

IF HE HADN'T known the country intimately, Joe thought, he could have easily driven right through the site of Lek 64 without recognizing it. The snows had smoothed out the tire tracks through the sagebrush, and predators had cleaned up the remains of the dead sage grouse. There were no longer feathers scattered everywhere on the ground, although there were a few pinfeathers caught in the brush. It was almost as if the birds had never been there at all.

This time, he let Daisy out. If there were any remaining grouse, she would find them. He let her work the brush, and he monitored her the way he did when they were bird-hunting. She flowed through the brush with her nose down and her tail straight up and wagging. For a minute, it appeared she had found something when her tail, like a supercharged metronome, suddenly picked up speed. Joe followed her, wondering how he'd catch a crippled grouse with his bare hands, where he'd store it for the ride down, and where he'd keep it.

Those thoughts vanished when a cottontail rabbit shot from the brush with Daisy in pursuit.

BEFORE JOE had put on his uniform and left for the breaklands, Marybeth had a long talk with the doctors in Billings. There was no bad news, but there was no good news, either. It was a miserable state of limbo.

The swelling on April's brain had gone down slightly, but it was a difficult thing to test. It didn't make Marybeth optimistic, but it confirmed that the hospital was doing all it could, she said.

Whether their insurance would pay for it all was also undetermined, despite daily calls Marybeth made to their provider.

Nate's condition was a mystery. All they knew was that he probably hadn't died. His wing of the ICU was locked down tight, per the orders of Special Agent Stan Dudley of the FBI. Dudley wouldn't take Marybeth's calls, and didn't return them. Joe had tried with the same result, and a call to Coon in Cheyenne had resulted in no information because, Coon said, Dudley communicated only with Washington and he didn't feel any obligation to let the locals in on Nate's prognosis. Even Nurse Reckling confided that Nate's condition was unknown to her and others she knew on staff. There had been more surgeries, but that's all she knew.

MORE NAILS had been hammered into Tilden Cudmore's coffin when it was learned by the sheriff's department that he'd been charged ten years earlier in Illinois for aggravated sexual assault. The victim was found walking down a rural road, and she'd accused Cudmore of giving her a ride and then pulling over and assaulting her. Unfortunately, she died several days later in a car wreck, before she could provide testimony against him in court. Cudmore was in custody at the time of the accident. The case was dropped.

Dulcie told Joe it showed a pattern that had eluded them until they learned of the Illinois charges. Long before he moved to Saddlestring, Cudmore had haunted the rural highways and picked up hitchhikers and women needing a ride. Once they were in his vehicle, he assaulted them and dumped them to fend for themselves. Dulcie said she'd asked Sheriff Reed to initiate an investigation to find out whether there were other victims of similar crimes through-out the state and region. Perhaps, she'd told Joe, Cudmore had been operating under their radar for years. His political causes and eccentricities, she thought, had masked his obsession.

BRENDA'S STORY about Dallas's journey home could not be disproved. He'd been thrown from the bull in Houston on Saturday, March 8. Brenda said he'd stayed in Houston most of Sunday as his pain got worse, then hit the road and drove twenty-two straight hours to arrive late Monday night. He was recovering at home and had been there for two days, she claimed, when April was attacked by Tilden Cudmore.

Unfortunately, Dulcie said, the Cateses could produce no credit card receipts for gasoline or food on Dallas's long ride home. Dallas, like most rodeo cowboys, paid his entry fees in cash and was paid in cash when he won. He rarely used a credit card except for the rare plane ticket or rental car.

No one had come forward to dispute any aspect of Brenda's explanation, Dulcie said. Until there was evidence otherwise, that line of inquiry was dead.

But Joe still had his doubts about Cudmore, and about Dallas.

AS HE TRAILED DAISY through the brush, he stopped and fixed his gaze on the southern horizon. He knew the Cates place was several miles in that direction. The bench he was parked on was flat, but a mile to the south it sloped down into a shallow valley. The BLM land abutted the twelve-acre Cates compound.

He turned slowly and studied the contours of the high bench. There were places, he thought, where the road he'd arrived on might be seen from below due to the high folds of the terrain. The angle might just be such that a vehicle on the road could be glimpsed from below in the valley in visual snapshots.

He called Daisy back and started his pickup and did a three-point turn, then slowly retraced his route.

At three different places along the two-track there were drainages to the south where he could see the valley below. At two of those drainages, he could see the distant cluster of buildings that belonged to the Cateses.

Joe stopped at the second swale, rolled his driver's-side window down three-quarters of the way, and mounted his Redfield spotting scope to the top of the glass. Because the Cates place was two miles away, he turned off the motor to stop the vibration through his cab so he could focus.

There was no activity on the place. After all, he thought, it was Saturday. He scoped the main house, a double-wide trailer, a barn, and several outbuildings. In the opening of a metal building he could see the chrome snouts of two pump trucks Eldon used to pump out septic systems.

As he watched, he saw the front door of the main house open and Cora Lee, Bull's wife, come out. She walked across the yard through a couple of old shacks. Her body language was surly, Joe thought, but then it always was. When Joe had arrested Bull for game violations, Cora Lee had called Joe every name in the book. She had a mouth on her.

Cora Lee stopped at what looked like a well, opened some doors, and tossed something down in it. A few minutes later, she pulled up a bucket and dumped it out near the opening. Then she threw the bucket back in, closed the doors, and returned to the house.

Could someone at the Cates place possibly have seen the vehicle of the person or persons who'd wiped out Lek 64? After all, if he could see the compound from where he was, they could see *him*.

Joe doubted it. Too much distance, and too quick of a look at a vehicle on the road.

But it gave him a pretense to pay them a visit. Director LGD would even approve of it.

Dulcie might be another story.

EVEN THOUGH the Cates compound was in plain view in the valley, it took twenty-five minutes for Joe to get there on ancient two-tracks that were barely roads at all. As the place got larger in his windshield and he bounced his tires over ruts and knee-high sagebrush, he thought that the family employed the same kind of defense sage grouse did: they hid in plain sight. The tough part wasn't finding them. The tough part was getting there.

And it would be impossible to sneak up on them.

He circumnavigated the fence line that defined the Cates property from BLM land and passed under a hand-lettered sign that read:

DULL KNIFE OUTFITTERS

C&C SEWER AND SEPTIC TANK SERVICE

BIRTHPLACE OF PRCA WORLD CHAMPION COWBOY

DALLAS CATES

Bull had emerged from inside the house and stood waiting for Joe with his hands on his hips outside the front door.

AS JOE SHUT OFF the engine and reached for the door handle, a pack of six big dogs thundered out, howling, from underneath the wooden porch Bull was standing on, and surrounded the pickup. They were mixed-breed short-haired mottled-color brutes with dark muzzles and flashing teeth. Joe guessed they were a mix of Rottweiler and Rhodesian ridgeback, a scary combination. One of them lunged at the passenger window and bounced off with a thump, leaving a smear of goo on the glass. Daisy cowered and backed up into Joe.

Bull whistled and called to them. The pack slunk back to the house. He opened the front door and one by one they went inside.

Joe told Daisy to get on the floor of the cab and stay. He shut off the engine and made a point of folding the seat down as he got out. Behind the seat, as always, was his 12-gauge shotgun.

Because if Bull opened the door and let the dogs out . . .

Bull rocked on the balls of his feet like a fighter in the ring and sneered at Joe.

"Hell of a brave dog you got there," Bull shouted.

He had to shout because of the din of a loud motor—likely a generator or air compressor—racketing from the garage where the pump trucks were parked. The sound was distracting.

"Daisy loves everybody," Joe shouted back. "She's not used to being attacked for no good reason."

"They got a reason," Bull said. "They're protecting their property from the man who dicked me around."

Joe said, "Then I guess you know why I'm here."

Bull's eyelids fluttered. A tell. But of what? Joe wondered. He paused by the grille of his pickup and waited to see if Bull would spill something. There was no doubt in Joe's mind he had something to hide.

Before Bull could respond, the screen door opened and hit him in the back.

"Move, son," Brenda Cates said, annoyed. "Let me come out." Behind her, the dogs barked to be let out.

Bull dropped his hands and stood to the side so his mother could come out on the porch. She squeezed out through the front door so the dogs were still inside.

Brenda emerged, wearing an apron embroidered with flowers, and she was in the process of cleaning her hands with a towel.

"You caught me in the middle of making some pies," she said to Joe. "So what brings you out here?"

Joe couldn't hear her well over the noise from the garage, but he could read her lips well enough to get the gist of what she was asking. He knew he'd lost his opportunity to get Bull to blurt something out or to come up with a lie. Brenda had saved her son whether she intended to or not.

"Can we get that racket back there shut off so we can talk?" Joe asked.

"Just say what you came to say," Bull shouted.

"I was wondering who might have been home a week ago last Thursday, in the evening," Joe said. "That would have been on March thirteenth."

Brenda eyed Joe coolly. Her face was hard to read. But she'd stopped wiping off her hands.

Bull turned his head to her as if waiting to follow her lead.

Joe took a few steps forward until he stood directly beneath them on the porch so he could hear them better.

"A week ago Thursday," she said. "Well, I was here. Dallas was here, of course. Bull and Cora Lee were out on a service call, right, Bull?"

"Yep," Bull said. "We didn't get back until late."

"They take the second pump truck out if Eldon is already on a job," Brenda said. "Sometimes when people call us, they can't wait for Eldon to get there. You know, like if it's a sewage emergency."

Joe nodded like he understood.

She said, "Now, why are you asking about Thursday the thirteenth?"

Joe pointed to the north. "Someone was up there on BLM land causing mischief. I was wondering if you or anyone might have seen a vehicle or heard anything."

Although Brenda had no reaction to the question, Joe saw Bull's shoulders relax. He knew that whatever dilemma he might have been facing had passed. Yet Bull clearly felt guilty about *something*.

"What was I supposed to see?" Brenda asked. "I'm usually in the kitchen at night. The window looks out the front of the house, not the side. So I really can't say I saw anything. Now, can I ask you a question?"

Joe nodded.

"What's the real reason you're here?"

"I just told you," Joe said. But he was afraid his face might betray him.

"You're here to see Dallas with your own eyes, aren't you?" she said. "You still think my Dallas had something to do with what happened to April, even though he was here at home and they caught the man who did it and hauled him to jail." She sounded both angry and disappointed with Joe. He felt a twinge of remorse.

A woman's voice from inside the house called out, "Who's out there, Bull?"

"Damned game warden," Bull said without turning his head.

"The one who put you out of business? *That* motherfucker?"

Cora Lee, Joe thought.

"Yep, it's him," Bull said.

"Tell him to get the fuck off our property," she said from inside. "Maybe I ought to let the dogs out to chase him away. He got no right comin' on private property if we don't invite him."

Brenda's eyes narrowed as she glared at Joe. "Is that true?" she asked.

"It is," he said. "But I'm not here looking for any trouble. I'm here trying to get some information on an ongoing investigation."

"An investigation of what?" Brenda asked, suspicious.

"I seen a truck up there," Eldon said from behind Joe. It surprised him, and he jumped. Eldon had been in the garage working on one of the pumpers, judging by the grease and muck on his bib overalls. The whine of the motor in the garage had covered his approach. There was a long, heavy wrench in his right hand.

Joe said, "How long have you been behind me?"

"Long enough to hear what you asked," Eldon said.

Joe nodded toward the garage. "Do you suppose you could shut that thing down so we can hear each other?"

"Naw," Eldon said. "I'm usin' it. I gotta power-wash them tanks out or they really start to smell rank. Especially now that it's gettin' warmer."

Frustrated, Joe said, "You saw a truck up there last Thursday night?"

"I did," Eldon said. "I got home in time for supper. I parked my pumper in the garage. As I was walkin' to the house, I looked up there in the hills and saw it. Then I heard a bunch of shots. I didn't think much of it at the time. People are always goin' up there and shootin' the shit out of things. There ain't a BLM sign or marker that ain't shot to shit."

It was true. Joe asked, "What did the truck look like?"

"White, new. I thought it was one of them fed trucks. I see them all over." He looked past Joe to Brenda. "Remember when those two federal knuckleheads came here last month asking about sage grouse? A man and a woman?"

"I do remember," Brenda said. "They wanted to know if we had any sage grouse on our land. It seemed like a dumb question."

Eldon said, "I told 'em if I did, I would have shot all them prairie chickens by now and roasted them. They didn't like that one bit."

Bull laughed at his dad's humor.

Eldon said, "You can't even eat the big ones, the bombers. They're no good for nothin' but jerky. But the young ones are pretty tender. Right, Brenda?"

"Right, they are," she said.

Joe had been watching the two of them, back and forth, as if viewing a tennis match. He found it interesting how both of these big men deferred to Brenda at all times.

Joe said to Eldon, "Are you talking about Annie Hatch of the BLM and Revis Wentworth of the Fish and Wildlife Service?"

"That sounds like their names," Eldon said. "They gave me their cards, but I used them to start a fire in the fireplace."

Bull snorted again. He thought that was a good one.

In the distance, Joe thought he heard a high-pitched scream from the air compressor.

"Better shut that thing off," Joe said.

"Why?" Eldon asked.

"Sounds like the bearings are going."

Eldon shrugged. "It's always something."

Joe gave up.

"Are you sure it was their truck you saw?" he asked.

"No," Eldon said. "I ain't sure. But that's what I thought at the time—'Those sage grouse feds are back.' But that's a hell of a long way up there, and I just saw the white truck for a few seconds. Then I heard a bunch of shooting."

Bull folded his arms over his chest and said to Joe, "There can't be that many new white pickups in the county, can there?"

Joe was thinking the same thing. He asked Eldon what time he'd seen the white truck.

Eldon shrugged and said, "Six-thirty, maybe?" He looked to Brenda for confirmation.

"That sounds right," she said. "We usually eat at six forty-five. We try to get done by the time *Wheel of Fortune* comes on."

The timing worked, Joe thought. But it didn't make sense—until he thought back on what Lucy had observed in regard to Hatch and Wentworth. Then it did.

"So," Brenda said to Joe, "you want to see Dallas?"

The offer took Joe aback. "Yup," he said.

"Come on in," she said. "You'll see that he's as banged up as I told you he is. Then maybe you'll finally believe us and leave us alone."

Bull said, "He can come back, Mom. Just so it's dark out and there's no witnesses for when I whup his ass."

"Damned straight, Bull," Cora Lee laughed from inside the house.

As Joe mounted the peeling steps of the porch, he glanced over his shoulder to see if Eldon was coming in. The man was lumbering back to the garage, swinging the wrench back and forth at his side.

Joe heard the air compressor whine again. He hoped the bearings would burn out and disable the engine so he could think clearly without the background noise.

Brenda cracked the front door and leaned inside. "Cora Lee, put them dogs out back in their run. We're comin' in."

15

The sound of the compressor muted as Joe stepped inside the house and the door was closed behind him. He removed his hat and held the brim with two hands.

"He's in the back," Brenda said.

Cora Lee was sprawled on a couch with one leg cocked over the arm. She was watching television, and she refused to look at Joe. That was okay with him. The show that blared from the flat-screen was something about spring break in Florida. Lots of bikinis and abs.

The house was small, cluttered, and close. It smelled of baked goods from the kitchen. The furnishings were familiar to Joe from so many visits to area homes: a unique combination of hunting memorabilia crossed with Wild West kitsch. An elk mount dominated the wall over a fireplace, and the fabric of the couch and chair was a motif of bucking horses and lariats. The low-hanging chandelier was a reproduction of a wagon wheel, with dusty little bulbs on each spoke. The adjacent wall, which melded into the hallway, was covered with cheaply framed photographs of rodeo action shots. Dallas riding a bull, Dallas on a saddle bronc, Dallas flying his hat like a Frisbee in an outdoor arena after a particularly good ride.

"That one is my favorite," Brenda said as Joe leaned in to the picture. "It was taken three years ago at Cheyenne Frontier Days when Dallas won it. The 'Daddy of 'Em All,'" she said.

A china hutch in the corner contained nothing but silver and gold buckles Dallas had won across the nation. There were four sparkling shelves of them.

As Joe passed by the wall, he searched for photos of the rest of the family and found one: an old shot of Bull, Timber, and Dallas with their arms around one another. It looked like it had been taken on a camping trip more than a decade ago. Bull's mouth was agape and he looked simple. Timber was wiry and lean, and his eyes were closed as he smiled. Both brothers towered over Dallas, who stared straight at the camera with a kind of alarming confidence for a boy that small. By the looks of the photo, Dallas would have been nine or ten at the time, Joe thought. That was it as far as photos of his brothers went. The rest of the front room was a shrine to Dallas Cates. A stranger entering the house could have reasonably assumed Dallas was an only child.

Joe inadvertently glanced at Bull, who stood glowering by the door. As if Bull could read Joe's mind, he winced and looked away. Joe almost—but not quite—felt sorry for him.

DALLAS RECLINED in an overstuffed chair in what appeared to be his old bedroom, judging by the yellowed rodeo posters on the walls and the photos of him playing football, wrestling, and running track as a Saddlestring High School Wrangler. He was watching a small television between his sock-clad feet. When Joe entered the room, Dallas turned his head stiffly and his eyes registered surprise when he recognized Joe. He lifted the remote and clicked off the set.

"Mr. Pickett," Dallas said.

"Dallas."

It wasn't a ruse, Joe quickly determined. Dallas *had* been seriously injured. His face was still puffy and his left eye was swollen shut. The bruises on his face and neck were entering the gruesome blue, green, and yellow phase. His left arm was in a sling.

"I thought I heard Mom talkin' to someone out there." Dallas's voice was muted and airier than Joe remembered. He attributed it to a throat injury.

Joe said, "Yup."

Dallas winced as he shifted his weight in the recliner to face Joe. Even in his condition, Dallas radiated a kind of raw physical power, Joe thought. Muscles danced and his tendons popped beneath his skin as he moved. Sinew corded in his neck.

"Nothin' hurts like busted ribs," Dallas said, and he lifted the front of his baggy sweatshirt. His midsection was wrapped, but Joe could see the bruised discoloration on Dallas's skin above and below the bandage.

"I broke my ribs once," Joe said. "I know how it hurts."

"It's not so bad," Dallas said with one of the big boxy grins he was famous for. "It only hurts when I breathe. Or talk. Or eat. Or try to move."

Joe nodded sympathetically.

"Dr. Jalbani at the clinic in town says the only thing I can do is rest and let the ribs heal on their own. There's nothing they can do to speed up the recovery. Did you know that?"

"I did."

"When did Saddlestring get a Pakistani doctor?" Dallas asked. "It seems kind of funky."

"He's been here for two years."

"Well," Dallas said, "that just shows you how much I've been around, I guess."

Dallas suddenly got serious, and said, "How's April doing, Mr. Pickett?"

Joe realized Brenda was standing in the door right behind him. Dallas had glanced over to her before he asked the question. Joe wondered if Brenda had silently prompted it.

"She's in bad shape," Joe said. "She's in a coma in a hospital in Billings."

"Man," Dallas said, "that's bad news." Then: "Is she going to make it?"

"We're optimistic," Joe lied.

Dallas nodded. And kept nodding. Then another quick glance to Brenda behind Joe's shoulder.

"Has she been able to communicate?" Dallas asked.

"No."

"Man, that's rough. Will she ever be able to talk?"

"We hope so."

Yet another glance. Joe considered whipping his head around so he could catch Brenda coaching her son, but he didn't.

"Well, if she recovers, I hope you'll tell her how sorry I am this happened to her," Dallas said. "I mean, we had our problems and all, especially at the end. But she means a lot to me. I can't stand to think of her stuck in some hospital room like that. So tell her I'm thinkin' about her, will you?"

Joe nodded.

"Maybe I'll be up and around soon," Dallas said. "Billings ain't that far."

He paused, then said, "If that's okay with you and Marybeth, I mean."

Joe didn't want to say, *There's nothing to see.* And he didn't like Dallas using his wife's name so casually. He said, "I'll let you know when she's better. Maybe we can work something out."

"That'd be great, Mr. Pickett."

He seemed almost sincere, almost eager. Joe thought perhaps he had always judged Dallas too harshly. He'd been put off by his mannerisms, his history, his too-eager-to-please persona.

But maybe, Joe conceded, it had as much to do with the fact that April had left with him while Joe and Marybeth were away. That it had been Dallas's fault as much as April's why she had left.

Joe asked, "How long have you been back, Dallas?"

"Since March tenth," he answered quickly.

"Oh, for Christ's sake," Brenda said from behind Joe.

"Not the thirteenth?" Joe pressed.

"Hell no," Dallas said, letting some heat show through, although the grin was still frozen on his face. "I see what you're doin' here."

"Just had to check," Joe said. "I'm sorry."

"You ought to be," Brenda said.

Joe looked back at her. She wasn't as angry as he'd expected. Oddly, she looked relieved.

"Well," Joe said to Dallas, "I hope you're up and around soon."

Dallas's grin turned into a bigger box. "The only good thing about it is, I couldn't have gotten busted up at a better time. I lost my entry fees on the Rodeo All-Star gig in Dallas, of course, but the big fun doesn't really start until June. By then, it'll be a rodeo a day, and sometimes two, through the rest of the summer. That'll be one paycheck after another. I plan to turn this setback right around and light up the PRCA all the way to the national finals. I ain't the first cowboy to get hurt, you know."

Joe agreed.

"You and Marybeth ought to come see me at the Daddy, last week of July," Dallas said, meaning Cheyenne. "I can get you some passes for the east-side stands."

"Maybe," Joe said.

"And you let me know how April's doin', okay?"

"Yup," Joe said.

"SO," BRENDA SAID as they went down the hall toward the living room, "are you finally satisfied?"

Joe said, "I have to say I am."

There was no way Dallas could have administered such a serious beating to April in his condition. The broken ribs alone would have prevented it, Joe knew. He remembered the searing pain he had experienced simply lacing up his boots. And how Dallas had managed to drive from Houston to Saddlestring in his condition was both foolish and heroic, Joe thought.

Brenda shook her head and said, "You're a hardheaded man."

"I just needed to be sure," Joe said. "I guess it still stings that April ran off."

Brenda reached out and grasped his elbow before he entered the front room, and he turned.

She nodded at the Cheyenne photo of Dallas flinging his hat and said, "You know, this community don't appreciate what we've got here."

Joe was momentarily puzzled.

"Dallas," she said. "He's a *champion*. He's our world-class athlete, and he comes from right here in Twelve Sleep County. There should be signs outside the town telling everyone they're entering the home of Dallas Cates. There should be parades every summer. We ought to name the high school after him, or at least the rodeo arena."

Her eyes were blazing.

"I talked to your wife about it a while back. I was trying to get her on board because I think she'd have some influence, bein' the head of the library and all. Maybe you can talk to her. Maybe you can let her know what a big deal that boy is back there. Sometimes I think people around here don't appreciate what they've got. They see Eldon pumping out their septic tanks and they don't think, 'That man— he's the father of a champion.' They just think, 'That man is pumping out my shit.'"

Her grip on his arm was surprisingly strong.

She leaned into him and said, "What do we have to do to get it through all the thick skulls around here that they've got a rodeo champion right here? Who grew up right here? What's wrong with them?"

"Brenda," Joe said, "I don't know that I'm the right guy to ask."

"That boy back there is special," she said. "He's one-in-a-million. Do you know how many people have asked me about how he's doing? Less than ten, I'll tell you that. The newspaper should have been out here. The mayor should have been out here."

"I hear you," Joe said. He meant that literally, not that he actually agreed. He thought, *Too many locals know about Dallas's role in the sexual assault when he was in high school. Too many locals had been beaten up or terrorized by Timber before he was sent to prison. Too many local hunters have been burned by Eldon or Bull while they're out trying to get meat for the winter. Too many locals have been harangued by Brenda about building monuments to her son.*

He said, "Have you thought about letting it be their idea instead of yours?"

Her face turned to stone. After a beat, she said, "It would never happen. They all look down on us. We know if we don't take care of ourselves, no one else will."

"That isn't my experience," Joe said. "People around here are pretty decent. Maybe you ought to give 'em a chance."

She looked at him with contempt.

"Thanks for letting me see him," he said, twisting away from her grip.

He clamped on his hat and reached for the doorknob. Behind him, Brenda Cates said, "Don't forget what we talked about here, Joe Pickett."

"Don't worry," he said. "I won't."

He couldn't get out of the Cates home fast enough.

JOE FROWNED against the sound of the air compressor until he was back in his pickup. Daisy was happy to see him, but she threw nervous looks toward the house as if expecting the pack of dogs to come out at any second. As Joe backed up and pointed the nose of his pickup toward the gate, he noted that Brenda was watching him out the kitchen window and that Bull had cocked back the curtains in the living room.

As he squared the pickup to leave, he saw Dallas's late-model four-wheel-drive pickup parked on the side of an equipment shed filled with a flatbed trailer with two snowmobiles on it. The pickup was a gleaming red Ford F-250 with a chrome cowcatcher and Texas plates. PRCA, PBR, and NFR stickers were on the windows. Anyone in the know would recognize the acronyms for the Professional Rodeo Cowboys Association, Professional Bull Riders, and National Finals Rodeo.

Eldon stood in the shadows inside the garage next to one of his pump trucks. Joe waved good-bye to him, but Eldon didn't wave back. Joe could see the compressor vibrating at Eldon's feet. Oddly, there didn't seem to be a pneumatic hose attached.

SOMEBODY LET THE DOGS out of their run and they followed Joe's pickup all the way to the county road. When he finally turned onto the graded road, he called Marybeth on his cell phone.

"I saw Dallas Cates," he said. "He didn't do it."

"You *saw* him? Where?"

"At his house. I was checking out this sage grouse thing and the Cates place was within sight, so I stopped by to see if they'd seen anything."

"How *convenient*," she said, deadpan.

He described Dallas's condition.

She said, "There was still a small part of me that was suspicious. Now I guess we can move on."

He agreed. "They're an odd bunch, though. Brenda buttonholed me about the town doing more to recognize her son. She might have a point, but she's a little scary when she gets going."

"She does that to everyone," Marybeth said.

"Oh, and I might have gotten a lead on who shot all those birds," he said.

"Who?"

"I'll tell you when I get back," Joe said, knowing he was about to hit a long dead zone for cell phone coverage. Then: "I'll have to tread real lightly on this one."

His phone blinked out and he didn't know if she'd heard that last part.

TEN MINUTES LATER, Liv heard the compressor shudder into silence. She knew what it meant and she fought back tears. Whoever had arrived was gone.

The footfalls came and she could tell there were two sets of them.

"Open that up," a woman said from above. Liv recognized the voice as belonging to the person who'd claimed she was Kitty Wells.

Dirt sifted into the root cellar when the doors were thrown back. Liv covered her face and eyes with her hands until it settled.

"You can go," the woman said to the man.

"Are you goin' down there?" Bull asked his mother with alarm.

"No. I just need to have a private conversation with this young lady. Go over there and help your dad."

Bull slunk away.

"I'm Brenda," the woman said, standing over the opening with her hands on her ample hips.

Liv brushed grit from her face and opened her eyes.

"I heard you screamin' down there. Luckily, nobody else did. Eldon can't hear much these days and the game warden thought it was the compressor goin' out."

Liv didn't know what to say. She'd screamed so hard she was still wet with sweat. She'd guessed her screams were drowned out by the motor. That was the reason, she was sure, they'd fired it up in the first place.

Brenda said, "If you ever do that again, I'll send Eldon out here to fill up this hole."

By the tone of her voice, Liv had no doubt she'd do it.

"I'm thinkin' you might go without dinner tonight," Brenda said.

Liv hugged herself but didn't respond. Brenda stood there, looking down at her.

Finally, Liv asked, "Why are you doing this?"

"You know, I ain't never had a daughter."

"What?"

"I always wanted a little girl," Brenda said wistfully, more to herself than to Liv. "I wanted a little girl so I could dress her up in dresses and brush her hair and sing songs with her, you know? Instead, I got boys. All they done was run wild, punch each other, and break things. Of course, my little girl would be a little paler than you."

Liv stayed quiet.

Brenda said, "But at least them boys didn't scream. I've gone my whole life without a screamin' female in it. I don't plan to start now."

With that, Brenda turned and vanished from the opening. Liv heard her say, "Bull, go close that back up now."

Two hours later, more footfalls. *Bull.* Liv was wondering if the game warden had been Nate's friend Joe Pickett, and she planned to try to get the name out of Bull. She dutifully threw off her blanket and relocated her chair to accommodate the ladder.

When the doors were open, Bull said, "We got meat loaf and apple pie tonight."

"Really?" Liv asked.

"I guess she changed her mind."

Bull leaned over and tied a knot in the handle of the feed bucket and lowered it down to Liv.

"Is Joe Pickett coming back?" she asked in a conversational tone.

"He better not," Bull said. "If he does, I'll put him down and let the dogs clean up the remains."

Liv nodded. "Aren't you coming down?"

"Naw," Bull said sullenly. "I ain't supposed to anymore. Cora Lee, she . . ." He let his point trail off. But it had been made.

Liv reached up and grasped the bottom of the bucket with both hands. The plastic was warm to the touch.

"Besides," Bull said, "what do you care if I come down there or not?"

Liv pretended she was thinking long and hard about what she was about to say. Then she said it.

"Because it gets kind of lonely down here."

Bull was silent. She looked up. He seemed to be frozen there. She couldn't see his face well because the sun was behind him, but she thought he might be blushing.

He closed the doors, locked them, turned, and went back toward the house.

Liv ate, but not because she was hungry. She ate because she needed fuel to survive.

As she did, those words came back.

I ain't never had a daughter before. It chilled Liv to the bone.

But the trap was set.

PART FIVE

THE READY
AREA

16

After his encounter with the Cates family, Joe drove on the highway toward his home. He knew Marybeth was planning a big dinner with all the items Lucy liked best—pasta, garlic bread, green salad—as a way to atone for the time she'd been in Billings and for Joe's food, and he wanted to be home for it. As he drove, a window opened in the storm clouds and he found himself suddenly bathed in warm yellow afternoon sun. The beam was small and concentrated, and the pool of light was no bigger than a half mile in every direction. It was as though he were the subject of some kind of cosmic spotlight. It felt good—*Summer was on the way*—although he was disappointed no revelation came along with it. It was just sun.

When his cell phone went off, he expected to see Marybeth's name on the screen. That wasn't the case.

"Governor," Joe said. "I didn't expect to hear from you on a Saturday evening."

"Damn, I'm so jet-lagged I don't even know what day it is," Rulon said. Joe imagined the governor pacing back and forth in his home office as he'd seen him do—one hand holding his phone to his face and the other gesticulating and wildly punching the air as he talked.

"I just got back from a two-week trip to Asia," Rulon said. "I was over there selling Wyoming coal—or trying to. We produce more coal than any other state, and the feds are shutting us down so they can stop global warming. The Asians want to grow so someday they can have First World problems like us. They want our coal, and as much of it as they can get. So we'll shut down our coal-fired utilities over here and pay higher utility bills while they build them up over there and provide power and air-conditioning to their people so they can make things and get wealthy. You know, like Americans used to do."

Joe smiled to himself. Rulon liked to rant. The governor said, "Somehow, we're going to stop global warming by shutting down our clean power plants so the Chinese can burn our coal in their dirty power plants. Ah, the geniuses in Washington! They never fail to constantly lower the bar on common sense. Anyway . . ."

"Anyway," Joe repeated.

"What's this I hear that our precious sage grouse are being wiped out in your district?"

Joe sighed. "It's true. I found an entire lek that had been—"

"I know all about it," Rulon said, cutting him off. "I read the report from the Sage Grouse Task Force."

Joe grunted.

"They're required to keep me informed of their activities. And it's attracting plenty of attention in the usual quarters, as you can imagine: 'Wyoming Neanderthals Fail to Protect Endangered Species.' That's not the actual title, but it sure as hell is the tone."

Rulon paused, then said, "Joe, I need you to clear up this sage grouse thing. I know you can't bring those birds back to life, but if you find out who did it and throw the book at them, it'll show the feds we aren't complacent. Plus, it will set an example for other yahoos who might have the same idea."

Before Joe could tell the governor what he'd learned, Rulon said, "The damned problem is the feds create reverse incentives and they don't even realize they're doing it. If you tell landowners that all their grazing land will be put off-limits for energy exploration or anything else if sage grouse are found up to two miles away, the incentive will be to *get rid of the damned birds*. Ranchers can't make money ranching anymore, so they have to make deals for wind towers, or solar, or some damned thing Washington loves. So where does that leave a guy who wants to use his property?"

"I considered that," Joe said. "The location where the grouse were shot is on BLM land."

"Is it two miles away from anyone?"

"Well," Joe said, "there's one family."

"Start with them."

Joe knew Rulon fancied himself an amateur detective. He said, "I did that."

"And?" Rulon prompted, ready to declare victory.

"They don't have enough land for wind towers or fracking, so I doubt they'd have any lease opportunities. That's not to say they might not be ornery enough to do something like this, but in this case I don't think so. But they gave me a lead I'm going to track down," Joe said. "If it goes where I think it could, we might have a bigger mess than we've got right now."

Joe could hear Rulon take a breath, ready to continue with one of his rants. Then he paused. Joe understood why. Cell phone conversations could be monitored.

Rulon said, "Let's meet tomorrow in my office. My afternoon's free and I'll try like hell to be lucid. Maybe I'll send somebody out to get me one of those energy drinks, I don't know. It'll take me a couple of days to get back on track, I'm afraid."

"I can drive down there tomorrow," Joe said.

Saddlestring to Cheyenne was four hours. Denver was two hours beyond that. He could kill two birds.

"I'll see you then," Rulon said. "My antennas are up now."

Two minutes later, Joe's phone lit up again. Rulon again.

"Joe, I heard about what happened to Romanowski and to your daughter. I meant to say how damned sorry I am, but I completely forgot when I called you the first time. Anyway: I'm damned sorry."

"Thank you," Joe said.

"Are they connected somehow?" Rulon asked, once again playing amateur detective.

Joe said, "No, sir. At least I don't think so."

"Two things like that happening in the same week in the same place," Rulon said. "It just seems hinky. But you're on the ground there, and I'm not. So how is your daughter doing?"

Joe told him.

"But they got the guy who did it?"

Joe hesitated before he said yes. Rulon had jarred him with his speculation.

"And the guy killed himself in his cell?"

"Yup."

"That's why I think we should issue nooses or electrical cords to every slimeball brought in on a nasty felony," Rulon said. "Maybe with a little instruction book on how to do yourself in. It would save us a lot of money and time if we did that."

Joe didn't comment.

"What about Romanowski? I give him a conditional deal and he goes out and gets himself shot the very next day. That guy is something else."

"As far as I know, he's alive," Joe said. "But the FBI has him under wraps. I can't get anything out of him."

Rulon cursed. He said, "I'll talk to those bastards tomorrow. This is that Dudley guy, right?"

"Yup."

"He's a crap-weasel. I'll go over his head. Maybe by the time you get here, we'll know more."

"I appreciate that," Joe said.

"I'm fading fast," Rulon said. "You're a good man, Joe. Good night."

"Good—"

Rulon had terminated the call before Joe said, "Bye."

IT WAS DUSK when Joe cruised through the rows of cars in the parking lot of the Holiday Inn. The lot was nearly full, which used to be unusual in March because it wasn't yet tourist season. Things had changed, though, because the lot was filled with muddy oil service trucks on their way to—or from—the oil boom in North Dakota. Saddlestring was a logical halfway point between Denver and the Bakken formation, where the oil had been discovered.

It didn't take long to find the white U.S. government pickup used by Annie Hatch and Revis Wentworth. For one thing, it was one of the few vehicles that had been recently run through a car wash. That in itself, Joe found interesting.

Since Wentworth was headquartered in Denver, he stayed at the hotel while he was in the area. Hatch lived in a rental in town, next door to her yoga studio.

Joe parked his pickup on the side of the hotel so it couldn't be seen from any of the south-facing guest-room windows, and he carried his evidence kit through the parking lot.

When he found the white truck, he ducked down and opened his valise. Despite the fact that the outside of the pickup was clean, he ran his hand under the inside of the rear wheel wells and found a coating of dried mud. If analysis later proved that the soil was picked up in the vicinity of Lek 64, Joe knew, it proved nothing. Wentworth and Hatch had been in that area several times, including the night Joe discovered the crime. But if he could find mud that was embedded with feathers or sage grouse blood, well, *even that was a reach*.

Joe did it anyway.

When the evidence envelopes were filled with flakes of mud and labeled, he carefully photographed the tread on all four tires. If the tracks he'd photographed in the middle of Lek 64 matched up with the tread of the government pickup, he might have something. The allegation could be corroborated by Eldon Cates.

Wentworth and Hatch could claim that *of course* they'd left tracks when they got lost that night in the snow, but the time stamp on Joe's shots would shoot that down.

It was circumstantial, but it was something, Joe thought.

And what about the shotgun shells? If he could find a half-empty box of 12-gauge shells in Wentworth's room or Hatch's home that were the same brand and shot quantity of the spent shells he'd found . . .

Then he smacked his forehead with the heel of his hand, nearly knocking his hat off. The realization hit him like a mule kick.

Hatch and Wentworth had been *very* concerned about the evidence Joe had gathered at Lek 64. Joe'd assumed they were concerned that he'd take too long, or that the state lab would somehow botch the analysis.

Given the circumstances, Joe had willingly handed over the box of evidence to them. He'd retained nothing but the photographs that were preserved on the memory card of his camera.

He thought:

What if they'd tampered with the evidence before sending it to Denver to their federal lab? Maybe changing out the photos he'd copied to a CD, or replacing or removing the spent shells?

What if they hadn't even bothered to send it in?

If either thing had happened, Joe knew, he had nothing to tie the government vehicle to Lek 64 the night the sage grouse were wiped out.

JOE SHOOK HIS HEAD as he returned to his pickup. Before ducking around the side of the building, he looked up to see if he had any observers in the four-floor building.

At the second window on the third floor, Revis Wentworth stepped back. A moment later, the curtain was pulled shut.

Joe had been caught, he knew.

So how would he play it now?

———

HE PULLED HIMSELF inside his vehicle and started it up while punching the speed dial on his phone to his home number.

When Marybeth answered, he asked, "How long before dinner?"

"Why?" she asked, suspicious.

"I might have a break in the sage grouse case, and I have to act fast. I don't want the suspects talking to each other before I get to them."

Marybeth sighed. It was a familiar conversation to both of them. "We eat at seven," she said. "You have an hour."

"That should be enough," he said, wheeling out of the parking lot.

WHILE JOE DROVE DOWN the streets of the subdivision Annie Hatch lived in, he mulled things over.

If his suspicions were correct, it meant two federal employees charged with preserving sage grouse and overseeing their protection had wiped out an entire flock.

It made no sense.

He again recalled what Lucy had observed out the front window of his house when Hatch and Wentworth had come to talk to him.

Maybe . . .

ANNIE HATCH lived in a small but well-appointed single-family home on Third Street. Next door was her Bighorn Valley Yoga Studio. A Prius in the driveway had bumper stickers that read CERTI-

FIED YOGA INSTRUCTOR and MY OTHER CAR IS A YOGA MAT. So she was home.

As he approached her door, he heard a phone buzzing from inside. He suspected it was Wentworth calling her to tell her what he'd seen in the parking lot. Joe knocked sharply, hoping she'd choose to answer her door before picking up her phone.

The phone continued to buzz and he heard no footfalls from inside. He knocked again, then leaned over the side of the porch so he could see into her living room from the nearby window. The television was on and a cat was curled up on top of a couch, staring at him. But no Annie.

For a moment, he thought the worst. Would an unanswered phone constitute enough probable cause to enter her home? He knew it wouldn't, but he twisted the screen door handle anyway. It wasn't locked. That wasn't unusual anywhere in Saddlestring.

He knocked again while he tried the doorknob. It was unlocked as well.

Joe glanced right and left down the street. It was deserted except for parked cars and trucks. No doubt the cool weather had kept the kids inside. He cracked the door open and leaned his head into the house.

"Annie? It's Joe Pickett."

No response. He looked around. There was a crumpled afghan on the couch in front of the television. It looked as though she'd thrown it aside moments before. He could smell popcorn from the direction of the kitchen.

"Annie?"

Her cell phone danced unanswered across a breakfast bar within view. Joe entered and snatched the phone up.

The display read: REVIS.

He quickly put it down and backed out toward the door. The cat watched him the whole time with dead button eyes and never flinched.

He was stepping out onto the porch when Annie Hatch said, "Joe, what are you doing in my house?" She was coming from the yoga studio, carrying a mop and bucket. And she was angry.

After being startled, he recovered and said, "I think you know why I'm here."

BUT SHE DIDN'T. Joe could tell from her expression and the way she lowered the bucket and crossed her arms over her breasts without taking her eyes off him that she was harboring no guilt about anything. She was just miffed she'd caught him coming out of her house.

"Just tell me what you were doing in there," she said.

"I heard the phone ringing inside, and when you didn't answer it, I got worried about your well-being," he said.

"That's nice, I guess," she said. "Still, you shouldn't enter someone's house."

"You're right," Joe said. "I shouldn't."

"Did you answer my phone?" she asked, curiosity working its way through her anger.

"Nope."

"Well, that's something, I suppose." She seemed no longer suspicious, just puzzled. She had a sweet soul, Joe thought.

He said, "I got a lead on Lek Sixty-four."

"You did?" She was genuinely surprised.

"Do you remember meeting the Cates family? They said they remember you."

She cupped her chin in her hand and searched the clouds, then said, "Are they the people who live just to the south of Lek Sixty-four? Kind of a junky place?"

"That's them."

"What do they have to do with this?"

"Eldon, the old man, said he saw a vehicle up on the bench the night the lek was wiped out. He said he heard shooting immediately afterward but he didn't think much about it at the time."

Her eyes widened, prompting him for more.

"He said it was a new-model white pickup. He said it looked just like the government truck that you and Wentworth drove out to his place."

She shook her head. "It couldn't be ours," she said. "We didn't go up there until the next night, if you'll remember. We went up there after you confirmed there had been a crime. Do you think Mr. Cates got his days wrong?"

"It's possible," Joe said. "But is there any chance you two were up there the night before? Like maybe you were lost or something?"

She looked at the underbelly of the clouds again, searching for the answer. Joe thought it must be some kind of yoga thing. He said, "It would have been Thursday, March thirteenth. I found the lek Friday."

Hatch shook her head. "No, that can't be right. I was in Casper at an agency meeting that day. I didn't even get back until Friday morning."

Joe let that settle, then asked, "Was Wentworth with you?"

"No. He stayed here . . ." And the doubt showed on her face. Everything Annie Hatch thought, it seemed, showed on her face.

"So Wentworth was here alone with his truck?" Joe asked.

"Why wouldn't he be?"

"Just asking," Joe said. "I remember you told me you first learned about Lek Sixty-four through a call to your tip line, right?"

"Right."

"Who retrieved the information, you or Wentworth?"

"Revis did."

"Did you ever figure out the identity of the tipster?" Joe asked.

"No, why?"

"Did you ever listen to the recording yourself?"

"No. But Revis heard it."

"Right. Is it still recorded somewhere?"

She shook her head. "You'd have to ask Revis."

She stepped back and put her hands on her hips. She shifted her gaze from the clouds to the lawn between her feet. "You're saying you think Revis had something to do with this?" she asked.

"I'm not blaming anyone yet," Joe said. "But I've got another question for you. Did you send that box of evidence to the lab in Denver?"

"Yes," she said. Then after a moment, she said, "Well, *we* did. I didn't personally send it."

"Were you there when Wentworth took it to the post office, or FedEx or wherever?"

"No. But he told me he sent it in."

Joe let *that* settle.

She shook her head again, as if ridding her hair of dust. "No," she said adamantly. "There is no way Revis had anything to do with it. You just want to pin the blame on someone. You just don't like him."

"Could be," Joe said. "I've got a request for you."

She looked up at him.

"Don't call Wentworth back for fifteen minutes. Will you promise me that?"

"Why should I?"

"Because it'll take that much time to clear him," Joe said.

After thinking it over, she said, "Fifteen minutes. But I'm sure you're wrong."

"I've been wrong before," Joe conceded.

As he raced back to the Holiday Inn, Joe had no confidence Hatch would restrain herself from contacting Wentworth. But it was worth a try.

He pulled his pickup in front of the lobby and went straight to the front desk of the hotel. The young female assistant manager on duty had purple-streaked hair and a nose ring and he recognized her as one of Sheridan's high school friends. She was texting with someone, but when she looked up she seemed to recognize him as well. Everybody knew the game warden.

He said, "Is Revis Wentworth still in the same room on the third floor? I need to ask him some questions and I'm pretty sure he told me it was room 348."

The girl looked on the computer and said, "No, he's in 343."

"Thank you," Joe said, tapping his fingers on the counter in thanks. "Good to see you again."

"No problem," she replied, and reached for her phone.

He'd had no idea of Wentworth's room number and he knew she wasn't authorized to give it out. He felt slightly guilty about the ruse.

JOE KNOCKED LOUDLY on the door of room 343. He stepped to the side so Wentworth couldn't see him out of the peephole and pretend he wasn't in.

Joe watched as the peephole darkened, then lightened again. From inside, Wentworth said, "Who is it?"

"Joe Pickett."

He heard a long sigh and the lock being thrown.

Wentworth wore sweats and gym shoes. A basketball game blared from the TV. His face was fixed in a snarl and he said, "I saw you out there sneaking around in the parking lot. What the hell was that all about?"

Annie Hatch had kept her word.

Joe said, "I was gathering evidence to prove that you slaughtered all the sage grouse in Lek Sixty-four. Annie is going to be very disappointed in you."

Wentworth's face drained of color and his mouth opened slightly. For a few seconds, his eyes went blank.

"You can't prove a thing," Wentworth said.

"That's the first thing guilty men always say. They don't say they didn't do it or that I don't know what I'm talking about. They always say I can't prove it." Joe smiled. Then: "I don't know much about women, but I don't think this was the most brilliant way for you to spend more time with Annie Hatch. After all, what would your wife think?"

"We're separated," Wentworth said. As he spoke, he unconsciously kneaded the naked ring finger of his left hand with his right.

Joe said, "That's your business."

Wentworth stepped aside as Joe entered the hotel room. The closet door was open and Joe peered inside. A 12-gauge pump shotgun was propped in the corner of the closet and an open box of Federal shells was on the shelf above the hanging rod. Joe could feel Wentworth tense up when he realized what Joe was looking at. Joe quickly withdrew his phone and snapped a photo of the shotgun and the shells.

"I'll be confiscating your weapon and the ammo," Joe said. "Don't worry—I'll give you a receipt."

"You can't do that," Wentworth said.

"Sure I can. Weapons suspected of being used in a wildlife crime can be confiscated until it's proved otherwise. So I'll be taking your shotgun with me for analysis."

Wentworth shook his head. He was trying to force a smile. He said, "I know shotgun pellets aren't like bullets. You can't match up the markings on pellets to a certain gun, and those Federal shells are a dime a dozen."

"Yup," Joe said, gathering the items. "But every shotgun leaves a unique firing-pin indentation on the primer. You can't see it with your naked eye, but a forensics lab can see it through a microscope. They'll know if this gun was used to kill those birds when they match it up with the spent shells I found at the scene."

"Bullshit."

"This time I'm sending the evidence to *my* lab," Joe said. "If I were you, I'd start a long conversation with myself about all this."

"So what are you going to do?" Wentworth talked like his mouth was dry. He looked at Joe with pleading eyes.

"Now?" Joe said. "I'm going to go home and have dinner with my family. But don't worry—I'll be in touch."

Wentworth's cell phone rang on a lamp table near his bed.

"That'll be Annie," Joe said while he backed out with the shotgun. "If I were you, I wouldn't pick up."

Joe's last glimpse of Wentworth as the door shut was of a man with his head in his hands.

THAT NIGHT, while Joe and Marybeth were getting ready for bed, Marybeth said, "I think we should go to church tomorrow. I know it's been a while, but I want to pray for April and Nate and to make sure they're on the church's prayer list. Lucy even said she wants to come along."

Joe said, "I have to go to Cheyenne and meet with the governor."

"On a Sunday?" She was distressed by the news.

"You know how he is."

"You have to go to Cheyenne on a Sunday to talk about wild birds?"

"Well, when you put it that way . . ."

"No, you go," she said. "The governor's been good to you and he won't be in office forever. I'll take Lucy with me to church and give everyone your regards."

"Thank you," he said. "I'll pray for them as I drive south."

"You do that."

———

AFTER MARYBETH had turned off her reading lamp, Joe said, "Do you think there is any connection between what happened to April and what happened to Nate?"

She hesitated for a moment, then clicked her light on again and propped herself up on her elbow.

"*What?*"

"It's something the governor mentioned today. He doesn't know all the details, but he thought it strange that two big events happened so close together. It's got me thinking, but I can't connect them at all."

"That's because there's nothing to connect," she said sharply.

"I'm sure you're right."

She reached over and doused the light again and settled under the covers with a huff.

"Thanks for giving me something to keep me awake all night," she said.

"Sorry."

17

Three hours later, Liv Brannan's eyes snapped open. Something—or somebody—was up there. Maybe it was the coyote or dog from a couple of nights ago. She'd heard it snuffling and padding around the closed doors. This time, though, it seemed heavier.

The Cateses unplugged the hanging trouble light at midnight, although they didn't unhook the extension cord that powered the space heater. She guessed it was an hour past, but she didn't know for sure. They'd taken her watch.

This was the first time she'd slept hard since they'd put her in the hole. The reason, she suspected, was that she was physically tired. Either that, or God forbid, she was getting used to being down here.

She was tired because, for the last day and a half, she'd spent every spare minute chipping away at the concrete-like compacted clay of the wall, trying to loosen a rock she'd discovered. The rock was round and smooth like a river rock but she had yet to find out how large it was. When she'd first uncovered the rock, the surface was no bigger around than a quarter. But when she began to dig around it with her fingernails, she found out it was much larger. Her fingernails were now sore and bleeding.

She'd used eating utensils after meals to dig deeper, using the tip of the butter knife and the handle of a spoon. More progress was made with the utensils, but she had to clean and return them so no one would suspect what she was doing. They always counted the silverware after they raised the bucket.

The face of the rock was getting bigger all the time. Her fear was that it was massive—too big to remove and too heavy to do her any good. Her hope was that it was medium-sized, maybe the size of a softball, and could be used as a lethal weapon.

Maybe they'd heard her digging and had come to punish her, she thought. But why after midnight?

The hasp snicked and the doors opened quietly. She looked up to see a large square filled with stars, and she felt a breath of cold air from outside.

Bull whispered, "Hey."

She closed her eyes and felt her heart race.

He said, "I'm puttin' the ladder down."

Not now, she thought. It was too soon. Not until she got the rock out of the wall.

She whispered back, "Bull, are you sure about this? What if somebody sees you?"

He snorted and said, "We went out tonight. Cora Lee is passed out on her fat ass and snoring like a hippo." He chuckled at his comparison.

Moonlight glinted off the rails of the aluminum ladder and she could sense it coming down. She shifted her position so the feet wouldn't hit her on her legs or pin her blankets to the floor. Then she was up, standing, rubbing her eyes. Her face was gritty with dirt and her mouth tasted like metal.

The ladder groaned as Bull descended rung by rung. If only she could yank that rock out of the wall . . .

"I've been . . . stoked . . . ever since you . . . told me you was lonely," he whispered. The exertion of climbing down made him short of breath. Exertion, plus gallons of alcohol. She could smell it on him as he descended. He was less sure-footed on the ladder than usual.

Her eyes adjusted to the dim starlight and she could see that even though he was "stoked," he hadn't forgotten the pistol in his waistband or the hot-shot that hung around his neck on a cord.

This wasn't how it was supposed to work, she thought. Her hints were supposed to have gnawed at him over several days until he finally gave in. By then she'd be ready with the rock. She'd wait until he turned his back to her to climb up the ladder and she'd bash in his skull. But here he was, the same day she'd set her plan in motion. And the rock was still in the wall and as stuck as when she'd discovered it.

"Bull, are you sure about this?" she said.

His boots were on the floor now and he turned and held out something to her.

"I brung you this," he said. It was a long-stemmed rose, the kind they sold for a dollar in bars. He'd probably bought it for Cora Lee and took it back while she was passed out.

She reached out for it and their hands brushed together. She guessed he liked that.

"Thank you," she lied.

He towered over her. Now that he was close, she could smell the stew of alcohol on his breath and cigarette smoke on his clothing. Then he was placing his huge hands on her shoulders, stroking her.

A moment later, he reached down and grasped her wrist.

"Here, look at what you do to me," he said as he pressed her palm to his groin. He was hard and huge beneath the rough denim fabric.

"What do you think about that?"

She purred. She didn't know what else to do.

"Want to see it out?"

She thought, *I'd like to rip it out by the root.* But she purred again instead.

"Now, don't try nothin' stupid," he said, "'cause you're in for a treat. First time Cora Lee saw it, she said, 'So that's why they call you Bull.'"

He chuckled deeply at this.

His other hand left her shoulder and she heard him unzip and start to fumble with his underwear.

"There," he said. "Where's your hand?"

She closed her eyes as he guided her hand to him. It was massive and hot.

He said, "I suppose you're used to this size."

Before she could reply, Liv was bathed in harsh white light. She flinched and turned away.

Cora Lee screamed, *"You fuckin' no-good cheatin' son of a bitch! I knew I'd find you down here with that whore!"*

"Now, Cora Lee," Bull said, stepping back and quickly stuffing his penis back in his pants and zipping up. "It ain't what you think."

"It sure as hell is!" she howled. "I ought to go get the shotgun and kill you both right now."

"Cora Lee . . ."

"I'll shoot you so many times, you'll be nothin' but a grease spot, you cheatin' bastard."

"Cora Lee, she lured me down here," Bull said, squinting his eyes against the beam of her flashlight. His voice was whiny.

"Right, and she held a gun to your head and made you show her your dick, you no-good cheatin' scumbag. I'm comin' back with that shotgun."

She started to yank the ladder out, but Bull realized what was happening and reached out and grabbed a rung. Bull and Cora Lee tugged drunkenly back and forth on the ladder for a half minute, Cora Lee screaming more obscenities at him the whole time.

Finally, Bull's strength won out and the feet of the ladder crashed to the floor of the cellar. Before he climbed up the ladder, he shot his arm toward Liv, threatening her with the hot-shot not to try and follow him. But he mistimed the threat and the hot-shot crackled when it touched her neck and the jolt threw her on her back.

"Sorry," he mumbled. Then he went up much faster than he'd come down.

"I'm gonna kill you, you cheatin' douche bag!" Cora Lee yelled.

When Bull got to the top, he pulled the ladder up so hard it went airborne and clanged on the ground as it landed. Liv trembled and hugged herself.

He leaned down over the opening and said, "Now see what you've done," and closed both doors so hard they sounded like gunshots.

With her eyes clamped shut, Liv heard Cora Lee and Bull go at each other over a mild buzzing in her ears. Cora Lee called him names Liv had never heard strung together before, and Bull kept shouting that he'd been tricked, that he only loved one woman, that he must have drunk too much and let the wrong head do all the "thinkin'."

After five minutes of shouting, an *actual* gunshot rang out.

Then silence.

Brenda's voice: "Shut up, the two of you, and go to bed. We'll sort this all out in the morning." She spoke calmly but with authority.

Cora Lee said, "I found him down there with his dick in her hand. The ladder was down and they was writhing around—"

"I said, shut up," Brenda said, barely raising her voice. "Or the next shot won't be in the air."

"Okay, Ma," Bull said. Liv thought he sounded like he was ten years old and had been caught stealing from her purse.

"I ain't sleepin' with *him* in the trailer," Cora Lee spat.

"You can sleep on our couch."

"C'mon, Cora Lee," Bull whined.

Cora Lee said, "It's *over*, you cheater. Over!"

"I bet the two of you woke up Dallas," Brenda said, sounding sad.

LIV WAITED. She wouldn't have been surprised if the cellar doors opened and Brenda, or Cora Lee, or Bull appeared holding the shotgun. There was no place to hide.

But they never came. There was nothing but silence until the coyote came back and sniffed around the opening.

FEELING SLOWLY RETURNED to Liv's body, but there was still a buzz in her ears. Two wounds, like a vampire bite, stung on her neck above her collarbone.

As her heartbeat returned to normal, she realized her hand hurt. She opened it to see that she had gripped the stem of the rose so hard the thorns had pierced her flesh. Her palm was sticky with coagulating blood.

Then, in the dark and with the stiff stem of the rose, she resumed chipping away the clay that held the rock.

Maybe she'd get it out by dawn.

18

Timber Cates sat alone at a round Formica table under a television set that was mounted high on the pale green cinder-block wall of the inmate visiting room. He had dark eyes and hollowed-out cheeks, and his prison uniform hung on his thin, tight frame. His dirty-blond hair was buzz-cut and the three-inch knife scar on his scalp showed through. When he got angry, which was often, the scar turned from white to pink.

Although his head and shoulders were still, his right leg kept a manic rhythm of its own under the table and he kneaded his fingers together on the tabletop. He exuded quiet menace. No one came near him. It was an aura and a look he'd worked on for years and still practiced in the polished-steel mirror of his cell. He could go for minutes without blinking his eyes.

A couple of small kids had wandered over ten minutes earlier, but when they saw him up close, they turned and ran back to their mother on the other side of the room. The mother shot him a disapproving look for upsetting her children and he didn't flinch. She turned away with a visible shiver and whispered something to her inmate partner. He refused to follow her gesture because he didn't want to get on the wrong side of Timber Cates.

Timber was fine with that kind of reaction from visitors and fellow inmates. He was used to it and it now afforded him a zone of peace.

It was Sunday, family day in the contact room at the Wyoming State Penitentiary in Rawlins and he was waiting for his family to arrive. He looked nervously at the clock on the wall above the reception desk, where a guard sat monitoring the inmates and the visitors in the room. The guard was old, fat, and bored. He had a comb-over that started an inch above his left ear. The guard would call out, "You two—that's enough," whenever an inmate and his woman hugged too long or made a display of their longing for each other. Hand-holding was permitted. Kissing, hugging, and fondling were not. Testosterone seemed to hang thick in the air like smoke from burnt meat on a barbecue.

Sometimes, inmates made deals with each other where one would distract the guard so the other could grope a quick feel or jam his woman's hand down his pants. They tried to do it out of view of the cameras. Even if the guard didn't see them, someone in the video room usually did. By the time the guy in the video room sent a message to the desk guard, it was too late.

Timber Cates didn't participate in bullshit like that. He had nothing to gain from it. The only female who ever visited him was his mother.

THEY CAME into the room fifteen minutes late. His father was wearing his gray C&C Sewer uniform shirt and a stained trucker hat he probably didn't even know was back in style. As always, his father kept his head down and looked furtively around the room. He was embarrassed to be here and felt put-upon by having to surrender his watch, pocketknife, coins, and anything else that was metal in the lobby.

Brenda trailed him. She had on a large print dress and heavy shoes. Her hair was up and looked welded to her head. She saw Timber first, and jabbed Eldon in the ribs and pointed him out. They waded through the children playing with toys on the floor and made their way to him.

Eldon sat heavily and leaned back in his plastic chair as if trying to maintain as much distance as possible from his son. He looked tired and beaten. Four hours in the pickup with Brenda could do that to a man, Timber thought.

"I didn't think you were coming," he said.

"Sorry we're late," Brenda responded, settling her bulk into a flimsy plastic chair directly across the table from him. "We had a long night. Bull and Cora Lee were going at it again. We had to stay long enough this morning to make sure they wouldn't wake up and remember the fight and try to kill each other."

"Cora Lee," Timber said derisively. "She's a real c—"

"Don't say that word," Brenda snapped. "You know I hate that word."

Timber bit his lip.

"You were right about Nate Romanowski's release from the feds," she said.

He nodded. "Guards talk to guards and things get around real fast in here. Some of us knew they were cutting him loose before *he* even did."

"You're wearing a blue shirt," Brenda said, studying him. "That's good."

Timber nodded. In prison, new inmates wore yellow, death row wore white, violent felons wore orange, and the general population wore blue or red. Up until a month ago, Timber had worn orange.

"So you're keepin' your nose clean," she said.

"Yeah."

"You're so pale and thin. Are you eating right?"

"The food is shit."

"You need to eat it anyway. I wish they would let me bring you some home cooking. You need to get strong again."

"I've been working out," Timber told her.

She said, "We got a letter stating you might be released tomorrow. Have they said anything to you about it?"

He scowled. "Nothin' official, but they moved me to a new cell. It's how they do it—they move you to a kind of holding area while the paperwork clears. Then they give you back the clothes you wore when you came in and let you go. I'm thinking they'll release me any day."

Brenda bobbed her head. She was thinking. He wondered if she'd ever get new glasses.

"I'm not fond of those tattoos on your neck," she said.

He raised his hands in a *What you gonna do?* gesture.

"Is that a skull?" she asked, peering at the left side of his neck.

"A *flaming* skull," Timber corrected.

"Oh, it has to be flaming, does it?"

He grinned, but he wasn't sure it looked like a grin as much as a grimace. Under the table, his leg twitched harder. He was afraid it might start drumming the bottom of the table like a jackhammer, so he slipped his hand down and tried to take control of it.

"Can you get it removed later?" she asked.

"Ma, is this what we're going to talk about? My *neck*? It's just a thing. It don't mean nothin'."

Brenda looked to Eldon, and Eldon said, "Don't sass her."

Timber leaned back and held his tongue. When he extended his leg, it didn't bounce so high. He wondered if she'd always have that effect on him.

SINCE HIS INCARCERATION, Brenda had sent him envelopes filled with newspaper clippings of Dallas winning rodeos all over the country. Sometimes she included a note. The note was usually about Dallas. If she knew that Timber tore up the clippings and never even read them, she'd disown him and he'd be out on his own with his demons. So he never told her to stop sending them. She assumed he was as proud of Dallas as she was, when all he wanted to know was, *What about me?*

He'd told his cellmate about the "Chicken Thigh Game" they used to play at home. Brenda would assemble all three of her young boys shoulder to shoulder in the kitchen and ask, "Who loves their mama the most?" The winner would get an extra fried chicken thigh.

Bull would go first. He'd say he loved his mama the most because she was the best cook in the world and he loved her food. Brenda would urge him to go deeper, but Bull had never been deep. Instead, he'd repeat what he'd said the first time, but with more emphasis.

Timber would say he loved his mama the most because she stood up to the neighbors and she was a good driver. He varied his response from game to game in an attempt to finally hit a chord that resonated with her. He said she was the smartest, prettiest, funniest. She'd nod along until it was Dallas's turn.

Dallas would squirm and smile and turn red. He looked cute doing it. He'd say, "I love my mama more'n anything in the whole wide world."

Dallas would get the chicken thigh.

Timber *still* didn't know what to say or do to make her love him best.

"You've got to stay clean and keep your head down for one more day until they let you go," she said to Timber. "You should have been out months ago. I want *all* my boys back home. It's time to be a family again. Dallas is there now, you know."

"You told me."

"So it's time for you to come home. Try not to get into any more trouble in here. It's only twenty-four hours. Sometimes you gotta turn the other cheek for the greater good of your people," she said. "You need to think long-term, which is something I know you've never been very good at. But if you lash out every time somebody does you wrong, you'll stay in this damned place forever."

Timber said, "If someone does something to you in here, you gotta retaliate or it just gets worse. This is a fuckin' jungle."

She looked around the room at the families, and the children scrambling around on the floor.

"It ain't like this inside," Timber said wearily. "There ain't a bunch of rug rats crawlin' around."

"I wouldn't know," Eldon said, "since I was never dumb enough to get caught and sent to prison."

That was his issue, Timber knew. It wasn't that his son was a convicted felon who was sent to the penitentiary in Rawlins. It was that he'd been dumb enough to get caught.

"I'm ready to come home," Timber said to Brenda. He ignored Eldon. Ignoring Eldon was getting easier to do.

"We're ready to *have* you back," she said, but with a beat of hesitation.

"What?" he asked, ready for another lecture about staying away from drugs and not hooking up with his old crew. She didn't realize that most of his old crew was either dead or in prison with him.

"Before you come straight home, we need to know you're with us," she said. She reached out with both hands and cupped his left. His right was still under the table, trying to control his leg. She stroked the back of his hand with her pudgy thumbs and studied him closely. She always seemed to know what he was thinking even when he tried to hide it from her. It was like she could see into his soul. Sometimes she knew what he was thinking before *he* was even sure.

She said, "We need to know you're willing to be part of the family again—that you'll contribute. We need some proof of your loyalty before we can welcome you back with open arms."

Timber stared at her. He knew she couldn't be overheard by the guard because of the noise in the room and the blaring television above his head. The CCTV would show them talking to each other, but there weren't recording devices to pick up what they said.

"Are you still working in the infirmary?" she asked.

The question came out of the blue. "Yes. But it's not like I have any responsibility. I just mop shit up."

"That's not important," she said. "What's important is that you know your way around a medical facility. Even if it's with a mop in your hand."

He sat back and tried to read her face for clues. As usual, she gave nothing away.

"We need you to do something for us where nobody knows you," she said. "It's got to be done in a way so it won't connect back to us in any way. But you can't do that unless they let you out of here free and clear and within the next couple of days. You've got to hold your temper and think long-term, like I said. Store up that angry feeling. *Don't* retaliate if someone does something to you."

"I've been good," he said defensively. "I done what you said. I've been a model prisoner for the last year. See that guy over there with the full sleeves?" He nodded toward a dark man with a black mustache, a shaved head, and a swirl of tattoos that covered each arm to his wrist. The inmate wore red and was whispering into his wife's ear while his two little boys wriggled around his legs.

Brenda looked over, then looked back.

"He stole my MP3 player from under my mattress. I know it was him. Two years ago, I would have ripped his throat out for what he done to me. But I let it go for now because I couldn't prove it and I want to get out of here. Did you hear me? I let it go."

"I'm glad," she said.

"Now, what is it I have to do before you'll take me back?" he asked.

"Don't put it like that," she said. "You know I love all my boys. But you also know that the most important thing in the world is to keep the family intact. We've all got to be working together or they'll tear us down. The town, the county—they all hate us for what we are."

Then she went on and on about how the community leaders refused to put up welcome signs on the outskirts of town that would read: Home of World Champion Rodeo Cowboy Dallas Cates.

He nodded. He'd heard it so many times from her over the years. "So what is it I have to do?" he asked.

"Before we get to that, I've got a question for you," she said. "Who loves their mama the most?"

19

"This kind of thing has happened before," Governor Rulon said to Joe in the governor's capitol building office. "Remember the Canada lynx debacle in Washington state?"

"No."

"Ah, a prelude to a story," Rulon said. He was wearing a snap-button cowboy shirt, jeans, and scuffed boots. No one else was in the building on Sunday except for a security guard dozing at the lobby counter.

Joe had left his home well before the sun came up. He toasted the memory of Chris LeDoux as he passed Kaycee, and he thought of Nate. The four-and-a-half-hour drive had included all four seasons: summer in Kaycee, winter near Midwest, fall in Casper, spring outside of Chugwater.

He'd also been thinking about the call they'd received the night before from Nurse Reckling in Billings. She said that she'd over-heard two of the doctors discussing the procedure for bringing April out of the coma. Reckling cautioned Marybeth about jumping to any conclusions, but promised she'd keep her posted. It was the first thread of good news they'd had on April's condition since she was placed in the drug-induced coma.

Sheridan had decided not to go on spring break to Arizona with her friends but to come home instead. She wanted to see April.

Marybeth told Joe that it just might be that the doctors would try to bring April back when the whole family could be at the hospital.

"That way," she said, "we'll all know at the same time if she'll make it or not."

He could tell by the look on her face that she was more than slightly terrified by the prospect.

RULON LEANED BACK in his chair, steepled his fingers, and said, "When I was U.S. Attorney, there was a big three-year study going on to determine if the rare and elusive Canada lynx existed in the forests of Washington. If the lynx could be proved to exist there, the Endangered Species Act would kick in and the feds would have to close all the roads, shut down the loggers, and seal off the forests to snowmobiles, skiers, four-wheelers, and on and on.

"Toward the end of the study period, with everyone holding their breath, there was an exciting discovery: Canada lynx hair had been found on three different rubbing posts. That proved that the lynx was there after all!

"Then somebody blew the whistle. It turns out that high-ranking U.S. Forest Service biologists had *planted* the hair samples on the posts. They'd gotten the hair from some zoo or a dead lynx and had *planted* it so it could be found. These biologists were true believers and they did it for their cause—to save the planet. How falsifying scientific evidence saves the planet is anyone's guess.

"Hell," Rulon said, slapping the desktop with the heel of his hand, "you got into a similar situation a couple of years ago with Butch Roberson and the EPA. This kind of petty crap by government bureaucrats shouldn't be new to you."

"It isn't," Joe said. "I just keep hoping that was a one-off."

"Oh, Joe," Rulon said almost sadly. "It's inevitable that when there are hundreds of thousands of bureaucrats with endless budgets, who have no accountability and can't be fired, that these things are bound to happen. They're just people, although too many of them like to think that they're special people with some kind of special insight. But when they have private agendas, watch out! That's what I keep hollering at anyone who will listen.

"What about the fact that they allow wind and solar companies to kill thousands of eagles and other birds without punishment or fines, but they throw the book at an oil company or power plant if a bird dies in *their* vicinity? Where's the fairness in that?"

Joe knew it was one of Rulon's constant themes, and one of the reasons he'd won more than seventy percent of the vote for his re-election, despite the fact that he was a Democrat in a thoroughly Republican state.

"So what you're telling me, Joe," Rulon said, "is that this Wentworth guy slaughtered an entire lek of sage grouse so he could spend more time with Annie Hatch, the fetching yoga instructor. Is that your theory?"

Joe nodded.

"Can you prove it?"

"Not yet," Joe said. "I need to check out the federal lab in Denver to see if the evidence box arrived there and what was in it. If it arrived intact, we should be able to match the tire tracks I photographed at the scene with the photos from Wentworth's truck and the shotgun and the shells. If the box was tampered with, we know the chain of evidence and who tampered with it. And if it didn't arrive at all, we know who supposedly sent it to them. I want to be at that lab when it opens tomorrow morning. I don't want to call ahead and tip them off.

"But," Joe continued, "judging by how Wentworth reacted yesterday, he might crumble and confess on his own. Especially if Annie Hatch puts pressure on him."

"I'm really liking this," Rulon said, grinning. "Keep digging, but keep what you find between us."

Joe was puzzled.

"You know he did it," Rulon said. "Now *I* know he did it. And this Wentworth guy sure as hell knows we know he did it. I want him to twist in the wind while you quietly build the case against him. Even when you have a solid case, I don't want you to talk to him or confront him."

"Why not?"

"Joe," Rulon said, "you're a good man. I'll miss working with you when my term is over. One of the reasons I like you is that you don't think like a politician. Your boss does, goodness knows, but you don't."

Joe wasn't sure if that was a compliment or an insult.

Rulon said, "With this in my pocket and at the ready, I have leverage against the feds if they decide to list the sage grouse as an endangered species. I can let them know through back channels that they better not rush to judgment. I'll let them know that if they try to rush studies or suddenly come to conclusions that the plight of the sage grouse will shut down our energy sector, I'll release the information that their own guy in the field killed an entire population of birds we tried to protect. I'll reveal it in a press conference on the steps of the U.S. Capitol. I'll wave your report around like I was McCarthy with his list of communists in the State Department!"

Joe groaned. But he admired Rulon's cunning, while at the same time hoping it would never be aimed at *him*.

"Go forth and build a box around this love-struck reprobate," Rulon said, tossing the back of his hand at Joe as if making a royal proclamation.

"So tell me more about your daughter and Romanowski," Rulon said.

Joe did.

As Joe put on his hat to leave, the governor said, "Are you going to the rodeo while you're in Denver?"

Joe paused. "What rodeo?"

"The Cinch Rodeo All-Star Shootout, of course," Rulon said. "You might just make it if you leave now. And if you see a bull rider named Cody McCoy, put some voodoo on him. I'm in a fantasy rodeo league, and if McCoy eats dirt this weekend I could win it all."

Joe shook his head. "You're in a fantasy rodeo league?"

"Of course," Rulon said, as if he were offended by the question. "Remember that name: Cody McCoy. Do some silent curses at him or something. Make a Cody McCoy voodoo doll and drop it into the dirt just before he rides. We can't have him win the Shootout."

There had been rumors prior to the last election that Spencer Rulon was going insane because of his erratic behavior. Joe hadn't paid any attention to the rumors. Now he wondered if he should have.

"Well, *go*," Rulon said, exasperated.

20

Like many westerners, Joe liked to seek out pockets of the rural west in any urban environment. Finding members of his tribe provided comfort. Although Denver was geographically in the west and there were plenty of remaining frontier vestiges—the Black American West Museum, the Buckhorn Exchange restaurant, the National Western Stock Show—it was also a large metro area of more than two million people, with funky hotels, restaurants, professional sports teams, gangs, and hipsters smoking legal weed and drinking craft beer. It was the anti-Saddlestring, and the politicians who ran Denver didn't like to play up its western roots.

The rodeo that Rulon had suggested offered a refuge, and Joe had nothing else to do before the federal lab opened in the morning. As soon as he bought his ticket and went inside the indoor National Western complex, he smelled familiar smells and encountered familiar-looking people. The men milling around the exhibition booths wore jeans, boots, and hats. Most left-side back Wrangler pockets showed Copenhagen chewing tobacco rings.

Unlike when walking around the 16th Street Mall downtown, he expected to meet someone he knew, and he did. The two brothers Stan and Dave Flitner ran the Lazy T Ranch outside of Saddlestring. They had a booth of their own and they were taking orders for bull semen in the hallway to the indoor rodeo arena.

"Look out!" Stan said in mock alarm when he recognized Joe. "It's the game warden! Dave, hide those fish!"

"Ha-ha," Joe said, shaking their hands. They both wore black hats because it was still technically winter. Within two months or so, they'd replace their felt hats with straw hats and summer would be official.

"What brings you down here?" Dave asked from behind the table.

"Just killing time," Joe said. "I've got a meeting in the morning."

"Want to buy some bull semen?" Stan asked. "We'll give you a ten percent discount on account of you're local."

"I'll have to pass," Joe said with a straight face. "I've still got a couple of gallons in my refrigerator."

"That's too bad," Stan laughed. "Business has been kind of slow."

THE CROWD INSIDE the arena was sparse, which was no doubt disappointing to the organizers of the event, Joe thought. Too much to do in Denver on a weekend, he guessed, as he settled into his seat. Still, those who were in the grandstands seemed to be hard-core rodeo fans by the way they cheered and applauded certain cowboys. They were probably in fantasy rodeo leagues, Joe thought.

While he watched the saddle bronc and bareback events, he followed the cowboys on the program.

The All-Star Shootout, he learned, was designed to attract only the top cowboys in each event. Unlike the PRCA circuit in the summer, where any cowboy with a PRCA card could pay an entry fee and ride, this was invitation-only. These were the names rodeo fans knew and followed, and Joe recognized a few of the top contestants.

As he read over the list of cowboys in the bull-riding section, he saw the name Cody McCoy. He didn't issue a voodoo curse, but he again recalled what Lucy had observed. Since she'd been right about Wentworth's desire for Annie Hatch, maybe she'd also been right about something else.

Lucy had said there was no way that April and Dallas Cates had gone their separate ways, even though Dallas—and Brenda—insisted on it. If April never regained consciousness, it might remain a mystery forever, one of those loose ends that would always nag at him.

Joe studied the names of the bull riders. They were from all over: Decatur, Texas; Terrebonne, Oregon; Donalda, Alberta, Canada; Waycross, Georgia; Oral, South Dakota; Winnemucca, Nevada; Los Lunas, New Mexico; Roosevelt, Utah; O'Brien, Florida; Stephenville, Texas.

Stephenville was where Dallas had moved to once he went professional.

Joe thought about it. These champion rodeo cowboys lived thousands of miles apart, yet they gathered together every weekend during the winter and practically every day in the summer at some rodeo or another. They traveled together, lived together, competed together. He thought there may very well be a couple of them, and maybe more, behind the chutes at that very minute who knew Dallas, and probably April as well. Maybe one of them could clear up the discrepancy.

He slapped the rodeo program against his leg and stood up. He was glad he was wearing his uniform.

IT WAS CALLED the "ready area" and it was located under the stands behind the chutes, out of view from the general public. Joe worked his way down there until he encountered a security guard who wouldn't let him through.

The guard wore a blue uniform shirt and eyed him warily.

"I'm not supposed to let anyone back there if they don't have a credential," the guard said.

"This is my credential," Joe said, pointing to the pronghorn antelope patch on his arm that said WYOMING GAME AND FISH DEPARTMENT and then his badge over his breast pocket. "I just need to talk to a couple of guys."

"What did they do?"

"They may know something about a situation I'm investigating," Joe said, keeping it truthful but vague.

"Man, I don't know," the guard said, looking around.

"Here's my card," Joe said, handing it over. "You can see I'm legit. And if you need to call your supervisor over, go ahead."

The man smiled. "I don't even know who my supervisor is. I'm just a weekend rent-a-cop. The Nuggets aren't playing today or I'd be at Pepsi Center, running one of the parking lots."

Joe waited.

"Oh, okay," the man said, stepping aside. "Don't get me in any trouble."

"I never promise *that*." Joe smiled.

THERE WERE A DOZEN private dramas unfolding within the ready area as Joe approached. The atmosphere inside the chain-link barrier was electric and intense.

Cowboys sat on saddles on the concrete floor with one hand on imaginary reins and the other in the air, acting out a ride to come.

Others slapped themselves across the face while they strode from one wall to the other like football players awaiting kickoff. Several stood with their eyes clamped shut, praying wordlessly.

As Joe entered, he stepped around a rodeo cowboy expertly taping his Wrangler jean legs around the shafts of his boots, and another tightening his riding glove by cinching a string of leather between his teeth.

He didn't know where to start.

In the arena, the saddle bronc competition ended and the cowboys who had ridden in it streamed into the ready area. They acted differently from the ones waiting to ride because they were *done*. Some joked and patted others on the back, some scowled at getting bucked off, one cowboy bitched about his score and said he'd been jobbed by "that fat judge with the stupid mustache." As the saddle bronc riders gathered up their gear, the bull riders filed out one by one. To a man, they seemed more wired and tightly wrapped than the bronc riders. Each cowboy had a friend or two with him who would help him out mounting the bull, getting set, and offering encouragement.

To Joe's left, through thick steel panels, the bulls were herded down a runway and into individual chutes. Some of the bulls were so stout, the arena attendants had trouble closing the gates to pen them in.

Joe approached a saddle bronc rider who looked affable and relaxed. The cowboy was stuffing tape and water bottles into a rodeo gear bag he'd sling over his back and take to the airport.

"How'd you do?" Joe asked.

"I got an 88," the cowboy said with a smile. He was missing a front tooth and he had a high, southern accent.

Joe knew the score was derived by judges in the arena who awarded up to fifty points on the animal and fifty points on the cowboy. The bull or bronco the cowboys rode was drawn at random. Eighty-eight was a good score.

"Congratulations," he said.

"I had a good draw," the cowboy said, meaning he'd drawn a good bronc. "I think that score'll hold up, so I'm in the money."

The cowboy introduced himself as Evan Lucey and said he was from Oklahoma City. He wore a necklace with a cross on it.

Joe gestured to the other cowboys in the ready area and said, "I suppose you guys all know each other pretty well."

"Yeah, I'd say we do," Lucey said. "I sat with most of 'em in Cowboy Church this mornin'."

"I'm trying to find a couple of cowboys who might know a guy I know."

"Who's that?"

"Dallas Cates."

At the mention of the name, Lucey physically recoiled. His affability vanished.

He looked down at his boots and said, "Yeah, everybody knows Dallas."

"Are you a friend of his?" Joe asked.

"Can't say I am."

He said it in a way that suggested the conversation was over as far as he was concerned.

"Can you point me to someone who is friends with him?"

"*Friends?* You got me there."

"Well, in that case, someone who knows him pretty well? I'm trying to get some information about him before he got injured."

Evan Lucey hoisted up his gear bag and threw it onto his back. He said, "Mister, you seem like a nice guy and I wish I could help you out. But I spent all my time stayin' away from Dallas Cates, and I'm not the only one."

Joe frowned. He said, "Is there anybody you can suggest?"

Lucey shrugged and said, "Maybe Little Robbie. He lives in Stephenville, and I think he and Dallas might have traveled together at some point."

"Little Robbie?"

"Rob Tassel. We call him Little Robbie. He's up right now," Lucey said, nodding the brim of his hat to the bull riders on deck.

"Thank you," Joe said. "And good luck in the standings."

"Thank you, sir," Lucey said, tipping his hat. "I'm sorry I couldn't help."

Before Lucey left, Joe said, "What is it about Dallas Cates? Why did you avoid him?"

Lucey hesitated, then looked straight into Joe's eyes and said, "Like I told you, these boys are good people. Just hard-workin' ranch kids tryin' to make a name for themselves and not step on each other doin' it. Dallas wasn't like that."

"How so?" Joe asked.

"I already said too much, sir. The Lord frowns on gossips."

And with that, Evan Lucey turned and went out through the gate.

CODY MCCOY SCORED a 92 and won the bull-riding competition. Governor Rulon, Joe guessed, would be beside himself. Rob Tassel got bucked off in two seconds. Joe wasn't sure he'd be in the mood to talk about Dallas Cates.

He noticed as the bull riders filed into the ready area that what Lucey had told him seemed accurate. It was almost impossible to discern who had won and who had lost by the way the riders chided each other and encouraged each other at the same time. Only when a couple of them clapped a cowboy on the back and said, "Good ride," did he know which one was Cody McCoy.

Joe gave them a few minutes to unwrap tape, change clothes, and pack up before he said, "Which one of you is Rob Tassel?"

A cowboy looked up from where he sat near his gear bag in the corner. He was dark, short, and compact. He had a scar on his cheek and warm brown eyes.

"That'd be me," Tassel said.

Joe squatted down next to Tassel. "Tough go out there."

Tassel shrugged. He said, "I rode that bull at Mesquite and got an eighty-nine. I thought I knowed him, but this time he zigged when he should have zagged."

"Mind if I ask you a couple of questions?"

"No, sir," Tassel said.

Joe wasn't used to being called "sir" twice in ten minutes. He introduced himself and dug out a business card.

Tassel read it. "Wyoming game warden? I don't know why you want to talk to me. I ain't never hunted there, and the one time I fished some beaver ponds outside Cheyenne, all I caught was a sucker."

"I'm doing some follow-up on a guy I've been told you know. Dallas Cates."

Tassel had the same reaction as Lucey, except more pronounced.

"I got nothin' to say about that guy."

"What is it about him?" Joe asked. "When I mention his name, people clam up."

"Is he a friend of yours or something?" Tassel asked.

"Nope. He went out with my daughter and I never liked it one bit."

"April Pickett?" Tassel asked, reading Joe's name badge again and finally putting two and two together. "April is your daughter?"

"Yup."

"Oh, man," Tassel said, looking around as if he were hoping someone would throw him a lifeline. "Oh, man."

"What?" Joe asked.

Tassel leaned closer to Joe. He said, "April's a sweetheart. I couldn't figure out why she hung around that guy."

Joe waited for more.

Tassel said, "I used to travel with him. We roomed together for a while on the road."

He paused and said, "He ain't like all these other guys."

"In what way?"

"Dallas," Tassel said, "he's just different. I ain't sayin' he's the devil, and he's a hell of a bull rider, but he ain't one of the guys, if you know what I mean."

"I don't," Joe said.

Tassel nodded his hat brim at the other cowboys in the ready area. He kept his voice down.

"All these guys you see around here will lend each other a hand. They'll see your draw and say, 'That bull spins left and crow-hops right out of the chute.' Dallas never done that. He couldn't care less. If he'd rode a particular bull before, he'd tell a cowboy who drew him lies about what that bull would do. That's so Dallas would keep the high score. We all learned we can't trust him. He's in this game just for himself. He's one selfish dude. Maybe that's how he stays focused and wins all the time, I don't know. I just know nobody else acts like that. We all try to get along, you know?"

Joe nodded.

"Dallas earned more money than any of us," Tassel said. "But he'd always be the first guy to leave the table at a restaurant and stick everyone else with the check. Or he'd say he'd split a hotel room with you and never pay it back.

"We're all like a football team, you know? Lots of camaraderie, if that's the right word. We watch out for one another and step in if a guy's going to get himself in trouble. It's easy on the road to take the wrong path. But Dallas, he's like the crazy egotistical wide receiver who's only in it for himself, you know? He's always bein' the big shot. Like he is better than anyone else and he makes sure you know it. And he *is* better. He's an incredible athlete. But he don't need to rub our noses in it, you know?

"That poor April," Tassel continued. "She didn't know Dallas had a girl or two in every town. He'd ask me to keep her busy so he could sneak off with every buckle bunny he could find. She is a *nice* girl, you know? You raised her right. I tried to tell her once what Dallas was like, but she didn't want to hear it. He had her buffaloed, you know?"

Joe felt the anger rising in his chest.

He said, "Do you know if they broke up before Dallas got injured?"

Tassel looked surprised. He said, "Not that I know of." Then: "Hell, if that had happened, I would have gone after April in a heartbeat . . ."

He caught himself and flushed. "Sorry, I shouldn't say that to her dad."

"No, you shouldn't," Joe said, "but I'd be a lot more comfortable with you around than I ever was with Dallas."

"Still, sorry."

"One more thing," Joe said. "Do you know if they left Houston together after Dallas got injured?"

Tassel thought about it. He said, "I guess I don't know for sure. I sort of assumed they did, since all of a sudden they were both gone, but I didn't see them leave together or nothin'."

"Would anyone know for sure?" Joe asked.

Tassel shook his head. "I doubt it. Dallas did his own thing, like I said. I was his only friend, and that's just because I'm stupid. He's the kind of guy who would just leave without sayin' nothin' to anyone."

Joe said, "Dallas told me that April broke up with him and played the field, trying to make him jealous."

"That no-good son of a bitch," Tassel said. He looked up at Joe with fire in his eyes. "Believe me, Mr. Pickett, that *never* happened."

"I believe you," Joe said, trying to keep his anger off his face. "Did he ever put his hands on her?"

"I never seen it," Tassel said. "But I wouldn't put it past him. I do remember she was wearing big old sunglasses for a week or so up at Calgary. She wouldn't take 'em off, even indoors. But I never seen him hit her."

"But you wouldn't put it past him?" Joe said.

"I wouldn't put nothin' past Dallas Cates."

Joe thanked Tassel and wished him the best of luck at the next rodeo.

As he turned to leave, Tassel said, "Mr. Pickett?"

Joe turned.

"You ain't gonna tell Dallas we talked, are you?"

"Why?"

"Because I don't want to be on the wrong side of that guy. Or his family."

Joe paused. "What about his family?"

"I met 'em a couple of times when they came to see Dallas ride. They ain't exactly a fun bunch, and that mom of his . . ."

"What?"

Tassel shook his head. "She's just scary, man. She don't want anybody to beat Dallas in nothin'. She'd say things to other bull riders like 'You better let Dallas win or I'll send my boys after you.' Things like that."

"Did you ever hear her say that?" Joe asked.

"Hell, she said it to *me* in Cheyenne," Tassel said, shaking his head. "She's got a thing about Dallas that ain't healthy."

That night, in his hotel room in downtown Denver, a few blocks from the federal forensics lab, after sending Governor Rulon his condolences regarding Cody McCoy's ninety-two-point ride, he called Marybeth and told her what he'd learned about Brenda and Dallas Cates at the rodeo.

"It sounds like he was talking about Ma Barker," she said.

"She scares men who ride sixteen-hundred-pound bulls," Joe said. "That's not nothing."

21

At the same time, four hundred miles to the north of Denver, Liv Brannan heard the screen door slam at the main house and she stepped away from the rock she'd been working on in the wall of the root cellar.

She'd been at it all day. The tips of her fingers on both hands were raw and bleeding from digging around the rock, and she'd resorted to working by covering her hands with her shirt and wearing only her bra. She'd tried to pry one of the rusty shelf braces out of the wall, but didn't have the leverage or the strength to get any out. She was finally able to bend and break a cross brace away from the angle iron early in the afternoon. When it finally came free, it was such an emotional victory that she stood and looked at the tongue depressor–sized piece of metal in her hand and cried.

Digging with the cross brace had doubled her progress around the rock. It was still stuck fast, but she guessed she was halfway there. The rock was oval and large, approximately the size of a football. If the hidden end was as round and even as the exposed side, she thought, she'd be able to lift it and it would cause serious damage. If she could ever get it out. And if she wasn't caught in the act of trying to remove it.

There had been no food deliveries during the day and they hadn't removed the waste bucket. The stench of urine hung in the dead space. The Cateses had either forgotten about her or were punishing her for what had happened with Bull the night before. Or they were simply gone. She'd guessed the latter.

Finally, midday, she had heard the sound of the Suburban entering the compound and the voices of Eldon and Brenda. They didn't look in on her.

An hour later, Liv had heard the main house screen door open and slam shut so hard it sounded like a gunshot.

Bull said, "Where in the hell are you going, Cora Lee?"

"Way the hell away from *you*!"

"You ain't takin' the truck."

"Fine, you son of a bitch—I'll walk."

"Oh, come on."

"I'm walkin'. See me walkin' away?"

There was a pause.

Then, in the distance, Cora Lee shouted: *"I'm still walkin'!"*

The door slammed shut again. Then a third time. A moment later, Brenda said, "Bull, go get her and bring her back."

Bull said, "Maybe I ought to let her go. It serves her right to have to walk twelve miles to town. Maybe she'll lose some weight."

Someone laughed. It was a new voice Liv hadn't heard before. A younger male.

"Hell, I ain't gonna go get her. I just got new shocks on my truck and I don't want the suspension screwed up. Maybe you could take the front-end loader and bring her back in the bucket."

"Dallas, you're no help," Brenda responded. She sounded annoyed but patient. Then: "Bull, go get her and bring her back. We can't have her tellin' her story all over town. If it gets out why she's mad, we've got big trouble."

Liv thought, *Dallas.* The special son.

Dallas said, "Maybe you should just run her over and be done with it."

"Dallas, *please*," Brenda said.

"Shit, I'll go get her," Bull whined.

His truck fired up a few minutes later, and Liv could hear the gravel popping under the tires as he left the compound.

He returned a half hour later, presumably with Cora Lee in the passenger seat.

Now, THOUGH, Liv heard two sets of footfalls.

She slid the thin cross brace into her jeans and pulled her shirt over her head and put it on. She hid her battered hands behind her back, out of sight, and looked up as the cellar doors opened.

It was night. The beam of a flashlight hit her in the face and temporarily blinded her.

"There she is," Brenda said to someone next to her.

Liv couldn't see who it was, just a form that blocked out the stars. He was wearing a cowboy hat.

Dallas said, "Not my type."

"I didn't think so," Brenda said.

"Maybe if you cleaned her up," he said, as if talking himself out of his first impression.

"Hey, how you doin' down there?" Dallas asked Liv.

"How do you think?" Liv said back.

"Better than me," Dallas said. "I got busted ribs and a dislocated shoulder. That ain't no fun, either."

Liv didn't reply.

"Luckily, I'm gettin' better by the hour," Dallas said. "By the end of the week, I'll be wrestling grizzly bears again. By the way, do you know who I am?"

"You're a rodeo star," Liv said.

"Damn, she knows," Dallas said, sounding impressed.

"She heard it from me," Brenda said. "She's from down south somewhere. She doesn't know rodeo."

"We got cowboys from down there," Dallas said. "I bet she knows some of 'em. Honey, do you know Piney Porter? Or Benny LeBeau? I've rodeoed with both of them."

"I don't know them," Liv confessed. Then, for some reason, she started to cry. She didn't know why.

"Are you hungry?" Brenda asked.

"Yes," she sniffed.

"Then I guess I better feed you. Sorry about breakfast and lunch. We had to go visit our oldest son down in Rawlins. I told Cora Lee to make you something, but I guess she forgot. Once she gets a mad on, it's like the rest of the world doesn't exist. I think the next time she decides she's gonna walk away, I'll let her."

Liv welcomed the bucket as it lowered. She snatched it down quickly so Brenda wouldn't see her damaged hands.

"We got chicken-fried steak, mashed potatoes, gravy, and green beans. Sorry there isn't that much gravy. Dallas ate like a horse, on account he's feeling better."

"Thank you," Liv said. She was starving, and she sat down on her mattress and removed the Tupperware containers one by one. Liv

dug into the chicken-fried steak and spooned out the mashed potatoes and gravy. Her eyes closed as she ate, and she moaned. The food
was delicious.

As she spooned gravy over the rest of the steak and potatoes, dirt
sifted down from the opening and sprinkled her dinner.

"Sorry," Brenda said. "Did I knock some dirt down?"

Liv didn't respond. She ate despite the sandy grit. She was *that*
hungry.

"Ma," Dallas said, "it just seems plumb weird to keep a woman
who don't know anything about rodeo in a hole on the property."

He said it, Liv thought, like she wasn't even down there.

"I remember when you put Timber down there for a week that
time after he wrecked the truck," Dallas said with a chuckle. "Me 'n'
Bull used to come out here at night and piss on his head. Man, that
made him mad."

"You were naughty boys," Brenda said.

"So why is she down there?" he asked.

"She wasn't supposed to be with him," Brenda said. "It was a surprise when the two of them showed up together."

Liv looked up, beam and all, and spoke directly to Dallas.

"If you let me out of here, I'll go on my way and never say a word
about this. I swear on my mother's grave. I know how to keep a
secret."

Silence. She assumed Brenda and Dallas were looking at each
other.

After a beat, Dallas said, "You aren't the first woman to ever lie to
me right to my face."

"I'm not lying," Liv said. But she had to look away. The beam of
light was making her eyes burn.

"Sure you are, honey," Dallas said. She wondered how he had gotten that Texas accent if he'd grown up on the compound.

"I told you she was wily," Brenda said.

"Maybe I ought to get Bull to come out here tonight," Dallas said. "We'll pretend you're Timber down there."

"No, you won't," Brenda said to Dallas, admonishing him. "You'll get your sleep and heal up the rest of the way."

"You're right," Dallas said, standing up and stretching. "She kind of bores me, if you want to know the truth."

As he started to walk away, Brenda said, "You want to stay and watch her eat?"

"Naw."

After a few minutes, Liv looked up to see that Brenda was still there.

After a long pause, Brenda said, "Men don't talk."

"Pardon me?"

"Men don't talk. They grunt at each other or they grunt at me. But they don't *talk*. I spend all my time out here on this place surrounded by men. I keep them in line, but they don't *talk*."

So that's why she stayed, Liv concluded. Maybe she could keep Brenda talking. Maybe she could convince her to come down into the cellar. Maybe she could get Brenda to lower the ladder . . .

"What about Cora Lee?" Liv asked.

"She talks, but she's dumber than a box of hair."

Liv faked a mild laugh.

"Did I tell you she walked away again? I know she did it just waiting for Bull to come get her. But this time I told him to let her go. She isn't worth the trouble. Not two times in one day. She'll probably end up with her ex-husband down in Oklahoma, and he'll probably put a bullet in her head. At least then there'll be something in there.

"I keep hopin' one of these boys brings a girl home I can talk to," Brenda continued. "You know, someone who can talk about something other than the Kardashians. Instead, I got Cora Lee."

Liv said, "I'm sorry I caused you trouble," even though she wasn't.

"You're trouble with a capital *T*. Bull never has had any sense, but luckily he lets me steer him around, just like his dad. But did you notice how Dallas took one look at you and sized up the situation and moved on? That's because he's the only one who can think ahead more than one step at a time."

Liv ignored the insult. The insult gave her strength. If she could get Brenda to come down into the cellar, she thought she might have enough incentive to pull that stone out of the wall.

Liv asked, "What are you going to do with me? You can't keep me down here forever."

"No, I guess we both know that."

"So why are you doing this to me?"

"I don't look at it that way," Brenda said. "It isn't aimed at *you*. I always cover my bases. Somebody around here has to. I figured if things really went screwy, we might need something to negotiate with, you know?"

The realization hit Liv hard. "You mean you're keeping me alive in case you need a hostage?"

"Yep. Although that doesn't look like it'll be necessary."

Which could mean only one thing.

Brenda didn't say anything for a long time. Finally: "I came up with a solution. I told Eldon, and he can get it done tomorrow or the next day."

"Get what done?"

"Hey, it was nice talking with you," Brenda said before she closed the doors. "It's kind of nice talking with somebody who has a brain in her head."

Then: "Honey, don't cry. Don't take none of this personal."

22

"Kelsea, this gentleman has been waiting for you since we opened up the doors at nine," the receptionist said the next morning.

Joe stood up, removed his hat, and thrust his hand out toward Kelsea Raymer, the chief forensics analyst of the U.S. Fish and Wildlife Forensics Center, which was located in the National Wildlife Property Repository on the grounds of the old Rocky Mountain Arsenal facility near Denver. Raymer was a tall, trim, and comely brunette in her mid-thirties, with a wide, open face and curious blue eyes. She shook Joe's hand and looked to the receptionist for an explanation.

"He says he's a game warden from Wyoming," the receptionist said with a shrug.

"We don't get many actual visitors here," Raymer said as she looked him over. "I'm surprised you found it."

"Me too," Joe said. It had taken him nearly thirty minutes of driving around to find Building Six within a compound of similar nondescript three-story brick structures that housed federal agencies and outposts.

She sized him up: studying his red uniform shirt, pronghorn sleeve patch, the badge that read GAME WARDEN 21, and the brass rectangular J. PICKETT nameplate over his breast pocket.

"What brings you to Denver?" she asked.

"I'm working on a case. I was hoping I could take a few minutes of your time."

"Put your hat back on and follow me," she said with a sly grin.

He followed.

When he looked over his shoulder at the receptionist, he could tell that she was puzzled by the warm reception as well.

"MY FATHER was a game warden in Montana," Raymer said as she gestured toward an empty visitor's chair in her office. There was no window, and the fluorescent lighting was harsh. The walls on each side of the room were lined with books and manuals. He noted a credenza filled with framed photos of her husband, her four tow-headed children—two boys and two girls—and the entire family on a white-water rafting trip.

"I grew up moving around the state," she said. "I was born in Choteau, went to grade school in Hamilton, middle school in Ekal-aka, and high school in Missoula and Great Falls. We followed my dad from place to place. I don't think he ever made more than twenty-four thousand dollars in a year, but I wouldn't trade my childhood for anything. Have you moved your kids around like that—provided you have some?"

"I do," Joe said. "Three girls. My wife and I bounced around Wyoming until I got the Saddlestring District up in the Bighorns. I was stationed in Jackson and Baggs for a short time, but that's a long story."

"The Bighorns are nice country," Raymer said. "They remind me of Montana. And what Colorado used to be," she added with a gentle smile. He liked her.

"I'm surprised you just showed up," she said.

He nodded.

"And what can I do for you?"

Joe explained finding the dead sage grouse—she cringed—and the gathering of the evidence. He left out the name Revis Wentworth but told her he had a suspicion the evidence had been tampered with or not sent at all.

She shook her head, puzzled.

"I know," he said. "It's kind of hard to believe. But I was hoping I could take a look at the package, provided it was received at all. I didn't call ahead and make an appointment because I didn't want to tip anyone off."

"You want to take it out of our chain of custody?" she asked.

"That's not necessary. I just want to see if it's here and what's inside. I don't want to take it back."

She closed one eye and said, "This is an odd request. No one has ever asked me to do this sort of thing before. We can't just open up sealed evidence to the general public, even if you are law enforcement. I'm sure there are rules about this."

"There probably are," Joe said. "But I was kind of hoping we could stay out of the rule book on this. I know if you ask somebody in Washington, their first response will be 'Don't do anything until we get a ruling on it.' That could take months. I don't have months."

She laughed. "You have some experience dealing with government agencies."

"I'm in one myself," he said.

She drummed her fingers on her desk for a minute and looked toward her bookcase, as if seeking an answer.

"I'm surprised you've gone to all this trouble," she said.

He sighed. "It's a high priority for my director and the governor. We're talking sage grouse, remember?"

"Oh, yes," she said. Then: "I don't get involved with the politics of all this. But I do know there is some concern if this bird gets listed as an endangered species."

"I try not to get involved, either, but I can't help it. And when it comes to sage grouse, there's a *lot* of concern," Joe said.

Finally, she said, "I guess it won't hurt anything to see if we even received it."

"How could it?" Joe said eagerly.

She booted up her computer. While they waited for the ancient desktop PC to become functional, she said, "I used to ride around with my dad sometimes. It was interesting to see him interact with all kinds of people."

"I've taken my oldest daughter out with me," Joe said.

"He could have gotten other jobs that paid more and weren't as dangerous. In fact, I know he interviewed for a couple in Helena after he was wounded in the leg by an elk poacher. But in the end, I think he decided he couldn't sit at a desk all day. Like me."

"He's a man after my own heart," Joe said.

"He died last year," she said.

Her eyes filled and she looked quickly away.

Joe said, "I'm sorry to hear that."

"He had a heart attack riding his old mule, Blue. That's the mule he used to patrol with before he retired."

Joe nodded.

"I think he died happy," she added ruefully.

"I'll bet he was happy for you, being the director of this whole operation," Joe said.

"He was," she said with a chuckle. "He said I was the only fed he ever liked."

Joe smiled.

"Here," she said, jabbing at the screen. "A package was sent from Agent Revis Wentworth in Saddlestring, Wyoming. It arrived over the weekend, and I assume it's in receiving."

Joe arched his eyebrows.

She said, "I suppose we can go look at it. But I don't want you touching anything or contaminating the evidence in any way, even if it's inadvertent."

"I understand," Joe said.

He stood up and stepped aside so she could pass.

"Receiving is in the basement," she said over her shoulder as they made their way down the nondescript hallway. As she walked, she pulled on her white lab coat.

The small cardboard evidence box was among several others in a canvas bag on a rolling cart. Joe recognized it as Raymer raised it out of the bag and placed it on a stainless-steel counter. The only other person in the receiving room was a Hispanic staffer who shot surreptitious glances at them over the top of his computer monitor.

"That's it," Joe said. "But it's been opened and retaped."

Raymer paused and said, "You're sure?"

He nodded. "That's my clear plastic tape under the new strapping tape he used. He must have cut it open and resealed it."

"Who would have done this?"

"The man who sent it to you."

"Why would he do that?" she asked. She was genuinely curious.

"Because I believe he is trying to contaminate the evidence so he can steer us away from who really did the shooting."

She stood back and put her hands on her hips. She kept her voice in an urgent whisper so the staffer couldn't overhear. "Are you telling me one of our own agents is trying to derail a case?"

"I'm not telling you that," Joe said. "I'm following up a theory."

She shushed him to keep his voice down.

"Maybe you could open it up," Joe whispered. "I'll know when I see what's inside."

She feigned impatience with him as she pulled on a pair of white rubber gloves from a dispenser of them and reached for a box cutter.

"Stand back," she cautioned.

Joe didn't approach her, but he did raise his height by balancing on the balls of his feet so he could see inside the box when she opened it.

"Shotgun shells," she said, plucking several out and placing them on the counter. "A beer can. A CD. A bag of dirt and some sage grouse feathers."

Then she looked up at Joe and said, "That's all."

He nodded and studied the items. He said, "These shell casings look weathered. They look weeks old—like they've been out in the sun and rain. I'm sure you can confirm that with testing. The ones I found were only a day or two old. The beer can and the feathers look like what I put in the box. No need to change them out. But who knows what's on the CD? I still have the original photos on my camera, so we can compare what I shot with what's on the disc."

She hesitated, then said to the curious staffer, "Juan, I need to use your computer for a minute. Isn't it time for your break?"

As Juan gathered up his things, Joe said to her, "You might want to dust that disc for prints just to see if mine are on it."

She looked at him with a withering glance that said, *I know how to do this job.*

Joe responded by putting his palms in the air in an apology.

But she dusted the disc. There were *no* prints.

"He wore gloves," Joe said. "I'm not that clever."

THE PHOTOS on the CD of the tire tracks didn't match the ones from the memory stick on Joe's camera. Unlike the shots he had taken in the killing field, the ones on the CD were of tire tracks squished through a grassy bog.

"Now look at this," Joe said, urging her to advance through the photos on his memory stick. She clucked her tongue while she toggled back and forth between the tracks on the sagebrush flat and the tread pattern of the tire on Wentworth's government pickup.

"These appear to match up," she said. "Further analysis is needed to confirm it, though."

"And the photos on the disc are obviously not taken in the same location," Joe said.

He pointed out the differences to Kelsea Raymer and she remarked on the disparity of the vegetation.

"He probably took those right off the edge of the parking lot of the Holiday Inn," Joe said. "And the shells probably came from the back of some oil-field worker's truck parked at the same hotel in Saddlestring. Believe me, I could wander through that lot myself and gather spent brass casings, shotgun shells, and beer cans out of twenty different trucks."

"Oh my," she said.

"THE TIRES IN MY PHOTO belong to a government truck," Joe said.

She winced as if he'd poked her with a pin, then said, "I still don't have enough evidence here to make any conclusions."

"I agree," Joe said. "But *I* can. I know what I packed in that box and I know that what was sent to you was tampered with."

She rolled her chair back. "It's not my job to investigate agency personnel," she said.

"I'm not asking you to investigate," Joe said. "In fact, you need to handle this the way you're supposed to handle it. All I ask is that you lock this box away along with the memory stick for my camera. If a guy named Revis Wentworth wants it back, I hope you'll throw up some bureaucratic roadblocks. You know, play dumb or tell him you're researching his request."

"That's his name? The agent who did this?"

Joe nodded.

"I've heard of him," she said. "He's supposed to be a sage grouse expert."

"Oh, he is," Joe said.

"But why would he do something like this?" she asked. "His job is to protect the species, not endanger it."

Joe told her Lucy's observation. While he did, Raymer shook her head in disbelief.

"If he did this, I hope he gets arrested," she said. "I don't like the thought of people like that in our agency."

"Good for you," Joe said. "Now I have another request."

She looked at him skeptically.

"I have his shotgun in my pickup and two spent shells I picked up out in the field that I didn't put into the original evidence box. I had completely forgotten about them until this morning, when I saw them rolling around in the back of my truck. You might be able to pull a couple of prints, or at least partials, off of the brass of the two shells. I think you'll find that the shotgun and the primer stamp on the spent shells match up. That will prove that he did the shooting."

She shook her head. "It might prove it to you, but it doesn't prove anything to me. All of this—*all of it*—is based on your assumptions."

Joe said, "That's right."

Raymer's phone chimed from a pocket in her lab coat and she instinctively drew it out and looked at the screen.

"How interesting," she said. "I just got an email from Revis Wentworth."

Joe smiled.

"He's asking me to confirm that we received a box of evidence in an important case," she said. "And he cautions me that, because of the magnitude of the crime, I may be contacted by local law enforcement attempting to influence our findings. I assume that would be you," she said, looking up.

"Yup."

"Does he know you're here?"

"Nope. He's trying to run interference. He's desperate."

She dropped the phone back in her pocket and looked at Joe squarely.

"So you're going to turn over every piece of evidence you have to me? The shells and the shotgun and the memory stick? How can you build your case if all of the evidence for it is here locked away in Denver?"

He said, "Because I trust you to keep it until we need it."

She cocked her head. "Why?"

"Because you're from Montana and your dad was a game warden," Joe said.

JOE HATED DENVER TRAFFIC and he kept both of his hands on the wheel and his pickup in the far right lane as cars zipped around him. It was as if every driver on the five-lane freeway had just downed three shots of vodka and had been handed the keys to Daddy's sports car. When his cell phone rang, he ignored it until he was nearly ten miles north of the city and the traffic finally eased up.

Marybeth.

She said, "The hospital called and the swelling on April's brain has gone down."

Joe blew out a breath of relief.

"They want to try and bring her out of it tonight or tomorrow. I need to be there, Joe."

"Of course you do," he said.

"I'm taking Sheridan and Lucy with me," she said. "They want to see their sister. They want to be there when she comes out of it."

Joe paused for a few seconds, trying to figure out how to frame his words, when Marybeth did it for him: "We talked it all out this morning. They know she may never be April again. They know that this may turn out to be one of the most difficult experiences of their lives, and so do I. But we have to be there, Joe."

He said, "I'm on my way, but you should all go now. I'll meet you at the hospital."

"I'll keep you posted after I talk to the doctors," she said.

Near Fort Collins, he called the governor's office. He used the private number Rulon had given him and the call went straight to voicemail.

Joe said, "We've got the goods on Wentworth. He slaughtered Lek Sixty-four and tried to cover it up.

"On another matter, I might be out of touch for a few days. There's news on my daughter's condition. The news could be good or bad."

23

Timber Cates refused to look back over his shoulder at the brick-and-glass front entrance of the Wyoming State Penitentiary in Rawlins. He vowed he would never look back at it, because he intended to *never* see it again for the rest of his life, and there was nothing good to remember about it anyway.

Not even when the corrections officer called out after him, "We'll keep the light on for you, Timber, my boy!"

What an asshole.

WHILE HE WAS BEING processed out, the CO had kept up a one-sided monologue that seemed intended to agitate Timber, as if baiting him one last time so he'd explode and get himself turned around and sent back inside.

"This seems like a whole lot of trouble when you'll probably be back here in a few months anyway," the CO said. He was short and stout, a fireplug, with a piglike face and a wispy goatee that looked unfinished. He had half-Asian features. Timber didn't like it when an Asian talked to him that way. Or when Asians tried to grow beards like real men. They weren't designed for it. He wished they would just give up and shave, for Christ's sake.

"It would probably save the taxpayers money if you just turned around right now and stayed inside. That way, we won't have to mess with trials and lawyers and all of that when you come back. And you *will* come back. Believe me, I've seen hundreds of convicts come through here. I know the look of one who never reflected on what he did to get in here in the first place. You're the type who thinks the only thing you did wrong was to get caught. You've been in here three years and you didn't get smarter, or learn a trade, or find the Lord while you were in here. It was your choice to remain ignorant and not to take any of the opportunities offered here to better yourself. You look harder and meaner than when you came in. Which means you'll be back, and some poor innocent people out there will pay the price. I can tell by your face. You've got that look, Cates, and you sure as hell have the wrong attitude."

When Timber didn't react, the CO said, "There's white trash and then there's *stupid* white trash. I think we both know which category *you* fit into."

Recalling what his mother had said, Timber closed his eyes and breathed in and out, in and out.

"Looks like you're picking a perfect time to get on the outside," the CO said. "They're predicting a major winter event in the next couple of days. That's what they call it now: an *event*. Like if they said 'blizzard,' we'd all throw up our hands and run around screaming like kids.

"Ten to twelve inches in town, eighteen to twenty-four in the mountains. That's what they're saying, Cates. You're getting out just in time to get your skinny ass buried in snow. And it couldn't happen to a nicer guy."

Timber had heard nothing of a big storm coming. And he didn't care.

HE WEAVED through the cars in the parking lot with his possessions wadded up and stuffed into a blue-black plastic garbage bag that he clutched to his chest. It was amazing even to him how everything he owned could fit into a garbage bag. Plus, most of it was truly ratty and shitty: a couple of pairs of boat shoes; his kit containing a toothbrush, toothpaste, a comb and a brush; another change of clothing; and a box of letters he'd mostly never read from his mom about his brother Dallas. If he lost the bag there wasn't much he would really miss. But since it was all he owned, all that was really his, he held it tight.

He tried not to think about how much he'd thrived in prison. He hated it with every fiber of his being, but he loved it at the same time. It was an easy life. Meals were rote. Clothing was provided. His job in the infirmary was easy. No one breathed down his neck. In all, it wasn't so bad.

And he'd never tell a single soul that he thought that way. That the asshole CO was right. He just didn't know how *much* he was right.

TIMBER WORE the same clothes—a black, extra-large Scorpions concert T-shirt, a torn denim jacket, jeans with grease spots—that he'd been arrested in three years earlier. The clothes didn't fit anymore. He *had* lost weight.

He picked up his pace as he weaved through the cars in the lot. He felt like he was getting away with something, that if he didn't leave the place soon they'd realize they had made a mistake and come after him. He banged his knee on the bumper of a Dodge pickup and cursed, but didn't pause to look at the bruise.

THE BLUE 1984 CHEVY CAVALIER his parents had left for him was parked in the farthest row from the front of the prison. It had a rusted roof, mismatched tires, and a cracked windshield. It was a crappy boxy car from a crappy era.

"Thanks, Pops," Timber said aloud to himself between epithets. "What—did you spend a whole four hundred fucking dollars on it?"

As they'd told him he would, he found the keys under the fender on top of the driver's-side tire. The car wasn't locked—*Who would steal it, anyway?*—and he threw the garbage bag on the backseat. The fabric of the seats was stained and ripped, and it smelled of old people.

Timber scooted in and put the key in the ignition. After a few seconds of a high-pitched grinding sound, the engine caught. In the cracked rearview mirror, he saw an ugly puff of black smoke blow out of the exhaust pipe.

There was less than eighty-five thousand miles on the odometer, which confirmed to Timber that the people who had previously owned it were old folks who'd probably driven it from their home to doctor's appointments and the mailbox and not much beyond that.

But when he engaged the transmission, the Cavalier lurched forward. It was underpowered and the suspension was mushy, but it moved. He guessed that if he could find the maintenance record it would show that the old geezers had changed the oil every three thousand miles on the dot and rotated the tires every ten thousand.

And that was all he could ask for at the moment.

THEY'D TOLD HIM to avoid the interstate highways as much as he could. No reason, they'd said, to draw any more attention to himself than necessary. So it was north to Lamont, then Three Forks. Jeffrey City, Moneta, Big Trails, Ten Sleep, Greybull, then Winchester, the back way. He knew the little towns and highways from when he was a high school athlete and they'd take the bus from town to town, to play football games. Wyoming was all like a small town with incredibly long streets.

After Winchester, he'd have to jump on Interstate 90 into Montana. Crow Agency, then Hardin, then his destination.

He'd been there a few times. But never like this.

His infirmary scrubs were on top of the pile of clothing in the trash bag in the backseat.

OUTSIDE OF JEFFREY CITY, which wasn't a city at all, he pulled over to the side of the highway after checking his mirrors. He couldn't shake the feeling that the Asian CO was following him. But he wasn't.

He kept the Cavalier idling and leaned over in his seat and popped open the glove compartment.

The sheet on top was a Google map of where he needed to go. He studied it and shook his head and folded it neatly in two. He'd pay more attention when he got closer. There was a printout of the face of a girl. She was a hottie. But at least he knew what she looked like.

On the bottom of the glove compartment was a bright green ceramic knife with a four-inch blade. It was a familiar knife, and he remembered his mother using it to slice onions and carrots in her kitchen. It touched him that she would give up that knife.

It looked battered, but it wouldn't show up if he had to walk through a metal detector. He wished it was bigger, but he knew it would work.

He placed the knife next to his right thigh and put the directions and the photo back into the glove box. He'd study them when it was time to study them.

Timber eased back out onto the old highway. In front of him, above the northern horizon, was a thick black band. The storm the CO had told him about was gathering.

SOUTH OF MONETA, in the middle of nowhere, in a high steppe desert of sand and thigh-high sagebrush, Timber tapped his brakes because a herd of sheep was up ahead on the road. The rancher on horseback driving them waved a sort of apology, but kept his herd trotting up the bad two-lane highway.

It had been years since Timber had seen sheep in Wyoming and he'd never liked sheep in the first place. Who ate sheep? Why did they even exist? He thought: *Range maggots.*

The rancher in charge rode a handsome buckskin and wore a wide-brimmed straw summer cowboy hat. He had a toothbrush mustache and a squared-off jaw and wore a pink scarf around his neck. Timber hated him immediately because of his good humor and attitude. *Of course there are sheep on the road*, he seemed to say, *but no one who takes the old highway south of Moneta would expect otherwise.*

There were other cowboys on the drive, but they looked Mexican or worse, Timber thought. He resisted the urge to plow through the herd of sheep and leave dozens of them writhing on the road.

After inching along for twenty minutes behind the sheep, he pulled to the side and let the herd get ahead of him.

But not all of them did.

Although the rancher and his Hispanic cowboys had moved the herd over the next rise, there was a single ewe struggling to keep up. Timber watched her and narrowed his eyes. She was obviously old and lame, and she had no fluidity to her gait. She pitched up and down with every step. The rancher and his hands probably didn't know they'd lost one.

IN PRISON, Timber had learned never to take revenge without really thinking it through. On this, his mother didn't have a clue. She only knew about the times he'd gotten into trouble. She didn't know about the times he'd carefully planned something.

He'd wait for the perfect scenario to occur. That involved making sure the COs weren't in the yard or were looking elsewhere. He'd do it where the closed-circuit cameras couldn't see him. He made sure his weapon was honed and reliable so it wouldn't snap in two on the initial impact.

So he eyed that straggling ewe.

When he didn't see either the rancher or the Mexicans come back for her, he leaned over and popped the button on the glove compartment.

———

THERE WAS DUST in the air from both the herd and the sheep cowboys. It just hung there.

The ewe was bawling, calling ahead, saying, *Wait for me.*

She paused when Timber walked up next to her. She looked at him with a blank expression only domesticated farm animals like cows and sheep are capable of, one of pure blind trust and incredible stupidity. She was large, nearly two-hundred pounds, all of it wool and mutton and dead dumb eyes.

Timber stabbed her with the knife behind her front shoulder, then he did it again. He stabbed her like a manic jackhammer, so many times and so quickly that he was out of breath.

The ewe collapsed, then rolled to her side. Her last breath rattled out in a sigh and she was still. Better that, he thought, than coyotes tearing her apart.

That's the secret, he thought as he backed away. It wasn't like the movies when a single knife thrust did them in. The more stab wounds, and the deeper they were, the better. It was exactly as he'd done in the yard to that son of a bitch who'd called him out for being white trash. Twenty-seven stab wounds in less than half a minute. There was no way that guy would live and identify his assailant. It had been so sudden and so violent that Timber would never have to worry about that guy again.

TIMBER WALKED BACK to the Cavalier with his entire right arm greasy with ewe blood and lanolin from the wool. The ceramic green knife was red.

He paused at a spring seep in the ground and plunged his right arm into it and watched curlicues of red form at the surface. When he withdrew his arm, there was no more sheep's blood on it and the green knife was clean.

He thought: *Do it fast and go home.*

WHEN TIMBER CATES got back into his car, he opened the Playmate cooler that Brenda had left for him. In the distance, the dust cloud formed by the herd of sheep was moving to the right, away from the highway. He'd have a clear shot now.

He found a large package of fried chicken wrapped in aluminum foil and he gleefully ate it all and threw the bones out the window. Even though it was cold, it was the best fried chicken—*the best food*—he'd had in three years.

She'd told him: *Don't forget to put on your scrubs.*

He reviewed the map to the hospital and the photo of the girl whose death would free Dallas once and for all, as she put it, and he thought:

Who loves his mama the most?

PART SIX

SPRING STORM

24

ight rain was changing to snow when Joe reached his home on Bighorn Road.

Spring storms in the Rockies always had the most impact. Unlike the powder snow that came down in the winter, spring snow was heavy with moisture. It piled up quickly and broke tree branches and downed power lines. Although it usually melted down within a day or so, the heavy wet blanket seemed like a cruel ending to a harsh winter, especially when the trees were starting to bud and baby animals had just been born.

His plan was to feed the horses and Daisy, grab a change of clothes, and head to Billings to meet up with the rest of his family before the storm hit.

A text from Marybeth and an unexpected visit from Revis Wentworth changed all that.

The text read:

> We made it safe and sound to Billings and the hospital in front of the storm. The doctors have postponed bringing April out of the coma until tomorrow or the next day. We're

getting two rooms at a motel, but no need to try to get here
tonight. Word is the highways may close anyway. I'll call
when we get settled.

xoxoxoxoxo,

MB

WENTWORTH'S WHITE PICKUP was parked at an odd angle in
front of Joe's house, but Wentworth didn't appear to be inside. Joe
parked in front of his garage and approached the pickup cautiously
with his hand on the grip of his Glock. The cab was unoccupied
except for an empty Wild Turkey bottle on the passenger seat.

Puzzled, Joe pushed through his front gate and walked across the
lawn. The snow was starting to stick to the grass, big thick flakes of
it, and he could feel it melting through his uniform shirt.

Several scenarios went through his mind when it came to Wentworth. He could imagine the man sitting in his lounge chair with a
shotgun across his lap, waiting for Joe to come in the door. Or he
was there with Annie Hatch and a new story to try and get Joe off
his trail.

Or . . .

He was drunk and passed out on their couch. Which he was.

Joe sighed and mounted the porch steps and entered his house. As
he walked through the mudroom, he heard Daisy whimper from
behind his closed bedroom door.

He stood over Wentworth, who had obviously found Joe's bottle
of bourbon and had drunk a quarter of it, judging by the level of
liquor in the bottle, and Joe said, "Hey, wake up."

Wentworth didn't move. He looked like he hadn't shaved or

showered since Joe had seen him last. He reeked of alcohol and sweat. His hair looked greasy and was pasted to his skull.

"Wake up, Revis," Joe said loudly, nudging Wentworth's foot with his boot tip.

Wentworth groaned but his eyes didn't open.

Joe thought about dousing the man with a bowl of ice water, but he didn't want to get his couch wet. Instead, he let Daisy out of the bedroom where Wentworth had obviously shut her inside.

After quivering and rubbing herself against Joe's legs to say hello, she romped into the living room and started licking Wentworth's face, just as planned. As she did, Joe got a digital micro-recorder out of his breast pocket and turned it on to record, then put it back while Daisy lapped away. At first, Wentworth responded by smiling and mewing. Joe could only guess what was going on in the man's mind and assumed it involved a vision of Annie Hatch. Then Wentworth cracked one eye, saw Daisy's mouth a few inches away, and screamed.

He shot up to a sitting position and raised his hands as if surrendering.

"Get that animal away from me."

"Daisy," Joe said, and his Labrador padded over to him.

"Stay."

Daisy sat on her haunches and looked from Joe to Wentworth, who was obviously terrified. Wentworth used his sleeves to dry his face and neck.

"Start by explaining why you're in my house or I'll . . ." Joe paused for effect. "Let her lick you again."

Wentworth lowered his hands and looked around. He shook his head. "I can't even remember getting here."

"But you did. What if my wife or girls had found you here? What if they'd called the sheriff on you?"

He obviously hadn't thought of that, and he winced as he reached out for Joe's bottle.

"Right, help yourself to more of my whiskey," Joe said. "Don't even bother to ask."

"I need it," Wentworth said, drinking straight from the bottle.

Then he looked at Joe with glassy eyes and said, "What can I do to get myself out of this? Is there something I can say or do? This could kill my whole career."

Joe remained standing. "So you're willing to admit it, then? You won't get fired. Nobody in a federal agency *ever* gets fired."

Wentworth's first reaction was to argue, but he fought against it. He said, "I could get reassigned to Bumfuck, North Dakota. Right now, no one down at the lab will return my calls. Annie won't even talk to me. The walls are closing in on me, and you know it."

"Yup," Joe said.

"So what can I do? I know I have a problem," he said, raising the bottle again and flirting with it. "I know I drink too much and get out of control and do things I later regret. Like coming here. Or that night out at Lek Sixty-four."

"So you admit you killed all those birds," Joe said.

Wentworth nodded. That wouldn't be an admission on the tape.

"Start by admitting it and we can go on from there," Joe said.

"I just did."

"Thank you," Joe said. "Then you tampered with the evidence I gathered and sent false evidence to your lab in Denver. I know because we opened the box this morning and looked at it."

Wentworth moaned. He said, "You were down there?"

"I met Kelsea Raymer," Joe said. "We opened the box together. Where did you get those spent shotgun shells?"

Wentworth tipped his head back and moaned again. Joe was getting tired of the moaning.

"I found 'em in the back of a guy's truck. It isn't hard to find shotgun shells around here."

"That's what I figured," Joe said. "And the tire tracks?"

Wentworth hesitated, then mumbled, "In an alley in back of the Stockman's Bar."

"Now, doesn't it feel good to come clean?"

"Not really," he said, sullen.

"Isn't that why you came here?"

"Kind of," he said. "I was kind of hoping you and I could work something out, you know?"

"Like a bribe?"

"Maybe. I've got some money in savings, and by looking around here you could use it."

Joe shook his head. "Have you been drinking since I saw you last?"

"Pretty much. I can't remember it all. I do remember going back up to Lek Sixty-four to see if you'd found all the shotgun shells. It was the second time I'd been up there since the incident."

"Did you find any?" Joe asked.

"A couple."

"It doesn't matter," Joe said. "I didn't send all of the originals in the evidence box. I held a couple out that came from your shotgun. Kelsea Raymer has them now. She'll no doubt find your fingerprints on them and determine they were fired from your shotgun."

Another moan.

"When is the last time you ate something?" Joe asked.

Wentworth shrugged.

"I'm going to scramble some eggs," Joe said. "Maybe you ought to put a cap on that bottle."

"It's a disease," Wentworth said. "I have a disease."

"Yeah, yeah."

As he cracked eggs into the skillet, Joe said, "In the state of Wyoming, only one party to a recorded conversation needs to be aware of it to serve as evidence in court."

He let that sink in for a minute.

When Wentworth staggered to his feet and leaned against the kitchen doorframe, Joe patted the recorder in his front pocket.

"So I'm fucked," Wentworth said.

"Yup."

"I just wanted to spend every second I could with Annie," he said.

"Judge Hewitt has a soft spot for crimes of passion."

"He does?"

"No," Joe said. "He doesn't."

THEY SAT AT THE KITCHEN TABLE. Joe watched Wentworth pick at his food at first, then cover it with ketchup and shovel it in like a wolf.

Joe said, "Do you feel bad about killing all those sage grouse? I mean, you're considered an expert on them. I would have thought you were serious about their survival."

Wentworth didn't respond, but just kept eating.

"Maybe if you explained it to me, I could understand," Joe said.

"Nothing to explain," Wentworth said. "Those birds are just a means to an end for me. Not all that much is known about them, so it wasn't all that hard to become an expert. Their population has boomed and crashed over the years. It's crashing now. If we can hold up a few oil rigs and slow the crash—well, good for us."

"What if they're crashing on their own? Without our help?" Joe asked. "I see it all the time. Some years, there are rabbits everywhere you look, and the next year there are coyotes and foxes in huge numbers eating rabbits. Then the rabbit population crashes and I don't see many coyotes or foxes for a few years. Could that be the case with sage grouse?"

"I don't know," Wentworth said. "It's above my pay grade to answer that question. It's just a job, okay? I don't have a personal investment in them."

"But the people out here have a personal investment in what you decide about those birds," Joe said. "It might mean either they have jobs or they don't."

"They can always change jobs," Wentworth said. "Or move. That's not my problem."

Joe frowned. Wentworth spooned more eggs onto his plate.

"What's happening outside?" Wentworth asked as he chewed.

"It's snowing."

"Crap. Can I make it back to the hotel?"

"You sure aren't staying *here*," Joe said.

WHILE DOING THE DISHES, Joe turned to Wentworth, who was still at the table sipping coffee.

"Didn't you just tell me you'd gone up to Lek Sixty-four before?" Joe asked. "I don't mean the night you shot up all the birds. I thought you said you'd gone up there looking for shotgun shells previously."

"Are you recording this?"

"Sure am."

"Can you shut it off?"

"No point now, Revis."

Wentworth sighed. He said, "Yeah, I went up there last week after you'd been up there. That's after I came up with the plan to send bad shells to Denver. I wanted to see if I could find any more of mine and get rid of them."

"When did you go?"

Wentworth surveyed the ceiling for a few minutes, then said, "Last Tuesday."

Joe thought back. Tuesday was when Nate was ambushed.

"Did you see anything unusual up there?" Joe asked.

"No. This whole state's unusual."

"Come on, Revis. *Think*."

Wentworth drummed his fingers on the table, and Joe watched his expression change. He'd recalled something.

"I'd been drinking," he said. "But I remember I was out there in the sagebrush and I heard a vehicle coming down that two-track. I thought it was you, so I got on the ground."

"Where was your pickup?"

"I hid it half a mile away, where it couldn't be seen from the road."

Joe nodded. "So who was it?"

"I don't know their *names*," he said with distaste. "But it was just a couple of locals. Two vehicles went by and I laid there thinking: 'Here I am, drunk and facedown in the mud. It has come to this.'"

Joe felt something tingle in his chest. He sat down at the table across from Wentworth.

"Two vehicles?"

"Yeah. One following the other."

"What did they look like?"

Wentworth said, "The first one was an old beat-up SUV. There was an old man driving it. The second was one of those white panel vans, you know? Like plumbers drive? A younger man—a big bruiser type—was driving that."

The tingle spread. Joe recalled Eldon and Brenda's battered Suburban in front of the courthouse. He'd seen it again at their place. The first driver sounded like Eldon. The second: Bull.

"The white van," Joe said, "was it new?"

"Newer than the beat-up piece of shit," Wentworth said.

"Was there any writing on the side of it?"

"Yeah. I couldn't see all that well down there, but it was something like 'Yahoo Falconry Services.' There was a picture of a bird on the side, like an eagle."

Joe leaned forward and his glare must have been intense because Wentworth sat back in his chair.

"Could it have been *Yarak* Falconry Services?"

"Yeah, maybe. I guess it could have been," Wentworth said. "That's a word I'm not familiar with. Why does it matter, anyway?"

Joe ignored him. "The SUV and the van were going which direction?"

"Toward the mountains."

"Did you see either one of them come back down later that night?"

"Naw—I was gone by then."

Joe guessed only one of the vehicles had returned, and he thought he knew which one.

Why would the Cateses have Nate's van? Where was Olivia Brannan?

The world tilted.

Joe asked, "Did you go up there again?"

Wentworth seemed surprised at the question. "How did you know?"

"Someone saw your truck up there Thursday night. I didn't suspect you until I heard about it."

"Who was it?"

"That isn't important now," Joe said. "So did you go back up there Thursday?"

"Yeah, I guess I did."

Joe said to Wentworth: "It's time for you to go."

Wentworth looked hurt. He said, "What should I do?"

"Go back to your room and bunker in. There's a storm coming. Just sit tight."

"But what about me?"

"What about you?" Joe said.

"I'm supposed to just sit at the Holiday Inn and wait to be arrested?"

"That's what I'd recommend," Joe said. "Dry out and get some sleep. Stay sober. Do the right thing. Now, *git*."

FROM THE FRONT WINDOW, Joe watched Wentworth's taillights vanish in the light snow.

He surveyed the sky. The snow wasn't falling as heavily as he'd thought it would. He might have a few hours before it really came down. It was still three hours until it got dark.

He turned and said, "Come on, Daisy. We're going to go find Eldon's secret elk camp."

25

At the same time, Liv heard footfalls approaching and she quickly stopped digging around the rock. Most of the rock was exposed now, but it was still stuck fast. Liv's fear that the stone was simply a spur of a much larger boulder had grown throughout the day but had recently been put to rest. The contours of the smooth ancient river rock were starting to round out at the back. It was, in fact, approximately the size and shape of a football. She'd cleaned enough of the packed clay from around it that she could now reach in and grab the top and bottom of the stone with both hands, although she couldn't get enough leverage yet to work it free. It would take more time and effort.

The doors opened and large flakes of snow floated down into the root cellar. The sky was cream-colored, the sun muted behind heavy clouds.

Brenda said, "I wanted to see if you liked pork chops."

"You're asking me what I want for dinner?" Liv asked, surprised.

"Not if it's something exotic the men won't eat. But what about pork chops?"

"I like pork chops."

"Then it's settled," Brenda said.

But instead of leaving, Brenda sat down on the lip of the doorframe. She was wearing an oversized barn coat over her housedress and her feet dangled down. Liv could see the woman's thick ankles and her heavy, old-fashioned shoes. She wore support hose and there was a bulge of white fat above the top of the hose.

"There's supposed to be a big winter storm coming," Brenda said. "By midnight tonight, we're supposed to really get hit. Is that heater working okay?"

"Yes."

"You got enough sleeping bags and all?"

"I think so. They don't smell so good, though."

"They smell like the guys," Brenda said. "Beggars can't be choosers, you know."

"That's not what I meant," Liv said, wondering if Brenda was going to go away.

After a long beat, Brenda said, "I brought this," and held something out in her hand. It was a hairbrush.

"I appreciate that," Liv said. "Are you going to drop it down to me?"

"I was actually thinking I'd come down there and brush your hair. It's something I've been thinking about. Would you be okay with that?"

Liv felt an equal mix of panic and revulsion. Brenda behind her, brushing her hair? The idea of it almost made her physically sick. But if she could actually get her down here . . .

Liv glanced at the stone in the wall. Maybe with enough adrenaline rushing through her she'd be able to jerk it out and brain Brenda.

"I'd love it," Liv said.

Brenda said over her shoulder, "Bull, lower that ladder."

Liv's heart sank. She hadn't realized Bull was right there with her, but out of view.

"Keep close and have that pistol handy," Brenda said to Bull. "Pop her if she tries anything."

"Okay, Ma."

Brenda said to Liv, "You're not going to do anything stupid, are you?"

Liv closed her eyes, fighting away tears. "No."

"You want your hair brushed?"

"Yes."

Liv sat with her back to the stone in the dirt wall so that when Brenda brushed her hair she wouldn't glance up and notice it. Liv wished she'd had more warning they were coming so she could have packed more loose dirt around the rock than she had.

The teeth of the brush actually felt good coursing down through her hair, although Brenda was a little rough at first, pulling it hard through tangles.

"Your hair is nice," Brenda said. "Is it always like this or do you treat it somehow?"

"I get it straightened."

"What would it be like otherwise?"

"It would be natural."

"You mean like an Afro?"

"Yes."

Brenda clucked her tongue. She said, "I can't even imagine."

Up at the compound, an engine started up with a high whine. Then it revved up fast.

Brenda called to Bull, "Did Dallas get that snowmobile started?"

"Sounds like he did."

Brenda chuckled. "That boy—he's a go-getter. There's nothing he loves more than getting up into the mountains on his snowmobile. When I told him about this storm moving in, he just lit up."

"Didn't he get injured at a rodeo?" Liv asked, making small talk.

"Yeah, sort of."

The answer perplexed Liv for what it didn't say.

Brenda said, "I've never seen a human recover so quick. He'll be back in the game in a few days at this rate. I wish I could come back after getting hurt like he does. But he's always been fast in whatever it is he chooses to do. He's an exceptional person, and I ain't just sayin' that because he's my boy. I just wish the folks around this county would give him his due."

"They should," Liv agreed, trying anything to establish common ground. "How did Dallas get injured? Was it a bull?"

"Yeah, in Houston. But he didn't get hurt that bad. Dallas got thrown in front of a big crowd of people and that probably hurt him more than anything else," Brenda said. "It wasn't until he got back here that he got those busted ribs and got his shoulder pulled out of the socket."

Liv was confused. Brenda must have sensed it.

"I had to have Eldon and Bull do it. Dallas agreed, but it isn't any fun to watch your husband and your oldest son beat the crap out of your youngest. Pulled his arm out of the socket and busted in his ribs. I had to turn my head when they done it."

"*Why?*"

"Oh, it's a long story," Brenda said. "Dallas did something he shouldn't have done. I had to figure out a way to keep him out of it. See, I'm the only one who does any thinking around here."

"I believe it," Liv said. "So why was injuring Dallas a good thing for him?"

"Wasn't just him. It was for the whole family. I look after my whole family and keep 'em on the right path. I don't let anyone get in our way. *Anyone.* I saw when they sent Timber away to Rawlins what happens when I don't stay on top of 'em. Timber's my middle son. He's the wildest of them all and he got out of prison this morning."

There was a pause. Brenda pulled the brush through and Liv mewed. It was a false emotion, but to Brenda it sounded genuine.

"You like that, huh?" she asked softly.

"I do," Liv said. Then: "It's too bad you didn't have daughters."

"Yeah," Brenda said wistfully. "Boys is all I know. It was the same growing up. I had two brothers and I was the only girl. I don't even know how to talk to other women—they always seem too soft and emotional to me. Most women, it seems to me, should get the crap kicked out of them by a couple of brothers like I did to toughen 'em up."

Liv lied and said, "My brother did the same thing to me growing up." In fact, she had no brothers.

Brenda said, "My dad bounced around between being a miner and a logger in the Ozarks. That's where my people are from: Jasper County, Missouri. A lot of the time he didn't work at all. But I was the apple of his eye."

"I thought I heard a little of the South in your accent," Liv said.

"Yeah, and I've never been back. I left when I was sixteen. I came to Wyoming to see Yellowstone Park with my uncle Harold. I'm still surprised my folks let him bring me out here, but they did. Uncle Harold raped me a few times and left me in one of those cabins they've got in the park. That's where I met Eldon. He was driving through Yellowstone to go hunting on the other side. He picked me up on the road. We caught up with Uncle Harold in Cody, and Eldon beat him half to death with a rifle butt near Heart Mountain. We've been together ever since."

Brenda's tone was calm. Liv swallowed hard.

"But back to my dad. When he was home, we'd listen to records together."

"Is that where you heard Kitty Wells?"

"Oh, that," Brenda laughed. "I must have been a sight back then, singing that song about cheating when I was just a little girl."

Liv hummed the tune, and to her surprise Brenda joined in.

"What the *hell* is going on down there?" Bull said from above.

Liv faked a laugh. "My mom used to sing it around the house."

"Did you have a daddy?" Brenda asked. She sounded curious.

"He worked on shrimping boats," Liv said. "He died when I was five."

"Mmmmm."

"I don't remember much about him."

"Better that," Brenda said, her voice hardening, "than him showing up whenever he felt like it. My brothers were animals, and they needed a man around to set them straight. He wasn't there when he should have been. He was mean when he got drunk and he knocked Mama around. Then he'd feel bad about it, but instead of making it up to everyone, he'd take off again.

"I swore back then that if I found a man, I'd make him stay close to me and his kids. I thought I could tame Eldon of his wild hairs, but over the years I've learned how to handle him instead. I'm close with my boys, and Eldon is . . . there. I wish he'd take more interest in them, but he's not much for ambition in any department except hunting and fishing. So I wore him down, which is the next best thing to having a good man in the first place. He doesn't even know how to think for himself anymore, which is a good thing, because I do it for him and I do it better. I know that sounds harsh, but it's the best for the family."

Liv thought: *She's proud of her boys?*

And she realized right then that Brenda was even crazier than she'd realized.

"MEN ARE SUCH SIMPLE CREATURES," Brenda said, keeping her voice down so that Bull couldn't overhear. "You and me, we have a thousand things going on in our minds at all times. It gets *noisy* in there. But men are different. They can't hold more than one thought in their brain at a time. It's 'I'm hungry,' or 'I'm horny,' or 'I need to fix the transmission or this truck won't run.' If they could ever get inside our brains, the hullabaloo going on would probably kill 'em in a few minutes. And if we could ever get inside theirs, I suspect we'd get bored real fast with all the peace and quiet.

"But you probably know that, because you're pretty and they fall all over themselves to get next to you. But when you're plain and you look like me and don't know fashion from cow plop, you learn to appeal to other base instincts, like food.

"If you look like me, you learn to cook. You find out what they like and you give it to 'em—and plenty of it. If you do that, they'll do anything you want. Fried chicken, mashed potatoes and gravy, chicken-fried steaks, pot roast—whatever. Waffles and fried chicken will be enough to convince them to go into a barn and gun down Nate Romanowski. It's simple, girl. Do you cook?"

"A little."

"Of course, you have other ways, don't you?"

"Like what?" Liv asked.

Brenda bent closer. "Like luring Bull down here."

"He did that himself."

"*Sure* he did."

"So why did Bull and Eldon beat up Dallas?" Liv asked. "I don't understand."

The question was met with silence. When Brenda spoke, her tone was flat.

"He had to look like a bull tore him up. He couldn't just fake it."

"But why?"

"I told you," Brenda said with annoyance. "Dallas could have gotten in trouble. This way, he got hurt a little, but he didn't get arrested or nothing. He's still with us and he's just about recovered."

Liv asked, "Why did Eldon and Bull ambush Nate? Did they have something against him?"

"Not at all," Brenda said. "In fact, I think they kind of liked him."

"Then why did they do it?"

Brenda scoffed. She said, "Anyone around this county knows that when the game warden gets in a situation, Nate Romanowski shows up to help him out. No one wants Nate around on the other side. That guy is *crazy*."

"I'm not following you," Liv confessed.

"I told you. Dallas did something stupid. It involved the game warden's daughter. We were able to handle the game warden—he's by the book and not that bright. He even came out here and saw Dallas, and he seen for himself that the boy was injured after all."

Liv recalled the item she'd read in the Casper newspaper about Joe's middle daughter being found beaten on the side of a road. Liv's stomach suddenly turned, but she tried hard not to show any reaction.

Brenda continued. "But Joe Pickett doesn't let things go. I've watched him over the years and I know that about him. If he told his buddy Nate that he suspected Dallas, even though he couldn't prove it, well, Nate may come a-calling. I didn't want Nate after my boy. So we put the word out there and lured you up and took him out before he could get together with his friend Joe Pickett and hear the story. It was a precautionary thing. We bought ourselves insurance, is all. Any mother would do the same thing for their boy if they thought they had to do it to keep him alive."

"So it was all a preliminary strike," Liv said. "You killed Nate *just in case*."

"Pretty much," Brenda said. "And it wasn't easy. I had to look my husband and son in the eye and say, 'Get in that barn and get ready. He's just a man. There's nothing special about him.' Finally, they went in there and got set up. I wasn't sure they'd go through with it until I heard the shots."

Liv boiled inside, but she tried not to show it.

"I didn't know you'd be with him," Brenda said. "You were sort of a kink in my plans."

"What happened to the van?"

"Eldon's good for something," Brenda said. "He knows every inch of this country out here because he guides hunters in the fall. He knows where to hide a vehicle where no one can find it."

"Why are you telling me all this now?"

Brenda went back to brushing Liv's hair. "Might as well."

Those words weren't chosen at random, Liv thought.

"You said you had a plan for me. Can you tell me what it is?"

"I'm not sure you want to know."

Liv said, "You could let me out of here. I could help you around the house. I could be the daughter you never had. Or I could leave and never say a word to anyone."

"You know neither one of those is a good choice," Brenda said. "If you stayed, somebody would see you and wonder why a black girl was living with us. They'd wonder where you came from and somebody would figure it out. And there's no way you can convince me you'd keep this all to yourself. Women aren't made that way."

"I am."

"Oh," Brenda said, bending forward again and whispering a few inches from Liv's ear, "if only that were true."

Liv closed her eyes. She thought about wheeling in her chair and plunging her thumbs into Brenda's throat. If Bull wasn't up there, she would have done it.

"I want to know," Liv said.

"I'm waiting on Eldon," Brenda said. "He's got to go get his tank filled up. Then instead of dumping it at the treatment plant, he's going to bring it back here."

It took a moment for Liv to realize what she'd just heard.

"He's going to dump sewage in the cellar?"

"Pretty much," Brenda said in a conversational tone. "Then he can fire up the Bobcat and fill the rest of the hole with dirt. If anybody ever gets a notion to dig it up, they'll realize this hole is full of sewage. There's no way they'd keep digging and eventually find a body. We'll just tell 'em our septic tank must have leaked."

Liv closed her eyes.

"So you were asking me about pork chops. Is that because it's my last meal?"

Brenda snorted, stopped brushing, and backed away.

She said, "Bull, cover me. I'm coming up."

Dirt sifted into the cellar from the edge as Bull bent over and peered in. Liv saw that he was holding her handgun.

She turned her head to see Brenda clumsily mount the ladder and start to climb. She grunted on each rung.

Liv stood and approached the clay wall and grasped the stone and pulled. It didn't budge.

As Brenda awkwardly climbed the ladder out of striking distance, she said, "Oh, I don't know about it being your last meal. I might bring you some breakfast, so put all those containers and the silverware back in the bucket tonight so I can pull it up."

When Brenda was out of the cellar, she said, "Thanks for letting me brush your hair. Maybe if it was different circumstances, we could have actually been friends, you know?"

Then to Bull: "Close it."

Liv waited until the footfalls faded away, then turned back to the stone.

It shredded her to know that she might have missed the only chance she'd ever have.

26

I t made a warped kind of sense, Joe thought. If Eldon Cates needed to hide a vehicle fast, where better than an elk camp that was unknown to everyone, including the game warden?

Revis Wentworth had given Joe an all-important clue to the location of the elk camp simply by describing which direction the two vehicles were going on the two-track road across the sagebrush bench. Joe had been on the road before, of course, when he'd found Lek 64. He'd taken a more established county road to the two-track, and when he intersected it, he'd turned east.

Several years ago, Joe had taken the road west through the foothills of the Bighorns and on into the timber. At the time, he was looking for a promontory, or high-altitude point, where he might "perch" and glass the terrain with his spotting scope. The road was little used, and Joe had given up looking for an opening in the timber as he ascended the mountain. It was difficult even finding a place to perform a three-point turn because the lodgepole pines were so thick.

His district was 1,800 square miles of mountains, plains, and broken country. There were hundreds of ancient two-tracks running through it, most leading nowhere in particular. If they didn't lead to an obvious destination or were rarely used by hunters or fishermen, he simply forgot about them, like he had with this nameless path.

The western direction of the two-track from the sagebrush bench into the mountains would be convenient for an elk outfitter like Eldon Cates, he thought. Eldon could access it from his compound down below in the valley and never cross a highway or county road, therefore not likely to be seen by hunters or anyone else. The land the two-track crossed was a confusing mix of BLM, U.S. Forest Service, and private land. It was a baffling checkerboard on the map and likely to deter visitors. So it was perfect for Eldon.

If Joe was guessing right, anyhow.

Something else made sense, now that he thought about it. He'd wondered how it was that April's possessions had been found at Tilden Cudmore's place and in his vehicle if Cudmore wasn't responsible for her attack. Or how Nate's assailants had accessed the HF Bar Ranch through a locked gate and not been seen.

Although he had to first confirm the existence of the secret elk camp and that the Yarak, Inc. van was hidden there, dots were suddenly connecting.

He hit the speed dial on his phone as his tires sizzled on the wet highway.

"County Sheriff's Department," the receptionist said.

"I need to talk to Sheriff Reed."

"Joe?"

"Yes."

"He's in a meeting."

"Get him out, please."

The snow was sticking to the green shoots of grass on the side of the highway, and the storm was moving over the tops of the mountains and coming down the western side like rolls of smoke. Joe had his windshield wipers on low and the defroster on. He thought he could find the camp and get out before dark and before the storm enveloped the Twelve Sleep Valley.

"Reed here. What is it, Joe? I'm in a budget meeting with the county commissioners."

"I got a lead," Joe said. "Revis Wentworth was at Lek Sixty-four last Tuesday and he said he saw two vehicles crossing the sagebrush into the mountains. One fits the description of Eldon Cates's old Suburban. The other fits the description of the white van Nate was driving the day he got ambushed."

Reed paused. "What are you saying exactly?"

"That the Cateses were involved in the shooting. Either they did it on their own or somebody hired them to remove Nate's van from the scene. They're implicated one way or another. Moving that van made everyone wonder where Olivia Brannan had gone after the shooting and made people think she must have been in on it. But it doesn't sound like she was there when Wentworth saw the two vehicles. The descriptions he gave me of the drivers sound like Eldon and Bull."

Reed said, "Why would they go after Romanowski? What's the connection there?"

"I don't know. I've been trying to figure it out myself."

"This is coming out of left field," Reed said. "How are we going to prove anything? Do you need a couple of my guys?"

"Not yet," Joe said. "But you might want to let them know what's going on so they'll be ready. I'm on my way up the mountain to see if I can find that van in Eldon Cates's elk camp. If I find it, we can go after Eldon."

"In this storm?"

"It's just snow, Mike," Joe said. "It doesn't look to be as bad as they were predicting. If we only worked in good weather, we wouldn't get much done around here, would we?"

Reed snorted.

"There's another thing," Joe said. "I've been thinking about Tilden Cudmore."

"What about him?"

"We all wondered how he could possibly be innocent in regard to April's attack after her stuff was found on his place and in his car, right?"

"Yes."

"Well, I want you to think about something," Joe said as he turned off the highway onto the county road that would lead him to the Lek 64 two-track. No one had driven on the road since the snow started, and it was untracked. "Think about patrolling this county every day. You—and me—always keep an eye out for anything unusual. We notice cars we've never seen before, or out-of-county plates. We notice out-of-state plates, or pickups with two or three men inside—that kind of thing. But what we don't notice is normal activities. We just kind of shunt them aside."

"I'm not quite getting what you're saying," Reed said.

Joe continued. "We don't even see the propane truck making its rounds. We don't notice the mail carrier on her route or the garbage service. We see them so often, they turn invisible, because we're only tuned to people and activities that aren't part of the day-to-day. They hide in plain sight."

Reed said, "Like a sewage-service pump truck."

"Exactly," Joe said. "Like C&C Sewer and Septic Tank Service. I probably see that truck, or trucks like it, five times a day and never even think about it. You probably do, too. They're all over, but we just don't see them."

Reed said, "Hold on." Joe could hear the sheriff speaking to someone while he held the phone away from his mouth. "Tell the commissioners it's going to be a minute."

Then back to Joe: "I see where you're going with this. You're saying Eldon could have planted evidence at Cudmore's place and in his vehicle and no one would have given a second glance. He could roll his pump truck onto Cudmore's property and no one would even look up."

"Right," Joe said. "And I bet if you take a look at that big key ring Eldon has on his belt, you'd find a key to the front gate of the HF Bar. They probably have a contract with him and they wouldn't even notice him when the ranch is in full swing. He comes and goes, and his pump truck is big, but it's also invisible."

"I hear you," Reed said. "But if what you're saying is true, you're back to thinking it was Dallas who beat April and dumped her. That the Cates family was covering for him by planting evidence at the Cudmore place."

Joe said, "Yup."

"It also means an innocent man hung himself in my jail because of the pressure we put on him."

"Unfortunately, yes."

"Tilden Cudmore ended up like Tilden Cudmore always thought he would: persecuted by the government."

"You said it, not me."

"That's a lot of speculation, Joe."

"It is."

"But it sort of makes sense."

"It does."

"We need real evidence before we can move on anything, but I'll run this by Dulcie and see if she can shoot any holes in it."

"Good."

"Still, though," Reed said, "it doesn't account for a couple of things. One, why did they ambush Nate Romanowski? Two, what happened to Olivia Brannan?"

Joe almost overran the two-track that intersected the county road, but he recognized it and turned right.

He said, "I just found the road into the mountains and I'm taking it. We may lose our connection real soon."

"Call me on my cell phone either way," Reed said. "I'll reschedule this damned meeting I'm in and call Dulcie. We'll be ready to move if you find something."

BECAUSE THE SNOW was coming from the west as the storm barreled down the mountain, it now swirled like a white kaleidoscope in front of the windshield. The volume of it had increased since he turned off the highway.

Joe couldn't focus his vision in the distance so he concentrated on keeping his front wheels in the two-track. Daisy seemed to sense his anxiety and she put her big head on his lap. She was warm so he didn't push her away.

The snowstorm was both good and bad, he thought. It was unlikely the Cateses would be out and about and see him on the road from their compound. But if the intensity of the snow kept building and turned into a patented Rocky Mountain spring whiteout, he ran the risk of getting lost or stuck.

Joe keyed the button on his dash-mounted GPS to record his current location. If nothing else, he'd be able to find his way back to where he started.

THE ONCOMING SNOW stopped swirling once he entered the trees at the base of the Bighorns. Instead, it sifted down through the pine branches like fine flour.

The lodgepoles closed in as the pickup serpentined up the mountain in a long series of switchbacks. A mile up the grade, the road got rougher and the canopy of branches closed in over the top of the cab. He remembered turning around at about this spot the first time he'd ventured up.

But it felt right, he thought. If Eldon's camp was up ahead, the last thing Eldon would do would be to improve the access road. The grade and condition of the road itself would turn back most visitors.

Then: *Whump.*

Joe nearly lost control of the steering wheel when something hit the passenger side of his truck. Daisy's head jerked up with alarm.

He looked over to see the mirror had struck a thick branch and had folded back against the passenger window. Joe looked at his reflection and observed, *He looks worried.*

And he was.

The tires ground over large slick rocks now, pitching the pickup right to left as it climbed. Snow-covered boughs smacked the windshield and dumped more wet snow over the hood.

Joe upped the speed of his wipers to compensate and to keep the glass clear.

"We're going to find it and get out," he assured Daisy. She looked up at him as if she understood.

HIS SITUATION CRYSTALLIZED as he shifted into four-wheel drive low to continue the ascent. Whether or not he found Eldon's camp, he could be in trouble. He could easily imagine getting high-centered and stuck on the boulder-strewn path during an epic spring storm. He was out of cell tower range and his radio crackled with static. Even the satellite phone he kept in his gear box in the bed of the pickup would likely not get a signal through the thick canopy of snow-covered branches overhead.

There were no openings in which to turn his truck around, and there was no way he could back it out down the switchbacks he'd taken. He had no choice but to keep going up.

SOUR THOUGHTS came to him as he climbed.

He'd assumed the Yarak, Inc. van had followed the Suburban up the trail. But how could a two-wheel-drive van have gotten up there, considering the fact that his pickup was barely making it?

He realized he might be completely wrong about the scenario he'd laid out for Reed.

Revis Wentworth could have lied about the two vehicles, or been so drunk he got the direction and the road they were on incorrect.

Joe imagined a fruitless grind up the eastern face of the Bighorn Mountains that resulted in him getting his pickup hopelessly stuck and him traipsing back down in knee-high snow at the same time his daughter was being brought out of her coma in a Billings hospital.

Then the road leveled, and even through the thick snowfall, he could see a slot in the rock wall ahead that appeared wide enough to drive his truck through.

THE STRIATION THAT FORMED the granite wall stretched out as far as he could see in either direction. Behind and above the twelve-foot wall, the timbered mountain continued to climb. But on the other side of the slot, there appeared to be an opening in the timber, a clearing.

He jumped out of his truck to move a log that blocked the entrance. As he moved it, he noticed how simply it came up and swung to the side. None of its branches were embedded in the ground and the base of the log was cut cleanly, meaning *it had been moved before*. Perhaps many times.

Joe got back in his pickup and slowly drove into the middle of Eldon Cates's elk camp.

WEATHERED GRAY CROSS POLES had been chained to the lodge-pole trunks to hang game carcasses. Each had a rusty block-and-tackle assembly at the midpoint of the game pole.

Several square-shaped tent sites were aligned around a blackened fire pit. Broken glass winked within the pit, as did beer bottle caps. Metal boxes were stacked against the inside granite wall. They were locked and bear-proof.

It was a terrific location for an elk camp, he thought. No wonder Eldon kept it a secret.

The white Yarak, Inc. panel van was located against the thick wall of trees on the south edge of the camp. It didn't look to be parked there as much as pushed there.

Joe approached it on foot with his shotgun barrel resting in the crook of his left arm. He noticed that both the front and back bumpers were practically wrenched from the van's frame, probably from tow chains they'd used to pull the vehicle up the rocky road.

He photographed the van from several angles as he got close to it. Other than the bumpers, it didn't appear to be damaged.

Joe took a breath before peering inside. He braced himself, hoping he wouldn't find Liv Brannan's body on the floor of the van. He exhaled his relief.

After pulling on a pair of leather gloves so he wouldn't leave additional fingerprints on the surfaces, he opened the vehicle and shot the interior with his camera. He recognized the hoods and jesses hanging from the inside walls as Nate's. Joe wondered what the Cateses had done with the falcons. He hoped they were still alive.

BACK AT HIS PICKUP, Joe tried again to see if he could raise a signal on his cell phone or radio. Nothing.

He dug his satellite phone from the back gear box and he tried to get a signal through the snowfall and tree canopy. It didn't work, either.

It was oddly quiet within the elk camp. Snow floated straight down and muted outside sound. There was about three inches of snow on the ground now, but not enough to be concerned about. How beautiful it looked, he thought. Even the worst scenes could be improved by a layer of white snow.

Joe placed the shotgun muzzle down on the floorboard and marked the location on his GPS for later. He called Daisy back into the cab and hoisted himself behind the wheel. He performed a three-point turn on the grounds of the campsite to head back down the mountain. There was an hour of daylight left and he thought there was no reason he shouldn't make it. Going down the switchback road would be faster than coming up. The only thing he had to worry about was not pushing too hard and sliding his tires off the rocks and the truck into the trees.

As he turned the wheel and pointed the nose of the pickup toward the slot, it suddenly filled with a pair of headlights that blocked the exit.

Joe recognized the pickup immediately by the steel pole and crossbeam in the bed: it belonged to Bull Cates.

IT HAPPENED FAST, so fast Joe almost didn't have time to react.

Bull slammed his truck into park and bailed out with a semiautomatic rifle loaded with a large magazine, the driver's-side door thumping the rock wall because it was such close quarters. He had to step back to close the door to give himself a shooting lane.

Joe considered flooring the accelerator of his own pickup in the hope that the head-on collision would knock Bull's vehicle out of the entrance. But Bull's truck was a three-quarter-ton four-wheel-drive, and Joe drove a half-ton Ford F-150. At best, he might push

Bull's vehicle back a few feet but he would probably injure himself in the process. Instead, Joe reached for his shotgun.

But Bull was faster. There was a sharp *crack*, a hole in Joe's windshield at eye level, and searing pain on the right side of his head.

He flopped more than dove to his right, pinning Daisy to the bench seat.

Bull was firing as quickly as he could pull the trigger.

Round after round punched through the windshield and exited through the back. Slivers of glass were everywhere, on Joe's clothing, in Daisy's coat, all over the seat, on the floorboards. As he writhed, trying to get even lower, he saw bright red blood on Daisy's head and shoulders, lots of it, but she didn't seem to be hurt.

Then he realized the blood was coming from *him*. Nothing bled like a head wound.

Bull apparently leveled his aim and Joe felt the bullets thump into the grille of his pickup and actually rock it back and forth on its springs. A bullet caromed off the front hood into the shattered windshield and the entire plate of glass imploded and fell into the cab like a collapsed roof.

Joe tried to recall how long the magazine was on Bull's rifle and tried to guess how many rounds he had left. He knew his truck had been hit at least twenty times, maybe more.

He reached up to the side of his head with his right hand and when he took it away it was covered with blood. He could actually hear it pattering on the fabric of the bench seat when it wasn't pouring onto Daisy. Joe couldn't tell how badly he was hit. His right eye socket was filled with blood and he wiped it clean with his shirt-sleeve to clear his vision. He recalled once encountering a hunter who flagged him down because he said he had a terrible headache. Turned out he had shot himself in the head. He died before the EMTs could arrive.

Suddenly, the cab filled with acrid steam. He recognized the smell as fluid pouring from the radiator through bullet holes onto the hot engine. It stung his eyes and made Daisy whimper.

Crack-crack-crack-crack-crack.

The pickup jerked with every shot, and it was remarkable how fast the punctured tires deflated.

Then silence.

TwENTY SECONDS OF SILENCE. Snow fell inside the cab through the frame of the missing windshield.

Joe could only guess what Bull was doing. Approaching the truck? Reloading? Waiting for Joe to rise up and look around so he could finish him?

Although his ears were ringing from the rifle shots, Joe heard a metal-on-metal sound and then the distinctive snap of a bolt being engaged.

Reloading.

Daisy whimpered again and Joe realized he was crushing her. He repositioned himself so she could breathe more easily. As he did, slivers of glass tinkled from the seat to the floorboards.

"Hey, game warden, are you in there?" Bull called.

Joe didn't respond.

"Good thing I took the long way home tonight and ran across them tire tracks in the snow. I followed them all the way here, but I didn't think it would be you."

The voice didn't sound any closer. Joe imagined Bull was still near his own truck, probably still on the side of it, since he'd been able to reach into the cab for his second magazine.

"I told you I'd get even with you for taking away my livelihood," Bull said. "I just never figured you'd come to *me*."

After a beat, Bull said, "Hey, I'm talking to you."

Joe didn't raise his head. He held Daisy down with his right hand and searched through the broken glass on the floor for his shotgun. When he closed his hand around the grip, he felt the piercing bite of dozens of tiny slivers of glass in the flesh of his palm.

Because she didn't like being confined, Daisy moaned.

Bull obviously heard it and mistook it as coming from Joe. He said, "What do you know? It sounds like you're hurt. I *thought* I got you with that first shot."

Joe pulled the shotgun closer to him.

"Since you seen that van, there was only one way this could go," Bull said. His voice was growing louder. He was cautiously approaching Joe's pickup. Joe could hear boots crunch in the snow.

Joe was at an odd position: facedown on the seat with a dog underneath him and the shotgun at his side. It would be difficult to scramble around to defend himself.

Slowly, he rolled to his back and squared his shoulders. He used Daisy as a pillow. He raised the shotgun so it was next to him on the seat, pointing toward the driver's-side door.

The crunching got closer.

Joe lowered his eyelids, but didn't shut them tight.

There was a beat of silence, then the top of Bull's face appeared in the driver's-side window. It vanished before Joe could react.

He waited, then Bull slowly raised back up. Joe saw the crown of Bull's cowboy hat with a dusting of snow on it, then the brim. Then Bull's narrow-set eyes. When Bull saw Joe's condition, saw the blood, his eyes scrunched in a smile.

Joe raised the muzzle and shot Bull in the forehead and he dropped out of view.

The sound of the discharge within the cab was so loud, all Joe could hear was a dull buzzing in his ears.

HE SAT UP and pulled on the door handle and kicked it open with his boot. The body, not two feet from the truck, thrashed in the snow for thirty seconds, then went still. A river of blood steamed through the snow like hot syrup. Bull died with the top half of his head gone and his arms and legs splayed out as if he were making a snow angel. The .223 Ruger Mini-14 tactical rifle lay at his side. The barrel was still so hot from all the firing, it had melted the snow around it.

Joe slid down from the seat. When his boots hit the ground, he swooned on rubber legs and he grasped the side mirror for support. Daisy jumped out and went straight to the body, sniffing it from top to bottom, her tail working like a metronome.

He was still holding the mirror bracket for support when he looked at his reflection. He thought, *No wonder Bull thought I was dead.*

Thick rivulets of blood covered his entire face. His collar and the front of his shirt were black with blood, and when he turned his head he could see where blood was still pulsing out of an ugly slash just above his right ear. He touched the wound with the tips of his fingers and found it numb. The bullet had broken skin and exposed a white line of slick bone. He'd never seen any of his skull before.

One more inch to the left and he would have been dead.

AFTER CLEANING HIS FACE with snow, Joe opened his first-aid kit and did the best job he could of taping a square of gauze over the wound. Within a few seconds, the gauze turned pink, but the blood had stopped flowing.

He was even able to clamp his hat back on.

When he turned and saw that Daisy was eating snow near Bull's body that had been colored with a mist of blood and bits of brain matter, he yelled harshly at her. She slunk away, looking humiliated.

Then he threw up between his boots and waited for the last of the adrenaline in his bloodstream to burn off.

27

Sheridan and Lucy Pickett stood shoulder to shoulder on a small open balcony they'd discovered on the fifth floor of the hospital—April's floor—and watched the snow fall on downtown Billings. Although it wasn't yet dark, the streetlights had come on below and they lit up the snowflakes like fireflies. The streets were black and wet and the girls could hear the distant sizzle of tires.

"God, I'm sick of winter," Sheridan said. "It seems like it's never going to end."

Lucy nodded in agreement. She was still a little surprised when her older sister talked to her like she was a peer. Although the circumstances that had brought them together were terrible, Lucy felt more mature and intelligent standing there next to Sheridan, who was both.

Since Sheridan had been away at college for three years, the family adjusted. When Sheridan came home for summers or holidays it got confusing because no one really knew what role to assume while she was back. Was it like before, or different? Sheridan seemed to want to maintain the independence she had gotten used to in Laramie, but at the same time she expected to be treated as she had been before she left, when it came time to having dinner, getting laundry done, and having her parents pay for everything. At the same time, her old responsibilities—feeding the dogs, putting away the dishes, vacuuming the living room—had fallen to Lucy, and Sheridan had no compulsion to take them back. The hospital seemed like a neutral location, though, neither home nor college. Lucy enjoyed being regarded as a peer by her sister. Finally.

"People use this balcony to smoke," Sheridan said, using the toe of her shoe to scrape flattened butts off the concrete. "I'm sure they're not supposed to, but they must come out here to light up when nobody is looking. You'd think doctors and nurses would know better, wouldn't you?"

"I guess."

"You'd be amazed how many kids I know who smoke cigarettes," Sheridan said. "Of course, even more of them smoke weed. It's just too easy to get down in Colorado now."

"I know some kids who smoke weed," Lucy said.

"That's too young."

"You should tell *them* that. I'm sure they'd stop," Lucy said with a sly smile.

Sheridan huffed. She obviously didn't like getting needled, even when she deserved it. Sheridan could be bossy and haughty because she was the oldest and most put-together. At least that's what everybody thought.

Sheridan said, "Don't *you* start smoking."

Lucy shook her head. "I tried it and it made my throat sore. I just didn't like it at all."

"Good."

"What about you?"

Sheridan watched an airplane descend toward the Billings airport up on the rimrocks above the city. She said, "I smoked weed with April once, back before she turned into a cowgirl. I guess I was trying to bond with her, sort of, during her outlaw period. I didn't like the way it made me feel. I *hate* not feeling in control. And don't you *dare* tell Mom and Dad."

"I won't. Was it yours or April's?"

"Hers." After a beat: *"Of course."*

"Do you think she'll ever be . . . normal?" Lucy asked her older sister.

"I don't know. She looks terrible."

"Mom said she looked worse last week."

Sheridan shook her head. "You just wonder, you know? What if she comes out of it with real brain damage? How are Mom and Dad going to cope with that? What if she needs constant care? If that's the case, maybe it would be better if . . ." Her voice trailed off.

"Don't say it," Lucy said.

"You're right."

The balcony door opened and Marybeth looked out and said, "There you two are." She sounded frustrated. "What are you doing?"

"Nothing," Sheridan said. "Just watching the snow. Did you think we were smoking?"

"Why would I think that?" Marybeth said.

"I was just kidding, Mom," Sheridan said, shaking her head.

"Aren't you getting cold?"

"A little," Sheridan said.

Lucy asked her mom, "How are *you* doing?"

"Fine," Marybeth said. "Well, not really. I can't get your father on the phone. I've called the house and his cell phone. Finally, I called the dispatcher and she said she'd try to raise him."

Both girls turned toward their mother. Whenever she referred to Joe as "your father," it meant she was angry with him. Sheridan said, "This sounds kind of familiar."

"I *know*," Marybeth said. "It happens all the time. But I don't want him to go off the grid *now*."

"You know Dad," Sheridan said. Lucy always envied her sister's close relationship with their dad. It was a result of being the oldest and also being the most willing to spend time in his world. At the same time, Lucy knew she couldn't fake interest in hunting, fishing, and driving around in a pickup, checking licenses.

Regarding Sheridan's comment, Marybeth just shook her head. Her eyes were hard.

"What does the doctor say?" Sheridan asked.

Marybeth took a deep breath as if to put her anger with Joe aside for a moment. "They've completely stopped the propofol drip. Now it's a waiting game. They're thinking she should regain consciousness by midmorning. They'll watch her vital signs all night and be on the alert for problems."

"What kinds of problems?" Lucy asked.

"Maybe a seizure," Marybeth said, reaching out and putting her hand on Lucy's shoulder. "It could be anything, I guess. But if she comes out of it on schedule and without problems, well, we'll know something tomorrow."

Lucy nodded.

"There's nothing we can do tonight except be with her and pray," Marybeth said softly.

"We could eat," Sheridan said. When both Marybeth and Lucy looked at her, she said, "Sorry, that sounded bad. What I meant was, we should have dinner and maybe get checked into the hotel. Then we could do shifts during the night so everyone gets at least a little sleep."

Marybeth considered it for a moment, then nodded briskly. Sheridan knew how much her mother loved a mission. "You're right. I'll call the hotel, and I'll get some dinner recommendations from the front desk. What do you girls want to eat?"

"Not elk steak," Lucy said.

"I'd *like* elk steak," Sheridan said, gently shoving her sister, who smiled. "I miss it."

Marybeth rolled her eyes, then told them she was off to make the calls. She said she also had to meet with the financial representative at the hospital administrative office about still-unresolved insurance issues.

"Are you two going to stay out here in the snow until it gets dark?" Marybeth asked.

Sheridan shrugged.

"Okay, I'll find you."

A few moments after their mother had left, Sheridan said, "Are you sure he's here?"

Lucy nodded.

"Where?"

"On the same floor. But they won't let us see him."

"We'll see about that. Follow me."

Lucy said, "Are we going to get in trouble?"

"Maybe. But he's my master falconer. I have a right to see him."

To Lucy, it sort of made sense. And if Sheridan was willing to try it, why shouldn't she?

SHERIDAN HAD DISCOVERED the storage room earlier that afternoon as she wandered the hallways. She told Lucy she'd watched a hospital staffer in scrubs push a laundry cart down the hallway to the door and press four buttons on a keypad to release the lock. The staffer didn't seem to notice that Sheridan was watching over his shoulder and that she could see which numbers he pressed. She'd waited for the man to leave before trying the code. It worked.

Sheridan pressed 7-7-7-1 and the two girls slipped inside and shut the door behind them.

The room seemed to serve as a transfer station between the hospital rooms and the laundry on some other floor. Carts of old scrubs and bed linens were crowded inside, and the walls were lined with shelving filled with clean bedsheets, towels, and other linens.

"Find something that will fit," Sheridan said, leaning over and rooting through the nearest cart. She pulled out a light green scrub top and held it to her chest, then discarded it as too large. "Try not to find something with blood on it."

Lucy froze.

"What, did you forget this was a hospital?"

"I'm not sure we should be doing this," Lucy said.

"It's an adventure," Sheridan said, pulling a pair of short, wrinkled scrub bottoms out of the pile. "Here—try these. An elf must have worn them and they might fit you."

"Funny," Lucy said drily.

"And look what we've got here," Sheridan said, opening the top drawer of a gray metal desk. Lucy could see it was filled with ID badges and lanyards.

"Probably people who don't work here anymore," Sheridan said, handing one to Lucy and looping another over her own head.

Lucy looked at the photo of a heavyset Hispanic woman on the ID Sheridan had given her, and said, "I don't look anything like Lupé Rodriguez."

Sheridan waved her off. "No one ever checks these things," she said, as if she'd done it a thousand times before. "Just watch my lead."

SHERIDAN CRACKED OPEN the door and peeked outside. Their streetclothes were on one of the shelves. Now Sheridan wore pale green and Lucy wore pale blue. Both sets of scrubs were wrinkled but clean.

"Clear," she said.

"Which way?" Sheridan asked Lucy once they were in the hallway. Lucy gestured toward the end of the hall, then right.

Sheridan walked with haste and whispered, "Move right along, Lucy. Pretend you have a purpose."

Lucy giggled.

"And don't giggle. Act like you belong here. And remember: if we get there, we've got to get in and get out fast before someone sees us or Mom comes back."

Lucy nodded. She glanced at their reflection in a window as they strode past. They looked authentic, she thought. She'd always liked dressing up, much more than Sheridan or April had.

When they turned the corner, there were two people in the hallway. A janitor in scrubs and blue vinyl gloves pushed a dust mop along the baseboard with his back to them. Next to him was a wheeled cart with a bright yellow Rubbermaid garbage bag, two shelves of cleaning supplies, and a sharps disposal tube on the side. A pop-up tent cone was set up where he was mopping that read CAUTION/CUIDADO. Farther down, a woman in a business suit with her back to them strode toward a closed door with a sign on it that read: AUTHORIZED PERSONNEL ONLY.

"Through there," Lucy said to Sheridan.

Her sister picked up her pace. She leaned in toward Lucy and said, "We need to get to the door before it closes."

Lucy nodded that she understood.

The woman in the business suit swiped a key card through a receptacle on the right side of the double doors and there was a soft click. Without turning around, she pushed through.

Sheridan sprinted ahead past the janitor and an empty nurses' station, Lucy on her heels.

As the doors wheezed shut, Sheridan slid her right foot on the polished floor and wedged it between the two doors before they closed and locked. It was a smooth move, Lucy thought. Sheridan reached back for her hand before pushing through.

The woman in the business suit kept going, her heels clicking like punctuation. She swiped her key card again and vanished inside an office.

As the doors closed behind them, Lucy saw Sheridan look over her shoulder. The janitor had seen them run past him, and Lucy guessed her sister wanted to make sure he wasn't dashing off to call security.

The doors closed tight and the lock clicked.

Sheridan said to Lucy, "Did that janitor look familiar to you?"

"I was running—I didn't look at him."

She shook her head. "There's no way I could know him, is there?"

Lucy shrugged.

"I got a really bad vibe from him," Sheridan said. "He's thin, but athletic-looking, I thought. He's got tattoos on his forearms and neck, but I guess everybody does these days. Did you see his eyes?"

"I told you I didn't get a good look at him," Lucy said.

"He's got a deadeye stare. He had cold eyes. I got a bad feeling off him. But I'm probably wrong."

Lucy thought Sheridan was doubting herself. She'd been wrong before, a few months ago, when she thought a fellow student was dangerous. She'd been wrong about the student and the result was tragic. Since then, no doubt, she'd not quite trusted her intuition as she once had. Lucy had never had that problem. She wished she could have gotten a better look at the janitor.

"Okay, never mind," Sheridan said. "Let's find Nate."

"There's some man who won't let anyone in," Lucy said. "Like a guard. I heard Mom and Dad talking about him."

"We made it this far. We have to try."

As she said it, a portly man in a sport jacket and tie appeared in the hallway. He was walking toward them, pulling on an overcoat. He didn't look like a doctor or an administrator and Lucy thought: *Oh no*.

"Come on," Sheridan said, sotto voce. "Act like you know where you're going."

Lucy fell in beside her. She hoped the man didn't look at her too closely and notice her age. Casually, Sheridan reached up and flipped her ID badge so that the photo and name couldn't be seen. Lucy did the same.

As the man got closer, he nodded to them. "Evening, ladies."

Sheridan turned on a smile and said, "Dinnertime?"

"It sure is," he said. Then he paused, looking hard at them. Especially at Sheridan, who stood with her head cocked and her mouth parted. Lucy was surprised how flirtatious and brazen Sheridan was being with him. It was a side of her sister she'd never seen before. Sheridan was drawing his attention toward her and away from Lucy, and Lucy was grateful.

While he looked deeply into Sheridan's eyes, Lucy took a glance at his credential and saw the name Dudley.

He said to Sheridan, "I don't suppose I could treat you to a quick bite?"

"What about my colleague?" Sheridan asked.

Dudley shot a glance at Lucy but she looked away as if embarrassed. She didn't want him to study her face.

"I'm kidding," Sheridan said. "I'm on duty. *We're* on duty."

"Maybe another time, then," Dudley said. "Do you work on this floor? I haven't seen you around."

"We fill in wherever they need us," Sheridan said.

"Well, I hope they need you around *here*," he said.

"Maybe."

"I'll keep my eye out for you," he said with a wink.

When he was gone, Sheridan said, "Creep."

"I think your instincts are right on about that one," Lucy said.

Sheridan tousled Lucy's hair as they walked down the hall. "Just follow my lead, little sister."

NATE'S ROOM WAS DIMLY LIT and he was the only one in it. An empty chair sat next to the bed with a paperback novel opened and turned facedown on the cushion. Probably where Dudley sat, Lucy thought.

Nate's eyes were closed and a plastic oxygen mask covered his nose and mouth. The covers of his bed were pulled up to his chin. His face was bruised and there was a bandage on his right cheek beneath his eye. Dozens of tubes and wires snaked up through the sheets, leading to monitors. His head was tilted to the side. If it weren't for the sounds of the machines clicking and the EKG screen that showed a heartbeat, Lucy thought he could have been dead.

He was a big man and he filled the hospital bed from end to end. Lucy had never seen him laid out like that.

"My God," Sheridan whispered. "At least he's still alive."

Lucy nodded, but stayed near the door while Sheridan approached him. Lucy could hear him breathing, in and out, through the oxygen mask. It was clouded with condensation.

Her sister said, "Nate, it's Sheridan, your apprentice. We're all up here to see April, down the hall. Well, Dad isn't here yet, but he will be.

"Look, you need to fight and get well. We need to fly falcons together someday, and you've got a lot still to teach me."

Lucy looked down at her shoes. Her eyes stung. Her sister sounded strong and sincere.

Then she heard Sheridan gasp, and when Lucy looked up, her sister had her hands to her mouth.

"What?"

Sheridan turned. Her eyes were huge. "He winked at me."

Lucy looked from Sheridan to Nate. He was just as still as he'd been when they'd entered the room. His head hadn't moved a half inch.

"He winked at me," Sheridan said again. "He opened his eyes and winked."

Lucy didn't respond.

"Really, he did," Sheridan insisted. She turned back to Nate and said, "Do it again. Show my sister I'm not crazy."

Nothing.

"Nate, come on. *Please.*"

After nearly a minute, Lucy said, "Sherry, maybe you *thought* you saw something. I believe you thought you saw him wink. But—"

"I *did*," Sheridan said.

Lucy shook her head, her palms up. "I'm not going to argue with you."

Minutes passed. Both Sheridan and Lucy studied Nate's face for some kind of movement, some kind of recognition from him that they were there.

Finally, Sheridan said, "We better get back."

Lucy agreed with her.

As they walked back down the hallway together toward the closed door, Sheridan said, "Maybe my mind is playing tricks on me."

"Okay."

"He opened his eyes for a second and he *winked* at me."

"Okay."

"Or maybe I just wanted him to so bad, I thought he did it."

"Maybe."

Sheridan reached out and pulled Lucy close as they walked to the storage room to change back into their clothes.

TIMBER CATES watched them pass by through a half-inch opening of the maintenance closet door where he'd found the cart.

He recognized the older one, although she'd been behind him in school by quite a few years. The younger one he'd never seen before, but they looked so similar they had to be sisters.

What were they doing wearing hospital scrubs? And did the older one know who he was?

He had two brothers and so had only known brothers. The

Picketts had three girls. They'd all grown up together in the same county a hundred and twenty miles to the south, but except for Dallas and April, the families had never interacted in any way. He thought how strange that was, but he couldn't really come up with how he felt about it.

The things he did for Dallas, he thought.

Or more accurately, the things he did for his *mother*. Dallas probably didn't even know he was out of prison.

Timber was assured that everything was fine and that he hadn't been recognized when the sisters emerged from the storage room. They'd changed from their scrubs to civilian clothing and they seemed to be joking with each other, the younger one teasing the oldest. They were good-looking girls, he thought. In any other circumstance, he'd probably make a run at them.

The mother, Marybeth, met them in the hallway, and the three of them went into the room of his target.

The ceramic knife was in his sock, hidden by the baggy right pant leg of his prison hospital scrubs. He hadn't even passed through a metal detector to gain entry to the hospital, so the precaution had been unnecessary. The prison ID, which he wore on a lanyard around his neck, looked similar enough to the ones they used at the hospital that it wasn't getting a second look.

Hell, he thought, he could have brought a gun. But the knife would do.

He'd wait. They'd all have to leave the room eventually.

28

Plumes of snow sprayed out from the tires as Joe barreled down the mountain in the foul-smelling cab of Bull's Ford F-250 meat wagon. Brass casings that had been ejected during the fusillade danced across the dashboard.

The snow wasn't falling as hard as it had been and there were breaks in the clouds. The big spring storm that had been predicted didn't turn out to be all that big, he thought, although it had dumped six to eight inches that would remain in the forest overnight and it made the road down the mountain slick and treacherous. He had less than an hour of light.

Joe had left his own pickup where Bull had shot it up in the elk camp. He doubted it could be repaired after being hit twenty to thirty times with high-powered rifle rounds.

He thought: *Another one.*

Daisy was on the bench seat beside him and Bull's lifeless body rolled around in the back. Joe had tried to wrestle the mass into the bed, but it was too heavy and ungainly. At one point, he'd sprained a muscle in his back while trying to lift Bull's upper torso onto the tailgate far enough that he could release his grip and push the legs up and over the lip, only to have the body slide off into the snow again. Bull's body was slick with blood. It was worse than loading a dead elk. At least with an elk, there were antlers to grab on to.

Rather than leave the body to the snow and predators, Joe had wrapped a chain around the legs and used Bull's own game winch to hoist the body into the air. He was then able to swing Cates's 280 pounds up and over the bed wall, where he lowered it into the back.

Despite the situation and the gore, Joe admired how well the game winch had been welded together. Probably Eldon's work, he thought. Bull was useless.

Had been useless.

JOE'S SHOTGUN LEANED AGAINST the bench seat, muzzle down. Next to it was Bull's Ruger Mini-14. It was still warm to the touch.

The inside of the cab reeked of sour, spilled beer and whiskey, bloodstains, motor oil, and rotting food in fast-food wrappers on the passenger-side floorboard. There was a long crack through the front windshield and a dead rabbit on the console that Bull must have shot along the way to the camp.

But the pickup ran well, and the tires gripped the slick rocks on the road better than Joe's pickup had on the way up. He was making good time.

He knew if the dispatcher was trying to reach him he was out of touch, since Bull's pickup obviously didn't have a radio. Joe realized he'd left his handheld radio in his pickup back at the elk camp and he cursed himself for forgetting it.

Then he checked his cell phone. Ten percent battery life and still no signal. Naturally, he'd left the charger back in his truck as well.

He glanced down at the gauges. Unless the fuel gauge was broken, it looked like the pickup was almost empty.

"Bull, you idiot," Joe said aloud.

He'd never make it all the way to the highway, he thought. The closest place that might have gasoline was the Cates compound.

And it was where he was headed anyway.

WHEN THE TREES CLEARED, Joe's phone came to life with a quick series of pings.

He pulled it from his pocket and saw there were five missed calls from Marybeth. His phone now had five percent battery life left, which would be just a few minutes of talk time.

Joe had a decision to make and he didn't like it, but he punched the preset for Sheriff Reed's cell phone. He didn't have enough time to go through the office's receptionist. When he raised the phone to his ear, he winced at the jolt of pain from the bullet wound.

"Joe?" Reed said through a mouthful of dinner.

"Mike, listen to me. I'm on my way down the mountain right now and my phone is about to die on me. I found Eldon's elk camp and Nate's van was ditched there. Bull showed up and started blasting away—"

"Are you hurt?"

"Mike, please. I'm fine. But Bull's dead. I'm in his pickup because mine was shot up. I'm headed toward the Cates place right now. I need you to put out a high-priority call to your guys and any LEs in the area to converge on the compound as quickly as they can get there. I don't even care if Chief Williamson fires up his MRAP, because we know Eldon will be armed. I don't know the connection between Nate and Eldon, but it's there."

"Jesus," Reed said.

Joe could picture the sheriff pushing his chair back from the table with one hand and wiping his mouth with a napkin held in the other.

"What about Olivia Brannan?" Reed asked.

"I didn't find her body. It's possible she's buried on the compound or maybe even still alive. I don't know."

"How soon will you get there?"

"Ten, fifteen minutes," Joe said.

He was on the two-track now. There were two sets of tire tracks in the road before him: his and Bull's.

"We can't get there that fast, Joe. Can you pull up and wait?"

He could look off the sagebrush bench now and catch glimpses of the Cates compound in the swale below. Although it was almost too dark to see, Joe could make out Eldon's red pump truck cruising across the untracked snow in the equipment yard, headed toward the edge of the outbuildings. Puffs of exhaust rose in the cold air from dual pipes.

"No," Joe said. "Something's going on down there."

"What?"

"I don't know."

"Okay," Reed said. "I'll put out the word and we'll get there as soon as we can. Joe, don't do anything stupid and don't get yourself hurt."

"Yup," Joe said. "Please call Marybeth. Tell her I'm all right and I'll call her as soon as—"

His phone died. He'd used up all of the battery and he had no idea whether Reed had heard any of his last message.

29

Brenda stood at the edge of the root cellar doors, wearing her heavy winter coat. Liv saw she was wearing the same scarf over her hair that she had worn when she introduced herself as Kitty Wells. It was almost dark out.

Brenda didn't look down. Instead, she peered off into the distance and motioned with her arms, indicating *Come on, come on.*

Liv was confused. But when she heard the low rumble of heavy equipment, she realized what drew Brenda's attention.

She said, "Brenda, *what's going on?*" Her voice was flushed with panic.

Brenda shushed her with her hand, then continued gesturing.

Liv could hear the sound of a truck entering the compound.

When Brenda finally bent slightly and looked down, Liv thought she could see tears on her cheeks.

"It's time, girl," Brenda said. "Eldon's back with a full load."

Liv closed her eyes.

"Put all them dishes and the silverware in the bucket. How'd you like the pork chops? I made 'em especially for you this time. Eldon and Bull will have to wait for theirs later on tonight. At least, if that damned Bull ever shows up. And Dallas, too. He saw this snow and took off an hour ago on that snowmobile. But I bet he'll be back later for his dinner."

She talked to Liv as if Liv cared about these details.

Liv said, "You don't have to do this, Brenda. I told you, I won't talk."

Brenda ignored her and started lowering the bucket hand over hand with the rope.

"Just put everything inside, sweetheart," Brenda said. "Don't make this any harder than it already is."

"Are you really going to bury me in raw sewage?"

"Don't think of it like that."

Liv felt cold fear spasm through her. "How in the hell can I think of it any other way?"

"Don't get hysterical, darling."

"Why are you doing this to me? Why don't you just shoot me and get it over with?"

"Shhhhhh."

The pump truck was coming toward the root cellar. It was still out of view. Liv heard a squeak of brakes. Then it began to back toward the opening.

Reep-reep-reep.

As it got closer, the warning increased in volume. Liv saw Brenda glance up at it and cock her head to the side to guide it in. She had moved to the other side of the opening so that the bumper of the truck wouldn't knock her into the root cellar.

Brenda was suddenly lit up in red from the taillights. Liv could smell the exhaust of the big truck now, and she saw a bronze valve, like a snout, ease over the opening of the cellar.

"Don't come any closer, Eldon," Brenda shouted. "You're far enough."

To Liv, she said, "Put them dishes in the bucket. I can't bear to lose a place setting."

The sheer unreality of the situation almost overwhelmed Liv. Brenda was concerned about her dishes getting buried in filth? *That's* what she was concerned about?

"Eldon," Brenda said. "That's good right there."

Liv raised up her hands for the bucket as it lowered. She looked up to see that Brenda was distracted by the proximity of the release valve of the pump truck.

Liv grabbed the top of the bucket in a firm grip and yanked down as hard as she could, putting all of her weight behind it. A guttural sound came out of her as she did it.

Instinctively, Brenda didn't let go in time. And now she pitched forward off balance, pausing for a half second on the edge of the opening and windmilling her arms before falling in.

Liv threw herself to the side of the wall so she wouldn't get hit. Brenda dropped fast, her body hitting the floor with a horrible crunching sound like a full bag of ice cubes dropped on pavement.

Reep-reep-reep.

The ear-piercing sound filled the hole.

Liv bent over Brenda, who had landed facedown. Her housedress was flopped up on her backside, exposing her thick white thighs and knee-high support hose, and her coat had bunched up on her shoulders. Brenda's arms were splayed out on either side. Her head was turned toward Liv and her eyes were open.

Brenda's eyes bore into Liv with so much hatred that Liv shuddered.

But she couldn't move. Brenda Cates was alive, but she'd broken her neck in the fall.

Liv's words were absorbed by the *reep-reep-reep* when she said, "God forgive me for what I'm about to do." Somehow, though, Brenda must have heard her because her eyes got even harder.

The *reep-reep-reep* sound suddenly cut out above and the motor sputtered to a stop.

"Brenda?"

It was Eldon. He'd shut the motor off and was clambering down out of the cab of his pump truck.

"Brenda, where are you? Where did you go?"

Liv knew if Eldon saw Brenda's damaged body down there, he'd likely grab his gun and start blasting. She knew she could try to wedge herself beneath Brenda's bulk, make herself harder to hit, or . . .

ELDON SAID, "Oh no. What the hell happened?"

He was bending over the opening, looking down, the beam of his flashlight moving gently over Brenda as if caressing her with light.

The pool of light found Liv. She was on her side, legs and arms splayed out as if *she'd* fallen, too. She kept her eyes closed even as the light turned the inside of her eyelids orange.

Then it was gone.

"Oh nooooo," he said, his voice choked with emotion.

When the light vanished, Liv opened her eyes a crack and found Brenda still glaring at her from a few feet away. Liv had never experienced so much raw, focused hate in her life. But this time, instead of shuddering, she grinned.

She whispered, "What's wrong? Cat got your tongue?"

Then: "You can watch what happens next."

AFTER THIRTY SECONDS of Eldon's panicked shouts to Bull for help, which went unanswered, and then to Dallas, who wasn't there, he slid the ladder into the root cellar. The feet of it settled between Brenda and Liv and broke up their staring contest.

As Eldon backed down the ladder, he grunted with each step. Liv closed her eyes again in case he shined the flashlight at her.

Eldon reached the floor and immediately turned to Brenda. He bent down over her, stroked her hair and back, and said with grateful astonishment, *"You're still breathing."*

Liv cracked her eyelids to see that Brenda's eyes were on Eldon in a sidewise glance. They looked desperate. She was trying to warn him.

"What happened? Did you fall in? Don't tell me I hit you with the back of the truck and knocked you in here."

As quietly and gracefully as she could, Liv rolled to her feet and grasped the rock in the wall. It pulled free, but it was heavy.

Brenda's eyes clicked back and forth between Eldon hovering over her and Liv approaching him from behind with the rock raised unsteadily over her head.

Eldon said, "Did that nigger bitch get you down here somehow?"

Before he could turn around, Liv smashed the stone down on the crown of Eldon's head and he rolled forward onto Brenda, whimpering like a wounded dog.

Blood streamed down the sides of his face onto Brenda's coat and back.

BEFORE SHE MOUNTED the ladder, Liv looked over her shoulder. Eldon's arms and legs were twitching slightly and the back folds of his C&C Sewer and Septic Tank Service uniform shirt tightened and relaxed. He was still breathing as well. He was a tough old man with a really hard head, she thought. That rock would have instantly killed anyone else.

She climbed the ladder recklessly, once losing her footing on a rung and nearly falling back into the cellar. The near-accident focused her attention and she climbed out very deliberately the rest of the way. But when she reached open air and felt the sting of the cold fresh wind on her face, she whooped.

Then she grasped the ladder and started to pull upward. It would not come free.

Liv yanked hard on it and there was some give, but not enough.

Was it stuck on something?

She peered down into the hole and cursed. Eldon's huge hand grasped the bottom rung. He was still on the ground, still on top of his wife, but he held the ladder in a death grip. Even with one hand, he had more strength than she did.

Liv looked around. The compound was silent. The only light was the porch light at the main house. Bull and Dallas were still away.

Maybe Eldon had some kind of tool in his truck, she thought. Something she could slide down the ladder or drop on Eldon to make him give up his grip.

She found a flathead shovel sticking up on the side of the pump unit and she pried it loose. Liv ran back to the root cellar and threw the shovel down blade-first like a spear. It bounced harmlessly off Eldon's back and clattered in the corner of the cellar. He still had that one-handed grip.

Then she thought about leverage. She couldn't outmuscle him, but . . .

SHE TWISTED THE LADDER hard to the right. It gave, but not enough. Then she violently reversed the twist to the left in a full rotation and it came free. She'd managed to wrench it out of his fingers.

When the ladder was up and out of the cellar and lying in the snow, she whooped again.

Hot tears stung her eyes and her cheeks. She didn't want to look back down in that hole, didn't want to see Eldon and Brenda Cates twitching down there like bloody salamanders.

She just wanted to be out of there.

That's when she looked up and saw headlights coming fast from the west.

30

The engine of Bull's pickup coughed, then raced, then coughed again. Joe glanced down and saw that the needle of the gas gauge was past the *E*, and he hoped he had enough fuel in the tank to get into the Cates compound.

He was surprised how dark it was now that the sun had finally dropped behind the mountains. There was still enough cloud cover to blot out most of the stars, and the only sign of life he could see ahead of him was a single porch light at the main house.

Where was everybody?

The motor shuddered and quit and the power steering went down and made the steering wheel taut. Joe pushed the transmission lever into neutral and coasted the last forty feet into the compound.

"That's it, Daisy," he said aloud.

As he reached down to kill the headlamps, he glimpsed movement on the far side of the compound in the vicinity of the outbuildings. Joe squinted to see better, but whoever it was had moved beyond the reach of the lights.

He started to get out with his shotgun but thought: Bull was a poacher. Poachers have spotlights. The grip for Bull's roof-mounted spotlight was overhead and Joe grasped it and thumbed it on.

There, shielding her eyes against the powerful beam, was Olivia Brannan. She was dirty and bloody and standing to the side of the

C&C Sewer and Septic Tank Service pump truck he'd seen moving across the yard from the sagebrush bench.

Joe closed his eyes for a second and breathed a sigh of relief. She was alive after all.

But she looked terrified.

"LIV BRANNAN," he called out while standing on the running board with the driver's-side door open, "it's Joe Pickett."

At the mention of his name, she froze for a second, then covered her face with her hands and dropped to her knees.

He could hear her sobbing as he ran though the snow toward her with his shotgun ready and Daisy on his heels. When she looked up, he was grateful they were tears of joy.

"What happened here?"

She hugged herself and said, "They kept me in that hole back there after they shot Nate. I just now got out. Just now."

He kneeled down in front of her and put his hand on her shoulder. He could feel her tremble. When she spoke, she was half crying and half smiling.

"It was the Cates family," she said. "They kept me down there since it happened. They'd lower food down to me in a bucket, but they didn't know what to do with me so they decided to murder me."

Joe rotated on his heels and looked around. "Where are they now?" he asked, suddenly aware of how vulnerable the both of them were since they were bathed in light from the spotlight.

"Luckily, I made Brenda fall into the hole and I'm pretty sure she broke her neck. I hit Eldon on the head with a thirty-pound rock. They're both still down there," she said, gesturing over her shoulder.

"Eldon's probably dead by now. I *hope* Brenda is alive a while longer. She needs to know what it feels like to be kept prisoner in a damned hole in the ground."

"Liv, you have to be kidding me, right?" Joe asked. "They're both in that root cellar?"

"Yes."

"But you're okay?"

"I think I can say I am," she said, closing her eyes and squeezing two more tears out. "I'm probably going to be half crazy, though."

Joe stood and walked around her to the open cellar doors. The pump truck was backed up to it so that the discharge valve was poised over the opening.

Liv said, "They were gonna pour raw sewage in that hole and drown me. Then they were going to fill it up. That was going to be my grave. They were all ready to do it when I yanked on the dinner bucket rope and pulled Brenda in on top of me. That's how she broke her neck. When Eldon came down to check on her, I brained him."

Joe paused and looked back at Liv. She was rattled enough that she could be saying just about anything.

But when he shined his flashlight into the root cellar, he saw that she was telling the truth. Eldon lay on top of Brenda, apparently pinning her down. Their bodies were in the shape of an X. Eldon's entire head was black with blood.

"I was going to open that valve," Liv said from behind him. "I was going to smother them with everything they have in that truck, but then you showed up."

"Glad I did," Joe said.

"We could still do it."

"Let's not."

"Whatever you do, don't go down there," she said. "They may look harmless, but those are two of the most dangerous psychotics you'll ever run across, especially Brenda. Just leave them where they are."

Joe said, "What you did . . . you are one tough lady."

"I am," she said.

Joe said, "The sheriff is on his way. I'm sure he'll call the EMTs. Those two may be rotten, but we don't just leave people in a hole."

"That's what they did to me," Liv said. Then: "What day is it?"

Joe had to think about it. "Monday, March Twenty-fourth."

"I was down there for six days," Liv said. "This was going to be my last night on earth."

Joe shook his head. It was a lot to take in.

She raised her hands to the sides of her face in alarm. "They're not all dead, though. Bull is out there somewhere and he should be back any minute for dinner. He *never* misses dinner. I thought when I saw your truck out there, it was him."

"You don't have to worry about him," Joe said. "He's going to miss dinner tonight."

"Good," she said. She didn't ask any more.

"What about Cora Lee?" Joe asked.

"Cora Lee is gone. She took off for good."

"And Dallas?"

"Dallas is out riding a snowmobile somewhere."

"Now?"

"That's what Brenda said."

Joe shouldered his shotgun and turned toward the mountains. He searched the far-off black timber for a single headlamp that would indicate Dallas coming home.

"They killed Nate," Liv said softly.

"You mean they shot him," Joe said. "Nate's alive."

"He *is*?" Liv said, getting to her feet. "My God. I had no idea. Where is he now?"

"It's not all good news," Joe said, telling her about Nate's condition in the hospital in Billings.

"I tried to see him when we went to visit April," Joe said.

Liv nodded. Her face was suddenly troubled and she closed the gap between them. "It was Dallas who hurt your daughter. Brenda told me."

Joe remained still.

"She said Dallas did something to your daughter, so they had to protect him. She said Eldon and Bull pulled his shoulder out of the socket and beat him up so he'd look more injured than he was. And they lured Nate and me up here so they could take Nate out before he could help you find the asshole who hurt April."

Joe was tight-lipped when he asked, "Did she say what Dallas did to April?"

"No. But I'm guessing you already know."

Joe said, "I do," but he could barely hear himself over the roaring in his ears.

"I'm sorry, Joe," she said. "I'm sorry for you and I'm sorry for Nate and I'm sorry for me."

Then she pointed toward the root cellar. "I'm *not* sorry for them. That's one toxic white trash family that's better off dead. Let's open the valve."

For a second, Joe considered doing it. But when he looked over her shoulder and saw a long stream of vehicles coming from the direction of Saddlestring, he said, "You stay right here. Don't open the valve. Just tell the sheriff everything you told me."

She said, "You're going after him, aren't you?"

"Yup."

"Before you do, tell me what happened to Bull."

Joe nodded his head in the direction of the F-250. "Bull's body is in the back of his pickup. He fired on me and I killed him."

"Is that what happened to your face?"

Joe reached up and touched the bandage. He'd forgotten about his wound. He nodded his head.

"Stay right here, Liv."

He turned on his heel and strode toward Eldon's equipment shed. He remembered seeing the trailer with two snowmobiles. He heard Liv behind him. She was standing over the opening of the root cellar, shouting down into it.

"Did you hear that, Brenda? Eldon's brains are bashed out. Bull's deader than hell. And your precious Dallas is next."

Joe paused and looked over his shoulder to make sure Liv wasn't trying to unscrew the valve. She wasn't. She was bending over the opening with her hands on her hips.

"Look up at me, Brenda. I want to see your eyes. I want you to see that I'm up here and you're down there and I'm ferocious. *Ferocious!*

"Oh, and your pork chops weren't really that good. Neither was the fried chicken. My mama can run circles around you in the kitchen, and so would I."

Joe thought, *Pork chops? Fried chicken?*

But there was no doubt in his mind that Liv was ferocious.

———

IT WAS THE SECOND TIME in recent memory that he'd found himself roaring through a winter forest on a borrowed snowmobile. This time, though, he was barely in control of his anger.

Dallas was easy to follow. There was only one snowmobile track that left the compound, crossing the sagebrush bench toward the mountains, and Joe rode right on top of it. He'd strapped the shotgun across the cowl with bungee cords. He'd not even bothered with snowmobile boots or a suit since the temperature was already rising above freezing after the storm passed.

He thought of April in the hospital bed, Dallas grinning at him with his boxlike smile, and Liv Brannan shouting like the devil herself into the hole in the ground.

He'd already killed one Cates brother tonight, and the two monsters who'd conceived him were crumpled on the floor of a root cellar.

THE TRACK VEERED as it got within a quarter mile of the timber on the side of the mountain. For whatever reason, Dallas had made a sudden turn. Joe overshot it but was soon back on his trail.

It wasn't long before Joe saw why Dallas had changed direction.

A five-by-five-point bull elk stood gasping in the snow-covered sagebrush, dual spouts of condensation pulsating out of its nose. The snow around it was churned up and mixed with bits of soil and sagebrush. It didn't run away even as Joe got within ten feet of it.

There were clumps of grass on the tips of the bull's antlers, snow on its shoulders and back, and a wild look in its eyes. The bull elk was exhausted and too tired to run away.

Joe slowed down as he passed it, then speeded back up with a twist of the hand throttle.

What had happened was obvious by the tracks in the snow. The storm had likely driven the elk herd down from the forest, onto the flats. Dallas had seen the herd coming down the mountain at dusk. He'd turned toward them and opened his throttle and chased the entire herd for a half mile or so, then closed in on a bull. Like a steer wrestler in a rodeo, he'd leapt from his snowmobile onto the bull and twisted it down by the antlers. He'd bulldogged an elk. The rumors Joe had heard years before were obviously true.

It was an astonishing athletic feat, Joe knew, but it was also foolish and cruel. Elk that survived the winter were weak by spring. Chasing them through snow and wrestling them down could stress them further and likely injure or kill them. Not that Dallas would care . . .

JOE FOUND ANOTHER BULL still on its side and breathing hard, a hundred yards into the forest. It must have been quite a battle, Joe observed. Chunks of bark had been sheared off pine trees by antler tips and pine needles carpeted the snow.

The animal had been injured somehow while being taken down, and blood was spritzed across the top of the snow.

DALLAS WASN'T DONE, though. The track went farther up the mountain, zigzagging across the churned-up trail of the fleeing elk herd. Joe stayed on it.

An old cow elk lay dead in the path and Joe almost hit her. He turned at the last second, and the left front sled nicked her haunch. She'd likely died from exhaustion, Joe knew. He could tell by her expanded form that she was pregnant with a calf.

Which made him even angrier.

THE TREES OPENED INTO a large mountain meadow painted dark blue by the starlight, and there was Dallas Cates, standing over the prone body of another bull elk, his snowmobile idle and rumbling thirty feet to the left of him.

He'd bulldogged another one.

When the beam of Joe's headlamp lit up Dallas's face, he was grinning and breathing hard from his latest conquest. There was blood and swatches of tawny elk hair on the front of his snowmobile suit.

He looked up and squinted, and the boxlike smile appeared. He was proud of himself, Joe thought. *Look at what I did. Three of 'em!*

He wanted to share the moment and be admired by whoever was coming his way on the snowmobile. Probably Eldon or his brother Timber. Dallas held out his hands, palms down, saying *Slow down*.

As Joe got closer and started to brake, Dallas's eyes narrowed. He recognized who was on the machine. Dallas's left hand shot up and unzipped the front of his suit and he reached inside with his right.

Joe caught a silver glimpse of the butt of a pistol. Dallas was trying to draw it out, but it had gotten caught on the inside of the bulky fabric of his snowmobile suit.

Instead of stopping, Joe cranked the right grip to full throttle and sat back and braced himself. The snowmobile surged forward as if kicked from behind.

Before Dallas could pull the gun, or duck to the side or run, the front end of the machine bucked and Joe ran him over. The headlamp exploded on impact and the plastic cowl cracked down the middle. Joe saw Dallas's arms flail and vanish underneath the machine, and he felt the big bump under the back end of the snowmobile as it passed over him.

Joe lost his grip on the handlebars for a second after the crash, but found them again in time to turn sharply and avoid smacking into a tree at the edge of the meadow. When he got the battered snowmobile looped around, he saw the writhing black smudge in the snow that was Dallas.

Joe cruised back and killed the engine. He dismounted and walked over to Dallas's snowmobile and shut it off, too.

After the high whine of his machine, the forest seemed silent and still. All he could hear was the ticking of the cooling engines, the labored breathing of the bull elk, and a moan from Dallas. Joe found the .45 semiauto in the snow ten feet from where Dallas lay.

Joe said, "I forgot to say 'Freeze.'"

Dallas moaned again and rolled painfully onto his side. Joe could tell from the odd angle of Dallas's left leg that it was broken. Dallas yelped when he drew a breath. Broken ribs again, too.

Joe said, "You shouldn't have gone for that pistol. Congratulations: you're my second Cates of the day."

THIRTY MINUTES LATER, Joe saw the lights of the Cates compound wink through the trees. Dallas was strapped to the back of the seat, facedown and groaning. Joe had taken Dallas's machine because the one he'd borrowed was a mess.

He was pleased on the way down to see that the first bull had recovered enough to wander back into the forest to rejoin the herd. Unfortunately, the second and third bulls had died from their injuries and exhaustion.

SHERIFF REED met him in the yard when Joe rumbled in and killed the motor. The flashers and lights of twelve law enforcement vehicles lit up the compound.

Reed looked at the writhing body on the back and said, "Dallas?"

"I was going to arrest him, but he pulled this," Joe said, handing the .45 butt-first to Reed.

Reed took it and said, "We found Bull in the back of his pickup. Not much left of his head, though."

Joe climbed off the machine. His knees and lower back ached from the ride.

"What happened to your face?" Reed asked.

"Bull shot me. Did you find Liv Brannan?"

Reed nodded. "She's in my car. Did you know . . ."

"Yup."

"My God," Reed said. "Six days. Did Brannan tell you that Dallas was the one who attacked April?"

Before Joe could answer, Reed gestured to Dallas tied onto the back of the machine and said, "Never mind. I can see that she did. I'll call for another ambulance."

Joe was puzzled.

"Brenda Cates is still alive. She's on her way to the clinic in the ambulance. She'll probably never have the use of her limbs again. I guess she's just too mean to die."

"Eldon, too?"

Reed shook his head. "He didn't make it."

Joe said, "Mike, I know there's a lot to sort out here, but I've got to get to Billings. Mind if I borrow one of your trucks?"

Reed groaned, and said, "You're hell on trucks, Joe. But sure. Take Deputy Boner's."

"Thank you."

Reed looked out over the compound and shook his head sadly. "The whole damned family," he said. "Except one."

31

Timber Cates waited in the maintenance closet after he'd seen the three Pickett females leave the hospital room. They'd left with their coats on and had walked together to the elevator.

Timber didn't know much about women, but he did know they always forgot something.

Three minutes after they'd left, the elevator chimed and the oldest daughter got out and returned to the room. She emerged clutching her phone.

He gave it another ten minutes, then he pushed his service cart through the door and let it shut behind him. The hallway was empty and the nurses' station was temporarily vacant.

The clock at the end of the hall said it was seven-fifteen p.m.

TIMBER DIDN'T GO STRAIGHT to the target room. Earlier that evening, he'd noted the closed-circuit camera located in a mirrored half-moon housing. If someone was monitoring the hallways, he thought, he didn't want to dash toward April Pickett's room and give them any reason to notice him.

He dry-mopped his way up the hallway, working the baseboards and keeping his face turned away from the camera. The open door to his target was less than twenty yards away.

Timber could feel the hard flat blade of the ceramic knife against his skin where his sock held it to his right ankle. He'd learned in Rawlins to always be aware of his hidden shiv and to practice pulling it out as swiftly as possible, but at the same time to never look down at it, even instinctively.

ONCE, he'd had a confrontation with a beaner who'd just arrived in the general population and didn't know enough to show Timber the deference he deserved. The two had squared off in the corner of the yard. Words were exchanged, and Timber held his ground. Then the man had glanced down toward his shoe right in the middle of the stare-down.

The beaner hadn't gone for it, but he didn't need to. He'd all but told Timber that, yes, he had a knife.

Timber hadn't hesitated. He'd pulled his own shiv and slashed the beaner's throat with one swift move, then discarded his knife through the chain-link fence. The beaner went down. Timber stood back and saw the guards pull a sharpened toothbrush from the beaner's sock.

They'd suspected Timber for the attack but couldn't prove it. And the beaner knew if he talked to them he'd never talk again.

SO TIMBER NEVER LOOKED down at his right ankle, even as he parked the service cart in front of the hospital room doorway, leaving just enough space for him to enter behind his mop.

She was in bed, of course. Her eyes were closed and she was breathing softly. Her face was slack and bruised, but he recognized her from the photo they'd provided him. She was a hottie, all right.

Dallas, he thought, was a damned fool.

TIMBER THOUGHT HE HEARD a door open out in the hallway, the door that was marked AUTHORIZED PERSONNEL ONLY, so even though he was now in the girl's room, he bent his head down and concentrated on mopping. If the person coming down the hall looked over the cart into the room, all they'd see was the hunched-over back of a janitor.

When he didn't hear footsteps, he guessed that whoever had opened the door had turned around and gone back down the hall. Probably a woman who'd forgotten something, he thought.

He leaned his mop handle against the foot of the girl's bed and bent to retrieve the ceramic knife. He fixed his eyes on her exposed white throat.

Timber started to hitch up his pant leg when he sensed a presence behind him. He rose quickly and reached for the mop handle to look the part when he felt a heavy blow on the right side of his head that disoriented him and made him let go of the mop.

Suddenly, roughly, he was physically turned around and shoved into the hallway. He ran into his cart and it rolled away. He tried to turn his head to see who was behind him, but another sharp blow created an explosion of stars in his eyes.

He was stunned and moving fast now—pushed and prodded so quickly he nearly tripped. He instinctively held his hands out in front of his face because he still couldn't see through the stars and he didn't want to be slammed into a concrete wall.

Timber felt a strong grip on the back of his belt, shoving him forward and guiding him at the same time. He shouted, *"Hey! Who are you?"*

His forearms thumped into a glass door, but he protected his face. It didn't matter, though, because the door gave way and it was cold and fresh-smelling, and whoever had him by the belt suddenly lifted him up just as his abdomen struck a metal rail of some kind.

The railing didn't stop his momentum and he was lifted up and over it, and he couldn't see or feel a thing for several seconds as he dropped through the air.

Then he did.

32

Joe winced as the emergency room doctor looped another stitch through his scalp to close the bullet wound. He kept his eyes averted and on Marybeth, who had marched him directly to the ER when he arrived at two in the morning. The doctor was a young South Asian man with a starter mustache and hipster glasses.

"Tell the financial people to put this on our tab," Marybeth said to the doctor, who smiled but indicated with a shrug he had nothing to do with billing.

"Don't worry," she said, sounding exasperated. "I'll tell them."

It was clear to Joe by the way she said it that the insurance coverage was still a mess. He tried not to worry about it now.

AFTER THE DOCTOR CONFIRMED that Joe hadn't had a concussion, he peeled off his gloves and said, "You look like you'll make it, but you'll probably have a pretty good scar."

Joe nodded.

"We're required to report bullet wounds."

"Go ahead," Joe said, "but I think they've got that part covered back in Wyoming."

"You people shoot each other a lot, don't you?" the doctor said with disdain.

"Not really."

"Don't you all have guns?"

"Yup. So do you folks in Montana."

"I'm from Islamabad, Pakistan," the doctor said.

"Ah, that peaceful place."

"I'll leave you two now," the doctor said haughtily. "There will be somebody in here in a few minutes to dress that injury."

"Thank you," Joe said. "You probably did a better job than I did in a truck mirror."

"Obviously, yes," the doctor said, rolling his eyes, as he turned and walked out the door.

"Pleasant fellow," Joe said to Marybeth.

"I have to say I like the doctors upstairs much better," she stated.

"I'M SO GLAD you made it here," Marybeth said, sitting on the raised vinyl half-bed with him. "April could regain consciousness any minute. She's coming out of the coma quicker than they thought she would. I called the girls and they're getting a ride here on the hotel shuttle."

She said, "It's been a crazy night here. Some hospital janitor jumped off the balcony on our floor—the same balcony Sheridan and Lucy were standing on earlier. It happened while the three of us were at dinner. They found him dead on the pavement five stories below. The local cops and hospital security were all over the place for a couple of hours."

"Did you know him?" Joe asked.

She shook her head. "I don't know. I've gotten to know quite a few of the employees here, but his description doesn't fit anyone I've met. They've been really hush-hush about the whole thing: no names or anything. Apparently, the security camera in the hall wasn't working for some reason, so they can't tell how it happened. But I did hear one of the night nurses say that he might have been a fraud— that he might have gotten into the hospital using a false credential. That's a scary thing to think about."

Joe had no idea what to make of it.

"Nothing like *your* night, though," she said, putting her head on his arm.

He'd told her what had happened when they talked on the phone as he drove to Billings. Her immediate concern was for him and the bullet wound and for Olivia Brannan's mental health. She was also worried that Joe might get investigated for running over Dallas.

He'd said, "I'd do it again."

She'd sighed and said, "I'm sure you would, too."

Marybeth slid off the bed when the door handle turned, but instead of the nurse they were expecting for Joe's stitches, it was one of the neurosurgeons she knew from the fifth floor.

"There you are," he said to Marybeth. He nodded a greeting to Joe and said, "We think she's coming out of it. She's not conscious yet, but there's a marked increase in eye movement."

Marybeth clutched Joe's arm. "That's a good sign," she told him. "Come up as soon as you get that bandage put on."

"To hell with that," Joe said, sliding off the bed.

"Okay, I'll dress it," the neurosurgeon said. He taped a bandage on and they followed the surgeon down the hall and into the elevator. Joe felt Marybeth find his hand and squeeze it.

The doctor wouldn't look at either of them in the elevator. Joe figured he was trying not to give anything away, not to signal whether he was optimistic or pessimistic.

Joe squeezed back.

SHERIDAN AND LUCY had just arrived when Joe and Marybeth entered April's room. Both looked groggy from being awakened. Joe gave Sheridan a quick hug and kissed Lucy on the top of her head.

When he realized she was staring at him with a grimace, he said, "I had an accident."

"He got shot," Sheridan said. She'd obviously talked with her mother since Joe's call.

"Are you all right?" Lucy asked him.

"Dandy."

"Girls," Marybeth said. There was both dread and excitement in the way she said the word, and they all turned toward April in her bed. The neurosurgeon stayed in the room with his arms crossed over his chest.

Joe didn't know what to say or what to think. He wasn't as versed as his wife in the Glasgow Coma Scale, only that Marybeth seemed pleased there was rapid eye movement.

He thought it seemed voyeuristic in a way to watch April's eyes move underneath her closed lids. He couldn't help but think of Daisy and Tube when they "chased rabbits" while sleeping. What was she seeing? What was she dreaming?

"April," Sheridan said softly. "Wake up now. We're all here."

April's expression froze. Joe felt his heart start to break.

Then she opened her eyes. They were glassy and unfocused, and they reminded Joe of the first look that newborn Sheridan had given him in the delivery room twenty-one years ago. She had looked in his direction, but he hadn't been sure she was really *seeing* him.

"Mom, Dad," April said. "How long have I been here?"

Her voice was weak, unpracticed. But lucid.

Lucy said, *"Yes,"* and grasped her sister's hand.

"Eleven days," Marybeth said through tears. "You've been here eleven days."

"Jesus," April said in a croak. "Where is 'here'?"

"Billings," Marybeth said through a crooked smile as she fought back tears. "You're at the hospital in Billings. You've been in a coma so your brain could heal."

"A coma?"

"Yes."

"Like the movies," April said.

Joe heard the doctor chuckle behind him.

"We're so glad you're okay, that you're right here with us," Marybeth said. "You've got some injuries, but you're healing up. It was always the head injury we were worried about."

"You've been here the whole time?" April said, as if she couldn't comprehend it.

"Most of it. For moral support, if nothing else. Everyone was praying for you."

"Well," April said, "I guess it worked."

"Do you remember what happened to you?" Marybeth asked.

The doctor stepped forward and placed a hand on Marybeth's

arm. He said, "You might want to give her a chance to get her bearings first."

"No, I'm okay," April said. "I remember."

The doctor stepped back.

April paused for a minute and searched the ceiling. Then her face darkened and she said, "Dallas was driving. We were coming back from the Houston Rodeo and we fought the whole way because I found out the son of a bitch cheated on me. I wanted to come straight home and Dallas wanted to go to his house first. I told him to let me out of the truck then, and he backhanded me."

Joe jerked back as if *he'd* been backhanded.

"I got mad and slapped him across the face and told him to stop the truck right there. I was so mad at him I couldn't see straight. He'd hit me before and he swore it would never happen again, and I'd told him, 'You're goddamned right it won't.'"

April's filter for cursing hadn't come out of the coma yet, Joe thought.

Before Marybeth could prompt her to go on, she did: "I got out and started walking. Dallas tried to coax me back into the truck, but I wasn't having any of that—or him."

She tried to swallow, and said, "Can I have a drink of water, please?"

Sheridan practically knocked Lucy over to find a water bottle, and she held it to her sister's mouth while she drank.

"Thanks, Sherry," April said. "It's good to see you . . . and even Lucy."

Lucy smiled through tears at that.

"April, what happened next?" Marybeth asked.

"I walked for a while, but it was getting cold," she said. "I would have called you guys, but my phone was dead. Then this old crazy asshole pulled up and said he'd give me a ride."

Joe and Marybeth exchanged looks.

"I wasn't going to go with him," April said. "He drove this big Humvee thing that had stickers all over it. I thought he was a creep, but he said he knew you guys really well and he could get me home in ten minutes. I know, Mom, I shouldn't have gotten in."

Marybeth could barely speak. She said, "No, you shouldn't have."

"I know. But I just wanted to get home, you know?"

"What did he do to you?"

"All I can remember is that when I shut the door, he started asking me what I thought about Obama and Bush and 9/11. I told him to shut up, and out of the blue he slugged me on the side of my head. I remember my head hitting the passenger-side window. And I guess he slugged me again after that. I don't really remember what happened next. He hit me a lot harder than Dallas ever had."

April indicated to Sheridan she needed another drink of water, and Sheridan gave it to her. When some spilled down the side of her mouth, Sheridan used the edge of the bedsheet to wipe it off.

April turned to Marybeth and said, "I can't remember anything else. Did he rape me?"

"No. He beat you and dumped you on a county road. You weren't found until the next day. You could have died of exposure out there."

April looked to Joe. "Why did he do it?"

"We'll never know," he said. "He was crazy. His name was Tilden Cudmore and he hanged himself in his cell."

Her eyes got wide, then narrowed. "I'm glad he's dead," she said.

Lucy looked up as if to say, *She's back, all right.*

Joe said, "You're sure about all of this? That it wasn't Dallas who beat you and dumped you?"

"He punched me for sure," she said. "And I slapped him a good one and told him to stop the truck. But he went home, I guess, so he could be with his wonderful mama."

Everyone stood in stunned silence.

Finally, April reached out for Marybeth and they grasped hands.

April said, "I'm never running off with another dumb-ass cowboy for the rest of my life."

To Lucy, she said, "And don't you do it, either, girlie."

Lucy seemed insulted and said, "I'd *never* do that."

"I HATE TO BREAK THIS UP, I really do," the doctor said, approaching the bed. "But we've got to run a whole bunch of tests right now to make sure everything really is as good as it seems to be."

As the family filed out of the room, he said to Marybeth, "I'm very optimistic."

"You hid it well," she said. "But I am, too."

In the hallway, Marybeth hugged Sheridan and Lucy and they cried together. Joe backed off and leaned against the radiator with his hands on his hips.

Tilden Cudmore. He'd never believed it.

And neither, he suddenly realized, had Brenda Cates.

"I need to talk to your dad," Marybeth said to Sheridan and Lucy.

THEY STOOD at the railing on the balcony where the janitor had fallen. Joe was surprised the Billings PD had not blocked it off with crime scene tape, and that told him they didn't consider that a crime had taken place. It was dark on the pavement below and he couldn't see where the janitor had hit.

A band of pink haloed the eastern rimrocks with the first hint of morning sun. The streets below were virtually absent of cars.

Marybeth said, "Are you going to call Mike Reed?"

"Soon," Joe said. "I'm still trying to wrap my mind around what April told us."

"Why would Dallas let Brenda make it look like he was hurt worse than he was? Why would he go along with that if he didn't do it?"

Joe shook his head. He said, "I'm speculating, but I think she always thought he did do it, even when he said he didn't. She knew what he was capable of and she probably figured since he'd backhanded April and kicked her out of his truck—he probably admitted that—she knew he'd be suspected of a much worse crime. And he would have been. She might have thought he didn't know his own strength and that he could have hurt her worse than he realized—or that he was spinning what really happened into the best possible light. Either way, she convinced Dallas to come up with a whole different scenario—that he'd come home a few days early, that they'd broken up, the whole thing. She was trying to protect him, she thought. And Dallas let himself be protected that way."

"What about Nate?" she asked.

"Brenda was so convinced that Dallas did it, she did a preemptive strike on Nate so he couldn't help me nail him. Liv told me that."

"My God," Marybeth said. "Think about the results: Eldon is dead. Bull is dead. Brenda herself is likely a quadriplegic, if she even makes it."

Joe nodded.

She asked, "What is Dallas going to do when he recovers?"

"*If* he recovers," Joe said. "I broke his leg and smashed in his ribs. I don't know about internal injuries. But it'll be a long time before he hits the rodeo circuit again."

"If ever," Marybeth said.

"Yup."

She said, "Don't blame yourself for any of it. This is all Brenda Cates's doing. She could have been honest and come clean and not tried to manipulate everything like some kind of evil spider. If she would have done that, none of this would have happened."

Joe tried to take solace in that.

But Marybeth said what Joe was thinking. "Dallas is a hothead and we know he can be violent. He'll want revenge."

Joe said, "We can put Dallas away for a few years. I'm sure Dulcie will agree to file charges for the assault on April and maybe even for conspiracy for aiding and abetting Brenda's crimes. I've got him for wanton destruction of those elk and pulling a gun on me. I don't know. Maybe he'll grow up a little in prison and realize it was his mother that put him on this path."

"Maybe," Marybeth said.

But she didn't sound convinced.

SHERIDAN AND LUCY burst through the balcony door with wide eyes.

Joe's first fear was that something had happened to April, but Sheridan said, "Nate's gone!"

"*What?*"

"We talked to a couple of the security people," Sheridan said. "They're looking everywhere for him."

Marybeth gasped and covered her mouth with her hand.

"I *knew* he winked at me," Sheridan said. "I knew he did."

"Wait here," Joe said.

He strode down the hallway in the direction of the restricted area and was surprised to see Special Agent Dudley coming toward him.

The man was disheveled and he had the distraught look on his face of a friend who had been asked to watch a neighbor's cat but had let it get away.

"Do you know anything about this?" Dudley asked when he recognized Joe.

"I just heard. I'm here because of my daughter. How long has he been gone?"

"Ten hours," Dudley said. "Man, I'm going to hear about this . . ."

"Never mind that. What happened?"

Dudley glared at him. His voice was monotone, as if he were tired of telling the story. "I came back from dinner last night and started to sit down in my chair when he got out of his bed and put me in a sleeper hold. I tried to fight back, but I could tell he's done this kind of thing before. The next thing I knew, I woke up, gagged with medical tape and tied up with electrical cords, and the bastard was gone."

Dudley shook his head and stared at something fixed on the wall behind Joe.

"I don't know how long he was contemplating it before he made his move. But on his way out of the hospital, he stopped by the security room and erased the video feeds from this floor."

"Sounds like Nate," Joe said.

"We'll find him," Dudley said. "We've got his description out to the locals, the state people, and the feds."

Joe nodded.

"He probably stole a car or carjacked somebody," Dudley said. "He could be halfway across Montana by now, or in another state. Tell me: Where would he go?"

Joe shrugged.

"He hasn't been in contact with you, has he?"

"Nope."

"You'll let me know if he does, right?"

"Probably not," Joe said. "You set him up by those conditions you put on him. I don't think he owes you much."

"Is that your brilliant legal opinion, game warden?" Dudley asked, his face flushing.

"It is."

JOE HAD A SPRING in his step as he rejoined his family on the balcony. He told them what he'd learned from Dudley. He noted how both Marybeth and Sheridan suppressed smiles. Lucy looked from her sister to her mother with a wary expression.

"I was just about to tell Mom another thing when you showed up," Sheridan said. "That janitor they found was an ex-con from Wyoming. He had a knife on him and the ID he wore around his neck was from the Wyoming State Penitentiary. His name was—"

"Timber Cates," Joe said.

Sheridan asked, "How did you know?"

"It all makes sense now. Brenda Cates sent Timber up here to keep April quiet."

"*Nate,*" Lucy said, her eyes wide.

They stood in silence for a moment as it all sank in.

"Look," Lucy whispered, pointing between Joe and Marybeth, toward the parking lot.

They turned as one.

A big man wearing hospital scrubs had his back to them as he slowly made his way through a row of cars to a waiting sedan under the dim glow of an overhead light. He had a blond ponytail and a pronounced limp.

When the passenger door of the sedan opened, the interior light came on. An attractive, dark woman was at the wheel. *Liv,* Joe thought.

Rather than flee immediately, Joe thought, Nate had obviously thought it all through. He'd erased the surveillance video and found a place to hide inside the hospital. Probably a room where he could change into scrubs and look like he belonged, just as Sheridan and Lucy had done. He'd contacted Liv to rent a car and come get him. Meanwhile, law enforcement was looking for him everywhere but here.

Nate turned and looked up.

Although Joe couldn't believe he could see them all up there, Nate gave them a thumbs-up before he climbed in and the car drove away.

"Girls," Marybeth said before Joe could say it, "he saved your sister's life. What we just saw needs to stay on this balcony."

Then: "Let's go talk to the doctors and see how soon we can take April home."

Stepping aside to let his family pass, Joe looked over his shoulder and down as the taillights of the sedan became pinpricks in the cold Montana dawn.

ACKNOWLEDGMENTS

The author would like to thank the many experts and first readers who assisted with aspects of this novel, including Bob Budd, the executive director of the Wyoming Wildlife and Natural Resource Trust; Hon. William F. Chinnock (Ret.); Vahé Alaverdian of Falcon Force (www.falconforce.com); Judge Peter Arnold (Ret.); Bill Haley, Wyoming Game Warden (Badge #1); Mark Nelson; and Dr. Charles Mackey.

Special thanks to my first readers Laurie Box, Becky Reif, Molly Donnell, and Roxanne Woods.

Thanks to Don Hajicek for cjbox.net and Jennifer Fonnesbeck for social media expertise and merchandise sales.

It's a sincere pleasure to work with professionals at Putnam, including the legendary Neil Nyren, Ivan Held, Kate Stark, Michael Barson, and Tom Colgan.

Ann Rittenberg, you're the greatest.

ACKNOWLEDGMENTS

The author would like to thank the many experts and first readers who assisted with aspects of this novel, including Bob Budd, the executive director of the Wyoming Wildlife and Natural Resource Trust; Hon. William F. Chinnock (Ret.); Vahé Alaverdian of Falcon Force (www.falconforce.com); Judge Peter Arnold (Ret.); Bill Haley, Wyoming Game Warden (Badge #1); Mark Nelson; and Dr. Charles Mackey.

Special thanks to my first readers Laurie Box, Becky Reif, Molly Donnell, and Roxanne Woods.

Thanks to Don Hajicek for cjbox.net and Jennifer Fonnesbeck for social media expertise and merchandise sales.

It's a sincere pleasure to work with professionals at Putnam, including the legendary Neil Nyren, Ivan Held, Kate Stark, Michael Barson, and Tom Colgan.

Ann Rittenberg, you're the greatest.